REPUBLIC FALLING

Advent of a New Dawn

By Michael J. Brooks

Wars of the New Humanity

Book One

About This Book

Content Warning

Republic Falling: Advent of a New Dawn is an action-filled science fiction book that contains violence, strong language, and detailed scenes of lovers making love.

2025 Edition

You are reading the 2025 edition of
Republic Falling: Advent of a New Dawn.

Paperback ISBN: 9781737929307
Ebook ISBN: 9781737929314

Library of Congress Control Number: 2021918972

Printed in the United States of America

Michael J. Brooks
Mount Rainier, Maryland 20712
www.authormbrooks.com

2025 edition

Praise for
Republic Falling
Advent of a New Dawn

The BookLife Prize

"A satisfying sci-fi thriller, the plot is evenly paced and the conflict is engaging."

"Action scenes are exciting and enjoyable."

"The fictional universe . . . features plenty of supporting details and technologies that flesh out the world."

"The characters are . . . presented with a sufficient complexity and internal conflict to help propel the plot and action satisfactorily."

Rabia Tanveer for *Readers' Favorite*

"While the topic of the fight between the upper class and the lower, less privileged is a common topic, very few authors have the skill to tackle it with grace and clarity. Kudos!"

Honorable Mention from the 2022 Hollywood Book Festival

Acknowledgments

I would like to thank my cover designer, Ida Jansson. She is truly a creative visionary. I would also like to thank every single person who chose to read this book. All of you have my utmost gratitude.

Glossary
(nonalphabetic order)

Earth Era: the era of humanity before intergalactic migration from Earth

Commonwealth: humanity's star nation consisting of four planets —Eden and satellites One, Two, and Three

Eden: humanity's utopian motherworld inhabited by three-fifths of the human population

Satellite One: humanity's dystopian secondary world inhabited by two-fifths of the human population

Satellites Two and Three: vacant worlds belonging to the Commonwealth, used for military training exercises and mineral excavation

Edenite/Eden citizen (synonymous terms): human beings living on Eden, whether born on the planet or during Earth Era

Highborn: a moniker referring specifically to human beings born on Eden

Colonist/colony citizen (synonymous terms): human beings living in the colonies of Satellite One, whether born on the planet or during Earth Era

Commonwealth Defense Force (CDF)/Defense Force
(synonymous terms): the Commonwealth's military force

Guardian: a soldier in the Commonwealth Defense Force

Cadet: a Guardian in training

Commonwealth Government/central government (synonymous terms): the governing body of the entire Commonwealth, which includes the Parliament and the Office of the Chief Executive

Republic of Unified Colonies (RUC): the republic formed by colonies One, Four, and Six after they declared sovereignty from the Commonwealth

The Three-Week War: the war initiated and won by the Commonwealth Government to reclaim colonies One, Four, and Six after they declared sovereignty from the Commonwealth

The Coalition of Rebel Factions/the Coalition (synonymous terms): a coalition of rebel factions formed by the remnant fighters of the RUC to continue combating the Commonwealth Government

The Interplanetary Union: the intergalactic alliance consisting of the Commonwealth and planets Ghanrax, Dhalgratt, Varsh'Ru, Zirkran, Rumanoah, and Taramassia

CHAPTER ONE

Armed dissidence: *avoidable armed retaliation resulting from long-term solvable friction between two or more disharmonious, uncooperative, or unaccommodating parties, for which the weaker party, feeling imperiled, is usually the retaliator*
—**Earth Era lexicon**—

Excited chatter echoed through the Academy's auditorium as the military graduates awaited their commencement ceremony. They stood tall and proud in their dress uniforms—earned at the expense of blood, pain, and sleepless nights. For the men, the uniform sported creased pants and oxfords. The women's uniform featured skirts, stockings, and heels. Affixed to both uniforms' jackets was a waist-length white cape symbolizing righteousness, the very ideal a Guardian embodied.

Momentarily, these young cadets would be officially inducted into the Commonwealth Defense Force (CDF). They were about to become the newest defenders of humanity's intergalactic republic, a republic fraught with homicidal war.

Twenty-two-year-old Cadet Randal Scott isolated himself in a lonesome corner, completely uninterested in joining the pre-ceremonial gabfest. Arms crossed, eyes shut, and chin tilted down, he was preoccupied with thoughts of getting payback.

He had sworn to exact revenge on the traitor responsible for his mother's death and the besmirching of his family's legacy. His father, a decorated serviceman he had once admired, was now a disgrace. In Randy's eyes, his sins could never be atoned for.

Being Linked *(cerebrally connected)* with his mother as she was atomized out of existence, Randy suffered both mentally and emotionally. Psychologists claimed that if a loved one's death was inhumane and brutal, being Linked during their demise could cause long-lasting psychic trauma, especially if psychological treatment was delayed.

The sharing of thoughts, emotions, and memories—courtesy of a nanochip beyond human ingenuity—was a scientific breakthrough credited solely to the Commonwealth's Union-approved trading partner, the Quilgarians.

A Link with another human being—upon mutually granted access—elevated empathy, rapport-building, and emotional intelligence. Such mental communion had been attempted but never achieved during humanity's bygone Earth Era.

Randy's psych evaluation for CDF admission had been conducted before the murder. Only he, his aunt, and his girlfriend, Cadet Stacie Spencer, knew he was Linked with his mother when she was obliterated. A new evaluation and some therapy would benefit him, but he couldn't risk a mental-health discharge, not until he made the bastard pay.

The skin between Randy's brows wrinkled as fond memories of his treacherous father tormented his mind. *Why?* he wondered. As he thought about his mother's funeral, the repulsion on his face worsened twofold.

He had once held the utmost respect for his father, Captain Arson Scott. The man had been a common laborer, toiling in the quarries of Colony Four on mankind's secondary world, a ringed planet designated Satellite One.

Arson later met the woman who would become his wife, a visiting Edenite named Kathleen Warner. Following in the footsteps of his father and grandfather, he left behind the drudgery of the quarry pits and answered a higher calling, enlisting in the military to assuage his yearning to serve humanity and provide for his wife and son.

Forging an esteemed career in the CDF, Arson fought in the Phazharian and Bhalkran wars, ultimately earning the Commonwealth Meritorious Service Medal, the highest commendation awarded.

Randy's admiration for his father inspired him to enlist in the Defense Force. The revered war hero had made his family and compatriots proud. Then, roughly six months ago, Arson mysteriously went AWOL, deserting his command post. His disappearance from the CDF had crushed Kathleen, inducing worry, sorrow, and recurring depression, some of which Randy experienced firsthand as a result of their Link.

At times, Kathleen would raise her firewalls to spare Randy's mind from being immersed in her personal distress.

Soon, rumors and allegations spread across Eden and Satellite One, claiming that Arson Scott had joined the terrorist insurgency opposing the Commonwealth Government. Randy later witnessed Arson take part in Kathleen's murder.

Vengeance became Randy's new motivation for enlisting. It fueled his drive to overcome the crucibles of Basic Combat

Training (BCT). During the intense mental and physical rigors he endured, his yen to see Arson pay gnawed at him constantly.

Determined to excel, he graduated from BCT as Warrior Extraordinaire, a recognition of outstanding achievement earned by performing at an exemplary level. Now he stood ready to take the Guardian's Oath and quell the outrage burning in his soul. He'd put an end to Arson Scott, whether it be by death or capture. Preferably the former.

A cherubic voice waded into his mind, saying, *Randy, it's me, honey.* Soft and soothing, the voice unmistakably belonged to . . .

Randy's eyes shot open. A luminescent, ghostly illusion of his mother shimmered before him. She wore a simple blue dress decorated with floral patterns. It was a favorite of hers, Randy recalled.

Leave the past in the past, Randy, Kathleen pled. *This vendetta of yours is decaying your soul. Move on.*

Randy shut his eyes. *Go away. You're just an apparition conjured from the pain and trauma recycled by my cerebral implant. Just a metaphysical figment of my subconscious spawned by alien tech that got overloaded with an influx of horror. You're the part of me wondering what my mother would say about me hunting down Dad. You're the boy in me crying for her to still be here, even if as some untouchable guardian angel. You are . . . my personal damnation.*

Kathleen said, *Randy, please—*

Go the fuck away! he demanded. Kathleen's voice disappeared.

Randy realized that these recurring manifestations of pain and longing in the image of his mother might be signs that fractures were forming in his mind. Maybe his unconquerable rage and thirst to eradicate his father were red alerts too. Still, he decided he'd gladly risk a lifetime of psychological damage if killing his father would bring serenity to his tortured soul.

A white-gloved hand clasped Randy's padded shoulder from behind. His eyes flicked open. On reflex, he spun, jerking his shoulder loose.

Standing smack-dab in his face was a striking blond woman. She had sun-kissed skin, cobalt-blue eyes, and a lovely red smile. She was Stacie Spencer—his peer, confidant, and significant other. And she was the only other class member to earn the mantle of Warrior Extraordinaire. *<Hey, you okay, Randy?>* the spirited young woman asked in a cheery voice through their Link.

Unrelated persons permitting access to each other's cerebral implants was one of the foremost acts of intimacy among the New Humanity. It topped or rivaled a touch, a kiss, or even intercourse. Access to a cerebral implant provided entry into the mind, a bridge to a wondrous symbiotic experience yielding unparalleled interconnectedness.

Proper-consent classes taught people to grant such a privilege judiciously. Even so, the granter could choose to safeguard specific feelings or memories, lowering their boundaries at their own pace.

Stacie's brows quirked in confusion. "Why the heck are you over here brooding?" she asked Randy aloud. "This is what we busted our asses for. Put some pride on that handsome face of yours." She playfully bumped her knuckles against his chest.

Though still perturbed, Randy dismissed her concern in a neutral tone. "I'm fine, Cadet Spencer." At the moment, there was no exorcising the anger plaguing his mind. Not here. Not in the same auditorium where, as a young boy, he had watched his father swear to uphold the very oath he was now about to take.

"Did you just call me 'Cadet Spencer'?" Stacie said in a feigned satirical tone, as if Randy had committed some heinous atrocity. It was a force of habit while in uniform, one he was still trying to shake. She placed a hand on her hip and wagged a finger at him.

"You and I are an item now, *remember?*" Her lips stretched tighter, and her tone shifted to something more perky. "So it's just 'Stacie' from now on, *even* in uniform. Got it?" She gave her boyfriend another energetic fist bump to the chest.

The past refusing to relinquish its stranglehold on Randy's peace of mind, he replied with a dull, curt, "Yeah, I got it." He didn't even crack a smile in return. Not even Stacie's vibrancy could liven him up, as it normally did.

Stacie folded her arms. Her smile deflated into a counterfeit frown. "Don't let me have to remind you again, *buster,*" she teased, her humor meant to brighten Randy's serious disposition.

Randy's expression remained rigid. "I won't. But hey, we'd better get back over there." He jerked a thumb over his shoulder at their fellow cadets. "The Master of Ceremony should be here anytime now." The Master of Ceremony was running late due to unforeseen circumstances but was said to be arriving within the hour. And the hour had just about expired.

The automatic sliding doors hissed open. Heads swiveled. Lively chatter faded to a murmur, then died completely.

In stepped a tall, thin colonel with a weathered face and a ring of shaggy gray hair crowning his balding scalp—the Master of Ceremony. He wore a green dress uniform, which had a long tailcoat. The ribbons, medals, and campaign badges pinned to his chest were proof of his work ethic, leadership, and dedication to duty.

"Oh, shit," Stacie said. "Let's move."

She and Randy hurried to rejoin their cohort.

With gravitas, the colonel strode down the aisle, wearing the sternest of expressions. There was no apology for his tardiness, only a silent, stringent expectation that the cadets fall in line at his mere presence. Excited, they formed a formation on both sides of the aisle, precisely as rehearsed. Then they composed themselves, straightening their uniforms.

As Warrior Extraordinaires, Randy and Stacie assumed their rightful place at the forefront of the class, their status signified by the patch on their left shoulders. The patch had a gold border shaped like an inverted triangle. On each line, black lettering spelled out "Extraordinaire." In the middle of the patch was a gold fist; a pair of gold thunderbolts intersected behind it.

Upon the colonel's approach, Randy and Stacie pivoted to face each other, making way for him. Once he passed, they spun back toward the stage, fell into position side by side, and steeled their posture—shoulders squared, heads high, eyes locked on the Master of Ceremony.

The colonel ascended a short set of wooden stairs to the top of the stage and stood behind a lectern. At his back hung a red tapestry that draped the entire wall. In its center, embroidery depicted the Commonwealth's emblem: Eden encircled by three smaller planets—satellites One, Two, and Three. Satellite One comprised the colonies inhabited by the remaining two-fifths of humanity. Satellites Two and Three were vacant worlds used for military training exercises and mineral excavation.

The Commonwealth was a member of the Interplanetary Union, an alliance of worlds. The seven races of the Union—Ghanrax, Dhalgratt, Varsh'Ru, Zirkran, Rumanoahan, Taramassian, and human—had united to pool resources and support one another. And all Union members were bound by the Union Charter, a system of rules, laws, and regulations.

Ready to induct the Defense Force's newest Guardians, the colonel cleared his throat and spoke into the mic. "I applaud each one of you for choosing to bear the burden of protecting the New Humanity," he said, loudspeakers amplifying his strong, raspy voice.

The tableau of cadets stood in silence, locked in the position of attention. Unable to contain their emotions, some cadets had tears in their eyes. They had made it to commencement, unlike those who had quit—or had become training casualties.

The pitch of the colonel's voice climbed. "You survived the infernal, insufferable temperatures of Satellite Two." Higher still. "You *valiantly* trudged through the arctic wasteland of Satellite Three."

Stacie winced and squeezed Randy's hand. He glanced at her from the corner of his eye.

A fleeting flashback of her nearly perishing from hypothermia stole her focus. She remembered being medevacked to the infirmary that day, and Randy had stayed by her side the entire flight. Later, she endured a severe viral infection, and Randy had visited her sickbed daily as she convalesced. A flurry of bonding moments reeled in her mind. During every grueling step of BCT, Randy had provided unwavering support and encouragement.

An "ahem" from Randy jolted her back to the here and now.

Realizing she'd broken ceremonial posture, she swallowed past the thickening lump in her throat, let go of Randy's hand, and snapped back to the position of attention. Then she simply said to him, cerebrally, < *Thank you.* >

"Everything was done to test your mettle," the colonel said. His histrionic gesticulations swept the air as he spoke. "Everything was done to break you, but you *did not* break!" Excitement suffused his veins as his fist hammered the lectern's surface. Some initiates flinched at the resounding *whack* that reverberated across the auditorium.

"Now you join the *mightiest* military force of the Interplanetary Union," the colonel continued, his fiery oration making chests swell with pride. "I welcome you to the family known as the

Commonwealth Defense Force, a force that repulsed the nefarious Phazharians and defeated the Bhalkrans.

"The enemy we *now* face, however, comes from within our own republic. They will tell you we are the tyrants. They will try to convince you that their actions are justified. Do not be swayed by their insidious lies, as some have."

Randy scowled, thinking about his father.

Arson's betrayal made no sense to him. Arson's own father had been denied Eden citizenship, even after devoting twenty years to U.S. military service. It didn't seem right to Arson. But by becoming a venerable war hero in the CDF, he had brought his father's—and his family's—years of selfless service during Earth Era into the public eye. Randy wondered why Arson had chosen to tarnish the Scott family's legacy. Why? Well, now it was up to him, Randal Scott, to uphold his family's honor.

The colonel lifted a hand. "Repeat after me." A sea of white-gloved hands rose in perfect unison. "I—"

A plethora of emotions flooded Randy's thoughts. "I, Randal Eugene Scott—"

Stacie's moist eyes shimmered. "I, Stacie Lyn Spencer—"

The colonel continued, voice steady and solemn. "—take this oath with no reservations." His words were echoed back in one powerful voice. "And I promise to protect the Commonwealth and its allies from all enemies, foreign and domestic." Again, word for word was repeated verbatim. "Till my final breath or till such time my commitment expires." Every voice rose high, saying the last of the Oath.

The colonel clapped a palm against his heart and then thrust his fist outward. The motion was mirrored with precision and crispness. "Congratulations," he said, "you have now officially transitioned from cadets to full-fledged Guardians of the

Commonwealth Defense Force. Welcome to the fight."

Class Alpha 9-5 became the eleventh class of this cycle to graduate. Since their specialization was Land Combatant, they'd be deploying straight to the war zones of Satellite One.

Cheers and hurrahs erupted, pounding eardrums. The noise level was so loud it practically vibrated the auditorium.

After the colonel exited, everyone began to mingle.

One male Guardian laughed and said to his comrade, "Do you remember that big-ass hairy monster on Satellite Three that attacked our camp? Looked like a four-armed man-ape or some shit."

The other Guardian smirked. "Yeah, I heard it ripped apart seven Echo Company cadets. I'm glad we survived the big ugly motherfucker."

Emotional from all the trials and tribulations she had triumphed over, Stacie sniffled, and her lashes fluttered. Unshed tears of joy surfaced. Today was a defining moment for her.

Randy brushed a few errant strands of ashy-blond hair from her face and pressed a kiss to her forehead. "I'm gonna go say hello to my aunt. It's been three months. I know she'd kill me if I left the Academy today without dropping by. So I'll see you tonight at the banquet, okay?" The appreciation on his face was a silent confession of how much Stacie meant to him.

For a moment, Stacie lost herself in Randy's caring, intelligent brown eyes, realizing just how fortunate she was to have him in her life. She returned his tenderness, cementing a kiss to his cheek. Still collecting herself, she felt her voice lose some of its strength. "Later then, handsome." She wiped away a tear.

Randy pivoted and made his way toward the exit.

Stacie watched him quietly maneuver through clusters of celebrants, avoiding the post-ceremony gabfest. After his mother's murder, he had become a solemn man who built walls around himself, allowing only a select few into his personal space. And though he excelled at everything he put his mind to—academics, sports, soldiering—he never let success go to his head. He remained humble.

The kudos and accolades that came with being exceptional meant little to him. They were a byproduct of hard work, not the motivator. For Randy, excellence wasn't about recognition; it was simply his personal standard, a way of life.

Stacie thought she and Randy seemed like a total mismatch, polar opposites. As an alpha woman, she loved the limelight. She craved recognition. And usually, she gravitated toward flashy men, men similar to her. It was a pattern that consistently yielded disappointment. Those kinds of men always ended up being jerks, especially the guy who preceded Randy.

Randy was a refreshing change, and she liked him. His high standards of conduct showed in every aspect of his life, especially in how he treated women. Sometimes, though, he needed to loosen up more. But she could help with that, just like the night during BCT when she finally cajoled him into a risky sexual escapade. They were lucky they didn't get caught in the act.

He was the yin to her yang, and vice versa. She was the remedy for his reclusiveness, and he was the remedy for her moral laxity and dissoluteness. They complemented each other's strengths and counteracted each other's flaws. And when it came to sex, they more than satisfied each other's needs.

Stacie felt she'd hit the jackpot. Tall, fit, and handsome, Randy stood out. He came from good genes. Even looking his worst after a day of BCT—golden-brown hair disheveled and uniform begrimed—didn't detract from his sex appeal. Naked, he was even more marvelous, her wet dream.

A brown-skinned Guardian swaggered up to Randy and stuck out his hand. He was Jarius Ford, aka "Mr. Larger Than Life," a nickname given to him by his peers. "Congrats, Randy," the young black man said exuberantly.

Randy clasped Jarius' hand and shook it firmly. "Congrats to you too." Though Randy remained straight-faced, he was glad to see Jarius.

"I saw the placement chart. You, I, and Stacie are gonna be stationed at Colony Four with Charlie Battalion's Lima Company." Jarius sounded pumped, his enthusiasm sky-high. "I guess it's no surprise. The training cadre said most of our class would probably end up at Four, since shit's so outta control there."

Randy responded with a slight nod and a terse, "Uh-huh."

He had connections within the CDF and knew many of the higher-ups, who had great respect for his family's generations of military and law-enforcement service. These high-ranking allies sympathized with his loss. They vowed to support him in any way they could as he sought to restore honor to his family name and eliminate his father—a man who had betrayed them, too, and embarrassed the CDF.

Because Randy had such a wide sphere of influence, he didn't have to leave any aspirations to happenstance or formal request. Colony Four, his father's home colony, was where his father was operating his resistance faction. Forgoing his personal values for the sake of vengeance, Randy pulled the necessary strings to get himself and Stacie stationed at Colony Four in the same company.

Arson had commanded Charlie Battalion's Lima Company Headquarters, and Randy thought the personnel there could answer the questions nagging him.

Jarius' eyes shifted to Stacie. She and two female Guardians were giggling together.

Jarius' downcast gaze climbed Stacie's well-developed calves up to her pert backside. "A *fine-ass* woman," he said, radiating high-octane energy. "*Whoo-wee*, you sure know how to pick 'em." He whistled licentiously, ogling the blond bombshell. "I heard she's a little on the wild n' dangerous side, though. But I can't understand why a wealthy heiress would join the CDF." Baffled, he cocked a brow. "She's a goddamn modern-day princess."

Stacie's family was one of the Eight, nicknamed the Eight Elite. They were a clandestine conglomerate of aristocratic families whose reach extended to top government officials, and their enterprises were the first private ventures to expand into intergalactic markets during Earth Era.

"Let's just say she has her reasons," Randy said. Not being in a social mood, he made short work of the chitchat, excusing himself. "I've gotta go. I've got something to take care of."

Jarius slapped Randy's back cheerfully. "Yeah, sure. I'll see you tonight at the banquet. And lighten the fuck up, will ya?"

Randy went on his way, giving off loner vibes. He enjoyed Jarius' brotherhood and was sure he'd go far in his military career. His charisma and magnetic personality drew many people to him. And he came just a few metrics short of Warrior Extraordinaire qualification. Randy figured Jarius would make a fine officer someday. With his type of dynamism, Jarius might've even been better suited for the Ambassador Corps. Anyhow, the Land Combatant Corps, the backbone of the CDF, was lucky to have him.

Randy walked into the corridor. To his left and right were white walls that had glass partitions. Behind them, students sat at desks in high-tech paperless learning environments.

The Academy was where onboarding and Phase One of BCT took place, which consisted of two weeks of basic-knowledge classes such as CDF history, weapon mechanics, drill and ceremonies, and customs and courtesies.

After completion of Phase One, cadets were shipped offworld for Phase Two—boot camp. The Academy was also where some of the more technical MOS schooling took place: Maintenance, Analysis, Intelligence, Administration.

In a classroom of fifty cadets, an instructor stood beside a holo projector generating a revolving 3-D representation of the CDF's mechanized combatwear. "This is what we call a Shell," she said to her students.

Model M-X02 was a dangerous wearable armament composed of smart fibers and gunmetal Kryoplaste armor. It had the aura of a cutting-edge superhero battle suit, engineered with sleek design aesthetics. The M-X02 was leaps and bounds beyond its predecessor, the clunkier unisex M-X01 exoskeleton—which resembled Earth Era war machines. The cadets were viewing the M-X02's male variant.

The instructor said, "Shells are thought-operated mechsuits that take commands via cerebral interface with your nanoimplant. They're fully weaponized—" Her voice faded from earshot as Randy walked further down the corridor, his footfalls clacking against the floor.

In another roomful of cadets, an instructor could be heard giving a history lesson. He explained that during the most recent war between the Falgoah and Chalderat clans of the Noshkanu province—a Commonwealth protectorate on planet Zelaforia—the Noshkanu High Council had requested CDF intervention to stop the genocide.

Because the Falgoah were the aggressors, the CDF sided with the Chalderat. After the Falgoah's surrender, the Parliament and Chief Executive invoked the Commonwealth's authority over its protectorate and exiled them. The instructor stressed that this decision had not only preserved countless lives but also prevented the Commonwealth's incorporated status—Union status—from being jeopardized. The Union didn't tolerate genocide on member planets or within their territorial holdings, such as protectorates.

Randy passed a purple-haired female and dark-haired male cadet exiting a lab. Technicians had just reformatted their implants for Shell-interface capability. Cringing in discomfort, the male cadet said, "I hope this fucking headache goes away soon."

Randy remembered how that felt.

He made a left into Corridor C, where the scent of chemical disinfectant permeated the air. A little dome-shaped scrubber golem crisscrossed the floor, its rotary buffer burnishing the tiles to a sheen. The bot chirped and paused to let Randy pass.

After entering classroom C-12, Randy lounged against the back wall to watch a batch of new military hopefuls receive an informative orientation. Their instructor was his aunt, Merriam Wells, whose knowledge and experience in military affairs were extensive.

Merriam noticed him as she took position behind the classroom lectern. She was a rather slim woman with neck-length silver hair. Milestones in genetic enhancement, due to the technology of other species, stretched the human lifespan and slowed aging, so she actually looked to be in her early forties instead of her mid-fifties, and she felt just as spry.

Her white instructor uniform had a black cape attached to her gold epaulets, symbolizing her status as a Master Instructor.

She acknowledged Randy, nodding once. Then she faced her class and put on a serious expression. "Good morning," she said into the mic. Static crackled from the loudspeakers. "I am Master Instructor Merriam Wells, and I'll be giving you a thirty-minute lesson on the history and inner workings of the terrorist organization that threatens the peace and stability of the Commonwealth, the Coalition of Rebel Factions."

Merriam laid a computer tablet on the lectern's surface, powered it on, and pressed a red icon onscreen. The video-wall behind her flashed to life, mirroring the display on her tablet—a star grid of humanity's sphere of planets, the Commonwealth.

"As you know, it was ten months ago that three of Satellite One's six colonies started the Independent Movement and unconstitutionally declared sovereignty from the Commonwealth, forming the Republic of Unified Colonies (RUC)." Merriam touched each settlement on her tablet's screen as she said their designations. "Colonies One, Four, and Six." Red circles flagged the trio of rogue settlements on the video-wall.

"Eden's Chief Executive and the Parliament launched a three-week military campaign that recovered the renegade colonies. Those colonies were then placed under martial law to eliminate the rebel remnants and prevent further rebellion."

Every cadet sat ramrod straight, ears tuned in, eyeballs unmoving. Failure to pay attention could lead to immediate discharge.

Merriam kept an eye out for anyone slouching or dozing off while she spoke. "The rebel remnants who fought for their colonies' liberation in the Three-Week War call themselves the Coalition of Rebel Factions. They believe they're some last bastion of hope for freedom from the external ordinance of the central government, which they allege to be cruel and autocratic.

"These underground factions mainly operate inside the occupied colonies. They carry out guerrilla warfare on government facilities and Defense Force bases. They try to spread their Independent Movement propaganda and Arman Reza's liberation philosophy to manipulate the gullible into joining their forlorn insurrection."

Merriam swiped a finger across her tablet's screen. On the video-wall, a news article replaced the graphic of the Commonwealth. The headline read: UNAFFILIATED TERRORIST-BOMBERS DETONATE EXPLOSIVES OUTSIDE CDF BASE IN COLONY SIX. A slideshow of articles with similar stories cycled.

Animosity weighted Merriam's voice. "Many citizens of the occupied colonies have become radicalized and secretly support the Coalition. They act as suppliers, financial backers, and even lone-wolf operators. These people *think* they're freedom fighters, but what they are is traitors. They've been transformed into radical dissidents, minds hijacked by Reza's liberation philosophy and this . . . Independent Movement nonsense.

"Reza's dogma has even now tainted minds here on Eden, breeding a small vocal minority of Independent Movement sympathizers. They argue the central government should've condoned treason and granted the RUC its independence. These *anarchists* have incited riots and formed armed extremist groups."

As Randy watched, memories of his own orientation session surfaced. He had sat where these cadets were now, listening to Merriam. Her patriotism, strict adherence to the Constitution, and the pride she took in being a Master Instructor were qualities that had made an impression on him.

"This Independent Movement *contagion* is spreading, and we are the cure." Merriam's tone grew uglier. "You will hear the anarchists say the central government was wrong for its aggression. That it should've attempted reconciliation first. That it should've tried *diplomacy.* These delusional halfwits act as if colonies One, Four, and Six were a sovereign entity to be negotiated with.

"Following the RUC's declaration of independence, the Chief Executive generously allowed them five days to cease and desist their treasonous actions. Those actions, unbeknownst to the central government, involved the illicit establishment of planetary partnerships to procure arms for their paramilitaries. *All* external commerce transactions *must be* authorized by the Union."

Worlds outside the Union underwent extensive vetting before the Commonwealth, or any Union member, conducted business with them. That way, the Union didn't end up funding governments with nefarious activities.

Merriam said, "By Commonwealth law, the central government is the only entity in our republic that can transact with external vetted partners. The RUC broke law after law. That cease and desist was their opportunity to set things right and avert war. Instead, they persisted in separating from the Commonwealth."

She suspected some cadets still believed that military action against the colonies had been excessive. She intended to shatter that illusion. "Declaring sovereignty is *treason*, as outlined in our Constitution," she said in a harsh tone. "So the five-day cease and desist was an act of benignity. Tell that to the simpletons who contest the government's civility."

Randy nodded in agreement, puzzled by why Arson started fraternizing with the enemy. Something volatile rose inside him, screaming for answers, screaming for retribution for his mother.

Merriam held up a finger, as if to stave off any forthcoming criticism. "And mobilization of troops to dismantle the RUC *did not* violate Article II of the Union Charter."

A cadet worked up the courage to raise his hand, challenging Merriam. "Excuse me, Ma'am. If the Commonwealth didn't violate Article II, as you say, then why was a proper-conduct investigation launched by the Union's planetary leaders?"

A coldness settled in Merriam's eyes, and the corners of her mouth turned downward.

Pressure built up in the cadet's chest, but he didn't back down. "They've had major doubts about the validity of our actions. For weeks, they've been reviewing our justification for use of force.

"When the emergency summit happens next week, they're going to present their deliberations. Some people believe those deliberations aren't going to be in our favor. We're basically going to be on trial. We might get exiled from the Union." He mentally patted himself on the back for speaking up.

A muscle twitched in Merriam's jaw, and she slammed her hands down on the lectern.

Color drained from frozen faces.

"Oh, shit," a female cadet whispered.

Merriam's voice tore through the air. "First of all, when a planetary leader enacts Article II's Exception to Force Clause without consulting the others—to stop an abrupt uprising—those leaders have the right to launch a proper-conduct investigation. It's standard procedure.

"Secondly, no matter what the critics say, we acted within the boundaries of the Exception to Force Clause. You should believe that beyond a shadow of a doubt," she added threateningly. The cadet spared himself expulsion, not challenging the Master Instructor any further. "The Commonwealth is always righteous. Now, does anyone else have anything to interject?"

A green-haired woman in her twenties, wearing square spectacles, raised her hand.

Merriam's eyes spotted the brave soul and glanced at her name tag. "Speak, Cadet Wilmington."

The lanky cadet took a bold stance and spoke her mind. "I lived in Colony One, my birth-colony, before the lottery granted me

Eden citizenship two years ago. Unfortunately, my parents weren't so lucky." She lowered her chin, concerned for her parents' well-being. A thought of them passed, and she lifted her gaze, meeting Merriam's cold grimace. "Like the other five colonies, the conditions there are dire." Despair bathed her features. "Temporary housing units are falling apart, filtration systems are malfunctioning, and—"

Merriam rolled her eyes and cut off Wilmington, who was grating on her nerves. "And your point is what?"

Wilmington asserted herself, saying, "My point is rebellion happened because the central government naysaid the colonies' plight. They failed to respond to people's grievances, galvanizing the citizens of colonies One, Four, and Six. Armed dissidence was bound to occur. So don't you think the government bears some responsibility for being remiss—?"

Merriam, about to blow her top, interrupted. "Cadet Wilmington, as Master Instructor, I pronounce you ill-suited for military service. You are hereby expelled from the Academy. Now remove yourself from my classroom."

Wilmington's face blanched. "But—"

"Leave," Merriam demanded in a livid tone, making a sweeping gesture with her hand.

Tears welled up in Wilmington's eyes and poured down her cheeks. She rose from her seat, head bowed, and stomped toward the doorway, muttering.

Randy, impassive to the outlier's predicament, silently watched her pout.

"*Bitch*," she mumbled, exiting the room.

Merriam tapped a sequence of icons on her tablet's screen, marking Wilmington's profile as "disloyal" and alerting Academy Enforcement. To question her about her subversive leanings, they would pinpoint the signal from her tracer beacon and intercept her before she could leave the building.

"That's what we get for letting immigrant nadir into the prestige of the Defense Force," a snooty female voice whispered from one of the rearmost seats.

"As you can see, anti-government sentiments *will not* be tolerated, and anyone caught listening to Arman Reza's rhetoric will be culled from our ranks as well," Merriam said ferociously. "Independent Movement sympathizers like Cadet Wilmington become defectors. That's what we don't want. Better to nip a problem in the bud now before it grows into a bigger one."

Merriam recovered from the distraction and resumed her lecture, adjusting her voice and posture. "You have been selected not only to defend the Commonwealth from foreign threats and protect our allies, but also to help maintain law and order in the colonies of our great republic. You should feel proud." She pressed a purple icon on her tablet's screen. "But the CDF's mission reaches far beyond the Commonwealth and the Union. Observe."

The lights in the room dimmed, and overhead, a wire-frame holographic projection of planets, moons, and stars spread out. It displayed a conflict grid marking the Commonwealth's Mission Worlds, which were located across multiple quadrants of the galaxy. These were all Tier 1 civilizations, fragile worlds where individual governments had become protectorates in exchange for military assistance or essential resources.

The terms of these agreements varied from one government to another. Some required surrendering a portion of trade profits to the Commonwealth, while others involved arms deals or long-term financial compensation that sometimes had negative effects on a protectorate's economy.

Agreements remained in effect until their expiration date,

which ranged from months to years. Then it could be renewed, renegotiated, or terminated.

The populations of some protectorates viewed the Commonwealth's intervention as benevolent service, while the populations of others saw it as imperial expansion driven by economic and political interests. Sometimes unrest and upheaval within protectorates resulted in opposition movements that sought to overturn existing governments using various means, including force, to cancel the Commonwealth's agreements.

There were Union leaders who had now grown concerned about the Commonwealth's lucrative planetary-impact missions. They feared these missions could infringe on sovereignty, disrupt people's well-being, or lead governments to become dependent on the Commonwealth. And there was a possibility that opponents of these missions might harbor animosity toward the entire Union.

Merriam deactivated the projection, and the room's lights brightened. She double-tapped a thumbnail on her home screen, and a picture of Arson Scott—the man once held in high esteem—enlarged on the video-wall. "This is one of the most-wanted terrorist leaders of the Coalition." In the image, Arson's dark hair was cropped short, and he had a deadly expression creasing the brow of his rugged face.

Randy glared at his father, his scathing countenance a mirror of his vengeful heart.

Merriam brought up the war criminal's prior CDF service sketch. On the video-wall, black text materialized against a blank backdrop. "As you can see, this *convert* isn't someone to take lightly," she said in a severe tone.

The text denoted Arson's military exploits, exploits that demanded respect and would even amaze some of the most seasoned warfighters. After giving the cadets a minute to internalize just how dangerous her brother-in-law could be, Merriam minimized the info and double-tapped another thumbnail.

Picture number two took over the video-wall: Arson, outfitted in CDF battle garb, tracking targets through the scope of a high-powered rifle. The black-and-gray camo-pattern uniform included a protective vest and a tactical belt carrying dual handguns.

"Arson Scott is one of the toughest sons of bitches this galaxy's ever seen," Merriam warned. "After the Three-Week War concluded and martial law in the renegade colonies commenced, he became influenced by the Coalition's doctrine. He defected, divulging CDF secrets, fighting against his own, and becoming one of the chief terrorist leaders of the Coalition." *And he ceased being a dedicated father to Randy and a loving husband to my younger sister,* she added silently.

Randy's heated glare stayed fixed on the picture of his father. His pulse quickened. The room seemed to shrink, suffocating him, and his mind took him back to the harrowing night the Coalition murdered his mother . . .

Randy guided his red sports cruiser across the night sky, enjoying the wind rushing through the open top. He landed the fancy flyer between two yellow lines, parking outside a three-story facility surrounded by forest.

The facility was A-1 Defense Solutions, a major defense contractor where his mother worked as a senior tech engineer. To celebrate her promotion to Chief Tech Engineer tomorrow, he was going to treat her to a meal.

He flipped a switch on the dash, and the engine purred off. He got out, smoothed back his windswept hair, and approached the building. It was after hours, and it was extremely rare for anyone to be at work at this time, especially since today was Commonwealth Observance Day, a holiday commemorating the inception of humanity's intergalactic republic.

Randy was nervous. Defense contractors had faced attacks from the Coalition. His mother's might be on their list.

Randy tapped the centerpiece of his wrist computer (wristcom). The electronic band beeped, ringing his mother's.

<Hey, honey, up here,> came Kathleen's voice from inside his mind. He looked up and saw her waving at him from one of the tall third-floor windows. Realizing she was within range of their Link, he canceled the call. <Be down in fifteen minutes,> she said.

"Wait, someone's still in there!" an outraged voice shouted from somewhere. "Intel said the building would be vacant tonight!"

Startled, Randy twisted left and right, sneakers scraping against the pavement. His eyes methodically combed the darkness.

<Randy, what's going on out there?> Kathleen asked, voice teeming with worry.

<Not sure,> Randy replied, swiveling his head. His panicking heart thumped frantically.

Suddenly . . . *FWOOSH!* The third floor erupted in a thunderous burst of flames. The second and first floors soon followed, explosions shattering windows into fragments.

The cruelest of pains burrowed into Randy's mind and razed every atom in his body, shivering his entire being.

He gripped his head, releasing a gut-wrenching, shrill scream that could wake the dead. The mental torment clawed at his psyche until it was in shambles. Speechless and disoriented, his face as pallid as a corpse, he died without dying. Then color returned to his face, and he heaved in ragged drags.

Lightheaded, tears upwelling, he sank to his knees.

Ash drifted, and wild undulating flames licked the air.

Randy stared at the inferno, shuddering, ears ringing. Intermittent throbs stung his mind. Words couldn't articulate the agony he had experienced.

A racket of gunshots stole his attention. Still on his knees, his vision blurred by tears, he canted his head to the left. His jaw dropped. Security personnel were discharging small-arms fire at three Coalition rebels geared up in modular vests and tactical equipment. One of them was Arson Scott.

One of the two men with Arson unslung his rifle and fired warning shots at the security guards. "Let's move!" His rifle's muzzle flashed, and expended shell casings pinged across the pavement.

All three rebels retreated into the trees.

"Where'd they go?" a guard said. He swept the darkness with the beam of his wrist light.

The rumble of an engine shook the forest. Birds cawed and chirped among rustling leaves. Twigs snapped. A heavily armored flyer emerged from a thicket of trees and climbed into the sky. As it zoomed away, its taillights disappeared into the night.

Randy stood up, whimpering. There was now a black hole in his heart that would never seal. His mother had been snatched away from him in an instant. The worst part was that his own father was involved in robbing him of his mother and mentally scarring him. Now, the war had become personal.

A guard ran up to Randy. "Hey, are you okay?"

Brows knitted in anger, the now-motherless son said nothing.

Emergency vehicles screeched onto the scene. Doors clicked open. Muffled chatter blared over radios.

Concerned, the guard asked Randy again, "Are you okay?"

Firemen hosed the conflagration using wheeled water cannons.

Randy remained silent, smoldering debris and the pungent scent of smoke wafting in the howling wind . . .

Randy's memory broke. The suffocating feeling lifted, and his muscles relaxed. He pulled himself together.

"I'm going to break here for ten minutes," Merriam said to her students. "You may stay or leave the classroom." At a brisk pace, she went toward her nephew, heels clicking the floor. Eyes followed her as she and Randy stepped outside.

Some students got up to leave; others explored the learning modules in their desks' info terminals.

Merriam grasped Randy's shoulders. "Dress Blues suit you." She brushed his shoulders and tugged on his uniform, straightening wrinkles. As she absorbed his appearance, the Warrior Extraordinaire patch registered. Her brows leapt. "And you graduated top-tier of your class. Fantastic. Your mother would've been *so* proud of you." She swung open her arms, and Randy embraced her.

A faint smile touched the corners of Randy's mouth, a pained one. He wanted his mother to see him graduate today.

Chatting as they left the canteen, two faculty members sauntered by, holding mugs of steaming brew.

Randy hugged Merriam tighter. "I wanted to let you know I received approval for my request," he said softly. They released each other. "I'm going to be stationed at Colony Four."

"Where your father is?" Merriam asked to confirm. Randy nodded, his expression tense. "I know, betrayal hurts. It stings. And rage burns inside you, as it does me." Her voice hardened. "But remember: duty first and foremost." She jabbed a finger against her nephew's chest. "You got that, Randal Scott?"

"Yes, Ma'am." He headed down the corridor. "I've got to get going. I'll call before I depart for my duty station."

"Anything you need, you let me know, Randy."

"I will," he replied, walking away.

• • •

Stacie moved down a corridor identical to all the others, on her way to leave the Academy. The loud and proud-sounding click-clack of her heels echoed. Her stride exuded confidence, and rightfully so. Not because she was ultrarich or because she had a body that turned heads—all of which inflated her ego. It was because she had transcended the expectations of naysayers and uncuffed herself from the prescribed lifestyle of the Eight by joining the CDF.

Thrilled about her first military deployment, she beamed.

Near the glass partition of the security office, three male cadets and one female lollygagged. Stacie slowed her stride and came up behind them, wondering what had their attention.

Wearing a black sleeveless spandex half-top and shorts, Cadet Wilmington sat in a chair with her hands bound behind her back.

Uniformed in dark blue, a tall, broad-shouldered Academy enforcement officer loomed over her. Hellbent on getting a confession, he pressed a shock baton to her chest.

Electricity buzzed and crackled.

Wilmington screamed.

"Are you a Coalition plant, Telisha Wilmington?" the officer demanded.

Tears pooled in Wilmington's large green eyes. "No! I already told you that!"

The officer clamped a hand around her jaw. "Are you a member of some other anti-government group?" he asked, while the female officer at the worktable behind him inspected Wilmington's uniform for nanosurveillance devices.

Wilmington's breath hitched. A cold film of sweat slickened her skin. "I'm not a member of *any* anti-government group," she replied, voice quavering.

"You sure?" The officer's shock baton discharged another jolt of electricity.

Wilmington winced, muscles coiled tight as she weathered the pain. "Yes, I'm sure!" Her face paled from the wave of fear that almost made her piss herself. "Now please stop! Please!"

Without a hint of compassion, the officer gestured for her to stand. "Get up so we can transfer you to detainment." Pure hatred strained his features.

Wilmington stood, her knobby knees trembling.

Stacie "tsked," shaking her head. *When will these sympathizers learn?* She walked away as the four onlookers pointed and giggled.

Stacie exited the Academy, stepping out onto the front portico.

Young cadets in battledress passed by her, going and coming.

A blue-haired male was in awe of her Warrior Extraordinaire patch. "Wow!" he exclaimed. "That's what I wanna be, Warrior Extraordinaire!"

The gawker's words pandered to Stacie's ego. She loved the recognition such an accomplishment brought her.

Under the lavish gazebos of the campus's sprawling courtyard, cadets sat on benches, engaged in free-ranging discussions.

A female Guardian, her back pressed against the Academy's wall, was making out with a male Guardian. Both were recent graduates. The woman's partner shoved his hand under the back of her skirt, nearly ready to have celebration sex right then and there.

Though strict during military exercises, assignments, and operations, the CDF was a far more relaxed fighting force than the militaries of Earth Era. Public displays of affection in uniform were permitted, aligning with Eden's permissive culture and the belief that excessive austerity for active-duty Guardians was unhealthy. Hair-color and tattoo regulations were also lenient, a stark contrast to the rigid codes of Earth Era's militaries.

A male cadet made a pass at a female, pinging her cerebral implant. Access was denied. Salty, he "humphed," and his face pulled into a pompous scowl.

Commotion broke out near the schoolhouse to Stacie's left. She turned. Two Academy enforcement officers wrestled an eighteen-year-old cadet to the ground.

"Get off!" the cadet yelled. His mop of teal hair brushed his forehead as he struggled to free himself. "I was just . . . trying to understand the enemy better, that's all!"

"Bullshit!" one officer blurted. "Now your ass is gonna be out-processed!"

The cadet's tablet lay beside him. He'd been viewing one of Arman Reza's incendiary orations on the net, a cyberspace nexus for information and communication, which was accessible to both Eden and Satellite One. Anytime cyber authorities took down one of Reza's vidcasts, it would resurface days later, and the location of the upload remained untraceable. No digital footprint. Nothing.

Using the net as his pulpit, over time Reza fathered the Independent Movement with his vehement declamations of colony equality.

No one had any idea who this dangerous inciter was, as he always wore a cowl and metal mask to conceal his identity. He also spoke through a vocoder, further ensuring he remained unidentifiable.

From the tablet, Reza's modified voice said, "The Commonwealth Government is undeniably wrong for our—"

One of the officers stomped the tablet repeatedly until it broke, silencing the harangue.

Stacie shook her head at the youngster. *Fucking idiot.*

Cadets milled around on the well-tended green spaces, chattering about what had just transpired.

Stacie spoke into her wristcom. "Options for transportation services." Following an electronic warping sound, a hololist materialized in midair. Stacie dragged a finger down the list, browsing various options. She touched the transport service she wanted, debiting her wayfare. Within three minutes of her transportation request, a driverless capsule-shaped flyer descended.

The overhead flip-up canopy snapped open. "Thank you for riding with Air Escort, the best in air-cab transportation," said a crisp artificial voice.

Stacie settled into the exotic leather interior, enjoying the luxury of massage seating. She recognized the flyer as having been manufactured by one of her family's acquisitions.

The canopy clicked shut.

"Destination, please," the computerized chauffeur requested.

Stacie buckled up and provided an address.

The nav-panel hummed to life, buttons blinking and go-lights flashing. Electronics chirped, navigation programs charting coordinates toward Stacie's given address.

"Destination logged," the computer reported as the flyer steadily ascended. "Now proceeding. Please sit back and enjoy the ride." The flyer cruised into an air lane.

Below was a magnificent panoramic view of Eden's capital, Cornerstone City. It was the epicenter of business, entertainment, politics, and commerce on the planet. The Academy, Parliament Building, Supreme Judiciary, and Chief Executive's Manor formed the Quad and were located in the center of the booming metropolis.

Maglev trains inside sky tunnels dipped and climbed at high velocities. Flyers whisked everywhere. A mass of ground transportation crawled to a gridlocked halt on the congested solar-paneled streets. Pissed-off motorists yelled obscenities and honked their vehicles' horns.

Men and women in lavish attire ambled along avenues of multifarious restaurants and storefronts. Behind clothing-store windows, holographic skins of mannequins cycled between the latest couture. Giant video banners across the city displayed colorful advertisements and infographics. In the major shopping district were large multiplex retail centers up to twelve stories. In the residential district, swanky high-rise apartment buildings loomed over the streets.

Many people were unaware that the Eight Elite's handprint was all over the city's construction.

Stacie's flyer soared by a business complex ten floors high. An employee in his office issued a voice command, causing the windows to become opaque for privacy.

Further out from Cornerstone, quiet rural suburbs provided relief from the hustle and bustle for those who liked life slower. To the east were colorful glades that were home to popular hot-spring resorts.

Though Eden was the utopia of the Commonwealth, a good deal of its citizens had resorted to illegal methods for generating wealth during humanity's turbulent transition period. So beneath Eden's glitz and glamour, a sinister underworld thrived. Evil and sin seemed to be the imperfections humanity couldn't extinguish, even in its new enlightened, evolved state.

Stacie said to her wristcom, "Call Mom." Rhythmic electronic chirps sounded. For the third time today, her mother refused to answer, letting her end go to voicemail. Stacie canceled the call, pressing a finger to her wristcom. Her face grimaced. *Three months and you don't want to talk to me?* "Figures." She expelled a heavy sigh. She needed a distraction. "News," she told the cab in an irritated tone. A holoscreen wobbled into view.

A stylish pod-shaped flyer whisked past hers, traveling in the opposite direction.

"Please designate a station," the cab's computer said.

"Any, as long as it's news." A blip on the holoscreen signaled the start of the autosearch. Seconds later, the system presented the first newscast it detected. With her fingers, Stacie stretched the screen to her preferred size. "Perfect."

A green-eyed, orange-haired reporter was onscreen. She said, "Lottery beneficiaries here on Eden have family living in the occupied colonies. Their loved ones have told them the CDF maintains law and order with extreme prejudice, raiding homes without warrants. They even say mandatory curfews are sometimes enforced with death. And eyewitness accounts are circulating about arbitrary arrests and forced confessions by means of intimidation and coercion."

Stacie heard the Master of Ceremony's words in her mind: *"They will tell you we are the tyrants. They will try to convince you that their actions are justified. Do not be swayed by their insidious lies—"*

Coalition propaganda, Stacie thought.

It wasn't beyond comprehension that some unjust acts were being perpetrated by Guardians. There were corrupt people in all professions and walks of life. But Stacie, like most Independent Movement antagonists, believed that the Coalition and their supporters were overexaggerating these rare occurrences—and completely fabricating some, to fool the masses.

"With me is one of the protesters who participated in an Independent Movement rally, here on Eden, just an hour ago," the reporter said.

A heavyset, fully bearded man spoke into the camera. "My daughter lives in Colony Six. She tells me all the time about how Guardians and military vehicles are always roaming the streets."

Stacie wanted to yell at the screen, *Yes, counterinsurgency operations are always ongoing, to catch the terrorists and defend the Commonwealth.*

"My daughter says Guardians have unfairly stopped, questioned, and frisked her and other law-abiding citizens," the man said. "Before the war, people in Colony Six received shitty treatment. Now they're being treated even shittier. And because of net restrictions, colonists can't expose what's happening and prove how lousy their living conditions are. The central government's got everything under lock n' key, to keep us on Eden oblivious to all the fuckery going on."

Stacie scoffed. *Stupid kook.* She had heard enough. "Another station."

On this newscast, a male anchorman in a blue suit sat at a sleek table. To his left sat a menacing, aged man with an aquiline nose, wearing a plethora of ribbons on his uniform. To his right sat a dark brown woman of African heritage in her middle years. Waist-length locs, decorated with colorful beads, framed her prominent facial features. Her attire for this interview consisted of a headdress and a purple robe bearing abstract patterns.

The anchorman, facing the camera, announced, "Joining me to discuss the Commonwealth's unrest are two members of the Parliament. First, we have Chairman Cornelius Gould." The camera panned to the man. His pallid face remained stoic. "In addition to his role as a chairman, he occupies the third highest government position, serving as Secretary of Defense *(Deputy Chief was the second highest government position)*." He also had a well-deserved reputation for being a master of manipulation, intimidation, and torture tactics. "He opposes the Independent Movement and favors the use of military force to suppress it."

The camera panned from the stern-faced combat guru to the colorfully dressed brown woman, a woman who had survived many hardships, a woman who had labored in the agricultural fields of Colony Two.

"Next, we have Chairwoman Oviereya Amaechi," the anchorman said. Oviereya's presence stood out on so many levels. "Just like Chairman Gould, she holds dual positions. She is also Chancellor of the Supreme Judiciary, the fourth highest position in the government.

"She doesn't approve of colony autonomy, yet she acknowledges the perspectives of colonists who desire independence. And she believes the Independent Movement was justified due to what she considers government negligence."

Election year was ahead. There were rumors that Oviereya and Cornelius might be vying for the Chief Executive seat. The people on Eden and Satellite One watching this interview considered it a preview of future debates between the two.

"Increase audio," Stacie said. The sound system's volume rose.

Oviereya had been the midwife for Stacie's mother, and she became a dear friend to Stacie. Though Stacie didn't always agree with her politics, she was glad that someone who had morals and a generous spirit had been elected to Parliament.

Oviereya, in a voice of assertion, spoke. "Inadequate housing, minimal access to health systems, unequal resource distribution, economic deterioration, rising poverty levels, and a lack of industrial development are what incited the civil unrest that sparked the Independent Movement. And who is to blame? The Chief Executive and the Parliament.

"The governors of the seceding colonies sat at the parliamentary meetings every cycle. Time after time they aired their people's grievances, with little ability to do anything else. All they could do was advocate for their colonies' welfare and submit proposals to the Chief Executive and Parliament regarding possible solutions, and those proposals were ignored. Two-fifths of humanity is living in today's Dark Ages."

Cornelius countered in a snide tone. "A new genesis for humanity isn't easy to accomplish. That is common sense. There were bound to be setbacks to intergalactic migration. Yes, the colonies' people need aid, but to say they're living in today's 'Dark Ages' is ridiculous." He let out an unsympathetic chuckle.

Oviereya's dark brows dipped. "No, quite the contrary."

To give her critics context behind her perspective, she decided to recount the events that had led to the rebellion, and perhaps she also intended to persuade voters for the upcoming election. Since most Edenites had never visited a colony, it was important that she offer an accurate portrayal of the colonies' dilemma—one that only a former colonist like herself, a lottery beneficiary, could provide.

Her shoulders tensed. Her throat turned dry. It was crucial that she get her message right. "This stratification of humanity began when we had to abandon Earth, a world that had fallen to pieces, to migrate to a new planetary habitat."

Humanity's venture into intergalactic arms procurement during Earth Era ignited an unprecedented arms race. Alien weapons of mass destruction fell into the hands of warlords, despots, and tyrannical regimes, plunging the world into an apocalypse.

Oviereya settled into the moment, anxiety draining from her body. Addressing such a large live audience was far from the hardest thing she had ever done. She told herself she had this under control. "With assistance from the Union Worlds and other intergalactic governments, we established the Commonwealth. But Eden, the Commonwealth's motherworld, has only a single continental landmass; it simply wasn't big enough to accommodate all of humanity. So a two-world solution was necessary.

"To avoid human bias in conceptualizing humanity's future, AEGIS (Advanced Exascale Global Information-collection System) was invented. It was supposed to formulate the best strategy for survival using logical calculations and unbiased reasoning. By analyzing census data from all nations, it decided who would inhabit Eden and who would inhabit the abject, substandard habitats of Satellite One, primarily consisting of manufactured housing units (MHUs)."

A tempest raged in Oviereya's eyes at the unjust classification labels assigned to colony selectees, determined by supposed value coefficients. She gazed straight into the camera, as though the people watching this interview were standing in front of her. "The AI stratified humanity into upper and lower-level classes. Those identified as being the most capable of pioneering the New Humanity were selected to inhabit Eden, as if they were the crème de la crème of the human race." About to erupt, she paused to gather herself.

Cornelius quietly growled at her "colony sympathizing."

Proceeding to pour out her soul, she said, "AEGIS categorized colony selectees as *inferior*, based on socioeconomic status, IQ, preexisting medical conditions, genetic predisposition, and other prejudices. They were determined to be the most expendable. They were told they were best suited to serve humanity as resource harvesters, merely *serfs* for the Commonwealth Government and Eden's megacorporations that—"

Cornelius spoke over her. "Typical progressionist blather, using manipulative, sympathy-inducing terms such as 'expendable' to further your agendas. Neither I nor any other government leader has described colonists, our own brethren, as 'expendable.'"

The chairwoman raised a hand. "No talking out of turn."

Cornelius grunted, eyes flaring.

The anchorman felt the tension between them escalating.

Oviereya collected her thoughts and continued her appeal to win over hearts and minds. "To pick up where I left off: AEGIS sent the lower-level classes to work as resource harvesters on Satellite One, where living conditions are harsh. The majority of time and assets were relegated to developing Eden's utopias, to give the upper-level classes—the chosen pioneers of the New Humanity—the best chance at persevering.

"Some people questioned the fairness of AEGIS's socioeconomic design, but not enough. Many were simply glad to have the chance to escape Earth and get a shot at survival. During that time of strife, most opponents of AEGIS didn't have the willpower or wherewithal to oppose Earth's highest orders. So they became compliant with the exodus directives designating them the lesser of humanity.

"But they remained hopeful; the low-grade living conditions were to be only temporary, a stepping stone. Their world was to become a paradise too, once or *if* the Eden migrants successfully completed their transition. Maybe that was the intention at first, but this promise got thrown by the wayside."

The anchorman appeared captivated by how soulfully Oviereya spoke. He had no doubt there were colonists watching who were in tears.

Oviereya said, "Over time, the migrants of Eden gave birth to the next generation of Homo sapiens. Their children underwent genetic editing, and they received genetic enhancement *(for gains in immunity, healing, pain tolerance, reflexes, physical strength, and other attributes).* No such human-performance augmentation was administered to the people of the colonies."

She became riled, remembering friends who had perished in her birth-colony, Colony Two, waiting for inoculations against diseases that Edenites were immune to contracting.

Her eyes narrowed. "It seemed Eden's people were being molded to be a sort of neohuman. The disparities between Eden and Satellite One grew as infrastructural development and life quality accelerated here but slowed in the colonies."

Nor did it need to accelerate in the colonies, Cornelius thought.

Passion infused Oviereya's words. "The years of colony progression that did happen appeased people at the time. Individual governments and an economy were established. The net was set up. Infrastructural growth was happening. But when the progression suddenly plateaued, people were no longer appeased.

"Colonists seemed to become a subclass of the New Humanity. They were being excluded from mankind's evolution technologically, genetically, and industrially. It was the people of Eden, AEGIS's chosen ones, who were prospering and becoming the new leaders of mankind."

Cornelius glowered at Oviereya. *As we were meant to be.*

Oviereya didn't miss a beat, maximizing every second she had to speak. "Humanity became divided into a privileged class and a sort of servant class. As more time went by without the central government resuming colony development, Eden-born became referred to as 'Highborn' by their colony brethren.

"Eventually, colony governors organized protests and conducted surveys to gauge their citizens' views on breaking away from the Commonwealth. These 'illegal' exodus polls were intended as a wake-up call to the central government. They revealed overwhelming support for secession in colonies One, Four, and Six, with eighty-four percent of their population voting 'yes.'

"The central government slapped the governors with fines and reduced their colonies' resources to punish them. After so many years, Eden's progression was still the top priority. The government's evolving development plan for the Commonwealth continued to discriminate against the colonies."

Cornelius listened on, his entire demeanor radiating pure apathy. Oviereya's words didn't move him or evoke any emotion.

Oviereya said, "Colonists felt like they were being dismissed. They felt like AEGIS's blueprint for humanity was being exploited to maintain a socioeconomic hierarchy that kept them at the bottom of the totem pole. Their anger grew.

"Sure, the colonies were given governors and even an annual lottery that allows several people to become registered Eden citizens each year, but that was only a *minuscule* step in the right direction. Don't get me wrong, though: I'm truly grateful the immigration lottery exists. I was a beneficiary of it."

Oviereya became an icon to the colony peoples. She was the first and only of them to be elected to Parliament. She was their homeworld heroine.

"However, colonists have started to believe their governors and the lottery are just ploys meant to keep them content. They were originally told their governors would give them a voice within the central government, but that wasn't the case. The status quo is being deliberately maintained because an AI has determined that colonists' value lies in hard labor."

Cornelius' fingers drummed the tabletop idly. Oviereya's opinionated historical recap bored him. "Thank you for your overblown, overly grim narrative the progressionists within the Parliament usually employ for political gain."

Oviereya's jaw tightened, and she shook her head. "My tale of events is no exaggeration. Chief Executives and the Parliament assured the colonies of change time after time, yet nothing happened. *Zilch.*

"Denialists within the central government claim we're an inclusive society and that the colonies have not been forgotten. At the moment, we *are not* an inclusive society. Colonists can't even enlist in the CDF unless they become lottery beneficiaries." Her inflection turned spiteful. "That doesn't sound fair to me."

Cornelius twisted his hands together beneath the table, fighting to repress the wave of disgust sprouting through him.

Oviereya said, "There were hopes that Chief Executive Jared Kerner would be different, but he's done little to alter the course set forth by his predecessors, which include his father.

"For too many years, it's been 'Eden first.' After the colonies had been neglected for so long, it's no surprise the governments of One, Four, and Six grew seditious and sought autonomy.

"They wanted to become self-governing entities and apply for Union membership independent of the Commonwealth. That way, they could engage in commerce transactions directly with other Union planets and external partners, no longer having to wait for hand-me-down resources from the central government.

"Chief Executive Kerner was never going to allow that. His failings, along with those of his predecessors, fueled colonists' dissatisfaction. Frustrated, the governors of colonies One, Four, and Six declared independence, an action most of their constituents supported, as the 'illegal' exodus polls indicated."

Cornelius' patience wore thin, every word from Oviereya chipping away at his composure. He rested his elbow on the table, cradling his forehead in his hand, while his eyes wandered to anything but her. He couldn't wait until it was his time to speak.

Oviereya was pleased to be irritating Cornelius. The two of

them getting along was impossible. Eager to share more of her thoughts, she persisted. "Discontent with the central government is rising among the other three colonies' populations. Rumors say Colony Five's governess, Samantha Hayley, is secretly supporting the Coalition. After all, her daughter lived in Colony Four and died fighting for its independence in the Three-Week War.

"Governor Rich of Colony Two has been suspected of forming backdoor alliances with outer worlds to boost economic growth and achieve self-sufficiency. He's finally become fed up with the central government's inertia. It may be only a matter of time before the unoccupied colonies push for independence."

Cornelius didn't care if the other three colonies rebelled. He'd just send in troops to restore order.

"If we don't end martial law, reinstate the imprisoned governors, and undertake drastic revitalization initiatives in the colonies, more rebellion will follow," Oviereya guaranteed. "Then what? We deploy more Guardians to engage in more homicide? We're already in jeopardy of violating Article II. This mercurial mess could easily implode if the government doesn't develop an action plan to address the colonies' poor state."

Cornelius seethed internally. He saw the chairwoman's words as a pitiful confession of weakness.

Oviereya kept delivering her message, her zeal matching that of someone campaigning for the Chief Executiveship. "Remember, the entire Interplanetary Union is watching us more closely than ever. When the Union leaders meet for the emergency summit next week, including our Chief Executive, the Commonwealth can be penalized or, worse, ousted by vote, if it is in violation of Article II *(which governed the use of force against a Union member's own people)* or even Article VI *(which mandated sound ethics)*."

We've outgrown our need for the Union, Cornelius thought.

Unlike him, Oviereya felt the Union was an indispensable ally. "To maintain incorporated status, we must comply with the Union Charter's articles. They're the criteria and guidelines that must be followed, or *else*. If we're expelled from the Union, times will get difficult. The Union Worlds are vital to our economy and defense.

"Without them, we'd be vulnerable in this vast galaxy, at the mercy of many technologically advanced foreign powers, like the Inkriex. The only reason hostile forces hesitate to attack the Commonwealth is because of our Union affiliation. If expelled, no one is coming to the Commonwealth's aid if it is attacked."

The anchorman signaled to Oviereya that her time was up. He had let her speak long enough and needed to be fair.

Cornelius grinned. His words were chambered like bullets, and he was ready to fire.

Her voice sharper than a knife, Oviereya gave her last statement. "While we've advanced technologically, economically, and militarily, it's still not enough to sever ties with the Union. Even if we could stand on our own, we're stronger together than apart."

"Mr. Gould, your thoughts?" the anchorman asked, now that the minority leader was done with her lengthy history analysis.

Cornelius spoke, his directness unadorned. "Rebuilding our *entire* civilization in this new galaxy takes time. It's important to remember that it's only been a few years since the Bhalkran and Phazharian conflicts. Those wars diminished resources and stalled progress on both Eden and Satellite One. Plus, the Commonwealth has an *astronomical* amount of debt to pay back to the intergalactic governments that helped establish our republic. That includes the Union Worlds."

He leaned forward slightly. "And yes, it's true that more funds are allocated to Eden than Satellite One, but there's a reason for that: Eden is the heart of humanity's intergalactic republic, and without the heart, all else dies. I'm not denying that more can be done to upgrade the colonies, but it's unrealistic for the government to undertake 'drastic revitalization initiatives' at this point."

Oviereya thought, *It's not unrealistic. You're just a coldhearted son of a bitch.*

Cornelius said, "I'm a man who gives people the reality of a situation, not what simply sounds good, unlike the chairwoman here." Oviereya grunted. Cornelius finished, saying, "An aid package would be sufficient to stabilize things."

Outrage engulfed Oviereya. "An aid package? That's like putting a bandage on a gunshot wound and hoping the bleeding stops. Again, a proposition that does zero to actually resolve the problem. We're spending billions of G-credits on military proliferation. I say we redirect funds from defense and use them to revitalize the colonies. And once the colonies' people experience progress, this internecine war will cease." She stared daggers at Cornelius, a look that could kill.

Cornelius shook his head. "Weakening the CDF's mission-essential functions would be detrimental to both the Commonwealth and the Union's safety. I believe we are fundamental to the Union's defense capability. That's why, even if I thought we had violated Article II, I wouldn't buy into the hysteria about us getting exiled. Without the Commonwealth, the Union would have fallen to the Phazharians, the Bhalkrans, or some other fiend."

Cornelius believed the Commonwealth had progressed enough to survive without the Union, and he saw the Charter's strict mandates on military force as a nuisance hindering the central government from delimiting the CDF. He also felt that the central government should have sole authority over planetary-partner approval, rather than waiting for the Union's consent, which he viewed as needless red tape.

In its infancy, the Commonwealth needed the Union, but much like a child that no longer needs a mother after reaching adulthood, Cornelius believed the Commonwealth had outgrown its dependency on the Union. The prior Chief, Jared Kerner's father, Thom Kerner, concurred.

Thom and Cornelius were military colleagues at one time and saw eye to eye on many affairs. Together, they set in motion a covert plan for the Commonwealth to achieve self-sufficiency. Military proliferation was a critical part of that plan, which was why Cornelius was hellbent on continuing to funnel G-credits into the defense-industrial complex instead of the colonies.

Leaving the Union to extricate the Commonwealth from the Charter was also part of the plan. Thom and Cornelius envisioned the Commonwealth evolving into an intergalactic superpower—essentially its own union of worlds—since other governments were becoming quasi-members as protectorates.

Therefore, for Cornelius, having the Commonwealth's incorporated status revoked would be a positive thing. But many of Cornelius' colleagues in Parliament, the people of the Commonwealth, and Chief Executive Jared Kerner opposed leaving the Union, so he catered to popular opinion to save face.

Cornelius added with cold aggression, "Right now, we cannot make grand promises to the colonies that we cannot keep, which is why I say an aid package must do for now."

To Oviereya, Cornelius was merely regurgitating the same dogma she had heard all her life, one designed to keep the colonies suppressed even longer.

Cornelius intended to drive his point home. "If we make

promises and fail to deliver, we'll face another wave of colonist transgression to combat, which could trigger yet another worrisome Union investigation.

"To end this internal conflict and keep the Union off our backs, we must intensify our efforts to wipe out the Coalition and other rebel groups, rather than give in to their demands. That's *another* reason to continue increasing military funding.

"Crushing these terrorists is the surest way to end the tiresome bid for independence from colonies One, Four, and Six—and to deter rebellion in the others."

Oviereya didn't like what she was hearing, and her face showed it. "So you believe more force is the only way to end the insurrection? There are no nonmilitary solutions?"

"Correct," Cornelius affirmed. "I also believe that to ensure the other colonies don't follow suit, additional . . . preventive measures are needed."

"Such as?" Oviereya asked calmly, camouflaging her disdain under a guise of professionalism.

"Routine inspections and audits of Two, Three, and Five's government operations. Permit mass surveillance of those *entire* colonies if necessary. In this State of Emergency, the Chief Executive has the power to do that. We need to keep tabs on *everything*. If we suspect any of the governments or citizens of those colonies are providing assistance to the Coalition or other rebel groups, then we launch investigations."

"More military-power expansion? Spoken like a power-hungry overlord," Oviereya said, tone tempered yet powerful.

A vein pulsed in Cornelius' temple. "No, spoken like someone who cares about his military and government too much to allow terrorists and their backers to beat them into passivity."

Time restraints forced the anchorman to end the debate and

ask his final question. "Election year is coming. The Chief Executive and Parliament seats are all up for grabs, and the political climate is very tense. Some people want a more aggressive solution to the war, such as Chairman Gould's; some want a peaceful one. But all are tired of it. People are seeking a new direction, a new vision. Rumors suggest both of you might run for the Chief Executive seat." He craned his head left, then right. "Any truth to that?"

"I have no comment at this time," Oviereya said.

Cornelius crossed his arms tightly over his chest. "Neither do I."

"Off," Stacie said. The holoscreen dematerialized into pixels and dissolved. "Maximum shade, please." The windows polarized, masking the sun's rays. "Set alarm for three minutes till landing."

"Alarm time logged," the flyer's computer said.

Stacie closed her eyes and dozed off.

• • •

Cornelius strode into the vestibule of the news station, shoved past a turnstile, and pushed his way out one of the four revolving doors. Outside, an armored black limo waited, flanked by an escort vehicle in front and another behind.

As he approached, one of the limo's doors clicked and hissed open. He ducked inside, settling beside a woman in a black pantsuit, her honey-blond pixie cut precise and professional. She was his executive assistant and apprentice, Gillian Bass.

"You did well, Sir," Gillian said.

Cornelius scoffed. Compliments meant nothing to him.

The lead escort vehicle slowly accelerated onto the four-lane street. At the proper interval, Cornelius' driver pulled behind it, and the rear escort vehicle followed in tandem.

A divider separated the front and passenger compartments,

allowing Cornelius to discuss confidential matters. "Any new developments from our intelligence on Orqron?" he asked Gillian.

She unlatched the attaché case on her lap, revealing a portable, high-efficiency information terminal.

She skimmed the report in front of her. "With the help of Orqron's Ministry of Defense, General Conlan's intelligence team has confirmed that—among the various tribes the Orqron Government is feuding with over land—the Nagamasulli Tribe was responsible for shooting down Zenith Combat Technologies' (ZCT) delivery transport.

"Perhaps if ZCT hadn't relied so heavily on the Orqron Government for protection and had bolstered its own security, this disaster could've been avoided."

"Perhaps," Cornelius replied. "But the Orqron Government is a Union-approved trading partner. Any interference with our arms industries' distribution services warrants a severe response. If it were up to me, I'd deploy a retaliation force to Orqron to obliterate the Nagamasulli Tribe. That would send a message to every tribe on the planet that the Commonwealth has zero tolerance for anyone attacking its people or disrupting its business practices.

"We need to instill fear in them. And though deploying a retaliation force to Orqron wouldn't violate the Union Charter, since the Nagamasulli drew first blood, Chief Executive Kerner believes engaging in active combat on Orqron isn't in the Commonwealth's best interest. He's too concerned about being perceived as a warmonger. We need a leader who prioritizes doing the right thing over their image, someone who isn't afraid to make tough calls, regardless of public scrutiny."

"Such as yourself, Sir?" Gillian asked, though she already knew the answer.

Cornelius didn't waste words. "Indeed. Now what of the

Falgoah Clan? Recently, I've become quite wary of them." Gillian fell silent as a growing sense of unease took hold. "Something bothering you?"

"It's just that . . . the central government casting an entire race of Zelaforians off their homeworld and turning them into refugees seems cruel," Gillian said ruefully. "The Falgoah and Chalderat are the only ones who should resolve their age-old feud."

There wasn't a detectable trace of compunction on Cornelius' face. "The Falgoah themselves are responsible for jeopardizing their existence," he replied frigidly. "The Ambassador Corps warned both the Falgoah and Chalderat about the consequences of violating the negotiated ceasefire. Instead of complying with it, the Falgoah made inroads into Chalderat territory and started another war.

"Disobedience and betrayal must have severe consequences. The Falgoah's belligerence could not be tolerated in the Commonwealth, just like the Coalition's belligerence cannot be tolerated. Now proceed with the report."

Gillian tapped a series of keys. A holovid ballooned from her info terminal. "Our surveillance drone recorded this footage. It shows a Falgoah clansman meeting with a man." She touched the holovid to enlarge the man's face. "Facial-recognition programs confirmed he is Drake Vikander, leader of the Vikander Faction."

Cornelius curled a finger around his chin, deep in thought. "So the Coalition has formed an alliance with the Falgoah."

"But why would the Falgoah ally with the Coalition? What do they stand to gain by the central government ceding to the Coalition's demands for independence or equality?"

"What they want is to return to their homeworld and reclaim their land from the Chalderat." The wheels in Cornelius' brain turned. "Perhaps the Coalition has grown exhausted with the government's refusal to compromise and is now planning a complete takeover of the government, which would allow them to invite the Falgoah back to Zelaforia."

Gillian powered off the info terminal. "That's a reasonable deduction."

"We should retaliate against the Nagamasulli Tribe. We should attack the Falgoah immediately; however, that video lacks sufficient proof that the Falgoah are working with our enemy. None of the Union leaders would authorize deploying Guardians to exterminate the Falgoah on the planet where they currently reside."

Gillian said, "Yes, and besides, the Union says the Falgoah have already paid their penalty with the Commonwealth's decision to exile them, ensuring they won't disrupt the peace in Noshkanu anymore. The Union claims there's no need either to attack or to monitor them. That means the video footage is illegal. So it can't be used to incriminate the Falgoah. In fact, it'd incriminate you."

"Not necessarily." Cornelius projected an air of certainty. "There are loopholes in every rule, regulation, and policy, loopholes a smart Chief Executive would exploit to keep an eye on a potential threat. We're surrounded by enemies seeking to tear apart our republic, and many of my confrères and the Chief Executive do *nothing*. Apparently, they'd rather be reactive than proactive, and inaction has negative consequences, as you know."

A memory of horrors beyond description seized Gillian's mind. She wrestled it away, then said, "Well, starting fights with our enemies before they've even tried to attack us might actually have negative consequences itself. If we do that, we could come off as the scourge of the universe, enabling our enemies to garner more support to overtake us."

Cornelius replied, "We'd simply crush their 'support' as well." Silent for a moment, he reflected. "I watched lands and oceans become mass graves because Earth's politicians hesitated to take preemptive action that could have prevented widespread Armageddon. I had to watch *billions* of people die.

"Those politicians wanted to be as *punctilious* as possible. They were frightened of being labeled as *belligerent*. Yet, their overly cautious approach to defense was the very thing that cost lives. I'll be damned if I let history repeat itself."

He gazed out the window. Uniquely shaped flyers soared high above. Richly dressed citizens, citizens he had sworn to protect, rode the slideways, which were moving conveyor-like sidewalks. Infographic pop-up holos appeared as the slideways transported the citizens past shops.

Cleaner golems sucked up trash and swept, keeping solar-paneled streets perfectly pristine. Far out, more buildings were being erected, their scaffolding and ironwork reaching a thousand feet heavenward. Construction flyers hovered.

Cornelius said, "Peacemongers like Chairwoman Amaechi want to divert funds from the defense budget to appease the colonists and cater to their emotional mandates. But our military might is why foreign hostiles have not overrun the Commonwealth and the Union. Debilitating our military, our greatest asset, would be disadvantageous.

"The chairwoman's compassion for the indigent is admirable, but right now, when we have enemies seeking to harm us, the indigent cannot be prioritized. If a few succumb to death in the meantime, so be it.

"The chairwoman's naiveté is further demonstrated by her willingness to placate the Coalition's demands. Giving in would make the central government appear weak."

Cornelius' motorcade swerved right, onto another street. A mix of Eden citizens and intergalactic tourists sauntered past storefronts and open-air cafés. Tourists from the Union Worlds and the Commonwealth's trading partners often flocked to Cornerstone City. It was a magnet for intergalactic tourism.

"The chairwoman also rebukes the social structure that AEGIS created." Cornelius' disdain for Oviereya seeped into his tone. "The system defined the proper function for everyone, ensuring we don't waste time, education, or resources preparing people for roles they aren't fit for. Some are simply better positioned for success in life as resource harvesters. The function AEGIS assigned to colonists aligns with the value they bring to society."

A grim mask settled on his face. "The integration of divisive immigrants into the CDF, such as the female cadet detained at the Academy today, proves that when AEGIS's social structure is deviated from, even slightly, the perfection of that structure is corrupted. The lottery experiment should be abolished."

Indignation rattled every fiber of his being. "Instead of worrying about colonists' frivolous woes, we need to expand our military's capability to hunt down the intergalactic sex traffickers, marauders, and other scourges terrorizing our great republic. Destroying this scum is the responsibility of the CDF.

"If I had the final say, I'd triple the number of expedition parties scouring the galaxies these fiends' operations span. They need to be annihilated completely, to rid the universe of them, so they will no longer harm us or any race of beings."

Cornelius had no limits when it came to doing what he thought was right to protect his people. When he was a U.S. soldier on Earth, his superiors reprimanded him for using unlawful interrogation tactics on POWs. As a general in the CDF during the Bhalkran War, he ordered bombs dropped on innocent Bhalkran villages to eradicate the Commonwealth's enemies hiding among them. He concluded that if a few must die to save the many, so be it, especially when the "many" were his own people. Such actions made him a controversial figure in the Commonwealth.

"We must have the strongest military possible," Cornelius declared. "We need to be feared. Neither Chairwoman Amaechi nor our feeble-minded Chief Executive is fit to lead the New Humanity. We must become the superpower we have the potential to be.

"No one knows what threats exist in the universe. It may be only a matter of time before something terrible comes to our doorstep. We must be ready."

Cornelius had tried to continue his and Thom's agenda to expand the military and its reach, an agenda hampered by filibuster and other bureaucratic red tape. It also didn't help that Jared was nowhere near the militant his father was, being more of a centrist.

"Truth is I'm hoping our incorporated status gets revoked, to unchain us from the Charter's constraints," Cornelius said. "Then we wouldn't have to play politics to fully utilize our military. Even if I were in the Chief Executive seat, it'd be next to impossible to convince two-thirds of the Parliament to rescind our incorporated status—because too many of my fellow conservatives have reservations about detaching from the Union. Maybe this civil war will be a blessing in disguise."

"So when *do* you plan to announce your intention to run?" Gillian asked.

"Next year's election is too far away. We need to steer the Commonwealth in a new direction as soon as possible. So I have decided to proceed with Operation New Wave."

"Kerner's assassination?"

"Yes. Not my favorite course of action but a necessary one, one to the liking of my . . . special benefactors." Benefactors who remained a mystery to Gillian. "Jared is nowhere near the Chief Executive his father was, a man I was proud to serve under. By decree, I'd be next in line to assume the Office of the Chief Executive once Kerner and Deputy Chief Norton are dead."

"What's your plan to eliminate them?"

"When Kerner—" In front of the limo, a burst of flames and smoke shot skyward, a ferocious boom assaulting the ears of every citizen outside. "What the hell?" The explosion flipped the lead escort vehicle onto its roof, glass and metal crunching.

The driver of the limo swerved around the ruined vehicle, tires squealing, then accelerated.

Both security personnel inside the mangled, flipped-over vehicle were dead.

Shouting, screaming pedestrians chaotically scrambled across the slideways.

Another explosion tossed the rear escort vehicle into a rollover. A third whipped the limo into an uncontrollable tailspin until it careered into a commercial van.

Breathing heavily, Gillian said to Cornelius, "Sir, you okay?"

Cornelius cringed. "Fine," he blurted. He reached a hand behind his neck, massaging the ache caused by whiplash.

Assassination attempts while traveling were the reason he preferred ground-based transportation. If he had been blown out of the sky in a flyer, he'd be dead.

What was left of the dashboard flashed colors and rang noisily. The driver's seat destroyed, Cornelius' chauffeur was dead.

Gillian stiffly reached for the sidepiece stowed in her harness, shoulder hurting. "Sir, stay inside." She pulled the door handle. A click sounded, yet the warped door remained stubbornly shut. "Damn it!"

She pulled the handle again and threw her throbbing shoulder into the door, prying it ajar. She rammed her shoulder into the door one more time, exacerbating the pain. It shrieked open, and she stepped out, heels clicking the pavement.

With a shaky two-handed grip, she extended her firearm and raked the air from left to right, searching for hostiles. Her heart thudded as her memory reunited her with the mayhem of urban warfare: people screaming all around her, staccato pops of gunfire, noisy sirens. It was a killing hell she didn't want to relive.

Her nervous eyes scanned the devastated street. A bead of sweat snaked down the bridge of her nose.

She spotted dead Union World citizens, two Rumanoahans and one Varsh'Ru. Nearby lay a dead Orsodonian from the Commonwealth's trading partner Orsodonia.

This was the first time foreigners had died on Eden soil. The incident was bound to cause political chaos. Gillian stood within history in the making.

She dragged a lungful of smoke-scented oxygen into her nostrils, exhaled, and stabilized her posture. It had been years since she was in a high-stress combat scenario.

She said into her government-issued wristcom, "Mayday." It was the call sign for Cornelius' emergency evac flyer.

A droning sound neared.

Alarmed, she spun to her right as a hoverbike whooshed to a stop in front of her. A helmeted man in dark clothing reached for the pistol holstered on his thigh.

Gillian's heart hammered her chest. "Fuck!" Military reflexes kicking in, she yanked the door closer and quickly sank down into a crouch.

Shots rang out. Sparks flew as a barrage of bullets ricocheted off the armored door. The mystery assassin emptied a full magazine and thumbed the release.

The sound of the magazine clattering to the ground was Gillian's cue. Her adrenaline spiked, and she rose, killer instinct in her gray eyes.

The assassin slapped a new magazine into his pistol, but it was too late. Gillian raised her gun and double-tapped the trigger. The weapon kicked in her hands as it discharged two shots.

The bullets slammed into the assassin's vest. He recoiled from the impact, and his pistol slipped from his grasp.

With deadly neohuman precision, Gillian locked him in her gun's sights and fired the fatal round. The bullet shattered the glass visor of his helmet, piercing his skull between the eyes.

A mist of red liquid spritzed the air as he fell to the ground.

Hands trembling, Gillian remained on high alert. Her eyes scanned the area for more assassins. "Stay inside, Sir!" she ordered Cornelius. "Your evac team is on the way!"

"I'm well aware of security protocol, Ms. Bass!" Cornelius snapped, a high level of agitation in his voice.

As the man responsible for implementing martial law, Cornelius had become a primary target for violent anti-government radicals and fringe groups. The mere rumor of him possibly running for Chief Executive only emboldened them further.

Gillian stood in front of the limo, maintaining her aplomb.

Sirens wailed, growing louder as they got closer. The roar of an incoming aircraft drew Gillian's attention skyward. Cornelius' evac flyer approached.

• • •

Stacie's air-cab closed in on a palatial mansion nestled in the lowlands on the outskirts of Cornerstone City, gliding above green pastures that extended as far as the eye could see.

The flyer's alarm chimed three minutes before touchdown, as programmed. Stacie stirred and rubbed her eyes.

"We have reached our destination," the computer informed her, lifting the windows' tinting to reveal the picturesque blue sky. The flyer slowly descended. A low pulsing hum was followed by a quiet clunk as it came to a stop. "Thank you for choosing Air Escort." A red flashing warning-notification told Stacie to yield movement. "Please ride with us again." The canopy opened, and all warning lights dimmed to black.

Stacie's seat belt unbuckled automatically. A chirp signaled it was safe to exit. She swung one stocking-covered leg out, then the other, and stood, stepping into the heat. She arched her back, stretching her stiff joints.

The cab received its next passenger's location and zoomed away.

Stacie approached the wrought-iron fence, her high heels making a soft clacking sound against the pavement. She pressed her palm to the electronic gate's biometric scanner. Once her identity was confirmed, the gate screeched open along its guiding rail, granting her entry into the immense, well-manicured yard.

She walked down a winding flagstone path framed by trimmed hedges. Above, birds chirped in green-leafed trees bearing brightly colored berries. All around the estate, colorful flowers bloomed. In the distance, greenhouses stood. They were where the Spencers' farmers cultivated crops for them.

The path looped around a sculpted fountain of an angel clothed in a tunic, her wings outstretched. It then continued onward.

Stacie reached the mansion, an incredible feat of modern architecture that had more windows than one could count. She walked up the five steps to the colonnaded veranda. The overhead shelter provided much-needed relief from the sun's simmering heat.

She wiped sweat from her glistening brow. Before she could scan her biometrics again, one of the large ornamental doors creaked open. An elderly bald man stood in the doorway. He had a bushy gray mustache and wore an elaborate purple tux.

"Greetings, Madam Spencer," the butler said. Security sensors had informed him of Stacie's arrival.

"Clifton, good to see you."

Clifton bowed from the waist. "You as well, Madam Spencer."

"I take it Mother and Father are furious."

"Indeed. You joined the Defense Force without their blessing."

Stacie scoffed. "I don't need their blessing." She turned her nose up and folded her arms, leaning her hip against the veranda's balustrade. "I'm a grown-ass woman, not a *fucking* child. I told them I was enlisting and that nothing they said could stop me."

Clifton had hoped the CDF had changed her, but it hadn't. He was still staring into blue eyes full of vanity, arrogance, and stubbornness. That, however, was her mother's fault.

Stacie took a long, slow breath, calming down from her rant, but a rant not without merit. She unsnapped the red fasteners on her service jacket. "So, where are Mom and Dad, at some *high-profile* meeting?" she asked, her tone rightfully snappish.

"Your mother awaits you in the common room. The baron is away on business."

Stacie wrestled off her jacket. Patches of sweat wet her white dress shirt.

After neatly folding the jacket and wrapping the cape around it, she passed the garment off to Clifton. Her voice carried a trace of worry as she asked, "How is Father, by the way?"

"His health has not been the best, but he is managing."

Stacie undid the first three buttons of her shirt and tugged on the collar for air. "Good." That news relieved her worry.

"Shall I escort?"

Stacie replied, "No, I'm a big girl. I can escort myself." She was direct and independent as usual, Clifton thought. Some of her better traits, though. "Take that uniform piece to my room for me."

"Yes, Madam."

"Thank you."

Stacie crossed a broad, lengthy hall, passing housekeeping golems tending to the mansion's upkeep. The skylights set into the ceiling spilled sunlight onto the expensive red carpet. She braced herself for confrontation, her features steeled by courage.

The hall widened into a grand oval foyer where a semicircle of family portraits hung. Stacie stilled and tilted her chin upward, staring thoughtfully at the hard-copy photos of the cute little girl with a long, plaited ponytail. The girl's adorable smile stretched from ear to ear, puffing out her cheeks. But that radiant smile was all show for the camera, a masquerade. Her small, innocent eyes were devoid of happiness.

Stacie's perfectionist mother had tolerated nothing short of excellence from her in academia and every single avocation she pursued. That constant pressure marred Stacie's childhood.

She thought back to the one-year horror of the Eight Elite's preparatory school, where they sent their seventeen-year-olds to prepare them for post-high school education. She dreaded the days spent learning how to "walk like a lady" or performing absurd exercises, such as balancing pewter dishes atop her palms or head to master balance and coordination.

It was no wonder that after enrolling at Cadwell Institute of Higher Learning for her undergraduate studies, she went totally wild. Her first two years revolved around alcohol, parties, recreational drugs, and sex binges. By year three, however, she longed for a life beyond frivolous decadence and the expectation of someday running the family business. So, after graduation, she enlisted in the CDF.

Stacie walked through the archway in the middle of the foyer and entered a richly decorated, well-furnished common room.

Dark rugs spanned the floor. Landscape paintings adorned the walls. Windows framed by lavish curtains let in sunshine.

Her daunting mother, Darlene Spencer, sat in a high-backed armchair fit for a queen, an unlit fireplace behind her. She wore a black dress with ruffled sleeves and an ankle-length ruffled hem. On her finger was a gold ring bearing the family crest—a man wearing a crown and holding a sword atop a horse standing on its hind legs. Glaring at Stacie intensely, she genteelly and silently sipped from a ceramic cup of hot tea.

Stacie went up to her. "Mother," she spat in a fiery tone, anticipating an earful of chastising.

The cup tinked the glass coffee table as Darlene set it down. Her expression spoke volumes about her feelings toward her daughter's new military career. Brows knitted, she heaved herself to her feet and then swung her hand, smacking Stacie's cheek.

Darlene was proud of the financial empire she and her husband had built. Stacie was the heir to it all, and to Darlene, it was time she started acting like it. "You insolent little degenerate. I thought we raised you better than this."

Stacie rubbed her stinging flesh. The slap that was all too familiar put a frown on her face. "Selfish? I—"

"Quiet," Darlene thundered, cutting her off. "Your father is ill, and you go off to play Guardian? You sully our estate with this . . . uniform?"

Stacie shot back, a hard edge in her voice. "This uniform is a symbol of prestige, Mother." Maybe to "regular" Edenites, but not the alpha, the Eight Elite. "And Father—"

Darlene interrupted Stacie again. "You have an obligation to your family. Your grooming to be our successor was to begin. You were supposed to attend the quarterly assemblies of the eight family heads. You were to familiarize yourself with our organizational structure. What the hell were you thinking?" She threw her arms up.

"I'll take up the torch after you guys croak," Stacie said, causing Darlene to freeze in shock. "Right now I need to—" Stacie searched for the right words. "I need to prove I'm more than . . . more than *this*." She whipped her arms out wide.

Darlene wrinkled her nose. "More than *what?*"

Stacie sighed. Her tone softened. "More than just some . . . some blue-blooded, silver-spoon nepo baby." Her eyes pled for a semblance of understanding. "Is that so hard for you to comprehend, Mother?"

Darlene shook her head in disappointment and huffed. "Your father could pass any year, any month, any day now. You are to succeed us. Instead, you risk getting yourself killed? Such fucking stupidity." Her tone became even frostier. "You need to live up to the responsibilities that come with being a Spencer."

Stacie rolled her eyes. "Forget it." She whirled around to leave, footsteps landing hard.

"Stacie Lynette Spencer, where do you think you're going?" Darlene demanded of her wayward daughter.

"To my room. I've got a graduation banquet to rest up for. Tomorrow, I leave for my duty station. Don't expect me to come to you in the morning to say bye."

Darlene pinged Stacie's implant. Stacie rejected her Link request, a sign of total disobedience for a daughter of the Eight.

Get lost, Mom, Stacie thought.

Darlene muttered under her breath. She figured maybe she should've slapped Stacie harder.

Stacie ascended the carpeted staircase to her room. She couldn't wait to arrive at her duty station, an escape from the stringent expectations that came with being a daughter of the Eight. Her parents expected her to take over the family business, leaving her no say in her own destiny. She was to always conduct herself in a moral, ethical, and honorable manner and never act in a way that would disgrace or humiliate the family.

She recalled the night she got her first DUI and totaled her car, which she probably should've put on autodrive. After explaining the incident to her parents, they subjected her to the archaic, draconian disciplinary measures outlined in the Eight Elite's rule book. Even the slightest infraction was unacceptable.

As the female head of household, Stacie's mother decided the punishment: ten belt lashes to her back. Just like when she was a child. Foolishness, in her eyes.

She opened the door to her room and toed off her heels. Next, she shrugged out of her shirt and slid off her stockings. Then she pushed her skirt down to her ankles and stepped out of it.

Clad in white cotton lingerie, she plopped onto her bed as the cool air conditioning soothed her skin. Beside her was her uniform's service jacket, placed there by Clifton.

Golden light poured in from the window, bathing her in its warmth. The stunning view of green meadows and rolling hills outside had always given her a sense of tranquility, even during the harshest moments of her childhood.

She glanced at the stark white walls surrounding her and flattened her lips together. After butting heads with her mother, she needed a more soothing color to clear her mind. "Change wall color to pink," she instructed the mansion's virtual assistant. A soft pink hue washed over the walls. Easily her favorite color. "Better."

She unscrewed the locking lid of the humidor on her nightstand, extracted a cigarette, and flicked a lighter to life. Tucking the cigarette between her lips, she inhaled deeply, letting the nicotine scour her mind of her and Darlene's past quarrels—memories dredged up by their argument downstairs. She was on the verge of ditching the habit, thanks to Randy—Mr. Righteousness, Health, and Fitness. But today would have to be a cheat day.

Her wristcom rang.

She ground out the cigarette in the ashtray and tapped her wristcom to accept the call.

Oviereya's voice flowed from the micro-speaker. "I just wanted to congratulate you on your graduation. I'm proud of you."

"At least someone is."

"Sounds like your parents aren't too thrilled?"

"Of course they aren't. You know them."

"Well, I commend you for making such a life-altering decision and redirecting your future down a path you desire. However, you still have family responsibilities. Don't forget about them."

"Yeah, yeah." Stacie changed the subject. "I saw you on a newscast earlier. Are you gonna run for Chief Executive?"

"I'm . . . considering it."

"I think you should totally do it."

"I have to go. Parliament has an emergency meeting in an hour. Again, congratulations." The call disconnected.

Stacie closed her drowsy eyes.

Her life was on the brink of transformation. Until now, every credit in her bank account had belonged to her parents, and they could take them all away on a whim. They owned her life, but not anymore. She was her own woman now. No more being caged.

She had postponed the burden of preparing to inherit Spencer Enterprises until she decided she was ready. She was *free*. And soon, she'd be on Satellite One, helping to end the insurrection. After that, maybe the CDF would send her unit to a Mission

World. And Randy would be with her. She envisioned a life of just helping people and making love to her boyfriend.

A calmness settled over her as she drifted off to sleep.

• • •

Randy, wearing a tailored black suit, escorted Stacie into a banquet hall filled with circular tables, his arm anchored around hers.

The sparkly red dress that clung to Stacie's frame made her a sight to behold. Although civilian attire was permitted for the evening, the thigh-high slit and the plunging neckline flaunting her breasts violated the dress code. Stacie's audacity knew no bounds. She had a splendid physique and wasn't bashful about showcasing it, always eager to be the center of attention.

Servers in white aprons set up buffets. A female chef, wearing a hairnet, wheeled in a rack of exquisite dishes from the kitchen. Until dinner was served, hundreds of sharply dressed graduates from multiple classes mingled.

Randy and Stacie strolled about, taking in the convivial atmosphere of the evening.

Jarius walked past them in a snazzy black tux and red bow tie, laughing merrily with his date, a well-endowed light brown woman sporting a silver halterneck dress and stilettos. "Lookin' good, Randy," he commented, his natural charm shining bright. He sipped his highball.

As Jarius and his cute n' curvy companion went to a table, she whispered something into his ear and pressed her glossy red lips to his cheek. He laughed out loud and rested his free hand on the small of her bare back. The evening seemed to be off to a good start for him.

"So how'd you and Specialist Ford become so buddy-buddy?" Stacie asked Randy.

"We met and became tight during our senior year at

Commonwealth University."

"I see."

Randy and Stacie navigated throngs of Guardians dressed in immaculate suits, tuxedos, gowns, and dresses. Some women eyed Stacie contemptuously, as her refusal to conform to clothing guidelines—to unapologetically show off—suggested she thought herself special. Men, though, welcomed the sight of her exposed flesh. After all, she was quite the physical specimen.

"Randal Scott!" came a powerful, jovial voice.

A man approached Randy and Stacie, his burgundy suit barely hiding his hefty physique. He had a neatly trimmed goatee, and a cybernetic prosthetic replaced his left hand.

Randy smiled upon seeing him. "General Conlan."

General Michael Conlan was the Chief of Defense Force Intelligence. His towering height, muscular physique, and booming voice could be intimidating when first encountered, but once you got to know him, you'd find him exceedingly affable.

He treated his subordinates as if he'd known them a lifetime, making them feel comfortable confiding in him about anything—family, relationships, career, and so on. Even during his time as a platoon leader, he'd fellowship with his men as if he were their friend. This informal attitude earned him tremendous respect.

However, those familiar with him knew that his kindness didn't equate to weakness. If you got on his bad side, disobeyed directives, or neglected responsibility and duty, you'd incur his wrath, receiving the harshest of reprimands.

"Randal, it's been a while," Conlan said. "I haven't seen you in —"—he curled a finger around his chin—"two years?"

"Sounds about right, Sir."

Awe lit Stacie's gaze as it lingered on her lover. "You know General Conlan?"

"He's a family friend," Randy replied.

Conlan shifted his friendly topaz eyes toward Stacie. Strong cheekbones; a thin, pretty nose; piercing blue eyes; and an attractive figure. Randy had snagged himself a treasure, Conlan thought. She reminded him of his late wife when she was her age. "And who might this *tantalizing* young woman be?" he asked.

Stacie replied, "Stacie Lyn Spencer, Sir."

Conlan's brows jumped. "Ah, daughter of Patrick and Darlene Spencer." He leaned his massive frame inward and politely kissed Stacie's hand. "A pleasure to meet you, dear."

Randy delicately coiled an arm around Stacie's waist. "Sweetheart, could the general and I have a moment?"

Stacie planted a kiss on his lips. "Ten minutes, babe, then I come hunting." She twirled and, with the elegance of a runway model, strutted past a male caterer balancing hors d'oeuvres atop a tray. He did a double take to be sure his eyes weren't exaggerating her beauty.

"Quite the catch," Conlan commented. "A member of the Scott and Spencer families getting together is a dynasty waiting to be born. She'll bear you excellent children."

"Let's not get ahead of ourselves. There are no wedding bells planned anytime soon. We're . . . still testing the waters."

"Well, everything happens in stages," Conlan provided.

Randy conspiratorially glanced left and right to ensure no one was within earshot and changed the subject, lowering his voice. "General, I'd like to thank you for making sure I got stationed at Lima Company. You have my deepest gratitude. Now I can see that my father pays for Mom's death."

Exercising forethought, Conlan gestured toward the balcony with a tilt of his head. He wanted to have a private conversation. "Let's step outside."

Randy looked bemused. What was this about? "Sure." He tucked his hands into his pants' pockets and followed the general.

Conlan pushed open the glass double doors leading out onto the curved balcony. He and Randy stepped into the warm night air.

The doors shut behind them, muting all the joyous merrymaking of the newly initiated Guardians.

Conlan relaxed his arms over the balcony's safety wall and sighed apprehensively, staring at the glowing city lights that went on forever in all directions.

A variety of flyers streaked here and there under the night sky's sparkling constellation.

Hands still in his pockets, Randy stood in silence, waiting for Conlan to speak.

Conlan contemplated his words carefully. "Randy—" He paused, reconsidering his decision. Putting aside his qualms, he continued. "—sometimes war isn't . . . black and white. There are . . . gray areas."

Randy cocked a brow. "What are you saying?"

Conlan said, "There are two sides to this war." No shit, Randy thought. "We . . . we choose the side we believe has the moral high ground. The side embodying our values the most."

Randy's brows came together. "Wait a minute. Are you trying to rationalize that bastard's betrayal?" The memory of A-1 Defense Solutions erupting in flames haunted his mind.

Conlan turned around. He pushed forward an open palm, halting the specialist from jumping to conclusions. "Listen, I'm just saying—"

Randy pointed a finger at Conlan and cut him off before he could form another word. "No, *you* listen. I wanted to fight the Coalition under my father's command. Imagine hearing, just two months before BCT, that your father, the man you wanted to emulate, had been confirmed to have gone rogue and joined the enemy.

"I thought it was some mistake. Maybe he was undercover or something. I came up with every excuse I could imagine. Then, three weeks before my departure date, the Coalition starts attacking the CDF's defense contractors here on Eden. A-1 Defense Solutions was hit, and my mother was killed. And who took part in that terrorist attack? My father. I was even Linked with Mom when that explosion stole her life."

Conlan lowered his chin in sympathy, chewing on Randy's words.

Randy said, "A week later, I attended my mother's funeral, but there was nothing left of her to lay to rest." Grief throbbed in his heart. "I will make my father pay."

"It's not like Arson premeditated her death. It was an accident, Randy. Arson didn't mean to—"

"It doesn't matter if it was an accident or not," Randy countered. He wondered how Conlan would feel if his dad had accidentally killed his mom. He wanted . . . No, he needed Arson to pay. Arson was the bane of his existence.

"He regretted what happened that night," Conlan insisted, his conviction absolute. "He never meant to cause Kathleen any hardship by leaving to—"

A questioning gleam entered Randy's eyes. "You sound as if you have firsthand knowledge of his thoughts and feelings. Did you have contact with him? Do you have contact with him now? Has there been any collusion between you two?" Stonewalling, the general said nothing. Randy's volume rose. "Conlan!" he pushed, in pursuit of answers.

The doors to the balcony squealed open, ending the standoff.

A tipsy Stacie strode forward, a wineglass of something strong in hand. She concentrated hard to maintain her balance. The alcohol had definitely taken hold. "Ten minutes are up, babe." She hooked her arm around Randy's. "C'mon, let's go," she said, voice unnecessarily loud and words slightly slurred.

Randy's feet stumbled as Stacie wrested him from the general. "Stacie, I—"

Conlan raked his fingers through the air, shooing Randy away. "We're done here, Specialist Scott. Go enjoy yourself."

As Stacie dragged Randy away, he peered over his shoulder at Conlan. Ire creased his brow. *This isn't over yet, General.* The balcony doors shut.

Conlan glared at his cybernetic prosthetic. *Thanks to you, Arson, I lost only a hand. I'm sorry you chose the other side, my friend.*

In Stacie's company, Randy forgot about his fallout with Conlan and engaged in dancing, dining, drinking, and conversation for the rest of the evening.

CHAPTER TWO

Arson Scott, his face black and blue, sat slumped against a dingy wall. Randy stood over him, grimacing, and leveled a pistol at his forehead. Hesitantly, he began squeezing the trigger. Then he suddenly froze. After three tense seconds, he fired. Arson's brains splattered over the wall and . . .

"Attention, we are nearing atmospheric entry," the shuttle pilot said over the intercom, taking Randy out of the dream.

He groaned awake as the hull shuddered.

The shuttle exited Hyperspace Leap, and the rainbow of colors outside the windows dissolved to reveal the black of normal space. Ahead, Satellite One was in view.

The fifty new Guardians assigned to Charlie Battalion's Lima Company sat in their BDUs, awaiting planetfall.

Randy ran a hand down his face. He stared through a porthole into the dark void, his expression unreadable. *Father.* Even in his sleep, the traitor bedeviled his mind.

Stacie awoke, too, rubbing her groggy eyes. She had slept off the hangover from all the drinking she did at last night's banquet.

"Hey, you okay, babe?" she asked, then yawned.

Randy's response came in the form of a quiet, unconvincing, "Yeah." He gripped his armrests tightly, banishing Arson from his thoughts for the time being.

Stacie didn't have to access their Link to know what was weighing on him. She knew he was thinking about his father. Wearing concern on her face, she placed a comforting hand over his. There was much chaos within him. She was happy to be a source of relief. After all, no one should have to hurt alone.

Jarius sat two rows up from them. Like all the Eden-born Guardians aboard, he had never actually visited a colony and seen the grim conditions the downtrodden complained about. He'd heard stories about newly trained Guardians, upon their first deployment to a colony, becoming so shaken by what they saw that they empathized with the locals and even defected. The unknown had him twiddling his thumbs. But he wasn't alone; everyone aboard was a little on edge.

As the shuttle penetrated Satellite One's atmosphere, the hull's metallic rattling grew louder. After planetfall, the shuttle descended into a sky of gray clouds, bumping against turbulence.

Once over Colony Four, the pilot routed a trajectory toward Annex 13, a small CDF outpost occupied by Charlie Battalion's Lima Company. Their mission was to keep the peace in Zone 03 of Sector 05. Zone 03 encompassed the towns of Halfin, Stanlow, Guthram, and Holbeck *(one urban district)*, along with a scattering of interim settlements. Captain Arnold Seymour led the company. He was Arson's XO and friend. He assumed command after Arson's desertion.

Three platoons currently made up the entire company. Because of the upcoming summit and the possibility of being expelled from the Union, Chief Executive Jared Kerner had mandated a troop surge to bolster the CDF's manpower. Now fifty of the recent Academy graduates were being sent to Lima Company to form a fourth platoon.

A platoon of callow Guardians with zero combat experience wasn't ideal, but desperate times called for desperate measures. Platoons of novices were being organized across the occupied colonies to dismantle the insurrection. The central government needed to convince the Union leaders that the revolt was under control.

Below stretched a patchwork of barren red earth and industrial towns. Infertile land made ninety percent of Colony Four unfarmable, but the colony was rich in valuable rocks and minerals. As a result, refineries, mines, and manufacturing plants served as the primary sources of income generation for its citizens. Colony Four also played a vital role in defense, as its citizens mined and refined sixty-seven percent of Satellite One's dimatanium, a metal element used to produce an armor alloy for the CDF's war machines.

With insurgent groups growing in number, anonymous hit-and-run attacks on Guardians becoming more frequent, and public displays of civil unrest escalating into violent clashes, Colony Four was becoming a powder keg.

Randy took in the magnificent, desolate mountains; valleys; and plateaus passing by below. *So this is your home colony, Father.* In Colony Four resided all of Arson's family, flesh and blood Randy hadn't met. Though he was born here, this would be his first time setting foot on its soil. Arson had told him a lot about the colony, but seeing it now made everything feel more real.

"This is Air Transit Control. Incoming aircraft, identify yourself," said a voice from the shuttle's comms, audio choppy.

"This is passenger shuttle niner-six-niner," the pilot replied.

"Requesting permission to land."

A burst of static followed before a response came through. "Permission granted."

The shuttle soared above a landing port crowded with aerodynes. As it slowed into a controlled vertical descent, its braking jets flared. After the landing struts deployed, it touched down between two boxy air freighters. Then the engines powered down with a hiss, followed by the creak of cooling metal.

The starboard hatch slid open, and a set of stairs extended to the tarmac.

Restraints clicked as the Guardians unbuckled themselves. Some stood from the fold-up seats and stretched, their stiff joints cricking.

Heavy, purposeful footfalls thudded up the stair-ramp. A six-foot-tall sergeant first class marched into the fuselage, sporting a white-blond crew cut. His unfriendly visage and the dangerous glint in his eyes made it clear he was all business.

Crossing his arms over his chest, he took care of the formalities. "I'm Sergeant First Class Lars Freeman. I'll be your platoon sergeant." He paced up and down the gangway, hands clasped behind his back.

There was an air of intimidation in the way Lars spoke and carried himself. He was clearly a no-nonsense person, a total hard case. "All of you survived hellacious warrior trials to wear that uniform. That means you have the heart of a warrior. But you're green. You've never been downrange, and trust me, it's a whole different beast in theater compared to BCT. So don't go thinking you're some sorta stud just because you aced some tac-sims and know how to operate a Shell."

Grouses, disgruntled muttering, and hard expressions came from Guardians who just got their pride hurt.

"Don't worry, you're in good hands," Lars said. "Your squad and team leaders are all adept combat professionals. I'm certainly no stranger to combat." The scar bisecting his brow and left cheek was a memento from one of his many missions, and his service sketch included the Phazharian and Bhalkran wars. "I can't promise all of you will live, but I can promise I'll do my damnedest to give you the best shot possible at staying alive.

"Some might say I'm a hard-ass, but if you follow my orders and are where you're supposed to be on time, then we're good. Do the opposite and *piss* me the fuck off, then . . . Well, let's just say you don't wanna cross that line. Am I clear, Fourth Platoon?"

Everyone shouted, "Yes, Sergeant!" Formalities taken care of.

"Good. Tomorrow, it's game on, because we have a mission. Mission brief starts at oh-seven-hundred hours. Leave your gear on board for now. You can off-load the shit after I give you the tour. Let's head out."

The Guardians filed out of the shuttle, down the stair-ramp, into the cool weather of the overcast day.

Annex 13 sat on the seaward edge of Halfin, providing a splendid, unobstructed view of the West Ocean. Off the coastline were scenic island landmasses lined with mountains.

While crossing the tarmac, Stacie heard a woman close behind her say, "Hey, princess, don't think you're gonna get special treatment. Your high n' mighty status doesn't mean squat here. Nobody's gonna hand you anything, especially not rank. And nobody's gonna coddle you or kiss your li'l privileged ass."

Stacie recognized the Russian-sounding voice and looked over her shoulder. A pale-skinned woman with an upturned nose and indigo eyes walked closely behind her. The woman's hot-pink highlights stood out boldly against the black tresses of her bobcut, and a conspicuous mole sat to the right of her mouth.

She was Private Emilia Rhineheart. Her adversarial relationship with Stacie had started during BCT. Emilia, a beneficiary of the lottery, was one of the few colony-born cadets in the class of Alpha 9-5. She formed a clique with the others, and Stacie, not only a Highborn but also a child of one of the Eight Elite—the uppermost echelon of the wealthy—became a prime target for their ire. Together, they bullied her and attempted to sabotage her success on more than one occasion.

I didn't know her ass was aboard, Stacie thought. "I'm not here for handouts," she snapped. "I work for my achievements, so can it, Private."

"The loudmouths yapping their goddamn traps need to shut the hell up," Lars said from the front of the platoon.

Stacie grunted. She had heard childish gibes like Emilia's too many times. That was part of why she'd nearly driven her body into the ground to earn the title of Warrior Extraordinaire, an accolade earned through blood, sweat, and grit.

Emilia knew Stacie was seething beneath her controlled facade. Determined to needle her, she lowered her voice so Lars wouldn't overhear. She couldn't help herself. "Pissed off, aren't you, princess?" She chuckled. *Your sensitivity meter's always been easy to push.*

Stacie smirked and whispered back. "All bases have a sparring suite, right? Meet me there at twenty-three-hundred hours so this princess can shut that big mouth of yours."

Emilia gave a smirk of her own. "Deal."

Randy fell into step beside Lars. "Can you tell us anything about the mission tomorrow?"

Eager to learn. I like that. Maybe he has leadership potential, Lars thought. Loudly, he said, "Listen up, everyone! Citizens for Change (CFC) is a nonviolent activist group here in Colony Four. They organize peaceful demonstrations and protests. They're staging several rallies in Halfin tomorrow. The problem is you never know what fanatics might join these rallies and turn them into anarchy.

"Lima Company has been tasked with keeping the peace and ensuring things don't get out of hand. It's basic crowd control. But don't let that dull your situational awareness. There are malcontents out there who know there'll be a CDF presence and can't wait to take potshots at us."

Lars showed his new Guardians the motor pool and outdoor track, then went indoors and showed them the mess hall, physical training center, infirmary, and the platoon's assembly room.

The group strode down a corridor. Two sergeants in civvies approached them from the open lounge area at an easy pace.

"These the newbies, Sergeant Freeman?" the blond one asked, then took a sip of the energy drink in his hand.

"Fourth Platoon, meet Staff Sergeant Jason Mansford, leader of First Squad." Lars' chummy smile conveyed Jason was a Guardian he held in high regard. "Depending on how the roster shapes up, he'll be the squad leader for some of you. And though he can be a cocky son of a bitch, he's one of L-Company's best. Check out his service sketch and you'll probably agree." He gestured to Jason's dark-haired buddy. "This is Sergeant Nico Fleming, leader of Second Squad." He put his business face back on and proceeded. "Now c'mon, we gotta finish up."

As Stacie walked by, her beauty caught Jason's eye. Eager to make contact, he pinged her implant.

A slight look of annoyance swept over Stacie's face as she rejected Jason's Link request. *Yeah, right, jerk. Like I'd ever Link with someone I don't know.*

Jason pulled his eyes away and moved on.

Nico jovially elbowed Jason's shoulder as they parted from the new arrivals. "Easy there. I know what's on your mind. You can't go sleeping with all the ladies now. Practice some self-restraint."

Stacie heard them, faintly. *Womanizers.*

Lars took the platoon into the armory through two automatic sliding doors. The room hummed with electrical current. Encased in glass-pod alcoves were rows of Shells plugged into power receptacles. Above the alcoves were digital displays of Guardians' names.

"This new model of Shell is a huge upgrade compared to the old M-X01 chassis you operated in BCT," Lars said. "More advanced weapons. A lighter, closer-fitting design to cut down on the bulk and reduce mobility lag." He patted one of the glass casings. "I think you'll like these babies a hell of a lot more. They even have a more advanced CPU incorporated and an AI Combat Assistant called Oracle."

"AI Combat Assistant?" a male Guardian whispered inquisitively.

Lars said, "As you know, a Guardian and their Shell are kinda yoked via cerebral interface. You and your Shell's CPU and the new AI assistant operate in concert as a single fighting entity.

"Your implant constantly feeds your suit's CPU data about your combat coefficients, such as ease of movement, aim, speed, reflexes, trigger squeeze, the works. Using that data as feedback, the CPU makes performance evaluations and calibrates your suit for optimal combat effectiveness. Your Oracle reads that same data, along with the CPU's evaluations, to learn more about you and better assist you."

Jarius chimed in. "So, there's like a running conversation going on between our cerebral implant, the CPU, and the Oracle. We transmit thought-commands and . . . brain data or something; then the Shell's tech receives and responds to what we transmit to help us out."

"Sounds about right, Specialist Ford," Lars said. "It's like a constant feedback loop."

"And this AI Combat Assistant, just how sentient can it get?"

"The bounds of the AI, and even the chip in our noggins, are still unknown to us and even the Quilgarians, who made it all." Lars went to a wall panel and keyed a three-digit code. The dials lit up, and a section of the wall shifted aside—one of two entries into the adjoining room beyond.

Fourth Platoon entered an octagonal space of computer workstations displaying complex nomenclature and mind-boggling reams of data. Seams along the walls and floor gleamed blue, and the room resounded with electronic chirping, humming, and buzzing.

"This is the Nerve Center," Lars said.

Gray-uniformed analysts sitting at the glowing panels and monitors spoke technical lingo.

A wall-mounted screen displayed a newscast. The anchorman said, "An hour ago, reporter Milan Jung caught up with Secretary Gould. Here's the exchange."

The replay showed Cornelius standing on the landing above the steps of the Parliament Building. The reporter and her cameraman hurriedly approached him from behind.

"Secretary Gould, a word?" Milan asked.

Cornelius turned. "Of course," he said. He wasn't in the mood for the press.

"What do you say to critics who call your execution of martial law in the colonies a mess?"

"I've said it before: The CDF had never handled this kind of operation. The early phase was bound to be rough. That phase is over. We've got everything under control now."

"Some people think your viceroys *(in charge of martial law)* have given the CDF too much leeway, transforming the colonies into a nightmare? Are your viceroys exempt from your supervision?"

"My viceroys give the CDF room to do their job, just like I give them room to do theirs," Cornelius said, his tone firm. "They don't need micromanaging. Neither do their forces."

"These viceroys are all former military colleagues appointed by you. Some call it an old-fashioned good-ole-boy network, and—"

The replay kept rolling as Fourth Platoon huddled around Lars.

Lars pointed to a row of analysts sitting at computer stations. "That's the Spec Ops team. Their telemetric systems capture everything that happens inside your Shell. Every thought you transmit to the CPU. Every movement. Your emotional state. Everything you can imagine.

"The team can pull that data and tell me whatever I need to know, like whether firefights are scaring you shitless or if you're reluctant to kill. That helps me identify who isn't measuring up." He zeroed in on one of the analysts. Her fingers danced over keyboards, eyes flitting from one screen to another. "Nijah, front and center."

The young analyst of Middle Eastern descent paused her busy fingers, took off her headset, and scooted her rolling chair back from the sophisticated console. She stood and walked over to Fourth Platoon.

"Nijah here will be Fourth Platoon's Overwatch," Lars said. "Her call sign is Overwatch 04."

Every platoon had an Overwatch assigned. Overwatches controlled platoons' Sentinels, aerial drones that transmitted a top-down view of the battlefield. Acting as Guardians' eyes in the sky, Overwatches provided intel and warned them of emerging threats.

Lars continued. "If they skipped this part in BCT, let me make it clear: You can't just tap into Sentinel 04 with your Shells. Nijah has to authorize access. Too many of you trying to sync with the drone would overload its circuits."

A smile traced Nijah's thin lips. "Good to meet you all. I've got your backs out there."

"Thanks, Nijah. You can return to your duties now," Lars said. She headed back to her workspace. "Alright, everyone, the tour's over. You're dismissed for today, and don't be a second late to my briefing tomorrow."

The Guardians filed out of the room to get settled in their quarters and get some R&R.

While leaving, Stacie and Emilia exchanged glares.

"Tonight, don't forget," Stacie said.

Emilia flashed a shark-like grin. "Wouldn't dream of it."

Stacie exited into the corridor. She thought back to the day during BCT when two female cadets had lured her outside. They told her a drill sergeant wanted to see her. As soon as she stepped onto the empty drill yard, Emilia and her clique ambushed her. They forced her to the ground, piled on top of her, and began hitting her repeatedly while hurling insults.

Stacie left that verbal and physical hazing bruised, bloody, humiliated, and wearing bedraggled, torn battledress. She wouldn't be able to make the rest of those miscreants pay, but she could at least teach Emilia a lesson, a painful one. She couldn't stand people of Emilia's ilk, and she was eager to humble her.

• • •

At 2300, the door to the sparring suite retracted. In came Stacie. Her hair was styled in a bun, and she wore a sports bra, spandex shorts, elbow and knee pads, and grappling gloves. She carried her headgear in her hand.

Her attire showed she was in peak physical condition.

Emilia was already there, dressed similarly, her outfit revealing the intricate tattoos on her arms, torso, and left leg. She punched the air, shadowboxing to warm up. *Now to teach this Highborn upstart a thing or two.*

Stacie appeared to have the advantage in height, standing a solid five-nine. Emilia was six inches shorter, though stoutly built.

"I wasn't sure you were gonna show, princess." Emilia cut the air with a blur of punches as she bounced on the balls of her feet.

Challenge in her eyes, Stacie slipped on her headgear and fastened the chin strap. "Wouldn't miss this chance for the world." She powered on the data-input kiosk to program the bout. "A hundred points to win?" she asked.

Emilia folded her arms confidently. "Whatever you want."

Stacie entered their surnames, the impact points needed to win, and pressed START.

A disembodied artificial voice said, "Combatants are Spencer and Rhineheart. Impact points needed for victory: one hundred."

Stacie warmed up, stretching her limbs. A thrill electrified her veins. In a sparring match, she could get some payback without earning a write-up in her service sketch. "You should've left your envy back at BCT. Hope you're ready to get your ass kicked, Private."

Narcissistic snob, I don't envy you. I don't wanna be anything like you, bitch. Adrenaline raging through her bloodstream, Emilia bumped her knuckles together. "Cut the banter, princess. Let's fight."

Stacie rolled her shoulders.

The two adversaries stepped onto the blue padded mat and shifted into the combat stance their training had instilled in them.

"Combatants are ready," said the computerized ref. "You may begin sparring."

Without preamble, Emilia lunged at Stacie like a rampaging

bull, taking her down with a vicious tackle.

They tumbled across the mat—wrestling, grappling, and trading choke holds. Emilia ended up on top of Stacie. Just as she raised her fist to nail Stacie in the face, Stacie twisted and tossed her aside.

"Impact points: thirty for Rhineheart, fifteen for Spencer," said the ref. A holographic scorecard flashed in the air: 30 POINTS-RHINEHEART / 15 POINTS–SPENCER.

Stacie rose. *Little twerp hits hard.*

Emilia stood up from the floor. "Too slow, princess. Why don't you request your release now and go back home to play with Mommy and Daddy's G-credit accounts? Go back to getting banged and shitfaced. Probably what you're actually good at."

"Your stupid wisecracks don't faze me. I've heard similar rubbish far too many times. Stuff like"—Stacie modulated her voice in mockery—"'you're just a rich tart who gets everything handed to her.'" Shifting her voice back to normal, she added, "But I graduated *Warrior Extraordinaire*. I proved I'm not just some . . . entitled brat.

"I don't have to ride my parents' coattails. I can achieve success on my own." Stacie beamed proudly. "I proved I'm willing to get my hands dirty and step away from the affluent lifestyle and predecided destiny that come with being the offspring of a baron and baroness. I'm the first child of an Eight to do this."

Emilia offered false applause, clapping her hands. "Bravo, nice speech." She cackled. "So you enlisting in the CDF was just about self-validation? You needed to do something unorthodox to show up Mommy and Daddy, is that it? Being a Guardian isn't something you do just so you can pat yourself on the back and say, '*There, I showed everyone.*' You're so sensitive and insecure I could vomit. Totally pathetic.

"Compared to the humiliation I've had to face, the teasers that get your fucking panties in a bunch all the time are nothing. I've been called slurs like 'nadir' by rich twits like you, and even fellow BCT cadets.

"And when I became a registered Eden citizen, I was supposed to receive my genetic upgrade, but apparently, we 'immigrants' aren't very high priority. It took me joining the CDF to get my upgrade, because it's absolutely required for enlistment."

Emilia's eyes blazed as she continued. "Isn't it funny how the government refers to us lottery beneficiaries as 'immigrants,' even though we're supposed to be equal citizens of humanity's intergalactic republic? If anyone should have a chip on their shoulder, it's me. You were birthed into privilege. You don't *really* have anything to be pissed about, princess."

Tired of being called princess and told she should be grateful for her perceived "fantastic" upbringing, Stacie channeled her unvoiced rage into a savage right hook, aimed as if she were trying to decapitate Emilia.

Emilia zagged to avoid the punch, Stacie's knuckles coming within a hair's reach of brushing her nose. Emilia immediately countered, kneeing Stacie in the kidney.

Stacie doubled over.

"Impact points: five for Rhineheart," the computerized ref announced. 5 POINTS flashed in midair.

"Just what I thought, princess: all mouth and no show," Emilia said, throwing a punch.

Stacie dodged the blow and quickly locked her arms around Emilia's outstretched limb. After applying an aggressive torque, she heard a satisfying *crack* as her pesterer's shoulder dislocated.

The pasty-skinned smart-mouth wheezed, her face twisted in pain.

Stacie derived satisfaction from hurting Emilia. After releasing her, she shoved her hard, throwing her off-balance.

Emilia staggered backward. Then, gritting her teeth, she popped her shoulder back into place.

She had underestimated Stacie's ruthlessness and fighting prowess. Before she could move again, Stacie took her legs out from under her with a sweeping kick, knocking her on her ass.

"Impact points: ten for Spencer," the ref announced. 10 POINTS flashed.

Stacie wore a cocky smile. "You're all mouth and no brains, Private. Probably why I'm a Warrior Extraordinaire and you're not."

Emilia sprang to her feet and charged, but Stacie caught her. Using Emilia's momentum to pivot into a flip toss, Stacie hurled her beyond the mat's boundaries.

Arms and legs flailing the air, Emilia landed back-first on the floor.

The ref declared the victor. "Combatant Rhineheart has left the sparring zone. Winner: Spencer."

A holographic WINNER! hovered over Stacie's head. Virtual confetti of all colors rained down.

Triumph fizzed through Stacie's veins.

Emilia undid her chin strap, gasping for air. She removed her headgear, its interior padding sweat-dampened. "A fluke win, princess. In a real fight, I would've whooped your ass," she muttered grudgingly.

Stacie walked toward the door. It whistled open. "Spoken like a true sore loser." Standing in the doorway, she said, "Oh, and I suggest you refine your stereotypical thinking, Private. Not every Highborn thinks lowly of colony citizens. My mother's midwife was Oviereya Amaechi, after all, and I love that woman as if she were my mother." *Maybe even more than my mother.* "So I'm not some . . . xenophobic, haughty bitch."

The door shut behind her.

As Stacie walked down the corridor, Emilia's words stalked her. So what if enlisting was about proving something to herself and people who doubted or badmouthed her? Not everyone joined the CDF out of some moral inclination to serve humanity. Some joined to build a career; others joined simply for money. Her reason didn't mean she was some insecure self-validation chaser, did it?

Jason Mansford fell in step behind her, following a little too close for comfort. He wore sleeping pants and a shirt. "Up late and in sparring gear. Needed a workout, huh?" He couldn't defeat the urge to give her backside—shown off in detail by her tight-fitting shorts—a once-over.

Stacie glanced over her shoulder. *Oh, go fuck yourself.* "Yeah, something like that," she replied harshly. She wanted to be left alone. *Damn it, do I need "Do not disturb" V-inked on my back?*

Jason strode up beside her, still lusting after her. She checked all his boxes. Abs? Check. Nice ass? Check. High and firm breasts? Check. And she was blond. "I'm just trying to break the ice and get to know you, Specialist, that's all."

Stacie quickened her pace and kept her eyes forward, not granting him any of her attention. *More like trying to bamboozle me into your bed.* "Good night, Sergeant. I have a briefing to rest up for," she said. *Not well-versed in the art of romantic seduction, are you?* She retreated into her quarters, feeling Jason's eyes on her the entire way.

Jason watched the door click shut. He'd been spurned again. *Oh, well.* He returned to his quarters as well.

• • •

Stacie entered Fourth Platoon's assembly room fifteen minutes late. She had overslept.

Lars was midway into his briefing. Everyone else had arrived promptly and was outfitted in their sleeves—black one-piece suits, with support padding at the joints, worn beneath their Shells. The formfitting flex material allowed ease of movement inside the combat machines.

Lars paused his briefing and made eye contact with Stacie. "Specialist Spencer!" he shouted, voice sharp and cutting.

Stacie jerked and froze in place. A wave of embarrassment rushed over her.

Lars nearly stared a hole through her pupils. "I don't know what they let you rich chits do at Cadwell, but *here*,"—he jabbed a finger toward the floor—"we don't just show up whenever the fuck we want. *Capiche?*"

Stacie's reserve wavered, her face flushing as anger took hold. She thought Emilia must be elated.

Her mouth opened for an angry retort, and boy, did she have a mouthful of unkind words for Lars, but she subdued them, clamping her trap shut. It was a no-win argument. She had goofed up and had to own it. Going off on a superior, on top of being late for her first mission brief, would only make her seem even more undisciplined—hardly fit for real soldiering, at least in the eyes of her comrades.

She stiffened her spine, forced the scowl off her face, and maintained military bearing. "Loud and clear, Sergeant."

"Good."

Her wandering eyes found Randy. He patted the aisle seat, which was to his left, letting her know he'd kept it off-limits for her.

She lowered herself beside him and crossed her arms.

"You okay?" Randy asked.

She nodded a yes. The lingering frown on her face and her body language said otherwise.

Lars continued his briefing. "Don't expect any aggression from the Coalition during these rallies. They only strike hard targets.

"This might come as a surprise to some of you, but the Coalition isn't foaming at the mouth to kill us Guardians. They try to avoid confrontation. They want to cripple the CDF and wear us down, with little to no fatalities if possible, all while trying to portray the central government in an unfavorable light and spread their ideals throughout the colonies to gain more supporters.

"They hope a combination of guerrilla warfare and growing support for colony autonomy will lead to one of two results: drastic revitalization efforts or full sovereignty." The latter was the least likely.

"So they're trying to beat us by attrition," a male Guardian said.

"Exactly," Lars confirmed. "However, if it comes down to us or them in a firefight, the Coalition will kill to defend themselves. And let me make something *absolutely* clear: The Coalition having a moral playbook and trying to be nice doesn't mean jack-shit. You hear me, Fourth Platoon?

"They are the enemy, and we always shoot to kill. You got that?" There was silence. "Let me hear a fucking 'Yes, Sergeant!'"

Lars' tone was so harsh that it made shoulders snap back.

Everyone shouted, "Yes, Sergeant!"

"Good. Now, though not nearly as powerful or influential, there are less prudent, more radical insurgent groups operating inside Colony Four who like to make statements whenever they can. Any opportunity to kill a Guardian, they take it. Those are the groups we need to be cognizant of while we're out there today."

Lars powered on his tablet. The wall screen synchronized with it, showing a man's face.

Lars gestured to the screen. "This is Eric Vaughn Ritter. Age twenty-seven. He's charismatic and knows how to appeal to the youth. He's also a maniacal sack of crap.

"He's an ex-Coalition rebel who believed the Coalition's actions weren't extreme enough. So he formed The People's Revolutionary Party of Colony Four. They aren't big in stature or numbers, yet. But they're growing.

"People who think the Coalition is being too soft join Ritter and other extremist groups like his. It's a power struggle for the minds of the rebellious, between the Coalition and these more radical groups.

"Ritter's Revolutionaries are nothing more than thugs who've appropriated some dangerous tech from inside and outside the Union. Be warned: Unlike the Coalition, these guys' mission is to off as many of us as possible. Two weeks ago, an off-duty Guardian was found dead in an alley."

Lars pressed a button on his tablet. The screen cleared and swapped Eric's mug for a macabre crime scene: a man lying next to a dumpster, his jugular lacerated. A grotesque amount of blood saturated the ground.

A female Guardian threw a hand over her eyes, goose bumps prickling her flesh.

Lars' voice toughened. "Sutherland, take your hand off your *fucking* eyes! You're not a little girly girl anymore! You're a goddamn Guardian!"

The young fair-skinned ginger jerked her hand away from her eyes. "Ye-yes, Sergeant." Her heart pumped in her ears.

Lars snorted, his contempt for weakness unmistakable. "This murder has the People's Revolutionary Party written all over it. Former Coalition rebels, and even some Guardians, make up about thirty percent of the group. They're all loony, anti-government ideologues like Ritter. Ten percent are teens off the streets, promised money, housing, and a sense of belonging. The remaining sixty percent are disgruntled adult citizens at odds with the central government."

Lars summarized more anti-government groups for fifteen minutes. Then he shut off the screen. "Alright, the briefing's over. I know some of you softies are already getting cold feet. I suggest you do whatever is necessary to shake off the nerves. Pray to your Almighty, or whatever."

"What do you do? To shake off the nerves, I mean," a male Guardian stuttered, hoping for some professional counsel.

Lars scoffed. "I don't get *nerves* anymore. But way back when I was a newbie like you, I just clung to my training and the gun in my hand. I sure as hell didn't sit around letting cowardly thoughts stew in my head. And since I don't pray, I didn't do that either."

Being a secular man, Lars found solace only in his training and the killing power of his Shell when in combat.

He said, "We leave in thirty mikes. Now get your fannies moving and get shelled so we can meet our hit time." He shot Stacie a withering glare. "Something some of us may not know a lot about." A verbal jab obviously aimed at her.

A smattering of chortles came from different directions.

Stacie's emotional buttons had been pushed, and her professional poise was on the verge of shattering. Randy settled a calming hand on her shoulder.

Everyone began orderly clearing out of the room.

Randy and Stacie got up and proceeded to leave as well.

Right behind Randy, Stacie was just about out the door when Jason Mansford approached her.

"Still ticked off, huh?" he remarked.

Stacie jutted out her chin. "No, I'm fine. I shook it off." By her intonation, that wasn't true in the least.

Jason saw right through her facade. "Don't let what Lars said get to you. I checked your service sketch. You graduated Warrior Extraordinaire, so you gotta be more than just a pretty face with riches, right?"

"Thanks," Stacie said casually, allowing some subtle warmth into her voice.

The room continued to thin out, Guardians chattering as they left.

"Just to let you know, you've been assigned to my squad," Jason informed Stacie. "I've designated you Alpha Team's sub-lead."

Stacie's face lit up. "Me?"

"Yeah, *you*, and don't worry, I didn't designate you sub-leader just to woo you or something. I'm a professional. A lot of thought and discernment goes into every decision I make. I did a deep dive into your service sketch, personality profile, and curriculum vitae. I genuinely think you have what it takes to fill that role." Stacie was a collegiate athlete, a Warrior Extraordinaire, an honors graduate from Cadwell, and a top-scorer on the CDF fitness test. Her credentials had impressed Jason.

Stacie thought, *Maybe I was wrong. Maybe he is more than just some playboy.*

"There'll be time to chat more later. For now, let's get shelled."

Stacie cracked an unexpected smile. "Right."

• • •

Randy stepped into the infrastructure of his Shell. The rear paneling of the powerful combatwear sealed, enclosing him. He drew his helmet from the magnetic catch on his hip and put it on. The featureless faceplate slid down. He said the suit's activation code: name and citizen registration number. "Scott: C-Seven-Three-Six-Seven."

His HUD booted up, populating with colored icons. Data scrolled, diagnostic check in progress. His mind pinged, cerebral implant tethering to the Shell's CPU. INTERFACE COMPLETE streamed across his HUD, and the CPU spoke to him, green-lighting all functions. The merger between mind and machine was complete.

The Shell made the necessary autoadjustments, morphing fibers conforming—snugly—to his height and size, creating the perfect custom fit. The outer chest, arm, and leg panels of Kryoplaste conformed as well, tiles of armor telescoping into place.

A little uncomfortable, he thought. Sensory receptors registered the haptic feedback, and the CPU refitted the suit. *Awesome.* The internal HVAC adjusted to his body temperature.

He tried out the CPU's syncing capabilities, accessing the net and bringing up juxtaposed street-camera feeds, all superimposed over his visuals in multiple windows.

People wondered if cerebral-interface technology would someday allow them to connect to more than just a Shell's CPU—such as personal computers, wristcoms, vehicular navigation systems, and even a home's mainframe.

People imagined what it would be like to access the net or control their homes' functions using only their implant. Cerebral-interface technology could likely evolve to that point, but the central government would never allow it. Such modifications posed serious security risks. Besides, the purpose of cerebral implants was to connect people more intimately, not to cybernize the human mind. The implant was meant to elevate people's humanity, not diminish it.

Randy tested his limbs, his movements flexing the morphing

fibers. The new model indeed had less armor density and far better reaction time. All his movements were quick and fluid.

He brought his Oracle online with a thought.

"Oracle now activated," an androgynous voice said.

"Great." Randy accessed the platoon roster published to the CDF's intranet cloud to learn the names of everyone assigned to First Squad, his designated squad. It read:

SSGT Jason Mansford (Squad Leader)

SGT Jack Holister (Alpha Team Leader)

SPC Stacie Spencer (Alpha Team Sub-Leader)

SPC Randal Scott

SPC Jarius Ford

PVT Emilia Rhineheart

SGT Olivia Slovak (Bravo Team Leader)

SPC Eli Manson (Bravo Team Sub-Leader)

PVT Ryoko Nahara

PVT Seth Youngblood

The roster window blinked away at Randy's mental command. He hoped the squad could find time to get to know each other. Squad bonding would build camaraderie.

Stacie moved her joints, getting acquainted with the M-X02. Actuators groaned. She felt powerful, unstoppable inside the suit—like a superwoman.

She explored the customizable weapons package on her HUD. The standard-issue ballistics carbine was the currently equipped primary weapon, though it could be swapped for others, like the heavy-duty Gatling gun, designed for extreme combat missions. The plasma-energy gun was the secondary. It was small, but every blast packed a hell of a punch.

More weapons were embedded in the Shell, such as extendable shoulder cannons for launching explosive rocket projectiles. Besides a battery of deadly weaponry, the Shells were equipped with stealth-cloak camouflaging technology.

Via cerebral interface, Guardians could also access manuals for weapons and vehicles, all stored in the CPU.

Stacie glanced down at the CDF insignia—a crossed sword and hammer—laser-engraved into the Shell's left shoulder. She was glad to be with Lima Company, representing the CDF, rather than attending some corporate meeting with her parents, where they'd be showing her the ropes.

Lars' voice came through the platoon's secure cerebral-communications (C-comm) channel. <<*Sergeant First Class Freeman, shelled and ready.*>>

The platoon responded with their rank, last name, and "shelled and ready."

Lars said, <<*If something crazy does kick off and you need to go lethal, remember to use plasma-energy weapons sparingly. The energy gun doesn't have many shots, and the energy weapons installed in your Shell sap a lotta power.*>>

Fourth Platoon proceeded to the motor pool to board Battle Utility Stations (BUSs), armored all-terrain lorries that would transport them to their respective rally sites. Lars joined First Squad for this op.

In transit to their rally sites, the new Guardians got culture-shocked by their first glimpse of the deteriorating infrastructure in the colony: dilapidated buildings, shanties, crumbling bridges, and crummy roads. It was a complete contrast to Eden's grandeur. The outdated fashion people wore and the vehicular relics they drove also astounded the Guardians.

Some now understood why colonists were so upset. It was revelations like these that caused Guardians to defect. But as Fourth Platoon arrived at their rally sites, the suffering of the people was pushed from their minds. It was game time.

• • •

Halfin was one of several unfinished towns in Zone 03. As shoddy as it was, it was upscale for Colony Four.

In front of Halfin's town hall, a large gathering of unruly CFP demonstrators waved signs and chanted in unison, "End the occupation! Peace, not war!" Citizens began to congregate and join in.

Viceroy McLaughlin, aware of today's protests, wasn't in his office inside the town hall. He was somewhere safe.

On the landing at the top of the town hall steps stood Lars and Alpha Team of First Squad, rifles at the ready. Bravo Team was stationed at another rally site. Parked beside the building was the BUS First Squad had arrived in. Its multiple gunports, twin pulse cannons, and spiked rims made the spacious, eight-wheeled vehicle a baleful sight.

The team had toggled their rifles' selector switch to NONLETHAL, to subdue the protesters with rubber rounds if they needed to.

As Randy's gaze swept over the area, his CPU fed him data about his immediate surroundings: approximate number of protesters, potential enemy approach routes, hiding spots, distance of passersby—everything. *Awesome,* he thought. The new, advanced CPU was giving him heightened tactical awareness.

"A lot of discontent out there," Jarius commented, noting the contemptuous faces in the crowd.

On a raised platform, a heavyset woman wearing round spectacles, a knee-length dress, and a denim vest took center stage. She spoke into a wireless handheld mic, her voice dripping outrage. "For too long we've seen our people get stopped, frisked, and questioned with no probable cause! We've had our homes barged into and searched, and we've seen people who have absolutely no Coalition ties get interrogated! Well, I say enough!"

The protesters gave the CFP mouthpiece a standing ovation, applauding and pumping their fists.

"You guys think there's any truth to that stuff?" Jarius asked.

Offended that a Guardian would dare entertain the idea that a government objector had a valid point, Lars was about ready to tear Jarius a new one. "Specialist Ford, are you questioning the moral standing of the Commonwealth Government?" he asked, voice gritty. He rested his thumb on his rifle's selector switch, ready to toggle it to LETHAL.

Jarius' brain scrambled to organize an acceptable response. He settled for an evasive, "Uh . . . no, Sergeant."

Lars took his thumb off the selector switch and turned back to the crowd. "Good." *Because I would've blown your ass away on the spot.* Which was completely permitted under CDF regulations if a Guardian exhibited behavioral signs of becoming an insider threat.

Curious to learn more about Colony Four's state of affairs, Jarius accessed open-source info from Satellite One's net. He browsed web articles, articles that couldn't be transmitted to Eden because of the net filters in place.

One article described how relief-aid nonprofits—created by humanitarian tycoons on Eden sympathetic toward the colonies—had built Assistance Living Centers, roads, and buildings and even provided some private-sector employment.

Jarius found pictures of deplorable living conditions and came across reports stating that depression and suicide rates were on the rise.

He thought, *Darn, after years of the government doing business with the Union Worlds and trading partners, you'd think it would've done more to advance the colonies. But then again, I ain't no subject-*

matter expert. This funding stuff's beyond my wheelhouse. Hopefully, plans are in the works to help the people here.

He continued searching the net and discovered some articles that detailed several accounts of Guardians mistreating civilians.

An article describing the miners' strike he had heard about, which took place in Colony Four a while back, caught his attention.

The strike had created a sizable labor shortage.

Cornelius had activated Reserve units to force the miners back to work. He cited their strike as destabilizing the Commonwealth's safety and prosperity, given the essential nature of the minerals being harvested. After being threatened with government charges, the miners had no choice but to return to work without securing their demands for better conditions. Otherwise, they risked jail time, leaving their families to starve.

The article slammed the central government, calling its retaliation against the miners' stand "egregious." It also claimed that Guardians opened fire on several defenseless miners, killing five.

Jarius found another article about the strike and read the headline: OUTRAGED PRIVATE AHMED HAWSAWI ATTACKS SERGEANT OVER SENSELESS KILLINGS.

A throaty male voice coming from his helmet's transceiver scolded him. "Specialist Ford, this is the Nerve Center. Is there a reason you, a dedicated Guardian of the Defense Force, are browsing Satellite One's net mid-mission, evaluating propagandist material defaming the central government?"

"Uh . . . sorry." Jarius quickly closed all articles and images. *Dang, is our every move monitored?*

The team's auditory comlink came alive with Nijah's voice. "This is Overwatch 04. Dubious activity detected at the zone's comms tower. There's a woman kneeling next to it with some sort of bag.

Could be an explosive ordnance."

"Randy, you're with me," Lars ordered. "Shouldn't take long."

"Gotcha," Randy acknowledged. *Finally, some damn action, instead of people watching all day.*

"I'll load Sentinel 04's snapshots of the woman into your suit's hard drive," Nijah said to Lars.

A message appeared on Lars' HUD: UPLOAD COMPLETE. With a mental command, he accessed the pics. In the top left corner of his HUD, pixels coalesced into an image of a scrappy-looking woman in a stylish black jacket, white tank top, and ripped jeans. Wild, dense ruby-red hair spilled from beneath a blue denim bandanna, reaching halfway down her back. Small gold studs adorned her nose and bottom lip.

<<Randy, I'm sending you pics of our person of interest,>> Lars relayed over the C-comm. He queued the images for transmission and mentally pressed SEND.

Randy's helmet chimed. DECLINE, in red, and ACCEPT, in green, flashed on his HUD. He instructed his CPU to accept the images. *<<Received,>>* he informed Lars.

They racked their weapons onto their backs. Then they dragged two hoverbikes from the rear of the BUS and mounted them.

Lifters powered up, displays came to life, and intake valves hissed open.

Randy and Lars twisted the hand throttles, and the bikes sailed off. They shot past cluttered markets, run-down shops, and towering stacks of tenements barely holding together.

Lars examined the graphic map superimposed over his visuals. Nijah had merged his Shell's navigation map with Sentinel 04's target tracker, which was keeping tabs on the woman.

Lars said to Randy, "Sentinel 04 shows our suspect leaving the comms tower and heading down Jefer Street on foot. We'll cut her off at the intersection up ahead."

A twist of the throttles gave the bikes a boost of power.

Lars pointed to the woman in the snapshots. "There she is."

The woman noticed Randy and Lars closing in on her at breakneck speed and darted into a grimy alleyway covered in anti-government graffiti.

Lars and Randy braked hard. The bikes sighed to a quick stop, whooshing up dust.

On the decaying balcony of a tenement looming over the streets, a shirtless hairy-chested man bellowed from his outdoor chair, "Damn CDF bastards, leave the lady alone!"

A gang of bystanders on the street backed him up. "Yeah, let her be," one of them said, wringing his fist.

Ignoring them, Lars jumped off his bike and sprinted through the mouth of the alley. "You, halt!" he said to the woman.

A scruffy critter scurried into a sewer grate.

The woman wedged her fingers into the gaps of a wire fence, preparing to climb over.

Lars' rifle clacked. "Don't make another goddamn move! That's a warning!"

Randy came in behind Lars.

The woman let go of the fence. Wire rattled. She froze in place. *Oh, fuck me. Just my damn luck.*

Lars visually inspected her for bombs or weapons.

"Did I do something wrong?" the woman asked, meeting Lars' menacing gaze.

Lars' voice shifted to a low, dangerous pitch. "What sorta mischief are you up to?" His eyes fell on the satchel slung over the woman's shoulder. "And what's in the bag?"

"Nothing," the woman retorted.

"Bullshit. Turn back around, nice n' slow." The woman spun and faced the fence. "Hands up and spread your feet." She dropped the satchel, raised her hands above her head, and spread her feet shoulder-width apart. Lars stepped a pace closer, an empty soda can crunching underfoot. "Where does your loyalty lie, with the Commonwealth Government or the Coalition of Rebel Factions?" he asked. The woman remained tight-lipped. "Are you an Independent Movement sympathizer?" Still no response. Lars pressed the muzzle of his rifle against her spine. "Speak up."

"Fuck off," the woman spat, revolt in her voice.

Lars rammed his rifle's buttstock into her back. She tumbled to the ground. This wasn't the first time her sassy mouth had landed her in trouble with a Guardian, and it probably wouldn't be the last.

Randy cringed, his heart flipping in his chest. He knew the blow hurt, especially for an unenhanced human. "Hey, lighten up, Sarge." He instinctively reached out a hand toward Lars' shoulder, but caught himself. He knew that laying a hand on a superior might get him reprimanded. "She hasn't done anything to warrant —"

"Quiet, rookie," Lars said sharply, ending Randy's protest. "We do things as we see fit."

Randy remembered what a drill sergeant had said to him and a bunch of cadets in formation on the drill yard: *Ruthlessness and fear are two of your greatest assets against your enemy! Soft hearts get you nowhere but the grave! And who is your enemy? Anyone shooting at you! Anyone who badmouths or defames the Defense Force or central government! It could be a civilian! It could even be the Guardian standing next to you! Whoever it may be, show them no mercy and treat them like the excrement they are, man or woman! Is that clear?*

The memory ended, and Randy thought, *We're human beings for goodness' sake. Does the CDF want us to be cold-blooded or something?*

"Get up," Lars said to the woman. She slowly pushed herself up onto her hands and knees. Becoming impatient, Lars raised his voice to a roar. "Hurry up! Stop wasting my fucking time!"

The woman's freckled features twisted into a pissed-off frown. "Kiss my fine ass, ya goddamn prick."

Lars savagely kicked her in the gut.

Unease rippled through Randy.

"You've got a big mouth, you know that, you snarky little bitch?" Lars growled.

"Why, thank you." The woman coughed. "Trash-talking's one of my most endearing traits," she added sarcastically, though her gut throbbed.

Lars snorted. "Enough jabber. Now get the hell up." The woman stood, raising chafed hands high above her head. "Check her, Specialist Scott."

Lars stepped back and continued to hold the facetious woman at gunpoint while Randy conducted the inspection.

"Hold still," Randy told her. He knelt and patted down her pant legs.

"Finest legs you'll ever touch, huh?" she joked.

"Lady, just shut up and let me do my job." Randy stood, checked her rear pockets, and extracted a plastic ID card.

"So who's Ms. Smart-ass here?" Lars asked, the business end of his weapon still aimed at the woman.

Randy dipped his chin, studying the credentials. "She's a courier for Dynamic Relief Provisions." He brought up the organization's webpage on his HUD. "They're the major relief-aid org on the planet. Her name's Kesley Whittaker." The credentials showed she was thirty-one.

A bloodcurdling boom diverted Lars and Randy's eyes from Kesley.

"What the hell?" Lars shouted. Smoke trails billowed from the rally site. "Lars to Overwatch 04, patch me in to Sentinel 04. I need eyes on the rally site." His visor interfaced with the drone, relaying him an overhead view of complete bedlam: fire, stampedes of people running, his Guardians discharging rounds. <<*Mansford, sitrep,*>> he sent over the C-comm.

<<*Multiple hostiles opening fire,*>> Jason responded. <<*They're Ritter's Revolutionaries. We got four civilian fatalities. Sergeant Holister's injured.*>>

The fence creaked. Randy and Lars wheeled around and saw Kesley climbing to the top of it. She swung to the other side with her satchel, gained her footing, and broke into a run, limping slightly from a sprained ankle.

"Forget her," Lars said. "Shit just hit the fan. We've gotta get back to the rally site."

"What about the comms tower?"

"I'll send someone to check for sabotage after the mission. Now let's go."

Randy deposited Kesley's ID in a personal compartment. He and Lars hopped on their hoverbikes. The plasma-charged aft boosters built up thrust, and the bikes soared off, thrumming.

"You struck that woman. That wasn't right, Sergeant," Randy said, a bitter undertone in his voice. "She didn't do anything to provoke that kind of force."

Lars glanced over his shoulder at Randy, who was following behind. "She was obviously hiding something. We needed to know what."

Randy and Lars sped past terribly maintained, half-built structures. They slowed the bikes to a smooth stop as they arrived at the rally site.

They saw battered phyocrete and injured noncombatants.

Jarius had a medpack and was kneeling beside one of the wounded, making good use of his Combat Lifesaver Skills. Jason was administering first aid while shouting commands. Emilia was trying to resuscitate a woman who was already gone, using the defibrillators in the fingertips of her suit. Sergeant Jack Holister, Alpha Team Leader, sat against a wall, the leg of his Shell breached.

Jack groaned. The injury hurt like hell. With him sidelined, Alpha Team's sub-lead, Specialist Stacie Spencer, was now in charge.

The injured civilians and casualties hadn't been intentional targets. They were collateral damage, the result of negligence by the reckless, untrained hostiles now lying dead. There were five of them, all young men no older than eighteen. They wore makeshift body armor slapped together from discolored scrap metals. Red armbands stitched with "RR" identified them as Ritter's Revolutionaries.

Lars shook his head in disgust. *Kids brainwashed into becoming martyrs for Ritter's insane cause. This bloodshed's gotta end.*

Stacie spoke over the C-comm. <<*So what do we—?"*>> A crackling cerulean blast exploded against her torso plating, bursting into a brilliant spray of sparks and propelling her backward like a thrown javelin.

She crashed to the ground back-first and skidded, her armor shrieking against the phyocrete. If not for her Shell's shock inhibitors, she would've felt the full brunt of the blast—and the impact of the landing.

She rose, armor darkly singed.

Everyone was on alert, scanning for the hostile.

Come on, where the hell are you? Stacie thought. Her targeting reticle panned left and right. Suddenly, another blast boomed, streaking past her shoulder. "Shit!"

A third, lower-powered shot clipped her helmet, whipping her neck back. Her helmet's optics damaged, she saw her visuals jump side to side.

Lars activated his helmet's external sound port, which amplified his voice like a bullhorn. "I'M SERGEANT FIRST CLASS LARS FREEMAN OF THE COMMONWEALTH DEFENSE FORCE! CEASE YOUR TRANSGRESSIONS AT ONCE!" Another haphazard shot exploded against the side of a building, raining rubble over his suit. "Fuck!"

"Hostile, three o'clock!" Jarius shouted, smoothing a medical slip over a civilian's leg wound. The slip's adhesive antiseptic membrane sealed the gash and staunched the bleeding.

Stacie turned toward the enemy, her mechanical joints whining.

One of Ritter's Revolutionaries was using a car for cover. A harness secured a heavy-caliber energy cannon to his armored torso. He clutched the outstretched handles and squeezed the discharge levers. The cannon's capacitor crackled as it built up enough energy for another shot. The longer he held the levers, the bigger and more devastating the blast would be. Stacie was lucky the shot that had clipped her was low-powered.

Her impaired vision made an accurate shot nearly impossible. She'd have to neutralize the hostile face-to-face.

As she ran toward him, her mechboots thumped against the ground.

He let go of the levers and recoiled as the cannon thundered, unleashing another energy blast.

Stacie crouched. Then her jumper struts launched her into a powered leap over the incoming shot. She could hardly believe how light she felt in the M-X02.

Behind her came a boom and the crash of shattering glass.

The roof of the car the hostile was using as cover screeched inward as Stacie landed atop it. Lacking time to fire another shot from such a slow-to-discharge weapon, he flinched.

Stacie hopped down. She leveled her rifle at his head. "Enough. It's over. Now remove the cannon, or I'll splatter your brains over the phyocrete, and I fucking mean it. Your call."

The hostile unstrapped the cumbersome armament and dropped it. Then he raised his hands in surrender, heart hammering his rib cage.

Stacie examined the foreign weapon, consulting her index for an ID. ARTIFACT UNRECOGNIZED flashed on her HUD, distorted by static and jagged lines.

The intergalactic innovation was likely illegally obtained from, and the brainchild of, a race outside the Union. It wasn't very advanced, though. All targeting was done via iron sights, and precision aiming was nearly impossible. But then again, this type of hardware wasn't meant for precision. It was meant for mass-scale destruction—the wrong choice of weaponry to take out a few Guardians without putting civilians at risk.

Stupid dipshits, Stacie thought. But Ritter incentivized enemy kills. And sometimes, young, battle-inexperienced men would go off half-cocked, grab some destructive weapon without thinking, and hunt for Guardians to slay.

<<*Good work, Spencer,*>> Lars said. <<*We—*>> A parked car vanished in an eruption of red-orange fire, cutting him off midthought. A shower of phyocrete fragments tinkled off his armor. "Damn it! We've got another hostile with one of those goddamn energy cannons!" he shouted. "Overwatch 04, we're taking fire! We need to know where from!" Lars swept the air with his rifle, hunting for the hostile.

"Already working on it," Nijah replied.

Another loud boom, softened by the Shells' noise reducers, rattled the scene. Crumbs of debris hailed down.

"Well, hurry the hell up!" Lars barked.

"Found him," Nijah said. "The hostile is atop the incomplete construction to your left."

"I got him!" Randy yelled, spotting the hostile. He considered his options. Given the hostile's elevation and distance, he couldn't make a manual kill shot, even with high-magnification targeting.

Suddenly, a bomb drone the size of a golf ball deployed from his armguard.

Randy said, "What the hell? I didn't deploy that—"

"Projectile launched," his Oracle said. It was helping to reduce a Guardian's cognitive load, as purposed. "Due to the target's distance and elevation, the optimal weapon is the Predator Bomb. Does the user disagree?"

Randy blinked, still shocked. "Uh . . . No, you're right on," he stammered. The Oracle had quickly formulated the best solution to achieve Randy's intended outcome: the hostile dead. Machine learning at its finest.

The Oracle input the seek-and-destroy prompt. Zigzagging through the air, the self-guided projectile homed in on its target.

On the rooftop, the hostile was screwing a fresh power-cell canister into his cannon. Before he could fire again, he heard a faint buzzing sound in his ear. From the corner of his eye, he caught a glimpse of the silvery sphere. "Oh, fuck!"

The bomb's glowing red iris blinked and beeped. The hostile drew his last breath, and then a sonic boom thundered, followed by a blue flash and a halo of shock waves. There one moment, gone the next, the hostile had been vaporized from existence—along with a chunk of the roof. That was the power of encapsulated plasma energy unleashed.

<<*Target neutralized,*>> Randy said.

The scent of plasma-burned ozone drifted.

"You're going to be put away for a long time for the mess you caused today," Stacie told her captive, who was now cuffed.

A clever grin played across his lips. "What if I could get you guys Arson Scott, in exchange for immunity?"

Randy removed his helmet and racked it on his hip. His brow furrowed. "*What?*" Mood darkening, he stormed up beside Stacie and seized the captive's throat in one hand. "Where is he?" His voice trembled. "If you know where that traitor is, tell me *right now.*"

"Stand down, Specialist Scott," Stacie ordered.

His mother's pain, never to be quieted, ignited a tension headache. Unable to rein in his emotions, he thoughtlessly squeezed the young man's throat, threatening to shut off his airway. He was slipping into a trance of rage.

Gagging, the near-asphyxiated captive wheezed.

"Spencer told you to stand the fuck down!" Lars barked.

Stacie batted Randy's arm away, armor clacking against armor. "That's enough, Specialist Scott," she said firmly.

The captive let out a long exhalation.

Taming the surge of emotion, Randy pulled back, shocked by his loss of control and violation of his own code of conduct.

Stacie stripped off her helmet, cursing the damaged HVAC as she undid her bun and let her sweat-laden hair spill free. Wisps of blond strands fell disheveled over her features. "Hey, Randy, I know you and I are involved," she said, alternating her finger between the two of them, "but out here in the field, I'm still your superior."

"Just got a little carried away, that's all," Randy spat smugly.

Amusement raised Stacie's left brow. She scoffed. "A little?"

Randy crossed his arms stubbornly. "Whatever, Stace."

Stacie's features twitched. *Whatever, Stace?* she thought.

The "Who the fuck do you think you're talking to?" look on her face was priceless—and had Jarius stifling a giggle.

Lars, helmet racked, barged between them, breaking up the squabble. Armor clanged. Stacie stumbled backward. He came nose-to-nose with Randy. "You were out of line, Specialist Scott!" He tapped his finger against Randy's chest plate. *Tink, tink.*

A matching scowl on his face, Randy gave the sergeant his comeuppance. "Just like you were out of line with that woman in the alley?" he snapped.

Lars' visage dared Randy to say one more goddamn word.

Fists clenched, Randy grunted and shouldered Lars aside. He walked away to cool off.

Irritation creased Lars' forehead. "Specialist Ford, Specialist Spencer, get the prisoner ready for transport," he ordered, voice hoarse from all the yelling he'd done today. He stared at Randy with a disapproving glower.

Jarius and Stacie replied simultaneously: "Yes, Sergeant." They went over to the captive, took an arm each, and heaved him to his feet.

Lars put on his helmet and lowered his faceplate. On his HUD, he brought up Randy's psych profile from the intranet, accessible only with the correct authorization code. Nothing adverse was logged, and his BCT dossier described him as smart, studious, and straitlaced. And from what Lars could see, he definitely had a backbone.

The dossier listed no demerits whatsoever. Randy was a promising young Guardian. However, whenever anyone mentioned his father, his temper flared. And he exhibited some antisocial tendencies.

Despite the clean record, Lars still questioned the fragility of

Randy's mental health. *Maybe I was wrong about that leadership potential. This hothead needs eyes kept on him.*

• • •

Randy, shirtless in his boxers, lay on his bed. Unrest churned in his soul. He wondered if the captive had given up Arson's location yet.

<*So what the heck was that all about today, with the prisoner?*> Stacie said from the glass-enclosed shower in the bathroom, water jets hissing.

<*I . . . I just got carried away. I realize sometimes my anger gets the best of me.*> Randy's emotions were indeed volatile, to say the least. <*I have to . . . compartmentalize better. It won't happen again.*>

<*Maybe you need that psych eval. You've obviously got some PTSD from your mom's death. An official diagnosis might—*>

<*You know I can't risk a mental-health discharge, Stace.*>

<*Well, you can't be so damn impulsive. You don't want a write-up for dishonorable conduct in your service sketch. And if you go bonkers again like you did today, Lars is gonna have the behavioral specialists order a psych eval anyway.*>

Stacie shut off the jets. Water gurgled down the drain. After the drying cycle, she emerged from the bathroom. Clad in silky pink lingerie, she displayed her sun-darkened, statuesque physique—which had been sculpted by grueling workouts.

Lips curved into a disarming smile, she sat next to Randy on the bed. "So, what are you thinking about now, babe, hmm? I know when you're feeling troubled about something." Her tone sounded chirpy.

Randy, staring glumly at the ceiling, said, "Conlan might've had contact with my dad. I don't know if there's been collusion between them. Both he and my dad have disappointed me, and I don't know if I'm even going to get my hands on my dad to make him pay for his misdeeds. So all the hurt, anger, and uncertainty have . . . just got my headspace all fucked up right now."

You spend too much time in your head, babe. "You need to take your mind off all that, and I think I have the solution," Stacie said in a sultry timbre. Her eyes twinkled.

Randy's attention drifted from the ceiling and settled on Stacie. Damn, she had the prettiest shade of tan he'd ever seen, and her musculature was hella impressive. She was temptation incarnate. Truth be told, he'd always been drawn to blond women with athletic builds.

Stacie crawled onto the bed and rose upright on her knees. The springs squeaked beneath her. She snared Randy's solid midriff between her thighs and peeled off her bra, tossing it aside. Then she leaned in, dangling her breasts over his face.

Randy fixed his eyes on her impeccable nipples. Exhilaration compounded in his groin, lengthening his lower extremity.

He couldn't ask for a better girlfriend: gorgeous, smart, affectionate, hypersexual. His eyes devoured every inch of her. Her figure was curved in all the right places and well-toned where it mattered.

Stacie smashed her lips against his, gifting him a breathtaking, ravenous kiss.

Randy cradled her scantily covered buttocks in his hands, sinking his fingers into her seamless flesh.

His mind revisited the night he and Stacie had snuck into the decommissioned barracks during BCT. He thought they'd just indulge in a little foreplay, but Stacie's bold aggressiveness shattered his commitment to rules and regulations, giving him one hell of a gut check.

Before that memorable night, they'd been limited to mindplay and dreamscape sex through their Link, experiencing external stimulation without physical touch.

Randy remembered the rush of dragging Stacie's underwear down her hips for the first time. In a five-second flash, his implant replayed their entire escapade, every vivid sensation, every breathless thrill . . .

Letting go of all restraint, Randy's high-tempo thrusts rocked the bunk, sating his hunger for Stacie's body. She squirmed and panted, clawing the bedsheets as they used their Link to guide each other in giving pleasure. Back and forth, she experienced his sensations, and he experienced hers.

Both mentally enshrined in a sex-induced delirium of physical and mental euphoria, Randy took Stacie's wrists and sank them into the mattress as he steamrolled more thrusts into her. Sixty seconds nestled between her legs seemed like a godsend, after being cooped up with a bunch of rowdy males for days on end.

Linking heightened bodily stimulation to thresholds unchipped minds couldn't fathom.

Randy nailed Stacie with a thrust that stiffened her nipples and sent her to the brink of unconscious bliss. From the overabundance of stimulation, her eyelids blinked, her pupils dilated, and a wheeze caught in her throat, morphing into a soft groan. Randy slackened up but kept fucking her.

Muscles convulsing, he yearned for a release. Somehow he mustered the will to pull out in time. He could only indulge so far without taking prophylactic measures.

In fear of getting caught, Randy and Stacie dressed and went back to their respective barracks, sleeping off the hangover produced by their cerebral implants' expansion of the human sexual experience . . .

Tonight, Randy and Stacie would have infinite time to test their bedroom stamina. Their orgasmic sensations from their previous night of pleasure had been archived, and Randy and Stacie were ready to explore new depths of bodily gratification.

Randy held Stacie at the waist and rolled her onto her back. Now on top of her, he gazed into her blue fuck-me eyes.

"What are you waiting for, an invitation?" she said.

Randy's starving lips trailed down her neck, each kiss a prelude to the carnality about to unfold. He sucked on one of her delectable nipples, causing it to perk up and harden in response.

The inebriating feel of Stacie's naked skin drove him wild. Every bit of her was perfect.

He slid his hand down her firm abs and into her panties. Then he claimed her with an unhurried, torturous rhythm until her mouth hung agape. She opened her legs wider, inviting him deeper into her. He obliged, pushing his fingers further. An expression of orgasmic pleasure drifted across her face.

Amping things up, Randy wrenched Stacie's panties down her lean, defined legs; tossed them away; and buried his face between her splayed thighs. His warm breath conjured sparks in her belly.

She arched her back, grinding her loins shamelessly against his mouth. As he flicked his tongue, her whimpers entertained his ears.

After orally fucking her nether region, he discarded his boxers and positioned himself above her. His body dying to release all the stress and tension from today, Randy's erection was as straight as a flagpole.

Not sparing another tormenting second, Randy sank into Stacie and thrust to his heart's content. Each collision of their loins soothed his needs and his frustrations.

Satisfaction danced in Stacie's eyes, and she made a raspy noise of approval.

Randy arranged her wrists above her head and burrowed into her with no intent of slowing down, her shallow gasps fueling him. This was going to be a night even more unforgettable than their BCT sex night.

• • •

The door to the Intensive Inquiry Unit slid open. Lars and Jason walked into the dank room. The prisoner sat in a metal interrogation chair bolted to the floor, wrists manacled to the armrests.

"We searched your name in the terrorist database," Jason said. "You're Nelson Weaver. Age twenty-one. Former Guardian with Zulu Battalion's Echo Company. You joined Arson Scott's faction but thought the Coalition was too passive for your tastes, so you joined Ritter."

"Yeah, that's right," Nelson confirmed.

"Alright, asshole, I'm not gonna play verbal ping-pong with you," Lars said. "Now where's Arson Scott?"

"First, I need assurance that I'm going to be off the hook if I give you that information," Nelson demanded. "I want to be free to go, and I want my name erased from the terrorist database."

Lars brutally drove his fist into Nelson's gut, knocking the wind out of him. "You're not in a position to be making demands, you little punk. Now I'm gonna ask you again, Where's Arson?"

Nelson coughed. "No deal, no Arson."

"Is that so?" Lars slugged him in the gut again.

Nelson wheezed in pain. "Physical abuse of POWs is illegal, last time I checked," he stuttered, laboring for breath.

Lars said, "Define physical abuse." He turned Nelson's face into a punching bag, mauling it until it was black and blue. "Where's Arson?" He slung Nelson's blood off his knuckles, and red spots mottled the dingy floor.

Nelson spewed a glob of blood. "*Go to hell.*" He spat out a loose tooth soaked in red.

Lars gripped Nelson's hair and hoicked his head back. "Resilient little bastard, aren't you?" He blew a disgusting spray of spittle into Nelson's wrecked face. "Come on, Sergeant Mansford, let's give this hardhead the night to come to his senses."

"We'll be back tomorrow," Jason said as he and Lars headed toward the door.

A line of blood oozed from Nelson's mouth. "Prisoners are required to have three meals! Where's my dinner?"

The door clanked shut. Locks clicked into place.

CHAPTER THREE

Kesley Whittaker woke to the blare of her alarm clock, squinting against the sunlight bleeding through the window.

Outside her third-story unit, the hum of midday traffic blended with the laughter of children frolicking around derelict structures—the usual sounds of the day.

After completing a late shift last night, she wished she could stay in bed longer, but the relief-aid org she worked for needed her.

Dragging her weary body out of bed, she sat upright and dropped her feet to the floor, eyes still adjusting to the sunlight. *Gotta get to it.*

Standing in the buff, she stretched until her joints cricked, basking in the sun's warmth. Every day she got to feel those rays on her skin was a blessing—lately, too many acquaintances had ended up dead or locked away, accused of supporting the Coalition. Ever since the troop surge, the CDF had been coming down harder, showing no mercy, no restraint.

Beginning her usual wake-up routine, she padded over to her worn-out laptop, voluminous red tresses brushing her back. She tapped the power button repeatedly. *Come on. Work, damn it.* When the outdated machine finally came to life, she opened a vidcast of Arman Reza for some words of aspiration and encouragement.

At the bathroom sink, she turned on the faucet. Recycled water belched out murky brown before clearing. While brushing her teeth, she listened to Reza preach hope, rebellion, and a future for the forgotten. His gospel always lifted her spirits.

After showering, she slipped on a pair of cutoff shorts and a white tee that hugged the buxom curves of her chest. Over the shirt, she wore a black jacket to hide a gun. Firearms were contraband under the current moratorium, but that never stopped her. A blue bandanna came next, then a crucifix necklace.

Done dressing, she gave herself a once-over in the cracked mirror before heading out.

Her feet clattered down the creaky metal stairs. Once she hit the ground floor, she stepped outside into the earthy-smelling air. Unpaved roads and bare rolling slopes stretched in every direction; not a single phyocrete street existed for miles.

Across from the residential complex she lived in was a row of ramshackle shops, their facades scarred and weathered signs barely readable. Built during the first phase of migration, they desperately needed renovation. Clearly, Eden's society was advancing while Satellite One's remained stagnant, lacking luxuries like airborne transportation and modern tech.

Kesley walked up to her flatbed carrier vehicle. Just as she was about to open the cabin door to get in, a voice called her name.

Startled, she spun around, heart racing. Consternation drove her to reach for the prohibited firearm stowed inside her jacket. "And you are?" she asked, eyeing the stranger.

It was Randy. His trained eyes noticed the bulge beneath her jacket. He approached calmly, careful not to escalate the situation.

"My name's Randal Scott. I'm a Guardian."

Kesley shot him a look of admonition, halting him in his tracks. "Hold it right there, soldier boy."

"I'm not here to harm you, ma'am," Randy assured her. He chanced another step forward.

Kesley's muscles tensed, her trembling hand tightening around the grip of her firearm. She held Randy's humble gaze with an incredulous stare. "What the fuck do you want with me?" she asked, distrust lacing her voice.

"I'm the Guardian who patted you down in the alley yesterday. I'm sorry about how my superior treated you. I just wanted—"

Kesley's lips pursed. "I already told you that—"

Randy reached into his pants' pocket and gingerly pulled out her credentials. "I just wanted to return this. That's all, Ms. Whittaker." He extended a sturdy arm, giving the feisty redhead her card.

Kesley cast her eyes on him for a long moment—evaluating, assessing, judging. Trusting her instincts, she made her call. Randy wasn't trying to hoodwink her. He was trustworthy.

Her muscles relaxed, and her heartbeat slowed. "Call me Kess," she said, her demeanor softening. "Sorry for being so uptight, but when strangers come calling my name, I get a little jumpy." She withdrew her hand from her jacket and took back her credentials. "I'm surprised. Guardians rarely do anything this courteous. They usually spend their time harassing civilians."

The irony in her words ticked Randy off. "You act like we're a bunch of dicks."

Kesley shrugged. "Most of you are."

Randy's brow creased. "We're fighting to bring peace and stability back to the Commonwealth."

Kesley fastened her hands on her curvaceous hips. "Depends on your point of view," she said with spunk.

"You're an Independent Movement sympathizer, aren't you?"

"I prefer 'advocate.'"

"All just semantics."

A dented, rusty clunker chugged by, its growling engine momentarily interrupting the squabble.

Once the noise subsided, Randy and Kesley resumed their conversation.

"Look," Kesley said, tone cooling but still edged, "you seem like one of the decent ones. After all, you returned my creds, and you didn't cop a feel when you frisked me, unlike most of your buddies." She yanked open her carrier's cabin door. "Ride with me while I pick up and drop off my delivery. Let me show you why the folks in Colony Four hate the Defense Force and central government so much."

"I've already seen some of Colony Four's infrastructure issues, down by Halfin Town Hall."

Kesley scoffed. "Then you ain't seen shit." She jerked her head toward the passenger side. "Get in."

Randy hesitated for half a beat. The duty rotation had Fourth Platoon off today and tomorrow. What harm could going with Kesley do? "Maybe I'll be the one doing the enlightening," he muttered, circling to the passenger side and hopping in.

The refurbished engine sputtered to life, coughing and rattling.

With the AC shot, the cabin was a sweatbox. Randy and Kesley rolled down their windows, letting in gusts of warm, dusty air.

The carrier lumbered over the dirt road, its exhaust stack spewing dark fumes. On Eden, environmental standards would've had the vehicle scrapped long ago.

Kesley's mobile phone buzzed. She grabbed it from the door cubby and held it to her ear while steering with the other hand. A voice crackled on the line. "Yeah, don't worry, I didn't forget," Kesley said. She hung up and tossed the phone back into the cubby.

"A mobile phone?" Randy said, brows raised and voice dripping with disbelief. Such a device was totally obsolete.

"Welcome to the colonies, Highborn. We don't get your fancy gizmos out here. This primitive tech is the best we've got. No wristcom upgrades for us."

Up ahead, Guardians in battledress were hectoring two seventeen-year-old boys. One of the teens mouthed something profane. A second later, he was eating dirt, shoved to the ground by one of the Guardians.

As the carrier rolled past, Kesley leaned halfway out the window and threw up the middle finger. "Fuck you, assholes!"

"Fuck you, bitch!" one of the Guardians shot back.

Randy grimaced at Kesley. He thought she must have gone crazy. "Are you outta your damn mind?"

"Fuckery begets fuckery, soldier boy. Those assholes treat us like garbage every damn day." The carrier rumbled past some Guardians going into a decrepit building. "Bet they're sniffing around for Coalition rebels again. Rebels like to use these ghost blocks to stage nearby ops. But that doesn't give Guardians the right to treat those boys like accomplices to murder or something. They were just kids minding their own damn business, out playing games and having fun n' shit."

"You don't know that," Randy retorted. "You don't know what that altercation was about. Those kids you claim are *innocent* might've been aiding and abetting rebels. There's not a lot you can discern while speeding by in a damn truck. So calm down."

Kesley snapped her head toward him, eyes full of fire, then refocused on the road. "You see? This is what I'm talking about!"

Her voice rose, sharp and hot. "You guys are like some kind of fucking mafia! You cover each other's asses no matter what!"

Randy checked his anger and adopted a gentler tone. "Listen, I understand that Guardians have committed some terrible acts, but I believe they're the minority. I'm truly sorry if the CDF has treated you or anyone you know unfairly."

Kesley calmed down. Randy's acknowledgment of Guardian misconduct renewed her faith in his rationality. "Well, that's a start. Maybe I shouldn't write you off just yet, soldier boy."

An awkward but defusing silence hung between them. As the carrier crested a hill, a cluster of interim housing units came into view.

"What are those?" Randy asked. Visibly disgusted, he stared at the drab box-like domiciles.

"Culture shock, huh, soldier boy?" Kesley said. "They were supposed to be temporary shelters during migration. But . . . 'temporary' kinda turned into 'indefinite.'"

"So families are stuck living in those abominations until the government decides to build them something better?" Disbelief crossed Randy's face.

Kesley nodded, her expression flat. "Something should've been done by now."

"The government *definitely* needs to do more for these people," Randy said, voice thick with sympathy. Barefoot children played with each other outside the units. A frail elderly woman watched over them. The sight hit Randy in the chest. *This is a humanitarian failure. Our leaders need to wake up.* He could only begin to grasp how deep Colony Four's struggles ran. On Eden, people would riot over conditions half this bad.

The carrier left the settlement and rumbled past a brick building that had the Coalition's motto spray-painted across its side: *Keep the Faith.*

The next stop on Randy's tour was a row of charred, near-collapsing slums. "What happened here?" he asked.

"A big firefight during the Three-Week War," Kesley replied. "The bureaucrats promised Colony Four restoration funds ages ago, but we're still waiting. We lost med clinics, as shabby as they were, and a hell of a lot of markets and shops. Now the people who live around here have to make a damn near two-hour trip just to get basic necessities.

"I don't know why the colonies always get the short end of the stick. With this area still in ruins, it's become a hotspot for black-market dealers." An arms broker, standing inside the skeleton of a bombed-out building, showed two younger men a selection of handguns tucked inside his trench coat. "I used to think all the destruction would've pushed the government to finally rebuild and renovate these buildings.

"They've been here since the first arks arrived. They need fixing. Hell, they were never meant to be permanent anyway." Memories surfacing, Kesley stopped the carrier. The brakes rasped. "A lot of people died here—men, women, children."

The devastation triggered a traumatic, eidetic flashback: streets awash in blood, lifeless bodies scattered everywhere, eerie green sensor scans from aircraft slicing through the night, bullets flying, and a cacophony of chilling screams echoing from all directions.

Amid the chaos, Kesley lost track of her brother. Coming out of an alley, she stumbled onto a grisly scene and found his small corpse lying among other war casualties. Weeping, she took the keepsake from around his neck, the very crucifix necklace she wore today.

Randy saw his own pain mirrored in Kesley's somber eyes. "I'm sorry for your loss."

Kesley snapped back to the present. "Huh, wha-?"

"I can see it in your face. You lost someone. Family?"

"Yeah. My kid brother," she said, grief in her voice. "He was seven. He got caught in some crossfire." Kesley took her foot off the brake and pressed the acceleration pedal. The cabin jerked, and the carrier rolled on. "So, you lose anyone? To the war, I mean."

"My mother. She died when the Coalition destroyed the building where she worked." Randy's expression darkened, the memory of Kathleen's death once again tormenting his mind. "And my father, Arson Scott, played a part in the incident," he added, brows knitting together.

Kesley's eyes widened. "You're the son of Arson Scott!"

Randy's features twitched. "Unfortunately."

"He's one of the most sought-after Coalition rebels."

"No fucking kidding."

CDF aircraft roared overhead, scouring the area for rebels.

Kesley switched on the net radio. A newscaster reported, "The number of fatalities from the terrorist attack that nearly claimed Secretary Gould's life has risen. Authorities have confirmed five additional deaths—three from Zanvetera and two from Nebosaa, both Union-approved trading partners.

"The emergency summit is scheduled for the day after tomorrow, and though the deaths of the visitors have placed the Commonwealth under intense scrutiny, Chief Executive Kerner assures the public that incorporated status will not be lost. Also today, Chairwoman Oviereya Amaechi made this announcement."

On the replay, Oviereya said, "I, Chairwoman Oviereya Amaechi, am announcing my candidacy for Chief Executive. I realize the RUC's declaration of independence was an illegal act that plunged the Commonwealth into war. And I despise war. I denounce it. But I understand the animus that incited the

Independent Movement. I understand why colony citizens feel ignored and oppressed. It's no mystery why they've reached their emotional apex.

"The central government has fostered downtrodden societies within its own republic. Martial law must be lifted, and our political system needs reform. Colony governors should have more autonomy, and all colonies should be allowed to engage directly with Union Worlds and external partners, so they won't have to—"

Kesley turned the volume knob all the way down. "I hope she comes out on top. Gould hasn't announced his intention to run, but you know he's going to, and he won't change a damn thing. I reckon things'll only get worse under his leadership. I hope that control freak keels over and breaks his fucking neck.

"Oviereya, I'm confident, will get the central government back on track. Hell, there've even been rumors the government's planning to fund the construction of artificial mini-islands, not for us poor bastards, of course, but as an attraction for intergalactic tourists. A project that'll take fucking *years*. *Hello?* Can someone please shine the spotlight back on colony development? Shit, has helping us become an afterthought?"

The carrier chugged onward south, passing roadkill.

• • •

After scrutinizing her appearance in her mirror, Stacie, clad in a sleeveless maroon dress that had a nice grip on her form and showed off her legs, left her quarters. She was in a good mood, having had Linked intercourse with her boyfriend last night—and again in the shower this morning. When he returned to base, it'd be time for round three.

She sashayed into the lounge, dress swishing over her thighs. Inside, Guardians in civvies were socializing, playing holo table-games, and scarfing down grub from the mess hall. Her eyes found

Jarius at a small round table.

A female Guardian—with Korean features, short cyan hair, and purple-dyed irises—was seated on his lap. She wore a crop top, blue jean shorts, and calf-high boots. After she and Jarius shared a laugh, she stood.

"Later, Yoon," Jarius said over the guffaws.

"Later, hotshot," she replied, walking away.

Jarius missed the warmth of her tush on his lap already.

Stacie came over. "Specialist Ford, mind if I sit?"

Jarius took a sip of his orange fizzing drink. "Not at all, Sub-Lead." Stacie sat opposite him and crossed her legs. "Look at you, all spruced up."

"Hey, what can I say? I enjoy being fashionable," Stacie remarked. She glanced around the room at everyone enjoying themselves. "Could you imagine being stuck in uniform twenty-four-seven on deployment? And no sex life on top of that?" She made a face. "*Bluh*, that'd suck."

"The old guard says that we new-gen soldiers are pampered way too much. They think we're undisciplined and that lax regulations have made us soft."

Stacie laughed. "Babe, I'm anything but soft."

"I'll give you that. You're a Warrior Extraordinaire, after all." Jarius couldn't deny she was one kick-ass lady.

Stacie activated the table's menu panel. She tapped the image of a blue cup on the order display. A boxy server golem floated from the mess hall to the table and set a frothing blue beverage in front of her, then zipped away.

Jarius took another sip of his drink. "So what made a woman of your stature join the CDF?" he asked conversationally. "You don't need the credits. Your parents set you up for life. Spencer Enterprises is basically a financial empire."

Aversion tightened Stacie's features. "That's my issue." Her voice was rough-edged. "I don't want an entire life built by my parents. I don't want my identity to revolve around being a daughter of the Eight." She quickly changed the subject, steering the conversation away from her parents and the Eight. Too many bad memories were being dredged up. "So what about you? Why'd you join?"

She spat out the question at rapid fire, with a grouchy tone. Jarius figured that he'd brought up a touchy subject. "There were many career tracks I could've taken, but they just seemed . . . unexciting." He gave Stacie a sharp grin. "And bland and boring ain't me."

The two kept chatting, gradually easing into lighter topics. As the tension faded, they discovered they had common interests. Both liked sports, surfing, and going to virtual arcades.

• • •

Kesley pulled the carrier up to a gate. Gravel crunched beneath the tires.

A small, weather-worn sign wired to the gate read: PROPERTY OF DYNAMIC RELIEF PROVISIONS.

A security officer in blue exited his booth.

"Am I going to be a problem?" Randy asked Kesley.

She shook her head. "Nah. As long as you're with me and I've got my creds, we're good."

The officer went up to Kesley's door. "Hey, Kess, how are you?"

"Doing as fine as I can, Steve." She showed him her creds.

He nodded and went into his booth. A few seconds later, the gate rolled aside. Kesley drove through, passing busy repositories.

She entered her usual loading station, a small warehouse packed with cargo containers, and slid the gearshift into PARK. The carrier's brakes scraped, and its engine compartment rattled and hissed.

The faint smell of metal and lubricant lingered.

Big rigs bearing the Dynamic Relief Provisions logo trundled in and out.

A train of freight crates, lined one behind the other, moved from station to station on an assembly line. At the midpoint, the double-pronged arm of a robo-loader set packages inside each crate.

A foreman entered Kesley's plate number into his tablet to access her daily manifest. He then gestured to the crane operator, a man in orange coveralls and a yellow hardhat.

The operator returned to his station and maneuvered the crane's magnetic clamp, suspended from the hoist, over a stack of containers. Once a container was secured, he lowered it onto the carrier's cargo bed. After releasing the magnetic clamp, he raised the hoist and swung it to the right to retrieve the next container.

"So how'd your mom and dad hook up?" Kesley asked Randy, waiting for her bed to be stacked.

"My father lived here and worked in the quarries. My mom, an Edenite, was sent here through her employer's temporary placement program for a voluntary special assignment. They hit it off, she got pregnant near the end of her stay, and after I was born, Dad made the lottery. Then they left to start a life together on Eden, got married, and lived . . . not so happily ever after."

So Randy was born here. He's essentially a Highborn with colony ties, Kesley thought.

Once her bed was loaded, Kesley drove off the premises to make her delivery. After some more get-to-know-you talk and a bit more verbal sparring over moral high grounds, Kesley and Randy arrived at Kesley's destination.

Randy eyed the brick building. "What is this place?"

Kesley rolled her eyes. "Don't you know anything?" Randy frowned in response. "It's an Assistance Living Center, one of three in this district. Dynamic Relief Provisions built all three. Children orphaned by the war and men and women who were displaced stay here. My payload is their food and supplies for the week. The place we left is one of Dynamic Relief Provisions' distribution hubs."

"I see," Randy said, compassion in his eyes. "We . . . on Eden hear about these things, but we don't see them unless we travel to a colony. And we rarely have a reason to."

Two ten-year-old boys zipped past the carrier on a pair of air scooters. Their laughter pealed.

"Time to give Joey and Kimberly their turn," a female service worker said, half stern.

Kesley stepped out of the carrier.

A middle-school-aged Indonesian girl and her two elementary-aged twin brothers rushed across the dirt path, excited to see Kesley. The girl wore a shirt and overalls, and she had inky-black pigtails that reached her shoulders. The twins wore matching yellow shirts and beige pants.

"Did you bring us candy this time?" one of the boys asked, his grin stretching ear to ear.

"Sure did, kiddo," Kesley replied. She mussed up his already-wild hair with her hand.

The girl squinted up at Randy, curiosity in her pearly dark eyes. "Who's he? Your boyfriend?"

Kesley laughed. "He's a friend of mine, from Eden."

The girl's jaw dropped. "You're a Highborn?" She pointed at Randy.

"Uh, yeah, I am," he said.

The girl's eyes lit up. "Are there really big, tall buildings on Eden called skyscrapers?" She spread her arms high and wide to mimic the scale. "And flying cars too?"

Randy bobbed his chin. "Uh-huh. Here, let me show you something." He pressed a button on his wristcom, and a shimmer of digital color morphed into a 3-D image of his sports cruiser.

"Cool, a hologram!" The girl snatched Randy's wrist.

Randy's feet stumbled forward as the girl pulled him closer to get a better look at the holo. "Whoa!" he exclaimed. The girl's adorable, innocent eyes gazed unblinkingly at the gleaming image. *The things that fascinate them are so ordinary for us Edenites. A shame,* Randy thought.

A bearded man—dark brown skin weathered from time and stress, bags under his eyes like he'd been fighting sleep for years— walked up to Kesley. A cigar smoldered between his lips, and he held a metal thermos in one hand. His jeans ragged and checkered flannel shirt wrinkled, he could be mistaken for a drifter.

He took the cigar out of his mouth. A dusting of ash slipped off the tip and scattered. "Who's he?" he asked, voice gravely.

"A Guardian," Kesley answered. She watched Randy play with the boys, drawing their laughter. "One of the good ones." *And a hunky one to boot,* she thought. She'd heard Highborn men, thanks to their genetic upgrades, were unreal in bed. But she'd never met one worth confirming that rumor with. Until now.

"Wasn't sure good ones existed," the smoker said. A sip of water from his thermos wet his dry throat. "I'll go grab the guys. We'll get some power pallets to unload everything." He tucked the cigar between his lips.

The limp in his leg, caused by an unjustified beating from some Guardians, made the short walk to the center feel like a trek.

Daylight waning, shades of orange emblazoned the sky.

As twilight fell, Kesley and Randy made the commute back to her residential complex. They spent most of it comparing their upbringings, which were like night and day. She had discontinued high school to help support her family; he had graduated from Commonwealth University. She had grown up in a small housing unit; he had grown up in a high-end family home. Her family had to be frugal; his didn't.

Kesley parked the carrier in the gravel lot, beside a hatchback that had seen better days. She and Randy got out.

Hyped, Kesley said, "Man, all the wonders of Eden you've been talking about and showing me on that doohickey wristband—I'd love to see them in person someday." Her voice was full of childlike enthusiasm. "I wanna see the skyscrapers and multiplex shopping centers. I wanna ride in a flyer."

Randy rested a hand on her shoulder. "How about we go there one week when I'm on leave?" he offered sincerely. "I'll show you everything. I'll even take you for a ride in my sports cruiser."

Kesley sighed. "It'd probably take forever just to get a two-week travel pass."

"What do you mean?" Randy felt chagrined by his lack of knowledge. "I don't really know how the pass process works. It's not something I've ever had to think about."

"Well," Kesley began, "after you get through security, you've gotta wait hours in a long screening line. First, you hit the ID-check station, where proctors thumb-print you to run a full background check, which now includes making sure you're not flagged in the terrorist database."

With feigned exhaustion, she went on. "*Then* you wait again, till they sit you in front of a computer to answer a long-ass checklist of *stupid* questions. And now it's stuff like, 'Have you ever been approached by anyone asking you to join an anti-government or terrorist organization?' or 'Do you have friends who are members of one?'" Annoyance clouded her face, and Randy looked unsettled. "Third," she continued, "a proctor takes you through a medical exam to make sure you don't have any communicable diseases, and that all your vaccinations are current."

Kesley's shoulders sagged. Just thinking about the process was exhausting. "The process was already a pain in the ass. I imagine now it's gonna be a *double* pain in the ass. And after all that, you still have to wait anywhere from six to twelve months. And there are way too few staff processing all the applications."

"I can see how irritating it is just to get a plastic card to go to Eden," Randy said. "The process needs to be streamlined."

Kesley scoffed. "Funny, isn't it? We're all supposed to be equal citizens of humanity's *great* intergalactic republic, but it's like we're together but separate. And if caught with an expired pass on Eden, you get locked up, so you better make sure your butt doesn't miss the return flight." She shook her head. "Hell, intergalactic tourists and vacationers get quicker access to Eden than us colonists, because they're feeding the economy."

"Total bullshit," Randy said.

"Yeah. And I get that you can't cram all of us colony folks onto Eden. It's only got one continental landmass, which ain't big enough for all of humanity. But still, you shouldn't have to go through a buncha hooey just to visit your fellow human beings."

"I agree," Randy said. "The goal, though, is to have Satellite One eventually become an 'Eden.'"

"Yeah, well, that's not happening anytime soon."

Randy's stomach growled.

Kesley giggled. "Guess you're pretty hungry, huh? Gotta be. We haven't eaten much all day." She started walking toward the complex's front door. "Let me take care of that stomach for you."

"I . . . I don't know. I should probably get back."

"What for? You're off the clock today. No one's searching for you, right? As long as you're back when you're supposed to be, no one really gives a hoot about how long you're offsite."

"Yeah, true," Randy said, still unsure if he should stick around.

Kesley gestured for him to follow. "Then c'mon."

Randy sighed and gave in. "Fine."

They went into the building and entered Kesley's third-story unit. The stale air permeated their nostrils.

Randy's eyes swooped over the cramped square space. The kitchenette, living area, and bathroom were all crammed together, boxed in by flaking white paint. To him, this place felt abysmal.

Without a beat of hesitation, Kesley wrestled her clammy shirt overhead, outright baring her naked flesh.

Randy flinched in surprise. "What are you—?" His heart stopped. Was this an unspoken invitation for . . . ?

"Just changing shirts, soldier boy. It's been a long, sweaty day." Free-spirited, Kesley strode over to her closet, completely unashamed. Her voluptuous breasts waggled with each step. "I'm not shy about showing some skin, if that's what's got you all dumbstruck. *Geesh*," she said. "Honestly, a devout nudist like me would rather be naked all the time."

The shape of Kesley's body was enticing. Randy couldn't help but stare, eyes drawn below her collarbones. She had a rack that was impossible to ignore—one with plenty of bounce.

She slipped a gauzy white tube top over her chest, and Randy's admiring gaze ended. The orange print on the shirt said SCREW THE GOVERNMENT. Randy hoped she wouldn't wear that shirt in public; the controversial words would attract attention.

Done changing, Kesley opened the fridge.

Randy wondered if she had a thing for him, if undressing in

front of him had been a seduction tactic. Maybe her choice of clothing was another—the thin tube top exposed the lower curves of her breasts and the outline of her nipples.

She pulled out two plastic containers of stew, slid them into the microwave heater, and tapped the two-minute timer. "Be ready in a jiffy. Just make yourself at home."

Randy took a seat on one of the two wooden crates at the table, its surface hidden by a white linen cloth.

When the microwave pinged, Kesley retrieved the containers and set them on the table. "Mom's recipe. You'll enjoy it, trust me." She grabbed two spoons from the cupboard and gave one to Randy. "Bon appétit."

Randy scooped a bite of stew into his mouth. The spicy flavor hit instantly, titillating his taste buds. "This is good. Your mom knows her stuff."

"Thanks."

As annoying as Kesley could be sometimes, Randy appreciated her taking him on her delivery run. The trip gave him a new perspective on colony life. "Hey, I want you to know that everything I saw today was a real eye-opener."

"Yeah, that's what I was hoping for. The route we took, so you could see all that, was intentional."

Randy blinked. "What do you mean?"

"That was the scenic route to the distribution hub. I could've gotten us there way faster." Kesley paused, letting that land. All the ruins and low-grade housing were intentional waypoints. "People like you might be able to make a difference, if you're aware of what's really going on here. Because as long as people stay in the dark, this oppression's gonna keep going. But if enough people like you open their eyes, maybe they'll actually do something for their fellow human beings."

"And what do you hope 'people like me' will do?"

"Stop turning a blind eye to pain and suffering. Divvy up some credits and donate to Assistance Living Centers. If you see Guardians messing with people, find your balls and stand up to them. Not too much to ask, right?"

"No, it's not." Randy downed some more stew.

Kesley was unlike most women he'd known. She was scrappy, street-smart, pushy, unrefined, and completely unfiltered. A far cry from the prissy women he'd befriended or dated in his home city, Frenchester Heights, or at Commonwealth University. He found that kind of attitude obnoxious but also . . . attractive.

After a few more spoonfuls of stew, Kesley added, "Who knows, maybe the more that open-minded people like you learn about what's going on here, the more likely it is that Oviereya becomes the next Chief. That's part of my hopes and dreams, anyway."

"Mine too." When Randy finished his meal, he stood. "Thanks for the hospitality, Kess. I should head back now."

Kesley walked him to the door. "It was nice getting to know you, Randy."

"You too. I'll definitely come back and visit." Randy's eyes landed on Kesley's satchel in the corner. "So, what were you doing at the comms tower yesterday?" The Guardian Lars had sent to check out the tower found no tampering.

"Nothing you need to be concerned about," Kesley said coyly. "But I've got a little gift for you to remember me by." A sensual smile tugged at her lips.

"What would that—?"

Kesley's mouth captured Randy's in a delightful, wet n' wild kiss. A kiss that almost knocked him off-balance. As she gradually pulled back, she pinched his lower lip with her teeth, a strand of saliva stretching between their mouths.

Warmth flooded Randy's cheeks. He'd been caught off guard. "I, uh—" His wristcom chirped. Lars had forwarded a message to the platoon. "Excuse me." Randy faced away from Kesley so she wouldn't see the confidential content.

Holowords in a text box said WE'RE GOING TO BE ON DUTY TOMORROW AFTER ALL. SO MAKE SURE YOU REST UP. OUR CAPTIVE JUST GAVE US ARSON SCOTT. WE KNOW WHERE HIS FACTION'S HIDEOUT IS.

Body pumped full of pain analeptics, Nelson had cracked fast. Even a finger poke evoked unspeakable agony thanks to the drugs.

Randy pressed a finger to his wristcom. The text dissolved. He turned back around, a rigid set to his jaw.

The heated look on his face—a look that could melt steel—gave Kesley goose bumps and made her take a step back. "Something up?"

Randy ground his teeth. The agony in his chest stabbed at his heart. A-1 Defense Solutions exploding into a burst of fire and smoke flashed in his mind, the last memory of his mother. "My platoon has a big impromptu mission tomorrow. I've gotta go." He yanked open the door and took off down the stairs.

Kesley closed the door behind him.

Randy made his way back to Lima Company on his hoverbike, speeding through a town. Arson temporarily off his mind, he thought about the bleak living conditions the people of Colony Four had to accept. *People on Eden who never visit the colonies might think their citizens are just bitching and moaning, but they do have a legit gripe.*

Randy heard the tumble of a trash receptacle and the sounds of a scuffle. As he shifted his body to the left, his hoverbike veered toward the commotion.

Two Guardians in battledress—one tall and brawny, the other short and stocky—slammed a man against a brick building. The sign in front read: MICKEY'S BAR.

"You a rebel?" the tall Guardian asked.

"I didn't do nothin'! Lemme go!" the man begged.

Randy decelerated, cut off the bike's engine, and dismounted. He bolted onto the scene, passing an inebriated civilian who was lumbering out of the bar and taking a swig from a flask.

Randy flashed his military ID. "What's going on here?"

The shorter Guardian replied, "In the bar, we overheard this bum making disparaging comments about the government. He could be a Coalition rebel."

"Last time I checked, anti-government discourse wasn't a crime," Randy said. "Are you really that paranoid?"

The tall Guardian replied, "We can't take any chances." He gripped the man's shirt and curled his fingers, bunching the fabric in his hand. "This gutter trash might be someone who kills one of our brothers-in-arms, and I sure as hell couldn't live with myself if that happens."

Randy's jaw clenched. "Yeah, but you can't compromise the integrity of the Defense Force—or deface its image—by roughing up every person you're suspicious of."

The short Guardian snorted. "Well, excuse the fuck out of us. The people of this mud-ball colony hate our guts and want us gone. Sounds like we've got a little cause to be concerned."

Randy pointed a finger at them. "You shouldn't have signed up for the job if you're gonna be so easily scared."

The tall Guardian flicked his hand, dismissing Randy. "Forget you. Get outta here."

Randy bristled at the insult. "Maybe you don't know who I am. I'm Randal Scott, and I've got connections to people who can have you mopping floors for the rest of your military careers."

The short Guardian let out a pissed grunt. "C'mon, let's go," he said to his comrade. They both left.

"You okay?" Randy asked the man they'd been hassling.

He tipped his head. "Yeah, I'll be alright."

"Need a ride or anything?"

"Nah, you go on. Thanks, though. Good to know there are Guardians like you who stand up to bullies like that."

"No problem at all."

Randy took off on his hoverbike.

He was fresh out of military training. He hadn't been a witness to the mistreatment of colonists by the CDF until coming to Colony Four. Guardians graduated from training with the belief that the CDF was always in the right, acting with the highest morality. He'd known the CDF had some imperfections, but maybe there were more cracks in the armor than he'd expected.

Guardians were told colonists were wrong for being anti-government, but after what he saw today, Randy understood why they were. That didn't mean he believed rebellion was the answer to their problems. After all, colonies Two, Three, and Five continued to enact change using a nonaggressive approach, rather than start a war.

It seemed the rogue colonies' citizens distrusted the central government because it had neglected them for so long, and they disliked Guardians because they were the government's enforcers, agents of the status quo. On the flip side, Guardians disliked the rogue colonies' citizens, viewing them as military-haters, whiners, and nonconformists. Their training conditioned them to see all government opponents that way. It was a difficult dilemma to fix.

Randy reached Lima Company and slowed to a stop at the checkpoint. After the Guardian on security detail confirmed his identity via retina scan, he drove past the gate and parked in the motor pool, in a row of hoverbikes. Ready to call it a night, he headed toward Annex 13.

For a moment, he thought about Kesley and their journey today, grateful for what it had shown him. Kesley had made an extraordinary impact on his thinking. His heart went out to her for the struggles she had endured and for the loss of her brother.

The memory of her mouth smothering his flashed across his thoughts. He guessed he'd made an impression on her as well, her planting a kiss on a Guardian. To deny she was sexually attractive would be foolish. He knew she'd make some man extremely happy, if he could stand her in-your-face attitude.

His mind refocused on business. Tomorrow, he'd have the opportunity he'd been waiting for. It was the reason he had Conlan get him stationed at Colony Four. Tomorrow, he'd confront his father . . . hopefully.

His implant pulsed like a warning siren—Stacie was near.

She burst through the front door, her face alight with energy. "You missed chow. Everything good?" she said, voice vibrant.

Randy didn't waste a second; he pinned her against the iron door, kissing her. His lips blazed a trail down to her cleavage. "Yeah, everything's good." He claimed her lips again, while reaching underneath her dress to stroke her thigh. Arson was a problem for tomorrow; tonight, more sex with Stacie awaited.

CHAPTER FOUR

Blue-to-red strobe lights flashed throughout Arson's stronghold. An earsplitting claxon-like alert blared. The sound of shoot-outs echoed.

"Hurry!" Arson shouted, racing down a corridor toward the shuttle bay with a slew of rebel troops, all armed. He and nine others wore white humanoid mechsuits, their headgear appearing to have an open-face design.

The reinforced entry door lowered behind them as they rushed into the bay, a cavernous space that resembled a warehouse.

A thunderous wham struck the blast door in front of them.

"They're using a battering ram!" a male rebel yelled.

Everyone fanned out, rifles in hand. They took defensive positions behind crates and containers.

Arson barked exhortations. Voices overlapped, rebels swearing and shouting in hysteria. Everywhere, there was heavy breathing. Terror swirled through minds.

One quivering young woman quietly recited the Coalition's motto. "Keep the faith, keep the faith, keep the faith."

An exhausted man ran up to Arson, fighting for breath. "The enemy has infiltrated every wing, sir," he panted. "We here in the bay are the only ones who have a shot at making it out alive. Everyone else is going to be killed or captured."

"Damn it! How'd they find us?" Arson blurted, wondering what security vulnerability led to this. He spun and gestured to the only pilot in the bay. "What are you waiting for, Richter? Get that shuttle prepped for takeoff! We're abandoning base!"

"Roger, sir!" the pilot replied. "Since the shuttle just came back from a run, it'll take at least fifteen minutes for the power banks to recharge enough for us to get anywhere!"

"Just get it done! And tell the incoming cargo ship that we've been compromised! They are to abort the delivery of the assets and reroute to Bravo Camp!"

The pilot sprinted off.

I can't believe we're it, Arson thought.

A rebel woman in a black tee and olive-green tactical pants came to his side. Her complexion wasn't as brown as her father's, nor as fair as her mother's. She had short dark brunette hair, deep brown eyes, and was in her late thirties. "Don't worry, we'll escape." She kissed Arson's lips.

"Thank you, Sariah." A boom buckled the blast door inward, metal screeching. "They're using a plasma cannon now! Get ready, everyone!" Arson heaved a deep sigh of remorse. *Once again, we're left with no choice but to fight back. It's us or them. Commonwealth Government, if only you'd end this madness. Then we wouldn't have to* —

Another boom blew an opening in the blast door, twisting, warping, and liquefying metal.

Lars and squads One and Two of Fourth Platoon bum-rushed the bay, footfalls pounding the floor. The rotary barrels of their

Gatling guns—the equipped primary weapon—spat an onslaught of heavy-caliber rounds, cutting unarmored rebels down into a bloody slush of limbs, organs, and body parts.

Rebels returned fire with a mix of bullets and energy blasts.

The backpacks feeding the ammunition belts into the Guardians' Gatling guns radiated heat as rounds tore through everything, shredding crates and containers, punching holes into walls.

The nodes on Arson's headgear illuminated. His rebels' mechsuits were operated by brain-computer interface, like Shells. At his mental command, interlocking plates enclosed his face, but not before Randy caught a glimpse of him.

Father, Randy thought.

Since Randy had last seen him, Arson had grown a thick dark beard, and his face bore a few stress-induced wrinkles.

"Careful, everyone!" Lars shouted. "I count ten with some sort of strange armored combat suit not cataloged in our index!" Including Arson, there were seven men and three women. The rest of the rebels wore plain, ragged clothes. Lars C-commed the leader of his third squad. <<*This is Sergeant First Class Freeman to Sergeant Thornton. Is the motor pool secure?*>>

Thornton's rifle rattled, a burst of bullets mowing down a rebel. Blood sprinkled over the phyocrete. <<*Motor pool is now secure,*>> he said to Lars. A hiss of steam escaped his rifle's barrel.

<<*Roger. Be advised: The enemy has unidentifiable mechsuits at their disposal, and there's no telling*—>> Combat interrupted Lars in mid-thought. <<*Gotta go.*>>

An assault vehicle blew apart in a shattering blast that hurled nearby Guardians into the air.

Shelled bodies, dust, and debris flew past Thornton. "Holy shit!"

The explosion slammed one Guardian against a vehicle's hood, cracking its windshield.

Thornton scanned the area for hostiles and caught a strange armored figure in his sights. *Must be what Lars was talking about.* "Target, left!"

The armored rebel held a sizzling sphere of plasma energy in his hands. With a kinetic push, he jettisoned the energy projectile at the infiltrators.

Guardians scattered, shouting colorful expletives. Another vehicle exploded, reduced to a heap of flaming wreckage.

The rebel balled more plasma energy with his hands. The complex, foreign tracery on his white armor glowed, and the suit emitted ghastly whistling noises.

"Open fire!" Thornton shouted.

Rifles rang as a conflux of bullets pelted the alien mechsuit.

Thornton saw the bullets fragmenting on impact. But how? The armor? Some kinetic output? Just like everyone else, he was awestruck. "Hold fire!" he ordered. *Fucking unbelievable.* "Switch to energy weapons!"

The rebel paused and dissolved the projectile. After a moment of stillness, he gave a nod, receiving a command to retreat.

His vernier jets ignited, launching him into the air.

Damn, these suits are aerial-combat capable too, Thornton thought. "Stand down, everyone!" Shells and weapons clattered. *Where the hell did these rebels get something like that?* he wondered.

"Arson," Sariah said, two pistols recoiling in her hands, "I've got your six!"

Arson was crouched behind a revetment. "Thanks, Sariah." He

stood and fired five shots from his energy rifle.

Jarius' Oracle analyzed the possible moves, tactics, and targets he was considering, then transmitted to him the best course of action. He took the advice, rotated left, and turned his Gatling gun on a rebel aiming at a fellow Guardian. Jarius' bullets riddled the rebel, ending his life.

"Get down!" Stacie shouted at Emilia. With her Gatling gun already depleted and discarded, she easily dove onto her adversary, tackling her to the floor and out of the path of incoming energy blasts.

Emilia, now sitting on her tailbone, stared at the smoking holes in the wall. *Whew, that was a close call.* "Nice save, princess."

Stacie, kneeling and facing her, said, "Yeah, thanks to my hardware." Heightened mental acuity was another perk of the upgraded CPU.

Streaks of energy zipped overhead, startling Stacie and Emilia.

"C'mon, let's get these motherfuckers," Emilia said.

Setting aside their mutual dislike, Stacie and Emilia jumped back into the fight as a team.

Stacie, using arm-mounted weapons, and Emilia, wielding her Gatling gun, concentrated their firepower into a fusillade that plowed down a group of rebels.

Bullets from Randy's Gatling gun spun bodies into bloody pirouettes. Shell casings spewed from the backpack's ejection port, pinging into a growing pile on the floor. Exhaust hissed along the gun's vents; then, suddenly, the trigger only clicked. AMMO DEPLETED flashed on Randy's HUD.

With a thought, he detached the backpack, sending it clanging against the floor. He dropped the heavy Gatling gun, and it thudded. His Oracle initiated the next step before he could give his CPU the command.

His secondary sprang up from a recess on his leg panel. He gripped the handgun, pulled it free from the securing clips, and drew it forward. "Thanks, Oracle."

"User is welcome," the AI replied.

The recess sealed. Randy discharged a deadly pulse of blue energy that exploded the chest of an unarmored rebel. A mess of red splotches and spalled flesh fragments sprayed in all directions. "Father!" He advanced toward Arson.

Arson turned to him, recognizing his son's voice. "Randal."

Randy commanded his faceplate to go away. It slipped up, exposing a seething expression.

It's been a while, Son, Arson thought.

Randy's faceplate resealed. He continued his pursuit of vengeance, firing blasts at anyone who got between him and his father, the betrayer who plagued his mind.

Closing the distance, Randy scored a shot to the abdomen of a plainclothes rebel. Bits of the rebel's body splattered grotesquely against his Shell. Another lethal blast burst a woman's head into a cocktail of blood and brain matter. Shot number three destroyed a man's leg below the kneecap.

A rebel jumped from behind the crates at Randy's six and ambushed him. A rocket launcher rested on the husky man's shoulder.

"No, wait," Arson said. But it was too late. The rebel had squeezed the trigger.

Randy craned his head. *Damn it.* He saw a rocket speeding toward him.

His Oracle made a tactical decision for him, activating his Shell's plasma-energy barrier.

A blue bubble ballooned around Randy. The explosive projectile collided with the energy field and scattered apart, metal shards darting across the bay. The Oracle expanded the barrier further, ensnaring the rebel in its wake. He screamed, the energy field incinerating him into ash.

The barrier deflated and crackled away as the Oracle dissolved it.

"Thanks again, Oracle," Randy said. The AI Combat Assistant was a true partner.

Randy checked his Shell's power cell. The vitality gauge on his readout was at level two, ten being full power. The cell was nearly depleted because of the barrier shield, but had the Oracle not activated it, he might be dead. Drawing from the auxiliary reservoir, he restored four units of power.

Sariah raised her pistol at Randy.

"No, don't get involved. That's an order," Arson said to her.

Bullets and energy blasts crisscrossed the bay in a barrage of destruction.

Randy checked his handgun's power-status indicator and saw the cell was drained. He sealed the weapon in the recharging holster and pressed a button on his armguard. Plasma energy coalesced into a flickering purple blade that extended from his wrist, his close-quarters weapon.

Rebel blood drenching his armor, Randy stared down Arson, an apoplectic look in his eyes. "I want answers, Father!" He swung his plasma saber, cutting the air.

Arson jinked, dodging Randy's swift attack.

A flurry of sizzling swings came at Arson. The blade sliced two gashes into his nanoengineered armor, but they instantly sealed.

Self-repairing tech? Randy thought.

Sariah jerked her pistol up at Randy. "Darling, I can help."

Darling? Randy thought, roiled. Was she his mom's replacement? It was bad enough that Arson had participated in his wife's murder, but now a new woman was in his life?

Enraged, Randy charged at Arson, screaming and brandishing his saber.

Arson kicked him onto his back, armor clanging against armor. Then he reiterated his order to Sariah. "I told you, *don't* get involved."

She lowered her pistol.

Randy leapt to his feet, the death of his mother consuming him.

A metal cable catapulted from a recess under Arson's wrist. The magnetic clamp clung to Randy's Shell.

"What the hell?" Randy said. He gripped the cable with his left hand and lifted the blade of his right. Before the blow could fall, a crippling plasma charge electrified the cable.

SYSTEM OVERLOADING blinked on his HUD, and circuits blew out. A harsh pang killed the cerebral link between his mind and the Shell. As his visuals flatlined, he let out an awful scream, and his legs buckled.

Arson retracted his taser coil and caught Randy's crumpling form in his arms, hauling him easily over his shoulder.

"Arson, Richter has informed me the shuttle is ready for takeoff," Sariah said.

"Everyone, fall back into the shuttle for evac!" Arson shouted.

The other nine armored rebels laid down suppression fire as their comrades withdrew into the craft through its rear-deck door. They took up staggered positions so they wouldn't get picked off easily. One of them generated an energy sphere in his hands, hurled it at a Guardian, and watched him disappear in a bright burst, remains blown all over the bay.

"Man, that's some crazy fucking firepower!" a female Guardian yelled.

A Shell would severely drain its power cell if it launched an energy attack that strong.

Jarius saw Arson heading into the shuttle with Randy. *Darn it,* he thought. *I've known you too long to let these guys take you from us. Hang on, buddy.* He activated his Shell's stealth cloak, which disguised him by replicating his surroundings.

Power consumption for stealth cloaking was on the high end, so Guardians couldn't stay cloaked for long. Jarius would have to move fast. How he and Randy would escape was still unclear, and he didn't have time to figure it out. Brave or stupid? Either way, it was too late to get cold feet now. He and Randy would have to improvise when the time came.

Jarius maneuvered into the shuttle, its rear-deck door slowly lowering. He'd have to be vigilant; stealth cloaks didn't make a Guardian completely unseeable or mute sound.

Lars shouted as the outgunned rebels fled into their escape craft, "Move in and take that shuttle out!"

The Guardians walked their gunfire forward, trying to overtake the retreating rebels.

The rear-deck door clamped shut. All the surviving rebels had made it inside. With them out of the line of fire, the shuttle's exterior gun batteries whined to life.

"Shit!" Lars yelled.

A salvo of hot slugs from the guns ripped into Guardians' Shells. Blood sprayed.

Guardians quickly bubbled themselves inside their barrier shields.

As the shuttle powered up for liftoff, the guns whined to a stop. An opening in the ceiling parted.

Nico lowered his shield. He extended his arm, and from a slot on his armguard, a tracer blasted out and tagged the undercarriage of the craft as it elevated into the sky, making a getaway.

Barrier shields went down, their shimmering auras crackling away. Cooling weapons hissed.

Nico thought, *The dog is injured and on the run. We've got you, Arson Scott.*

Lars said, "Sergeant Mansford and Sergeant Fleming, check your people and give me an ACE Report."

A Guardian removed her helmet and vomited, unable to withstand the sight of all the massacred bodies, CDF and rebel alike.

"Someone, help," a barely alive Guardian drawled through a mouthful of blood. His Shell had been breached and organs damaged.

In the aftermath of the violent skirmish came a din of pain-filled wails, plaintive cries for help, panicked voices, and shouted instructions.

Team leaders got headcounts, logging who hadn't survived.

Stacie, breathless and fatigued, said to Lars, "They got Randy." Dents, fractures, and sooty marks blemished her Shell, and red blotches of blood stained the gunmetal Kryoplaste. Her faceplate slid up. The inflection of her voice soared to a dramatic pitch. "What are we going to do?" In a knee-jerk reaction, she gripped Lars' shoulders with her suited palms.

"Nothing we can do," Lars replied laconically. "And Jarius is missing. A Guardian said he saw him cloak and go after Randy."

"Can't the Nerve Center track Randy's signature?" Despair cast its shadow over Stacie's face. Worry swarmed in her belly.

Lars said, "Already tried. His Shell's gone dark. It's completely off the tracking grid. Must be offline."

Stacie expelled an acquiescing sigh.

Lars hated losing any of his Guardians, whether by death or

capture. "Randy's my soldier, no matter how much of a pain in the ass he is, so I don't like it either." He walked away.

A knot of dread settled in Stacie's chest. She prayed Randy would somehow return safely.

Looking at the carnage sent a chill traveling down her spine. When her eyes landed on a sight too graphic for words, her mouth fell open. Emilia's body had been torn apart. Swimming in her blood was a grotesque mix of entrails, minced flesh, and Shell scraps—all hers. This was the handiwork of a plasma-energy attack from one of those alien mechsuits.

Still acting as First Squad's interim Alpha Team Leader while Holister recovered from injury, Stacie logged Emilia as "killed in action." *Great job, Stacie,* she thought bitterly. *One KIA and two MIA.*

Nausea churned in her stomach. She averted her eyes from the gore and covered her mouth with her hand, shaking in horror.

As Guardians scrambled to help their injured comrades, the blood-soaked floor squelched beneath their mechboots.

"I am detecting elevated levels of psychological stress," said Stacie's Oracle. "Should I administer the SR-21 sedative to help —?"

"No! No psychotropic drugs," Stacie replied. She shut off her Oracle, removed her helmet, and racked it.

Jason Mansford went up to her and placed a hand on her shoulder. "Don't worry, the psychs are on duty tonight if anyone needs them. The chaplain's available too. I know this stuff can really mess with your head." He pulled out a cigarette from his chest plate's personal compartment, holding it out to her. "Want one? It helps."

Stacie eyed the offering and took it from him. "Oh, what the hell," she said. "Thanks."

Jason produced a lighter and lit the cigarette.

Stacie said, "I've been trying to quit, but under the circumstances—" Her voice was ragged. She shuddered at all the destroyed human bodies. "*Ugh*, gross." She felt herself getting queasy. "You always keep these on hand?"

"We have to use personal compartments for something."

Stacie drew smoke into her lungs, nicotine alleviating her nausea. She exhaled a mist. "They got Randy. Hope they don't harm him." Her voice quavered, and her thoughts were a tangled mess of worst-case scenarios.

"Well, Arson is his old man, so I don't think his life is in any danger."

"I hope not." At the mercy of the unknown, Stacie closed her eyes and kept smoking.

Subjected to combat stress for the first time, young Guardians —who had never fought in an actual battle or taken lives—sat on containers to decompress.

A Guardian studied the bay. "So what was this place?" he asked Lars.

"It was originally an alloy-processing facility for Mining Absolute, a top mining corp on Eden, owned by some entrepreneurial bigwig named Kenneth Lords. Apparently, the Scott Faction repurposed it as a base. Since Arson was a quarry worker, he naturally had industry connections, and private property off-limits to the CDF without proper justification made for the perfect hideout.

"Whether Lords is a Coalition supporter and was aware one of his decommissioned facilities was being used as the Scott Faction's base remains to be seen. Could be one of his quarry managers was helping Arson under his nose. He's being taken into custody for questioning."

Stacie pondered how Randy was doing as the glowing tip of her cigarette smoldered.

<<*Spencer,*>> she heard over the C-comm. It was Lars. <<*You can calm down a little. Sergeant Fleming has just informed me he tagged the shuttle with a tracer. We might be getting Randy back soon.*>>

Stacie's spirits lifted, and a subtle smile of relief livened her face.

Lars transitioned to audio. "Listen up, everyone. Sergeant Fleming tagged the shuttle. I've gotten permission from higher to dispatch a squad to follow it, while the rest of us stay behind to secure the facility and harvest any beneficial data. I'm guessing most of it's been scrubbed.

"Mansford, you and your squad will pursue the shuttle. Wherever it lands, you are to stand by for backup and observe. Under no circumstances should you engage. That clear?"

"Understood," Jason replied. He C-commed his remaining squad members: SPC Stacie Spencer, SGT Olivia Slovak, SPC Eli Manson, PVT Ryoko Nahara, and PVT Seth Youngblood. <<*Alright, no recess for us, people. Get your asses in gear, and let's get into a BUS and tail that craft.*>>

They all C-commed back "Roger."

•••

Randy came to. Through his slitted lids, the bright overhead light stung his eyes. He winced and rubbed them with his forearm. He was lying face-up on a metal bench in his sleeve, his head throbbing. The whirring of turbines reached his ears. Obviously, he was still aboard Arson's evac shuttle.

Randy brought himself to a sitting position and took in his surroundings. Metal walls boxed him into a constricted square space that had a barred window. He was in a detention cell.

He got to his feet. His back ached from lying on the hard metal surface.

The thunderhead outside crackled and flashed, promising a violent storm.

He moved to the cell door and peered through its small rectangular grille. Two rebels were guarding him. One had almond-colored skin, a thick build, and a close-cropped dark beard streaked with gray. The other was of Vietnamese descent, had a medium build, and appeared to be in his mid-twenties. He wore his dark hair in a neck-length ponytail, and scruff covered his jaw. They were watching a newscast on the tablet the bearded rebel held.

An anchorwoman onscreen said, "The emergency summit happens tomorrow. People are on edge. We now know the assassin who tried to kill Chairman Gould was a lone wolf inspired by Arman Reza's anti-government rhetoric—"

Randy rapped the cell door with his knuckles. "Hey."

"You're awake," said the bearded rebel.

The ponytailed rebel contacted Arson using a palm-sized comm-set. "Sir, your son is awake."

The comm-set squawked. "Bring him," Arson replied.

"Yes, sir." The comm-set beeped and went silent.

The bearded rebel punched a code into a wall module. Locks clacked. The cell door screeched open. "Come on, we're taking you to your father, and don't cause a commotion like your comrade did." He kept his weapon trained on Randy.

"What comrade?" Randy asked, his voice a low rumble.

"Guy's name is Jarius. He stupidly sneaked aboard to play hero." Jarius' heroics had simply ushered him straight into enemy hands.

"Was he harmed?"

"He's fine. Just locked up."

"Well, you don't have to worry about me trying to escape,"

Randy assured the two rebels. Venom in his voice, he added, "I'm actually looking forward to this."

Randy's escorts led him down the shuttle's central corridor.

A downpour pummeled the craft's hull.

With his patience fraying and emotions high, the short walk felt like an eternity to Randy.

As he thought about his mother, the phosphorescent illusion of her appeared again, levitating beside him.

Remember what I taught you about forgiveness, Kathleen's voice whispered in his mind.

Get lost, he replied.

Son, I—

Randy's nostrils flared. "Go away!" he said aloud.

The cerebral specter vanished.

His escorts stared at him as if he'd lost his mind.

"Who the hell are you talking to?" the ponytailed rebel asked.

"Just take me to my father," Randy demanded, seeing red.

The walk continued.

Randy wondered if his mother's consciousness had transferred into him when she died, now living as some kind of entity within his cerebral implant. It sounded far-fetched. Then again, the unforeseen possibilities of the Quilgarian technology were vast. Or maybe he was simply teetering on the edge of insanity.

The rebels marched him past two automatic sliding doors, finally ending his wait. But his arena, a featureless all-white room with a single wall screen, was devoid of Arson.

"What the hell? There's no one here," Randy said.

A holo of Arson took shape, flickering and shifting until it stabilized. "Leave us," Arson commanded his men.

The rebels exited, and the door whisked shut behind them.

Rage burned in Randy's eyes. "You don't even have the courage to face me man-to-man."

"No, that's not it," Arson replied matter-of-factly. "I'm just not interested in fisticuffs with my only son. Last time we met in person, you tried to maim me with a plasma saber. This way, no one gets hurt."

Randy grunted.

Arson said, "Hear me out. Kathleen's death was an accident. A-1 Defense Solutions was my op. My intel said the building would be vacant that night and—"

"Well, your intel was wrong!" Randy lashed out, venting the anger that had been festering inside him for months.

Arson's chin touched his chest, and he pressed a hand to his forehead. The impact of Randy's words had hit hard. "Yes, it was. And I take full responsibility for what happened that night. I constantly think about what I could've done differently, to prevent Kathleen's death." Repentance was written all over his face. "I ask myself, 'Was there any way to reconfirm the floors were clear before detonating the explosives? Should I have called Kathleen to make sure she wasn't at work?'

"My wife's death has traumatized me. I have nightmares about that night. Hell, I was the one who thumbed the detonator." The anguish in his voice rose. "In *no way* has this been easy for me. So spare me your vitriol. I'm not some heartless monster. If it weren't for Sariah, I don't know if I would've been able to go on living."

Bastard. Hurt and indignation compounded, launching Randy into an emotional tirade. "You shouldn't have left! I had to be there for Mom because you weren't! You neglected *your* responsibility as a father and husband—as a man! Who abandons his wife and son to go off and join some terrorist outfit?"

Arson shook his head. "One man's terrorist is another man's revolutionary." As the shuttle bumped against turbulence, the holographic transmission blinked and sizzled.

Randy looked at Arson with an expression that seemed to ask "Are you serious?"

Randy said, "So that's what you think you are, a revolutionary?"

Arson adopted a defensive tone. "It's the *truth*. This is a war the central government caused, after all."

Condemnation enveloped Randy's face. "Your mind's been so deluded by the Coalition's doctrine that you can't think straight."

"Maybe it's your mind that's been indoctrinated and institutionalized to where *you* can't think straight. You've seen the despicable housing conditions and eroding infrastructure. You've witnessed the degradation of people under martial law. The Independent Movement is a revolution.

"Initially, colony selectees, including my parents and me, were thrilled to finally leave a desecrated Earth. We accepted the temporary living arrangements built in the colonies, as subpar as they were. It was understandable. Intergalactic colonization wasn't going to be all rose petals and rainbows, but people believed something better was on the horizon, or so they thought.

"Colony development ramped up with help from the other Union planets, and then it slowed. Colonists watched Eden flourish while their own conditions remained unchanged. The disparities between Eden and Satellite One only grew.

"In my early manhood, I was complacent, working in the quarry pits for decent wages. Then I met your mother while she was on assignment, and she got pregnant.

"I wanted to make something of myself and create a stable life for my family. I wanted you both to have a better life than the one I had growing up. So seven years after obtaining Eden citizenship and working as a manager for JMD Intergalactic, I enlisted in the CDF and fought in the Phazharian and Bhalkran wars.

"When the RUC formed and declared independence, I became angry. I had fought to keep the colonies safe from our enemies, and then the governors of colonies One, Four, and Six, with majority public support, disavowed our Constitution. They *knew* declaring independence would lead to civil war.

"But though I was angry, I understood why people wanted independence. They'd been suffering and ignored for far too long.

"And I could relate to them, not only because I was once a colony citizen, but also because I faced unfair treatment in the CDF from comrades who thought an immigrant had no place as a Guardian. They believed AEGIS had chosen only *them* to be the Commonwealth's protectors. I proved them wrong, though.

"Despite my own experiences and the colonies' hardships, I kept telling myself there had to be another way to achieve equality than disavowing our Constitution. So I fought to reclaim the renegade colonies in the Three-Week War. After that, my superiors assigned me to command Charlie Battalion's Lima Company to help restore law and order.

"Under martial law, I watched people's rights get stripped away —the right to bear arms, to question authority, to even listen to someone like Arman Reza if they chose to. People were being mistreated and oppressed.

"It was like the freedoms I'd sworn to protect were being torn away from my own people by my own government. I felt like I had betrayed my friends, my relatives, my community." Arson paused, working to contain his fury. "Randy, this martial law flagrantly violates human rights!" he shouted, the firestorm inside him becoming more turbulent.

He calmed. "I felt terrible. I asked myself, 'What would my family think of me? What would you, my son, think of me after I betrayed my people?' But what could I do? As a Guardian, I was duty-bound to enforce the government's will.

"Then I met Arman Reza, the catalyst of the Independent Movement." Arson struggled to articulate his admiration of Reza. "His words penetrate your soul and enlighten your mind. He's a messenger of an extraordinary kind.

"Reza made me realize there's no shame in fighting the government. He showed me that I wouldn't be disgracing myself by joining the Coalition. In fact, I'd be honoring the very promises and freedoms this intergalactic republic was supposed to stand for.

"It's like a man once said, 'A great revolution is never the fault of the people, but of the government.'"

Randy chastised Arson for admiring Reza, saying, "Reza's idealistic crusade is the reason that the fanatic who tried to assassinate Gould got those intergalactic visitors killed."

"Reza isn't responsible for every lunatic who misuses, misinterprets, or radicalizes his teachings," Arson countered. "After meeting him, I knew I had to rectify the wrong that I had played a small part in creating. How could I live with myself if I did otherwise? I have family here, living in the nightmare created by the central government stalling development and imposing martial law. I *had* to do something. So I joined the Coalition."

"You didn't have to! I know the colonies have problems, but there were other ways to achieve change. Starting this war was wrong! Colonies Two, Three, and Five didn't result to violence! Instead, they—"

"Haven't done shit!" Arson growled. "The Coalition is the answer to bettering life in the colonies. We give hope to disillusioned people."

In a moment of uncertainty, Randy began second-guessing himself. Had he misjudged his father?

Arson said, "I would've explained to you and Kathleen my

reason for leaving, but who knows what tabs the CDF might've been keeping on you guys to get to me."

Under Commonwealth law, any communication—intentional or not—with war criminals had to be reported to the Defense Department. Failure to do so meant arrest on conspiracy charges. Arson didn't want to put his family at risk. He had communicated with Conlan, but even with the utmost precautions, he couldn't entirely eliminate the possibility of endangering him.

Feelings of betrayal roared within Randy. "You shouldn't have left. Mom suffered because of your decision."

Arson looked mournful, caught in guilt's viselike grip. He had never meant to cause his wife any pain. "I thought Kathleen's family, especially Merriam, would help her cope and—"

Randy would hear no more. "Save your excuses, Father. You need to pay for hurting Mom, dishonoring our family's generations of service, and your dereliction of duty."

A wave of repulsion permeated Arson's voice. "No, it's the politicians who need to pay for *their* dereliction of duty."

"What the hell's that mean?"

A crash of thunder punctuated the moment.

Arson said, "At first, the Coalition's goal was to wear down the government and the CDF until we got what we wanted: an action plan to modernize the colonies or autonomy. But we've concluded that we must overthrow and rebuild the entire government, regardless of whether they give in to our demands. The Coalition's new goal is to end the government as it stands."

The Coalition's new goal gave Randy pause. "So the Coalition is planning a *complete takeover?*" He emphasized "complete takeover" as if the Coalition had crossed a moral line, switching from liberators to would-be dictators.

"What we're planning," Arson said, "is to overhaul this broken system for the betterment and dignity of the *entire* Commonwealth, not just the amelioration of the colonies. What began as a war for colony liberation has become a war to free the Commonwealth from corruption, so it can become the virtuous republic it was always meant to be."

Curiosity got the best of Randy. Arson had piqued his interest. He reeled in his animosity, for now, but it simmered beneath the surface.

He adjusted his tone to sound a little more polite. "Go on." Wrestling with the discomfort of having a civil conversation with his father, he briefly wrenched his gaze from the holo.

"The Coalition has gotten some people within the government to defect," Arson said. "Those inside informants, and a few anonymous whistleblowers sympathetic to the colonies, provided us with some very damning information about several members of the Parliament and lower-level officials."

"Alright, humor me," Randy said. Arson was apparently beginning to break through his son's intransigence.

The screen in front of Randy flickered to life, showing a bracket displaying headshots of Parliament members. At the top of the bracket was Cornelius Gould. The screen zoomed in on him.

"This man is dangerous," Arson said. "Especially in the position he holds. Many people believe he'll run for CE in the next election. If he wins, he'll be even more dangerous.

"What the public doesn't know is that most of the funding for his campaign as a Chairman of the Parliament came from the CEOs of these corporations." Logos of various corporations populated the screen, which included Zenith Combat Technologies and A-1 Defense Solutions.

Randy said, "So, what you're saying is that Gould is indebted to those CEOs. Sure, politics is a dirty game, but what you're describing isn't illegal. A CEO can make a personal donation. He just can't use corporate funds to do it. And yeah, maybe Gould's giving kickbacks for those donations, but that's how the game is played. Not saying I'm okay with it."

"Well, there's more," Arson replied, not done yet. "These corporations are owned by one of the Eight Elite, the Spencer family."

Randy's brow creased. What did Stacie's family have to do with any of this?

"Patrick and Darlene Spencer gave each of these CEOs the maximum number of G-credits allowed for individuals to donate to political campaigns," Arson explained. "All of those credits went to Gould's. The Spencers bypassed the law capping a registered donor's credit limit by illegally funneling donations through their CEOs.

"And we have undeniable proof that it *was* the Spencers' money, not the CEOs', that funded Gould's campaign. Those CEOs were just smokescreens, obedient yes-men used to launder money and cheat the donor tracking system—put in place to cap the wealthy's influence in elections. In exchange for their . . . 'generosity,' Gould awarded the Spencers' corporations lucrative contracts to supply the CDF with tech and weapons.

"So, if a defense contractor isn't part of the Spencers' network, it stands little chance of getting CDF contracts. In essence, Gould is stuffing the Spencers' coffers in return for their support."

Randy said, "What the Spencers and Gould are doing is definitely illegal. But beyond Gould agreeing to award contracts to the Spencers' companies, how much influence do you really think they have over him? He doesn't strike me as someone who'd let himself be anyone's puppet."

"Maybe not," Arson conceded, "but the Spencers have real clout in the government, possibly more than the constituents who elected our officials. And with whatever influence they have over Gould, the planetary partners they want, for expanding their intergalactic enterprise, will be some of the first on his list for Union approval if he becomes Chief. The Spencers could easily become 'first-serve.'

"Think about it. If Gould wins the election, that means one of the Eight Elite would have some influence over the Commonwealth's leader. I'm betting Gould would offer government positions to any of the Spencers' sycophants that they want in his administration, as a favor.

"And Gould isn't the only government official, chairman or lower, being influenced by one of the Eight." The screen flashed, and the bracket of chairpersons reappeared. One frame glowed red. "This is Parliament Chairman Markum Weiss. He's taking bribes from the North family."

Another frame lit up. "Jason Wen, Marshal of Commonwealth Law Enforcement. He's making it harder for our police to take down a specific trafficking operation that's selling our women and children to intergalactic slave networks. That operation belongs to the Prosser family, another of the Eight Elite. Wen's on their payroll, doing what he can to keep the police off their trail."

Arson briefly stopped talking, letting Randy digest what he'd heard so far, then continued. "The Eight are nothing more than a consortium of criminal entrepreneurs, and their crimes go all the way back to Earth Era. Our intel shows many government officials are being corrupted by criminal organizations, but the Eight Elite are by far the most powerful of them.

"We believe other Elite families may also be backing CE candidates. They could all be vying for influence over the highest seat in the government. But we don't think they're at odds with each other, at least not in any serious way. It's more like a friendly game of one-upmanship between them."

A chirp from Randy's wristcom stole a second of his attention.

Arson said, "I've forwarded some of the intel from our inside sources to your wristcom. There's a lot there. Take your time, Son. This shit will blow your mind. And if you're thinking about contacting your company with your wristcom, don't bother. The signal's blocked aboard the shuttle."

Randy's sense of justice had been stirred, but his scholarly mindset kept him from making premature decisions. He'd study the info thoroughly before deciding what to do. "I'll review everything with an open mind."

"Good." Arson sounded glad. "Not every government official is corrupt, but the ones who are need to be incarcerated. The whole system needs to be overhauled, for the colonies' survival and the good of the central government. If no one takes a stand, this corruption will never end. I don't know about you, but I signed up to fight for our republic, not the Eight Elite and a bunch of dirty politicians."

Randy, though still upset with his father for leaving and inadvertently partaking in Kathleen's murder, found the corruption revealed today disturbing. "Let's not pretend. Even without this evidence, the Coalition still would've tried to overthrow the government, because all your efforts haven't amounted to much, and victory is starting to seem inconceivable. This corruption was just the smoking gun needed to make government overthrow more justified."

After a beat of contemplation, Arson said, "Maybe."

"So, what's the plan for this . . . Eden invasion?"

Arson found the phrase "Eden invasion" abhorrent. "It's called Operation Hammer Fall. And the first move is exposing the corruption to the public. But we need a distribution channel with enough range and bandwidth to disseminate the info across Eden and all the colonies simultaneously. It has to bypass net restrictions and stay online long enough for everyone to access it."

"So the Coalition needs to take possession of the Parliament Building to gain control of its broadcast center," Randy deduced. Before tech had advanced, the Chief Executive would use the broadcast center to vidcast all their addresses to the entire Commonwealth, and still used it occasionally. "From there, net restrictions can be lifted, and this info can reach everyone on Satellite One and Eden."

Arson nodded. "Correct. But we're not just taking the Parliament Building. For strategic purposes, we'll also be seizing the Chief's Manor and the Academy."

"How does the Coalition's assault force plan to enter Eden airspace without detection?"

"We've got a starship being fitted with cloaking technology."

Well, that's impressive, Randy thought.

He wondered what race of beings had given the Coalition tech advanced enough to cloak an entire ship. Shells couldn't stay cloaked for long without suffering a massive power drain. Cloaking an entire ship, long enough to breach Eden airspace and reach the Parliament Building, was a feat the CDF hadn't even pulled off yet.

"Tell me, after the Coalition topples the government, then what?" Randy asked. "You guys just establish an illegitimate oligarchy?"

The mere thought of setting up an autocracy turned Arson's stomach. "No, we're not dictators, but yes, we do intend to have input. We plan to collaborate with the honest officials and the public to reform the government and achieve equal footing between Eden and the colonies. We'll let democracy take its course.

The people will decide who replaces the corrupt, and due process will decide their fate."

"So who's spearheading this mission? Who's directing the Coalition's moves and procedures?" Randy asked.

Arson stood silently.

Randy pressed, voicing a suspicion held by many but never proven. "Is it Reza? Is Reza the Coalition's head honcho?"

Arson went ahead with the truth. "Yes, he's the overall decision maker for all the factions."

"What's the makeup of this assault force?"

"It'll consist of three elements composed of armored and unarmored troops, totaling a few hundred. The Reldaldri built the mechsuits you saw some of us wearing at my base, and they're essential for Operation Hammer Fall. My faction's final shipment of suits was en route before your people attacked.

"The shipment was rerouted to my Bravo Force's camp, the second and only other unit of my faction. Those suits are crucial to give us the firepower we need to succeed. We're headed to Bravo Force's camp now to receive the shipment and recuperate."

Never one to be indirect, Randy demanded more info. "So, what's the *full* plan for Hammer Fall?" He wanted the breakdown, the ins and outs.

"The three elements of the assault force—Red, Blue, and Gold —will airdrop onto their respective targets and take them over. Then shield generators will be set up at each site. It's that simple."

Randy considered the plan weak. It certainly didn't inspire any confidence in him. "So it's gonna be a cakewalk, huh?" he said doubtfully. The Academy taught him that piss-poor plans produced piss-poor results.

Arson understood why Randy would be concerned about the odds of success, but it was the best plan the Coalition had for ending the war. "Well, it's a surprise attack. No one could possibly anticipate what we're about to attempt. But we are expecting an intense battle. After all, we both know how fast the CDF's Rapid Response Teams can deploy to reinforce the Quad's security forces.

"So, best-case scenario: we deal with the security forces and Rapid Response Teams, with minimal to no loss of Guardian lives, and get the shield generators in place before hundreds more activated Guardians converge on the Quad to overpower us. Worst-case scenario: we end up battling a massive number of Guardians, and a firefight like no other erupts on Eden soil. We're hoping for the former. We don't want too many Guardian lives put in danger. None, actually.

"Reza has entrusted me with overseeing Hammer Fall's entire contingent. He's also appointed me leader of Red Force, which is tasked with taking over the Manor. Blue will take the Academy. Gold will take the Parliament Building.

"Once activated, the shields will buy us, I'd say, at least seven hours before the CDF figures out how to neutralize them. That's plenty of time to cast the info over the net, let people process it, and allow Reza and the uncorrupted Parliament members to negotiate a peace deal.

"The info will undoubtedly turn the Commonwealth's citizens and the CDF against the central government. I can't imagine anyone wanting a bunch of scumbags to remain in office."

Randy wasn't sold. "Plan sounds kind of iffy to me. Needs more refinement."

This wasn't Arson's first war. As a captain in the CDF, he'd learned that you didn't always have the resources, troops, or time to perfect a plan. And the longer you waited to strike, the more ground the enemy gained. "Nothing's foolproof, Randy. Things don't always go a hundred percent as planned, but we're ready to adapt and modify as needed.

"I want you to join me. Join this revolution. Reza's dream is to create a Commonwealth free of corruption and a CDF that doesn't blow away its own Guardians just for having a heart or difference of opinion, a CDF with true checks and balances. You'll see that the Coalition, if you choose to join, doesn't retaliate against its own, treat opposition forces or Edenites with cruelty, or take prisoners just to torture and beat."

Randy thought about Lars assaulting Kesley. He also thought about the civilian he had saved from an unnecessary beating by two Guardians.

Arson said, "Reza doesn't condone any of that nonsense, and he truly wants all the Commonwealth's peoples to coexist peacefully. And I get it: Just because corruption exists doesn't mean you go join a rebel outfit and betray the oath you took as a Guardian. You're probably thinking there are other ways to oust corruption and ensure the colonies achieve equality. You have to decide for yourself who the good guys and bad guys are."

Randy thought about what Conlan had said: *"There are two sides to this war. We . . . we choose the side we believe has the moral high ground. The side embodying our values the most."*

"Maybe I shouldn't have left you and Kathleen. Maybe I should've let others fight the war for colony equality," Arson said. "If that's so, I'm sorry. But you have to understand, it was my honor and dedication to what the Commonwealth stands for that drove me to fight for the Coalition. To me, joining them was no different from leaving you and Kathleen for a long-term deployment."

Deployments are mandatory. You leaving wasn't. And families know where their loved ones are being deployed to. Just more excuses for abandoning us, Randy thought. "What if I don't want to be a part of this?" he asked.

"Then we release you somewhere safe, and you can return to your duty station. Like I said, we don't have a use for prisoners, and we don't interrogate, torture, or do any of that garbage. But please, Son, give joining us some genuine thought."

Locks clacked, freeing the room's door to open. The two escorts came in.

Arson said, "They'll be taking you back to your cell. Sorry we don't have better accommodations, but we'll be landing in a little over an hour. So you won't be in there long."

The ponytailed rebel took Randy's arm. "Come on."

As Randy was being steered away by the men, Arson said, "I really hope you join us."

Almost at the door, Randy stopped. "Tell me, has there been any collusion between you and Conlan?"

"I relayed to him my reasoning for joining the Coalition, and I expressed my grief after Kathleen's death, but no, there was never any collusion. His loyalty to the CDF is without question."

Randy let the two rebels take him out of the room. The holo faded into a blurry haze and vanished.

While Randy was being escorted back to his cell, his thoughts wandered. He was actually starting to believe the Coalition had the moral high ground. After yesterday's eye-opening trip with Kesley, and the damning information his father provided today, he was questioning his military indoctrination.

As he neared the brig, he thought about Stacie. He wondered if she was keeping secrets, if she was involved in her family's illegal dealings. His heart sank at the possibility.

After being taken back to the brig, Randy sat on his cell's bench and powered on his wristcom, accessing the recent download. A holographic folder-selection menu appeared above his wrist. He touched the tag labeled GOULD, and a dozen virtual files materialized.

Using a fingertip, he dragged three files to the right and three to the left. He touched them one by one, opening each in its own window. Suspended in midair were emails, soft-copy documents, G-credit transaction data, graphs, account numbers, and other evidence confirming his father's accusations about the Spencers.

Randy devoured the information, processing every detail.

He accessed the folder on the Prosser family and their trafficking operation, poring over trade-route schematics, expenditures between the family and their field handlers, and even pictures of abducted young women. There was also data confirming Wen's assistance.

Thirty minutes in, Randy still wasn't done. The corruption was real. Gazing at the thirty-plus windows open around him, he had a heart-to-heart with himself. Something had to be done.

Although his rancor toward his father remained, he was able to put it aside for now. He still believed Arson shouldn't have left, triggering Kathleen's moments of mental and emotional collapse, but Arson wasn't the terrible person he'd thought he was. Arson truly believed his reason for fighting with the Coalition was valid.

Randy wouldn't have left to fight in a rebellion at his family's expense if he were in Arson's shoes, but that was him. He and Arson had two opposing schools of thought.

As Randy delved deeper into the information, he considered the unthinkable: He might join the Coalition himself. But he wasn't sure if Reza was truly what he claimed to be—a savior—or just a ruse, a wolf in sheep's clothing, a manipulator seeking power. Randy was determined to find out, and the truth about Reza might ultimately decide where he placed his allegiance. In the meantime, he hoped to avoid any confrontation with the CDF.

"We are now landing," the shuttle's pilot reported over the

intercom.

Time had seemed to pass quickly while Randy studied the files.

The shuttle closed in on Bravo Force's camp, isolated from any sign of civilization.

Randy looked out the barred window. The shuttle was banking downward, seemingly on a collision course with a cliff. He jerked back. *What the hell is—?* The cliff warped, rippled, and fractured as the shuttle phased through it. *Stupid me,* Randy thought, his heart rate slowing to normal. A holographic mirage.

The CDF wouldn't search a no-man's-land for Coalition hideouts without concrete evidence they were operating there, especially since all hot zones were concentrated in Colony Four's urban districts. Still, the mirage added an extra layer of protection for Bravo Force's open camp, just in case.

Once the shuttle was stationary, Randy's cell door slid open.

Sariah Manard walked in. Two lime-green smart jackets hung from her right forearm. She extended her free hand to Randy. "It's a pleasure to meet you, Randal. Arson's always spoken fondly of you." Her voice had a warm, dulcet resonance. It was deep and soothing. Quite a lovely sound.

Randy took her hand and shook it. "Thank you." Though he was still uncomfortable with his father getting involved with another woman, he had no ill feelings toward Sariah.

"Come on, let's get outside," Sariah said. "And put that on. The rain's not coming down heavy anymore, but it's still drizzling."

Randy slid into the jacket and zipped it up.

They left the cell and followed a corridor.

"So, what's the story between you and my father?" Randy asked as two rebels passed them.

"I was a nurse at a medical clinic in Halfin. Like many, I got sick of the injustice, so I joined the Coalition. I learned how to fight. Learned battle tactics. Became a leader. Your father and I fought together often. During his grief, I was there for him, and we fell in love.

"After Kathleen's death, he wasn't sure if he could love again, wasn't sure if he should *allow* himself to.

"But even though we're together, I still see the love he has for Kathleen in his eyes. Your father's a good man. And I don't think Kathleen would want you two at odds."

Randy's features compressed into something close to irritation. He wouldn't be warming up to his father anytime soon.

He and Sariah exited the shuttle into an old dig site, which was steeped in the pitch-blackness of night. Only four spotlights lit up the tarp shelters, portable housing modules, and freight containers converted into domiciles.

They raised their jacket hoods as a light rain fell. Wind whooshed, flinging warm droplets into Randy's face.

He and Sariah swiped the left sleeves of their jackets. The water-repellent material glowed neon green.

Ahead, a handful of rebels ran toward a saucer-shaped spacecraft, their boots squelching in the soggy earth. They wore glow-in-the-dark jackets similar to Randy and Sariah's, the glow lighting their way through the camp. They also used wrist lights.

By the spacecraft, Randy saw rebels speaking with a lavender-skinned, roughly humanoid race. Their robe-like garments, which had numerous pouches, were utilitarian rather than fashionable. A black cloth wrap covered their hairless scalps, and they wore eccentric goggles over their frog-like eyes.

Randy figured they were the Reldaldri and that the craft was the rerouted ship carrying the suits Arson's faction was supposed to receive before the CDF attacked his base.

The cargo hold door groaned open to reveal containers packed with the suits.

Some of the Reldaldri spoke in their native tongue, loudly and harshly. They were clearly irate about the course diversion.

One of them held out a device. A rebel pressed his palm against it. The device beeped. Some sort of signature confirmation of receipt, Randy guessed.

"So, where's Arson?" he asked Sariah.

"Doing damage control," she replied. "Alpha Force was decimated. He owes the chain of command a sitrep."

"Chain of command? You mean Reza?"

"Yes."

A man walked up to them. "Sariah, I'm glad you and Arson made it safely."

Randy estimated him to be in his early forties.

"Randy," Sariah said, "this is David Larkin, leader of Arson's Bravo Force. Larkin, this is Randal Scott, Arson's son."

"Nice to meet you, Randy," David said in a welcoming tone. "I wish I had time to chat, but I have to supervise the offload. Take care." He took off jogging toward the delivery ship.

Sariah walked forward, mud caking the soles of her boots. "Come, Randy, I'll take you to your tent."

"Wait," Randy said. Sariah stopped mid-stride. "A friend of mine infiltrated the shuttle in a rescue attempt. His name is—"

"Jarius Ford. I know. He's fine. No one's going to harm him. But because he can't be trusted, he'll remain detained for now."

Randy couldn't shake his worry for his friend. "I want to see him."

"Tomorrow, you can see both your friend and your father. For now, I'll take you to your tent so you can get some rest. And I'll bring you something to eat."

Inside his tent, Randy sat in a dented metal folding chair. He forked some meat into his mouth from the tray on the makeshift table in front of him. It was a reasonably sized tent, offering enough room to stand comfortably. At his feet, a cell-powered glow-lamp buzzed softly.

He searched the rest of the Gould files for anything that might implicate Stacie—a breadcrumb, a message, some form of proof connecting her to her family's criminal activities. More covert communications and deep-pocket dealings between Gould and the Spencers appeared.

Realization dawned on him. He was fooling himself. He wouldn't find any evidence showing Stacie was directly involved in her parents' schemes. She'd joined the CDF to distance herself from their operations. But that didn't necessarily mean she hadn't known about them. And if she didn't, what would she think when he told her?

Randy shut off his wristcom and eased himself into the hammock strung between four worn wooden poles. Rain tapped the tarp above, a steady, restless patter. He closed his eyes. In all the bombardment of information, he had forgotten the emergency summit was tomorrow. And if the Commonwealth got booted from the Union, chaos would ensue. Tomorrow was going to be a hell of a day.

The roar of a distant liftoff was the last sound he heard before his consciousness receded into sleep.

First Squad of Fourth Platoon was conducting reconnaissance atop a precipice overlooking the camp. Jason's reticle zeroed in on the outbound Reldaldri ship thundering into the drizzly sky, its undercarriage lit by multicolored lights.

He tightened the zoom on his reticle and snapped some

pictures. *Who are you, and what were you doing at that camp?* Rain tinkled off his armor as he ran the pics through his CPU's spacecraft index, hoping for identification. The query came back as UNIDENTIFIABLE, as he'd expected. *Wonder who the Coalition is in cahoots with.*

"Any new developments?" Stacie asked, approaching Jason in her Shell, her helmet racked at her hip. The soft, wet ground made sucking noises as each mechboot sank into it.

Jason shook his head. "Nah, not much movement besides that ship finally leaving. I got some clear pics, but no ID."

The rain stopped, and a shroud of fog crept over the ridge.

Time seemed to drag for Stacie. "So when's the cavalry getting here?" The angst in her chest wouldn't subside.

"The company has just finished securing Arson's hideout and mining its databases. They've got to get back to HQ to recharge their Shells and reequip. We took a lot of casualties, and hell, some Shells aren't even mission capable. I'm operating at seventy percent functionality myself. And the company needs rest. Plus, Commander Seymour wants more intel, so we don't go in blind. It's going to be a while."

"Damn it." Stacie kicked pebbles and wet earth. "Shit!"

"Hey, calm the fuck down, Specialist. I know you're worried about Randy, but I think he'll be okay. Besides, us going down there blind won't do a damn thing to help him. Which is why we need to conduct recon. Hell, we don't know what was off-loaded from that alien ship. Better to go in as prepared as we can be than half-cocked and get our asses handed to us."

Stacie exhaled a frustrated sigh. "Yeah, you're right."

"I'm sending a recon drone down there. You should try to rest up. I know the BUS isn't exactly the best of accommodations, but out here, it's better than the dirt."

"Roger, Sergeant." Stacie started toward the BUS.

"Hey," Jason called out, stopping her.

Stacie turned halfway. "Yeah?"

"After seeing all that carnage back there—and given how worried you are about your boy toy—are you in the right headspace for the fight that's coming? Because when we storm that camp, it's gonna get real—fast. I can't afford any liabilities."

"And you won't have one," Stacie said firmly. "When it's go-time, my head will be exactly where it needs to be."

"It'd better be," Jason warned. If he thought her mind wasn't clear enough for combat, he'd bench her. And to make sure she stayed put, he'd command override her Shell to lock her out of it.

Stacie went into the BUS without another word.

A globe-shaped microdrone deployed from Jason's suit. He activated its stealth cloak and guided it down into the camp. He'd have to be careful. If the rebels spotted the drone, they'd evacuate, ruining the CDF's chance of capturing or killing Arson Scott.

CHAPTER FIVE

Outside the Chief Executive's Manor, a media frenzy was in full swing. Union leaders were arriving for the emergency summit, and the press was there to capture every moment.

News networks provided wall-to-wall coverage, with commentary and recaps detailing how this day came about. Orange-and-black-striped barricades blocked off streets, air traffic near the Manor was restricted, and additional Executive Protection Agents (EPAs) were stationed at the gates.

A hover ferry sailed toward the Manor, flanked by an entourage of battlecruisers. The first of the Union leaders had arrived, Queen Pappalonie of planet Taramassia.

The ferry carried the young queen and her driver, while her sentries rode the battlecruisers in powered exoskeletons, fully prepared to neutralize any threat to her safety.

The antigrav vehicles whisked to a stop. Cameras flashed, and reporters jabbered excitedly into their mics.

The vehicles settled onto the ground.

The ferry's overhead energy dome powered down, blinking and

crackling. The lift descended, bringing Her Majesty down to the phyocrete.

The crowd greeted her with oohs and aahs, as if she were a luminary.

Cameras clicked in a frenzy.

The Taramassians had dark teal skin, outstretched fox-like ears, and tendrils in place of hair, each adorned with gold rings. The yellow sclera of their eyes contrasted with their midnight-blue irises. Four round silver markings decorated their foreheads, matching the color of their eyebrows.

Their planet's ecosphere was a fusion of jungle and technology, as they held nature in high regard.

The queen wore a gold top and skirt made of a sheeny metallic fabric. On her feet were sandals with straps crisscrossing up her stout little calves. On her forehead gleamed a magnificent jeweled tiara, the sign of her position as Taramassia's leader.

As she strolled gracefully toward the Manor's gate with her sentries, her jewelry jingled. She was only five feet tall, so her towering protectors looked like titans beside her.

A wiry reporter rushed forward to snap photos, too close for one sentry's comfort. The sentry growled a warning. The reporter quickly backed up, stumbling and falling onto his backside.

EPAs kept the media at bay as the queen and her guards passed. The media would only be allowed onto the lawn once the Chief was ready to announce the results of the summit.

In the distance, a spectacle of antigrav vehicles hovered toward the Manor, more Union leaders arriving.

In the Chief Executive's office, an overwhelmed Jared Kerner sat behind his polished, commanding desk. Deputy Chief Angela

Norton occupied the brown armchair in front of him.

The space resembled a typical high-ranking executive's: a wall monitor, large windows, tasteful art, and plush, high-end carpeting.

Jared gazed down at a holographic picture of his young Asian wife and seven-year-old daughter, suspended above his wristcom. His careworn expression was a telling sign he was coming apart at the seams.

His eyes were bloodshot, and his appearance was unkempt, hair disheveled, stubble speckling his jaw, suit coat rumpled. Angela, by contrast, was the picture of composure. She was dressed in a well-pressed beige pantsuit that complemented her caramel skin, and her indigo curls were perfectly styled.

Jared shifted his woeful eyes toward Angela, silently pleading for some kind of reassurance that he was still fit to lead humanity's intergalactic republic. "Where did it all go downhill?" he asked ruefully. "After the Three-Week War, stabilization operations were supposed to be simple: send in the CDF, impose martial law for a few weeks, round up the last of the rebels, and restore order.

"But things . . . didn't go that way." He thumbed the slider on the side of his chair, reclining the backrest. Then he gripped his head with both hands. "And now there are uprisings even on Eden, and our incorporated status hangs by a thread."

"Nothing is ever simple," Angela said calmly.

Jared shut off the picture. It flickered, jittered side to side, and then vanished.

He adjusted his rimless square glasses. "Was I too quick to let Gould talk me into going to war with the RUC? Should I have tried alternative solutions? Sent the Ambassador Corps instead? What would my father have done?"

"We can't unmake the past, Jared," Angela said curtly.

It still irked her that Jared had overtaken her in the primaries, riding on the coattails of his father's popularity. He'd been thirty during the election, with far less time in politics than her. She was a decade older and far more qualified to be Chief Executive.

Somehow, youth, vigor, and charisma had triumphed over wisdom and experience. But now Jared's inadequacies, once masked by hype, were coming to light. People increasingly saw him as a figurehead, assuming his advisory committee and trusted consultants like Cornelius were the true masterminds behind the government's ongoing success.

At first, Angela had questioned whether she should accept the nomination for Deputy Chief and serve in what she viewed as a mismanaged Jared Kerner administration. But ultimately, she decided it was a smart move. Having Deputy Chief on her resume would only strengthen her candidacy when the time came to run again.

Jared thumbed the slider forward, elevating the backrest of his chair, and removed his glasses, setting them on the desk. He buried his face in his hands, anxiety overtaking him. "Maybe I shouldn't have let Gould pressure me into going to war so quickly. Then again, he served under my father, and my father always trusted his judgment in military matters."

Such an insecure weakling. So easy to manipulate, Angela thought with disdain. "Well," she said aloud, "our Constitution clearly states that declaring independence is an act of treason. You took Gould's advice and exercised your authority to declare a State of Emergency, authorizing the deployment of troops to squash the insurrection, after giving the renegade colonies a generous five days to cease and desist.

"Parliament had thirty days to vote on vetoing the State of Emergency and withdrawing the troops. They took no such vote, fully aware that treason violated the Constitution.

"Though the Parliament could've intervened and didn't, you could've terminated the State of Emergency and didn't. As CE, you're the Commonwealth's point man; it's ultimately up to you to decide what's best. As for Gould, he's a military hard-liner whose mindset has been shaped by war. He acted the only way he knows how: by going on the offensive.

"If your intuition told you to explore other solutions before deploying troops, then perhaps you should have."

"Well, like you said, we can't undo what's been done. Now we're in a bind: Either we can concede defeat—making the Three-Week War pointless—or keep fighting the Coalition and risk losing our incorporated status, which might happen today anyway."

"I pray to Allah it doesn't." Angela sincerely meant that.

Jared's wristcom chirped. He answered the call. Light and pixels swirled and merged into a chiseled face with a dimpled chin. "Sir," the dark-haired man said, "the Union leaders have all arrived and are being escorted to the master stateroom now."

"On my way." Jared ended the call, and the holo dispersed. He put his glasses back on, pushed his rolling chair away from the desk, and stood. "Come on, let's get this dog and pony show over with."

Jared and Angela traversed the Manor's West Wing, where a red carpet stretched beneath golden chandeliers, and animated wall displays depicted key moments in human history. They passed door after brown door before entering the master stateroom.

In cushioned armchairs, the six other Union leaders sat around the room's rectangular table. Each wore an earpiece that would translate every spoken language into their native tongue.

Jared and Angela sat side by side at the table and put on their earpieces.

The Union leaders noticed Jared's tired, dry eyes. They could see the weight of managing the Commonwealth's chaos was wearing him down.

"My fellow planetary leaders, I welcome you all to Eden. Let the summit now be in session," Jared said.

Following custom, each leader introduced themselves.

"I, Durgraso T'Horbelis of planet Ghanrax, am present," declared a male leader clad in animal skins and fur.

The Ghanrax were a semi-aquatic race. Though they primarily lived on land, they often traveled and hunted underwater. Leathery yellowish skin covered their faces and torsos, while bluish scales coated the rest of their bodies. Small spines bristled along their shoulders, and their webbed fingers and slightly protruding eyes added to their amphibian look.

They were known as a methodical, quick-tempered race.

"I, Ziltilda Ca'Rúshe of planet Dhalgratt, am present," said a female leader. Her muted brown eyes and long, silky black hair made her stand out. She was one of only two female planetary leaders in attendance, the other being Queen Pappalonie, the Eminence of Taramassia.

The Dhalgratt's appearance was defined by their lean, stout builds, sand-colored skin, and the subtle ridges of their low foreheads. Notably, intricate dark markings embellished their backs and broad shoulders. The clothing they wore reflected their need for comfort in their world's hot climate.

"I, Orphazel Khaphadelis of planet Varsh'Ru, am present."

The Varsh'Ru had white skin and lithe bodies with elongated, flexible limbs. Their faces featured slitted nostrils, lipless mouths, and black opaque eyes.

Traditional dress for their planetary leader and top officials consisted of snug purple garments overlaid with gold chain mail.

"I, Baraphelis Da'Nophzar of planet Zirkran, am present."

Zirkrans, known for their high intellect, usually stood between seven and eight feet tall. They were further distinguished by their orange-red skin, a short chin tendril, and deep-set dark eyes beneath sloping, hairless brows.

Baraphelis sat poised in the robe-like garment and decorative shoulder sash customary to his position.

"I, ZorKeld Levatorg of planet Rumanoah, am present."

Broad cheekbones, high foreheads, wide noses, and long, untamed hair were typical of the Rumanoahan people. Their coarse yellowish-gray skin was a natural armor, notoriously hard to penetrate.

ZorKeld, dressed in dark sleeveless attire, sported silver studs in his earlobes and a ring through his nostrils. Already not considered the most attractive fellow by his people's standards, ZorKeld bore a disfigurement from the arena combat sports he regularly engaged in, and dominated.

"I, Pappalonie Valasirus Cetreon of Taramassia, am present."

"I, Chief Executive Jared Kerner of the Commonwealth, am present, accompanied by Deputy Chief Angela Norton," Jared announced.

Durgraso fixed a reproving glare on Jared. "We have assembled here today to discuss the instability and dysfunction of the Union member known as the Commonwealth," he said in a guttural timbre, pointing a finger at Jared. "Represented by its leader, Chief Executive Kerner." From his nostrils came a loud snort of contempt, and the gill-like slits on his neck hissed.

ZorKeld rested his forearms on the table and steepled his fingers. His eyes grew cold as he thought about the two Rumanoahans killed during the assassination attempt on Gould, deaths he considered the result of an avoidable war instigated by the Commonwealth Government.

Animosity laced his voice, directed squarely at Jared. "The Commonwealth has been embroiled in internal conflict for some time. Article II of the Union Charter clearly states that all planetary members agree to abstain from acts of violence, aggression, or any form of belligerence against each other and their own peoples. As stewards of peace and goodwill, we have pledged to leave such barbarism in the bygone eras of our civilizations.

"Article II's Exception to Force Clause does permit the use of force against one's own population for planetary policing or quelling hostile uprisings."

"Correct," Jared quickly interjected. "Three of the Commonwealth's six colonies—One, Four, and Six—revolted against humanity's main governing body. Therefore, we enacted the Exception to Force Clause and launched an offensive to reclaim those renegade settlements."

ZorKeld responded coolly. "Yes, but we have been evaluating the Commonwealth's justification for use of force, Mr. Kerner. During this process, we reviewed the monthly reports your governors were required to send you. Those reports revealed your colonies in a state of immiseration. Your governors attempted to cooperate with you and proposed corrective actions to resolve the situation. You failed to act on any of those proposals."

"We didn't have the resources to implement them," Jared said.

ZorKeld refuted him. "That is debatable."

Jared's expression tightened in protest.

"Now," ZorKeld continued, "our investigative team has been touring your colonies to examine the conditions that the separatist colonies claim led them to seek independence. The team also interviewed the imprisoned governors in person. After much discernment, our consensus is this: The central government's use of force was not justified."

Jared's face paled. Angela's brows twitched with anger. Pappalonie fidgeted, grappling with feelings of regret; she had reluctantly come to the same conclusion as the other leaders.

ZorKeld clarified their reasoning. "Article II defines an uprising as 'the use of violence by an armed group to overthrow a sovereign government.' We do not consider the breakaway colonies' attempt to abandon your star nation *(more than one planet inhabited by a race)* an 'uprising.' We deem it a peaceful retaliatory response to your dereliction of duty.

"Therefore, you, Chief Executive Kerner, are the one who has committed treason, not against your nation, but against the Union Charter. As outlined in Article VI, every planetary leader must guarantee the welfare, well-being, and livelihood of their citizens. They must provide the essentials for survival and must not show prejudice or indifference toward any individual.

"Yes, it is a tall order, but it is the standard required of all Union members. We hold ourselves to high moral expectations. Our shared integrity is what attracts trade and visitors. These expectations are precisely why we conduct thorough investigations of every prospective trading partner."

Jared aimed a thumb at himself. "So, wait, you're saying I'm the bad guy here?"

ZorKeld replied, "You did not act with malicious intent. But you failed to respond to your people's suffering and resorted to force to prevent them from leaving your star nation, which they felt they had to do in order to survive.

"Do you understand what I am saying?" His voice became grittier. "Your people were crying out for a better life, and you failed to provide it."

"Wait, so the formation of the RUC was a *justified* uprising?" Jared's voice rose in astonishment. "Justified treason?" It climbed a tad higher. "Is that it?"

Ziltilda entered the fray, casting her eyes on Jared. "Chief Executive Kerner, as ZorKeld said, we have chosen not to categorize the formation of the RUC as an uprising at all. They did not fire the first shots or attempt a violent overthrow of your government."

To Jared, and to opponents of the Independent Movement, abandoning the Commonwealth *was* the first shot.

Ziltilda said, "You are ignoring your own failings, which incited what we deem to be an understandable act of retaliation."

So these fools think the RUC declaring sovereignty is no different from picketing or sit-ins, Jared grumbled inwardly.

ZorKeld, not yet finished, continued. "The case of the Three-Week War has been an onerous one to review. We initially assumed an uprising had occurred, which would have made your military response permissible. We gave you the benefit of the doubt, as we would any of ourselves when faced with a potential coup or violent disruption.

"But as we examined the findings of our investigative team, we could not endorse your actions. Instead, we came to support the actions of the RUC, which had no intent to commit aggression. They were merely trying to escape what we view as oppression, and oppression has no place in the Union."

Jared's lips pressed into a firm line. So many articles of the Charter were unambiguous. Others, though, were the exact opposite—vague, open to interpretation and debate. Depending on a person's indignation, leanings, or the sway of their heart, they could bend those articles to serve almost any perspective.

Orphazel now spoke. "Our understanding is that after the CDF defeated the RUC's paramilitaries, the remnants of those forces organized into several unified factions known as the

Coalition of Rebel Factions, or simply, the Coalition. Additional pockets of resistance, independent of the Coalition, later emerged. I believe you categorize all these resistance groups as 'terrorists.'

"We questioned whether we could classify these other resistance groups as hostile anti-government aggressors, or, in other words, 'uprisers.' But after much deliberation, we concluded it ultimately did not matter. Your poor leadership was the genesis of your star nation's meltdown."

Jared's mounting frustration made it hard to maintain his professional poise. "So this is all my fault?"

Durgraso snarled. "There is cause and effect, Chief Executive Kerner. The rebellion resulted from your inadequate leadership. We know your laws say a colony declaring sovereignty is treason, thus warranting a forceful response. However, the Union does not view standing up to oppression as treason."

Orphazel reentered the conversation. "What concerns me is that an end to this rampant disorder is nowhere in sight."

"Not so," Jared said. "Just yesterday, we dismantled a major Coalition faction, and we've increased our manpower in the colonies under martial law. The CDF is conducting a large-scale operation to flush out and defeat the insurrectionists who started this mess."

Angela backed Jared up, saying, "Also, rebuilding an entire civilization is a gradual process, and we've incurred massive debts and fought external wars that drained our resources.

"We're doing the best we can and are developing a plan to improve conditions in the colonies. The insurrectionists should have understood that. Instead, they tried to break away from the Commonwealth, recklessly endangering the rest of humanity, because the colonies' resources are vital to our shared survival."

Ziltilda said, "Still, the current state of your colonies is the best you can manage after all these years? *Unacceptable.*"

Durgraso drummed his webbed fingers on the table. "I had extreme reservations about allowing you Earthlings into the Union," he growled. The gills on his neck hissed. "I did not want a race that nearly wiped itself out to bring its belligerence here. The Union was meant to be a place of peace. But I voted to accept you Earthlings. As I feared, perhaps I voted wrong.

"Your war has now cost the lives of Varsh'Ru, Rumanoahans, and others outside the Union. Those outside races are furious, and they are demanding reparations from the Union, reparations we are passing on to you. The Union's reputation as a haven of peace, comfort, and safety has been tarnished."

"We're sorry for those losses," Jared said sincerely, "and we understand we must compensate those worlds with reparations, and we will."

ZorKeld, his features set in a brooding expression, made eye contact with each of his colleagues. "We have spoken enough. It is time to get to the point," he said darkly.

Pappalonie shifted uncomfortably in her chair, her pointy ears twitching and jewelry jangling. She dropped her chin in disapproval of the verdict about to be delivered.

ZorKeld said, "Chief Executive Kerner, by a five-to-one vote, it is at our behest that you resign as the Commonwealth's leading official."

Jared jerked, jaw falling. A Chief Executive had just been impeached—not by the people of the Commonwealth, but by an outside body of adjudicators. Perhaps his father had been right in trying to withdraw from the Union.

ZorKeld said, "According to your laws, Deputy Chief Norton now assumes leadership. Norton, you have five days to end this domestic crisis. After five days, we will reconvene to decide the next course of action and whether to impose additional penalties. If you fail to end the conflict within five days, disciplinary measures will begin, including the potential rescinding of the Commonwealth's incorporated status."

Durgraso added, "And during these five days, all tourism must cease."

Pappalonie objected to the five-day deadline—just like she had objected to impeaching Jared. "While I agree that halting tourism is necessary to prevent more innocent lives from being lost to crossfire, five days is insufficient for the new Chief to resolve the conflict. By the authority vested in me as a planetary leader, I cast a vote to extend the time frame by an additional five days."

Ziltilda said, "By a show of hands, shall we extend the time frame?" Only Pappalonie and Baraphelis raised their hands. "It is decided. The time frame for Chief Executive Norton to resolve the Commonwealth's war shall remain five days."

Jared and Pappalonie's eyes met. Unspoken doubt passed between the two leaders.

"We are done here," ZorKeld said.

As everyone filed out, an icy silence lingered.

Pappalonie paused beside Jared. "If there is anything I can do to help the human race, let me know."

"Thank you, Your Eminence. You've always been the most compassionate of the Union leaders."

"I wish you the best, Jared Kerner." Pappalonie walked out.

"I'm sorry, Jared," Angela said with faux sympathy. She was glad to be in charge.

"Thank you." Jared sighed. "Let's not keep the media circus and the public waiting."

They left the room and proceeded down the hall, headed to the outdoor stage on the lawn, where the press awaited.

Jared said, "No matter what, don't let word get out that the Union leaders sided with the rebels. Who knows what the fallout would be. Personally, I don't want to find out." Such controversy could breed more Independent Movement supporters, or it could make people angry at the Union.

Jared and Angela exited the Manor through double doors and walked out onto the stage. The press pool waited to be addressed.

Camera drones transmitted signals to the Parliament Building's broadcast center, which relayed the feed to viewing devices on Eden and Satellite One.

Jared stepped up to the lectern, his demeanor hinting that the summit hadn't gone well. Three EPAs in black suits formed up behind him. Angela stood off to his right.

His gaze swept over the well-dressed reporters. He swallowed, still coming to terms with his expulsion from office. "Members of Parliament, Justices, government officials, and citizens of the Commonwealth, the Union leaders have mandated that I resign from office," he announced, voice dull. The crowd gasped. "They've determined that my leadership no longer meets Union standards. Some of you may agree. Some of you may not. But the decision is final. Deputy Chief Norton will now assume the role of Chief Executive."

Stepping aside, the deposed Chief shook Angela's hand, passing a torch he no longer had the right to carry.

She went up to the lectern confidently. "Citizens of the Commonwealth, the Union leaders have given me five days to end the Coalition's war. First, do not panic—"

BOOM! The stage erupted in a plasma explosion, shattering into a cloud of lethal shrapnel.

Nearby reporters were flung into the air.

The explosion's shock wave disfigured faces beyond recognition, melting features into grotesque smears.

A female reporter's shriek tore through the aftermath.

One EPA writhed, his left arm flayed to the muscle.

A shudder crawled down a reporter's spine as he caught sight of a woman who was little more than a roasted corpse. He screamed into his mic, "The CE and DC have just been killed! Everyone near the stage has suffered injuries!"

Inside the Manor, alarms blared, launching EPAs into action. They flooded the halls, locking down every access point.

In the Executive Bedroom, Jared's wife, Mei Ling Kerner, sat on the canopied bed, holding their terrified daughter. She prayed the commotion in the halls was just a drill or a false alarm.

An EPA burst into the room. "Your husband's been assassinated," he said. Mei Ling gasped. "I'm taking you to the bunker."

EPAs rushed the Union leaders into the reinforced underground bunker. A shadow of confusion and concern fell over the Union leaders' faces.

Outside the Manor, Cornelius sat comfortably in the back of his limo. Through the tinted window, he smiled triumphantly at the raging fire consuming the stage. His sinister plan had gone off without a hitch.

He spoke to Gillian over his wristcom. "It's done. The CE and DC are dead. Time for phase two of Operation New Wave."

Ambulance flyers landed to evacuate the wounded, while fire crews battled the blaze, shooting jets of foam from their vehicles' cannons.

Cornelius' limo rolled off. Now, he would be the incoming Chief Executive.

• • •

Jason and his squad were still atop the cliff overlooking Bravo Camp. They had spent the night conducting recon in shifts, taking turns operating the camera drone. Their nourishment came from meal cubes and nutrient bars.

At some point, they tuned in to the multiplanet simulcast through their Shells, witnessing the first political assassination in Commonwealth history.

As Jason began his next recon shift, he monitored the camp, the camera drone feeding a steady stream of footage to his HUD. He continuously updated Lars, who, in turn, kept Commander Seymour updated while the company rested, regrouped, and rearmed after the assault on Arson's base.

"So, when's backup getting here?" asked Specialist Eli Manson. "We can't let Arson get away. He's one of the Commonwealth's most-wanted terrorists. This could be our only shot."

Jason looked back at the young mocha-skinned man behind him. "Reinforcements should be here in sixty mikes."

"So, what effects do you think the assassination will have on the Commonwealth?"

Jason exhaled. "Gould's already blaming the Coalition. That's going to rile up Independent Movement opponents even more.

"Independent Movement supporters are already crying foul. They're saying Gould orchestrated the whole thing so he could take power and push a hard-line military agenda, one that doesn't just tighten control over the occupied colonies, but expands it to the unoccupied ones. Who knows what new extremes anti-government groups will resort to. They fear this guy."

"Do you think he was behind the assassination?"

Jason shrugged. "Anything's possible."

In her Shell, Stacie leaned against the BUS, anxious to go rescue Randy. She thought of him, and her cerebral implant responded by projecting memories across her HUD as stills: a stroll in a park after their return to Eden from BCT, a shared laugh, a kiss.

Stacie cleared her mind, and the stills disappeared. *Fifty-five mikes until backup gets here. Just fifty-five mikes.*

• • •

Inside his tent, Randy, dressed in some old clothes provided to him, had watched the assassination on a tablet. He then watched Gould swear in and address the public. The new Chief Executive claimed the fiends behind Jared's death were none other than the Coalition. An obvious lie. The Coalition was becoming a scapegoat for everything that went wrong in the Commonwealth.

Randy suspected Gould would exploit the crisis to push the Parliament into expanding Defense Department authority. As he stated in his interview days ago, he wanted special provisions, like surveillance and audits of colony governments that hadn't been indicted for aiding rebel groups.

Randy knew the Commonwealth was about to change, and the Spencers might've known about the assassination, maybe even played a part in it.

The tent flaps rustled. Sariah pulled them aside and poked her head in. "Good morning, Randy. I brought your friend." She and Jarius stepped into the tent's roomy interior. She unlocked the cuffs around his wrists. "Please don't run or do anything foolish." Jarius nodded silently, striving to suppress his growing exasperation. "Randy, I'll be back in thirty minutes with your father."

As Sariah exited, Jarius moved further inside. "I've been worried about you, man. And what the hell is going on? Why are they giving you the royal treatment? Roaming free, private tent—feels like you've got VIP status."

"I'll explain in a bit. There's something I want you to see."

188

Randy pulled up some of the corruption files, windows of data projecting from his wristcom.

Over the next several minutes, Randy showed Jarius irrefutable evidence that many government officials were corrupt. He also shared details of his revelatory sightseeing trip with Kesley and talked about his conflicting feelings regarding which side, if any, to fight for.

Jarius ran a hand through his hair. "I've been kinda feeling the same way after seeing how messed up things are here in Colony Four. I get why people rebelled. They don't see a better future unless they take drastic steps. But . . . fighting for the Coalition?" He shook his head. "I don't know. We took an oath. And like you said, we don't know if this Reza guy's legit or just another sleazeball trying to acquire power. Could be another Ritter."

"Yeah," Randy agreed. "But I'm gonna stick with the Coalition a little longer and see what I can learn. Trust me, they'll let you go unharmed if that's what you want. They've got no use for prisoners. But I'd like you to stay and check things out for yourself before making that call."

Sariah parted the tent flaps and peered inside. "Randy, your father's outside." She stepped in, holding Jarius' cuffs in her left hand.

"Are those still necessary?" Randy asked, irritated.

"Only until we find the right time to let him go. Maybe tomorrow."

Randy said to Jarius, "I guess you've got until then to decide if you want to stay or head back to the company."

"Who's to say Arson would trust him enough to let him stay?" Sariah said. "Just because he trusts you without supervision doesn't mean he'll have the same confidence in your friend."

"I'd take full responsibility for Jarius," Randy said.

Jarius held out his wrists without protest. Sariah locked the cuffs around them and marched him out of the tent.

Randy exited and found Arson waiting for him. The pain was still there, but it no longer consumed Randy. It didn't control him. That didn't mean he and Arson would suddenly become close. But at least they could exist in the same space without Randy wanting to put a bullet in Arson's skull. A renewed father-son relationship would take time, if it could happen at all.

"Everything's changed," Arson said grimly, holding a tin cup of hot java. "We have to expedite Hammer Fall. Reza knows that militant madman Gould is bad news. With him in power, martial law will get worse, and the hunt for us will only intensify. We have to stop him."

He took a sip from his cup and then continued. "Reza's making an announcement from his stronghold tonight, broadcasting to all Coalition factions via holovid. He's setting a new timetable for Hammer Fall. The good news is that last night's shipment of suits made it safely to his stronghold, just like he wanted.

"That's where the rest of the Reldaldri mechsuits are, and it's where the main assault force will deploy from. He wants me and what's left of my faction there ASAP. I'm guessing that means he's planning to launch the op soon. We're leaving to go there in a few hours."

"So where exactly is Reza's stronghold?" Randy asked.

Arson's eyes flicked away. He hesitated. Randy hadn't chosen a side yet, and that made him a liability. Arson had to tread carefully. After a long pause, he answered. "Colony Five. With no suspected rebel activity there, it's outside the CDF's area of concern."

Randy had been half-expecting that exact answer. "So all the speculation is true. Governess Hayley is supporting the Coalition."

"Yes. She wants the Coalition to win. The only problem is that eighty percent of Colony Five's population feels neutral about the war. They don't want to fight the central government or break away from the Commonwealth, unlike the people in colonies One, Four, and Six. Sure, they want change, but they're fine with pursuing it using political pressure.

"Despite their neutrality, Hayley's been quietly helping the Coalition, offering Reza a safe haven. She's careful, though. She limits how much freedom we have in Colony Five. She doesn't want her people, or the central government, catching on to her support." Arson placed a hand on Randy's shoulder. "I meant for us to catch up, but given recent events, that'll have to wait."

Randy twisted away, escaping Arson's grasp. "I wasn't in the mood anyway," he said with a bite. The resentment over his father's abandonment still lingered, though he understood why he left. They simply had different concepts of right and wrong. "It can wait."

Arson accepted that rebuilding trust would take time. "Okay." He started to leave with Sariah and Jarius, then paused after a few steps. "Have you decided whether to join us yet?" he asked Randy.

"Still thinking."

"Take all the time you need." Arson pointed to a row of improvised shelters. "Chow tent's that way. Get some food. I'll see you later."

Randy walked in the opposite direction from Arson, Sariah, and Jarius.

Kathleen's metaphysical imitation appeared, floating beside him. *Your father's not the insensitive man you thought he was, is he?*

Randy replied, *Maybe not, but that doesn't mean he made the right choice, leaving you and me.*

He made a choice I didn't like, but your father did what he had to do. Knowing his people were suffering was eating at his soul. He wouldn't have been the father or husband he needed to be with that kind of weight on his mind. That's just . . . the man I married. Let go of your bitterness, Son.

Randy scoffed at himself for having a conversation with someone who didn't exist. She was an amalgamation of thoughts, emotions, and memories molded into a lifelike personality he could confide in—an impersonation brought to life by his implant. *Enough of this nonsense.*

Kathleen faded from view.

Randy proceeded to the chow tent, passing weary souls wearing old, tattered clothes. Rebels recovering from injuries moved slowly; some wore slings or bandages, while others were missing limbs. The war had clearly taken its toll on them.

• • •

On the cliff above Bravo Camp, the rest of Fourth Platoon had arrived with Second and Third, while First Platoon remained at the annex.

Captain Seymour himself had come to oversee the crucial op. "Alright, everyone, let's not squander this." His voice conveyed the authority of someone who had braved countless battles and had insurmountable combat knowledge. "Command wants Arson brought in alive. If that's not possible, his corpse is the next best thing.

"And remember, two of our own are down there being held captive. Specialist Scott and Specialist Ford. If you find them, get them out. Now let's go into stealth mode and burn that damn place to kingdom come." *You betrayed us, old friend. Now you pay.*

Before the Guardians advanced, they activated their stealth cloaks, the holographic skins mimicking the surrounding terrain.

• • •

Randy walked back from the chow tent, thoughts still muddled.

He came to a training ground.

A man lay prone beside a woman, coaching her through marksmanship training. "Nose to the charging handle," he instructed. She followed his lead. "Now adjust your aim."

The woman lined up her energy rifle's sights with a large flat rock, slowed her breathing, and pulled the trigger. A pulse of energy vaporized the rock into dust. "Yes!" she cheered.

Nearby, one rebel showed another how to deconstruct a rifle for maintenance. Off to the right, two men sparred in hand-to-hand combat, their chatter suggesting they were enjoying the friendly match. All around Randy was purposeful activity.

He saw good people conscripted into war by desperation, people with heart and a genuine drive to improve colony life. The Coalition wasn't some terrorist outfit bent on seizing control of the Commonwealth. These people were fighting to make it better. And every one of them had treated him with generosity.

Five young rebels stood around a sinewy brown-skinned woman with close-cropped blond hair. She wore black stretch pants, an olive-green tank top, and boots.

She was briefing the five newcomers on the Coalition's ethos.

"First and foremost, we carry out our attacks with the intention of causing little to no casualties," she said. "We are not tyrants or vengeful murderers, no matter what the central government or media say."

She believed in the ethos, and her voice carried a bone-deep commitment to uphold it and instill it in the newcomers. "Edenite or colonist, we want what's best for all," she said, gesturing inclusively with her hands. "Not just what benefits the colonies. We want the original vision of the Commonwealth to be recognized."

His dreadlocks swaying, a swarthy young man raised a hand. "Excuse me, Ms. Lovelace, Why not just take over the central government and treat Edenites the way they've treated us? Like crap. An eye for an eye, you know?"

"Because that's not our way, Malachi. And many Edenites are simply misguided. Their poor opinion of colonists comes from a perception of us as ungrateful grumblers who should accept the status quo. Most are unaware of the inhospitable conditions we endure because the net filters suppress the truth. Let us be the ones who enlighten the New Humanity."

What Randy heard charmed his soul. He understood what his father had meant. The Coalition wasn't like the CDF. Respect for everyone, even the enemy, was the foundation of its ethos. This was the culture Randy had expected the CDF to have.

These rebels were good people guided by moral precepts.

Suddenly, guilt twisted in Randy's chest as he thought about the rebels he had killed at Arson's base. *I'm sorry.*

Emotion clogged his throat.

He swallowed and continued walking as Lovelace kept speaking. He passed an elderly Earth Era war veteran wearing an eyepatch, venting to a younger man with facial scars *(Earth Era war vets were utilized as trainers)*.

The vet said, "I fought wars on Earth, and AEGIS classifies me as nothing more than a manual laborer, like I got nothing to offer society. That damn computer disqualified my wife's sister from Eden citizenship because she's supposedly predisposed to cancer. Hell, people infected by those alien biochem weapons *(during Armageddon)* didn't make the cut either. What happened to them wasn't their fault."

"What a buncha bullshit," the younger man said.

Bullshit indeed, Randy thought.

A young fair-skinned woman pranced up beside him, wearing a white shirt and brown leather pants. Her blond hair was arranged in a long braid. "So, you're Arson's son?" she asked politely, her French accent easily noticeable.

Miffed, Randy let out a breath. Though not in the mood, he stopped to entertain a conversation. "I am." He gently shook the woman's hand.

"I'm Mandy Bardot. Welcome to the Coalition. If there's anything I can help you with, just—" Loud, thudding explosions drowned out the rest of her words, and fear pulled her delicate features taut.

A stray blast punctured her back and tore open her midsection. The blood spray was immense.

Randy's face took on an expression of terror. He stepped back as Mandy's body went limp.

Energy blasts hammered the camp.

A rebel felt his gut lurch from anxiety. "We're under attack!"

An explosion wiped out a section of tents.

Cloaked Guardians atop high slopes opened fire. Their Shells' holographic skins dissolved on command.

"Move! Move!" a rebel barked. He and four others dashed past Randy, jumping into the fight.

Boom after *boom* threw the camp into chaos.

A group of Guardians skated down the slopes, traction skids engaged. They uncloaked and unleashed a hail of energy blasts.

A rebel's chest erupted in a geyser of blood.

Randy's heart began beating rapidly.

When a blast cratered the ground in front of him, rock and dirt peppered his body. *Shit!*

Yelling and swearing reached a fever pitch.

Explosions pulverizing the camp startled napping animals, sending them scurrying into burrows and crevices.

Guardians and rebels peeked out from behind berms, stones,

rock formations, and the camp's makeshift shelters, discharging shots before ducking back under cover.

Randy's implant pinged, tethering to Stacie's. *She's out here somewhere.*

To avoid being an easy target, he sprinted for cover. He came upon the decapitated body of a rebel woman and stopped, cringing. Realizing he might have to defend himself, he leaned down and snatched the energy gun lying next to the headless corpse.

Randy stared at the weapon, hoping he wouldn't have to use it. He dreaded the thought of opening fire on his fellow Guardians. And if he did have to defend any of the rebels, that would imply to the CDF that he had officially joined the Coalition.

"Randy!" a woman's voice cried out.

Randy turned and tucked the handgun between his belt and pants. "Stacie!"

She had followed the signal of their Link.

Her faceplate slid up. Randy was a sight for sore eyes. "Thank goodness you're okay." She exhaled in reprieve and took hold of his wrist. "Let's get you away from here and—"

Randy yanked his arm free. "I can't go. I'm sorry."

Stacie's joy withered. "What do you mean?" Her brows quirked in confusion.

From afar, a boom roared.

"It's hard to explain," Randy said. "Let's just say the Coalition is planning something big, and I want to investigate more."

"You mean play turncoat to go undercover or something?"

Randy brought up a holo-menu from his wristcom. "Quickly, sync with my wristcom. We don't have much time."

"Okay, but can you fill me in?" Stacie asked, perplexed. Her faceplate dropped into place. SYNC COMPLETED displayed on her HUD.

"The info I'm about to send will explain everything." Randy entered a series of numbers and letters on the menu. The wristcom chirped. "There's a video message from me appended." He forwarded the data and the message. Stacie permitted her CPU to accept it. A chime from Randy's wristcom confirmed the transfer. "You may not understand my reasoning for what I'm doing. I hope you will."

Stacie's faceplate rose again, her expression shifting from confusion to worry. "Randy, you're not making sense. What exactly do you intend to—?" He pressed a see-you-soon kiss to her cheek.

"I've gotta go," he said, running away to find Arson.

Hollering, explosions, and the sound of energy blasts merged into a single cacophony.

Frustrated, Stacie threw her hands up. "Randy, what the heck?" Blasts whisked past her, chewing up the ground near her feet and disintegrating rocks. She tossed her head back, zeroing in on where the shots came from. Two rebel men were targeting her from atop an incline. "Shit!" She backpedaled to dodge the next wave of blasts.

Her Oracle instantly lowered her faceplate. More blasts followed. She retaliated with a rapid burst of counterfire from her wrist gun.

Randy glanced back. "Stacie!" His pulse became a frantic rhythm that thrummed in his very throat. He tried to shelve his worry and keep moving. Stacie was in a Shell; she'd be okay, he thought. But his emotional connection to her wouldn't let him leave.

One of the rebels hurled a plasma grenade at Stacie.

Caught off guard, she froze.

Her Oracle made the save, summoning her barrier shield. Energy crackled, ballooning into a protective dome.

The grenade landed in front of Stacie and detonated against the shield. Competing plasma energies ignited a concussive backlash that tore at her legs. "Shit!"

The world around Stacie exploded in a brilliant flash. A blue torrent of destruction with the force of a hurricane yanked her off her feet and cartwheeled her through the air. The overwhelming surge of energy knocked out her visual sensors, plunging her into darkness as she went barrel-rolling across the harsh landscape.

Outside the blast radius, Randy threw a forearm over his eyes to block the blinding light.

Stacie tumbled side to side and bounced against the rocky surface. Her armor clanked and clacked with each impact.

In the explosion's wake, a deep, smoldering crater had formed. Zigzagging fissures spiderwebbed the ground and surrounding rock formations.

The force unleashed provided a demonstration of just how dangerous plasma energy could be.

Damn it, Randy thought. He ran back to Stacie, over fractured earth, and squatted beside her. Heat from the crater radiated against his back. "Stace, you okay?" He touched her hot armor. Mistake. His face pinched, and he jerked his hand away. "Stacie, are you okay?" She didn't respond, incapacitated.

The two rebels sped down the incline to off their target. "Move, Randy," one of them demanded, closing in fast and brandishing his weapon.

"Enough, there's no need to kill her."

"Blowing away a woman doesn't feel right to us," the rebel said. He leveled the barrel of his gun at Stacie. "But in this case, we've got no choice. She's with the people trying to kill us right now. We can't risk her waking up and taking our lives or those of our friends."

Randy rose to his feet unflinchingly, arms outstretched. "You'll have to kill me before I let you touch her."

The two rebels stalked closer.

"You're the boss's son. Just whose side are you on?" the other rebel asked.

"Right now, the side of human life," Randy responded. It sounded heroically corny, but hell, it was the best he could come up with.

"We don't have time for this nonsense," the rebel said, shoving Randy to the ground as he and his comrade moved forward.

Stacie's Oracle rebooted. A slot on her armored thigh popped open, and mini autoguns jutted forth.

Shock paralyzed the rebels. In execution style, a horrific bombardment of bullets riddled their defenseless bodies. Bits and pieces of them littered the ground, soaked in their blood.

Randy, sitting on the dirt, shut his eyes, sickened by the grotesque sight.

The gentle hum of an approaching hover vehicle made him open his eyes. It was a combat sled, a roofless two-seater equipped with blasters on each side and a gun turret at the rear. The sole occupant was a woman at the controls, dressed in a short-sleeved black shirt, loose-fitting pants, and a dark balaclava.

The sled hissed to a stop in front of Randy and the still-unconscious Stacie.

Randy got to his feet, ready to protect his lover.

The driver peeled off her balaclava.

Randy blinked, unable to believe his eyes. The driver was Kesley Whittaker. Fate and circumstance, it seemed, had intertwined their lives once again.

Wind ruffled Kesley's unruly red hair. "Well, don't just fucking stand there, get in."

So she is a rebel. "I can't leave—"

Stacie stirred.

At that moment, Randy made his choice. He jumped into the seat beside Kesley and strapped in. She stamped the acceleration pedal, and the sled zoomed away, dust billowing behind.

Stacie groaned as lucidity returned. Equilibrium off-kilter, she staggered to her feet. Structural damage hampered her every movement.

Her HUD displayed a message moving from left to right: MOBILITY RESPONSIVENESS 30% DECLINE.

She watched Randy speed away with Kesley. *Randy, I hope you know what you're doing.*

Against the bedlam of explosions and gunfire, Arson bellowed instructions, his face guard retracted. He had already issued the order to abandon camp.

"Scott!" a voice called out.

Arson pivoted. Gravel crunched underfoot. "Arnold."

The two former comrades faced each other.

They had endured BCT together, fought wars together, and conquered Officer Candidate School together. But now they were adversaries, fighting on opposite sides of the war.

"Arson, if you come along quietly, I won't harm you," Seymour said.

"You know me too well to think I'd ever surrender without a fight."

"Why, Arson? Why? Why'd you choose the Coalition over the CDF? Why disgrace yourself like this? You spat on the oath you swore to uphold."

In the distance, a high-pitched boom reverberated, followed by a terrible scream. The battle was growing fiercer.

"Quite the contrary," Arson replied, eyes locked on his old friend. "I was dishonoring myself by enforcing a system of oppression that should never have existed. You've seen how colonists live."

"The government was working to improve life for *everyone* in the Commonwealth. Just because you didn't like the pace doesn't mean you get to force it to accelerate by blowing up contractors, attacking military bases, and killing Guardians."

"Change doesn't happen by sitting around and doing nothing. Now enough. I won't surrender, and I refuse to let you berate me and question the love I have for the Defense Force, an institution I still credit for shaping me into the man I am today." With that, Arson activated his face guard.

"Then you've chosen the hard way."

Fléchette explosives dispersed from Seymour's shoulder cannon. They detonated against Arson's chest plate, staggering him backward and shaving away fractions of armor. Exposed structural components crackled.

Arson exhaled through clenched teeth as his armor sparked. Seymour fired energy blasts from his handgun. To make his former XO work for a direct hit, Arson engaged his vernier jets, flying above him.

Seymour elevated his aim, firing wildly in an upward arc.

Arson came down fast, his armored knee striking Seymour's faceplate.

Seymour's teeth rattled on impact. Disoriented, he toppled backward, then got up.

Arson landed, momentum sending him into a forward skid.

Before Seymour could fully recover, Arson spun around. Four spider-leg-like appendages sprouted from the back of his Reldaldri mechsuit. They were blasters.

The gleaming nozzles lit up and discharged energy beams. Two struck Seymour in the chest. Another two tagged his leg panels. He fell down on all fours, smoke rising from the damaged armor.

A warning lit up Seymour's HUD: UPPER TORSO DAMAGE 20% / LEG DAMAGE 15%.

Arson rushed forward and delivered a brutal kick to Seymour's helmet, knocking him flat. Then Arson ignited his vernier jets and blasted into the sky. *So long, Arnold. I hope our paths don't have to cross again.*

Seymour got to his feet, knee actuators creaking. *Damn you, Arson. You won't keep getting away. Your luck will run out.*

The sounds of battle dwindled into sporadic pops and zaps. The firefight at the camp had ended, with the CDF scoring a critical victory.

Miles away, Randy and Kesley's combat sled sat parked beneath the ridge of a plateau, surrounded by barren desert.

Smoke trails coming from the camp snaked into the sky.

Something resembling a purple one-eyed donkey galloped by, hooves trampling parched earth.

Kesley pressed a button on the dashboard to comm Arson. "This is Kesley to Commander Scott. Your son is with me, unscathed."

Arson's reply came instantaneously. "Thank you, Kess. I'm with Sariah and two of my men. We're safe as well. I've confirmed thirty others made it out of that fight too."

"What now?"

"We head to Colony Five, as Reza requested. We'll rendezvous at the abandoned depot. There's a shuttle stashed there."

"Roger." Shifting toward Randy, Kesley hooked her arm over the back of her seat's headrest. "So, you mad I didn't tell you?"

"No," Randy said casually, "I get why you couldn't. I probably would've arrested you on the spot."

"You could've gone back with your company just now. Why didn't you? You on our side now?"

Randy leaned back and cupped his hands behind his head, sinking into the seat's worn cushion. He gazed up at the sky. "I've .. . kind of had a change of heart."

"Kind of? What the fuck does that mean?"

Absentmindedly watching black winged mammals traverse the skies, Randy put his thoughts in order. "Arson showed me how corrupt the central government is. I don't want to fight for them, and I sure as hell don't want to fight for Gould. And after everything you showed me, I get it now: Not nearly enough is being done to help the colonies' people.

"Still, I'm not convinced rebellion was the only way to change things. But I understand why the people of colonies One, Four, and Six became disillusioned with the government. At the same time, it's hard for me to betray the oath I swore to uphold. And I'm not totally sold on Reza." *I might not want to fight for him, either.*

Agitated, Kesley flung her palms skyward. "So are you gonna fight with us or not?" she asked demandingly, tired of Randy's oscillating loyalties.

"For now, I'm neutral in this," Randy replied. Well, it was a start for Kesley. "I'm not committing to anyone's side right now. Hell, maybe I'll just go home and watch everything play out from the sidelines."

Kesley's lips stretched into a teasing grin. "If you do end up joining us: Like father, like son, huh?"

Mortified, Randy snapped upright and twisted toward her. His brow furrowed with scorn. "Even if I joined you guys, I don't have a wife and child," he shot back hotly. "If I did, I wouldn't have ghosted them to join someone's goddamn rebellion."

Kesley gave him a "C'mon, really!" kind of look. "You're a grown-ass man, Randy." She giggled, ticking him off even more. "It's not like he left you when you were some wee li'l boy."

"He caused my mother depression! Don't lecture me! How would you feel if your dad just up and vanished without a word?" Kesley fell silent, no comeback in sight. Point made. "That's what I thought. Now drive . . . to wherever the hell we're headed. It's likely my company has already sent out search teams to hunt down any rebel survivors." He crossed his arms and let out a contemptuous "humph."

The engine cranked, and the sled whizzed over the arid terrain, passing a family of taloned bipeds pecking insects off the ground with their yellow beaks.

The sled entered the mouth of a canyon.

Five minutes of mundane sightseeing helped diffuse most of Randy's tension. "So, relief-aid worker by day, rebel by night," he said, tone tinged with some residual hostility. "How'd you get hooked up with the Coalition?"

Kesley swerved around an outcrop. "Well, I was working for Dynamic Relief Provisions before the Three-Week War, and we were doing a lot of good. Then the war started. After it ended, I saw people getting disrespected even more under martial law.

"Dynamic Relief Provisions wasn't enough for me anymore. I wasn't content. I wanted to empower myself against the central government. I caught wind of a secret Coalition meetup, and I joined. Now here I am, doing good on two fronts—one as a relief-aid worker, the other as a rebel fighter."

"And what were you doing at the comms tower?" Randy asked.

"Arson wanted it rigged so we could try tapping into CDF comms transmissions. I haven't had a chance to go back and finish up." Energy blasts went off behind them. "Shit!"

A CDF hover vehicle glided out of a valley and stayed on their tail. The cannon on its prow fired again.

Kesley recoiled. "A search team found us! Hang on!"

She yanked a lever on the dashboard. Plasma energy lit up the aft boosters, and the sled kicked into high velocity, wind howling. She executed evasive maneuvers, zigzagging to dodge incoming fire.

Blasts struck the canyon walls.

A chip of rock smacked Randy's forehead. "Damn it!"

Kesley veered left and right, avoiding collisions with large craggy formations.

A blast grazed her side of the sled, scorching its surface. Another blast hit the stern, and the sled lurched into a tailspin.

Kesley was unable to regain control. "Fuck!"

The sled ricocheted off the canyon wall, then skidded across the ground, smashing a cluster of furry mammals. It slammed into a jagged outcrop with a metallic crunch, coming to a full stop.

Steam and smoke rose from blown gaskets. The engine sputtered under the crumpled hood.

The CDF vehicle whooshed to a halt beside the wrecked sled.

The Guardian at the controls killed the engine, and he and his battle-buddy disembarked.

Their faceplates retracted and locked into place. One of the men was dark brown with rugged features. His name tag said CLAY. The other was fair-skinned and had a tank-like build. His name tag said BLAIR. Both were privates.

"Alright, get out," Clay demanded, pointing his rifle at Randy and Kesley.

The sled's scrunched-up doors groaned as Randy and Kesley pried them open. They got out with their hands up.

Blair recognized Randy from his prisoner profile. "Hey, that's one of the captives, Randal Scott," he said to Clay.

"You okay, Specialist?" Clay asked.

Randy realized they didn't know he was with Kesley willingly. "Uh, yeah." He lowered his hands and stepped away from her. "Thanks for saving me from these guys," he said, playing along. He wondered how the hell they were going to get out of this mess.

Kesley whipped her energy gun from its holster and pulled the trigger. The muzzle flashed, but the rushed shot missed its intended target, Blair.

"Rebel bitch!" Blair charged, mechboots hammering the ground. Desperate, unfocused shots blazed past him. One blast struck his side, leaving a smoking burn. With a running shoulder attack, he knocked Kesley off her feet. The gun flew from her grip, and her head hit a stone. Blunt force trauma blotted out all consciousness.

Blair undressed her with his eyes, wondering about her dimensions. Her perfect hourglass figure drove him into a state of wild lust. *Damn, she's fucking stacked.* His Shell's rear paneling hissed open, and he took a few steps backward, exiting the suit. It stood idle while he knelt beside Kesley's defenseless body. *To the victor go the spoils of war.*

"Hey, what are you doing?" Randy asked, his voice as sharp as a blade.

Predatory amusement stretched across Blair's square-jawed face. "Chill out." He tossed a toothy grin Randy's way. "I'm just gonna have a little fun with this riffraff before I slit her throat."

Clay exited his Shell. "I'm next."

Randy's hands curled into fists, knuckles turning white. He was about to go berserk on these two depraved Guardians.

Blair straddled Kesley and pulled a knife from the green sheath on his belt, eager to slice open her shirt.

Just then, Kesley's eyes popped open, widening in panic.

Recalling stories from women she knew who had survived assaults by Guardians, she imagined the horror of becoming a victim herself. "Keep your filthy paws off me!" She thrashed against Blair, bucking her hips to try to throw him off.

"Oh, I love it when they fight back," Blair sneered, his voice full of arousal. He fixated on Kesley's writhing body. "Fucking hell, you're hot."

Randy screamed internally.

Kesley knocked the knife from Blair's grip. He responded by backhanding her with brute force, the slap resounding like a gunshot. Her head violently snapped to the side, and she tasted the metallic tang of blood in her mouth. Refusing to give in, she pushed through the pain, her instincts driving her to fight.

A thunderous expression strained the muscles of Randy's face. "Stop it!"

Blair was beyond stopping, beyond listening. He leaned down and dragged his tongue up the side of Kesley's neck.

She raked her nails across his face, gouging his flesh.

He yowled, the wounds searing. "You bitch!" He grabbed her wrists and forced them to the ground. "Be a good girl and stay still!"

Kesley spat in his face, her saliva hitting him square in the eye. "Fuck you, motherfucker!"

Infuriated, he shoved a hand under her shirt, his violating fingers trailing along her rib cage.

Kesley jerked a knee up to fend him off but failed to hit him. Her hips shifted as she fought to free herself. "Get the hell off me!"

"Stop moving!" Blair slid his hands from her midriff to her pants and unbuttoned them.

Randy refused to be a witness of a sexual assault. "Enough!" In a swift motion, he drew his gun and fired a precise shot into Blair's back. Blood splattered, seeping into the fine-grained sand.

Blair's eyes bulged, his mouth hung open in shock, and he collapsed on top of Kesley. She grunted, muscling his body off to the side, struggling to draw breath.

For a second, Clay stood frozen, surprise etched on his face. "Damn you, Specialist!" He punched Randy in the jaw, knocking him flat on his back. "Traitor!"

"It's Guardian misconduct to rape a woman," Randy said, getting up. "He was defacing the Defense Force's good name!"

An energy blast struck Clay in the leg, and he fell down, screaming in agony. Kesley was on her feet, rubbing the back of her head with one hand while her other held her handgun.

Blair's blood had stained her already-dirty clothes.

Perspiring, she walked over to Clay and leveled her gun at him, ready to finish the job.

Randy clutched her shoulder. "That's enough."

"Enough? We should kill the son of a bitch!" The memory of Blair's grimy tongue on her neck made her shudder.

"No, no more killing." Randy's eyes met hers. "The scumbag who tried to violate you is dead. This guy didn't do anything."

"Yeah, he didn't do *anything* to stop his buddy."

"Let's just take their vehicle and go, Kess!" Randy wasn't in the mood to argue.

"*Fine.*" Kesley gave Blair's dead body a parting kick to the ribs. *Bitch-ass motherfucking sicko.* She spat on him.

Clay, in pain, contacted the company with his comm-set. "This is Private Clay. I'm down. Private Blair is dead. The captive, Randal

Scott, has switched sides."

The CDF was now under the impression that Randy had defected. Whether he wanted to join the Coalition or not no longer mattered. The decision had been made for him. His life had descended further into limbo. *Oh, well,* he thought. He knew killing Blair would cause Clay to believe he had joined the Coalition, but he had no other choice.

A gust of wind swirled grit and sand into the air.

Kesley holstered her gun. "Told you we should've killed the bastard."

"Let's just get moving before it's too late!" Randy hollered. "All the noise is bound to attract more search teams! It's probably only a matter of minutes before they're on our asses!"

They jumped into the CDF vehicle and shot off toward their destination.

• • •

At the ravaged camp, Captain Seymour waited for updates from the search parties.

Stacie had heard Clay's APB for Randy over the comms. Confusion and worry squeezed her heart. *Okay, babe, what's going on with you?* She brought up Randy's video message on her HUD, suspense gripping her.

In the recording, Randy explained the same things he had told Kesley: that learning about the government's corruption and witnessing the colonists' suffering had changed his perspective. He still wasn't convinced rebellion was the answer, but he couldn't stomach fighting for a corrupt government.

He had conflicting feelings about the war. He was weighing everything, trying to figure out which side to fight for, if any. But before making a decision, he needed to know more about the Coalition. He needed to understand their grand plan.

The very possibility of Randy joining the Coalition felt surreal to Stacie.

In the last thirty seconds of the message, he gave her the hard truth, telling her the biggest criminal factor in government corruption today was the Eight Elite, including her family.

She tensed.

He told her to check out the folder on Gould. Then the message ended, dissolving into static waves.

She opened Gould's folder with haste. Her eyes widened at the illegal financing of his campaign, all traced back to her parents. *No,* she thought. "Fuck, fuck, fuck," she let loose, just above a whisper.

As she dug deeper, she uncovered more financial kickbacks, not only between her parents and Gould but also between her parents and other politicians. Then she accessed files on the rest of the Eight Elite. What she found shook her to the core: scandals, human trafficking, money laundering. What exactly were her parents involved in, a crime syndicate? Was everything they gave her, everything they owned, bought with dirty money?

Her blood boiled. She needed answers. She needed to know the extent of her parents' criminal activities. What else didn't she know? Were her parents just as malevolent as some of the other Eight families?

When she was a child, she often saw family heads and politicians visit her parents. Her father frequently attended gatherings he vaguely described as "important business meetings." She was unaware of the details of these meetings or how her parents had accumulated their wealth.

She didn't bother asking many questions, as she wasn't particularly interested in her parents' business dealings. Whenever she did inquire about them, the responses she got were always along the lines of "You'll know when it's time." Well, there was no more time to remain ignorant and naive about Spencer Enterprises. "The time" had arrived.

• • •

Randy and Kesley's vehicle exited the canyon and glided over sand dunes of varying sizes.

Randy sat in silence, unpacking everything that had transpired. If he ended up deciding not to fight for the Coalition, what would he do? Could he go back to the CDF, smooth things over, and salvage his military career? As he struggled to envision his future, he cursed himself for getting embroiled in this quandary.

The hover vehicle's boosters powered it up a steep elevation, and then it cruised down the other side.

His strength wilting, Randy was ready to board the shuttle and just snooze for a while, letting sleep's peace sanitize his mind of his unfortunate circumstances.

Though quiet, Kesley was still horrified by how close someone had come to violating her.

They arrived at the rally point, a dark and dreary disused facility.

"This is it," Kesley said somberly. She unclipped a comm-set from her belt and held it against her ear. "This is Kesley to Commander Scott. Your son and I are outside."

Arson replied, "Sariah, myself, and twenty of my men are inside. Open the loading-dock door and get in here. We'll take off as soon as my other ten survivors arrive."

"You heard the man, let's move," Randy said.

Exhausted, they went to the dock door. Kesley slapped the big blue button on a control box, and the roll-up door slowly screeched upward, revealing a shuttle from yesteryear.

They walked into the musty-scented dock. Cobwebs hung from the corners. Old inert machinery, long out of service, sat covered in rust.

Randy studied the craft's makeup. "This thing's an antique." A spooked gray critter resembling a mouse scampered by his foot. "Must be one of the first models developed."

Arson came down the shuttle's stair-ramp, plain-clothed. "Randy, Kesley, glad you made it," he said as he approached them.

Tolerating Arson's closeness brought a look of discomfort to Randy's face, but after a moment, his features settled.

Explosions, muffled by distance, thundered across the desert.

"Commander Scott," a woman said over the comm-set on Arson's belt, "this is Lovelace. The enemy has caught up to us. We're outnumbered and—" After another explosion, the comms channel went dead.

"She's gone," Arson said grimly. "Along with the other nine."

A small weeping sound escaped Kesley. She had obviously known the woman.

Overwhelmed by raw emotion, she clenched her fists, ready to strike something—a wall, a crate, anything.

Randy delicately framed her face in his hands, his touch warm. Sadness glossed her eyes, and rivulets of tears ran down her cheeks. "Hey, I'm sorry," Randy said.

Arson gestured sharply. "Quickly, inside the shuttle."

Arson, Randy, and Kesley hastened up the stair-ramp.

Randy spotted Jarius. "You stuck around, huh?"

Jarius replied, "I talked to your dad. I told him we were collegemates and that I wanted to follow your lead and continue checking things out. He was okay with it."

"Glad you're here."

"I figured someone's gotta keep you outta trouble."

At the controls, the pilot cranked the old engine. It sputtered, cronked, and then died. "Damn it! Come on!"

Now, everyone aboard was on edge.

Holy fucking shit, Randy thought, nervous. *Some escape craft.*

The pilot tapped buttons on the control panel, trying to get the shuttle to behave. The engine coughed and died again. Grimacing, the pilot kept troubleshooting. Finally, the resuscitated engine growled to life.

A collective cheer broke out among everyone.

The landing wheels rolled the craft outdoors, just as three CDF hover vehicles pulled up. Gunners perched at the rear turrets unleashed flurries of bullets.

The shuttle lifted into the sky, sunlight winking off its scarred metal surface. The landing gear retracted, and the old plasma thrusters flared.

The gunners kept firing until the shuttle soared out of range, speeding toward safer territory.

"Damn it," a sergeant in one of the vehicles blurted. He swore again and commed Commander Seymour. "This is Sergeant Downey. Arson's gotten away."

Commander Seymour replied, his voice steady, "Roger, Sergeant. Return to the campsite."

Though Arson had escaped, the day was still a success. The second—and remaining—body of the Scott Faction had been squashed.

Everyone in the escape shuttle was now at ease, out of harm's clutches.

Randy sat next to Kesley. The growing ache in her heart from Lovelace's death washed a sorrowful expression over her features.

Sympathy emanated from Randy. "You two were tight, huh?"

A sob caught in Kesley's throat. "Lovelace was my guide when I first joined the Coalition. She taught me a lot. We became besties, almost like sisters."

Randy wrapped an arm around her and drew her close.

"Thanks." Burnt out and heartbroken, Kesley leaned her head on his shoulder and shut her eyes. A tear slid down her cheek, and he wiped it away for her. "Thanks again," she said, her voice faint.

"No problem." Randy continued holding her.

Kesley felt comforted by his presence. And he had saved her from a horrible fate today. She was in his debt.

Despite her tendency to irritate him, Randy appreciated Kesley. The broadening of his perspectives and evolving view of the war had started with her.

If he were honest with himself, he had developed a crush on her.

Both of them dozed off as the shuttle made its way toward Colony Five.

CHAPTER SIX

The survivors of the attack on Bravo Camp walked from the outlying landing spot for aircraft toward a small, unassuming prefab. They were in a jungle in Colony Five, moving through a makeshift compound. The prefab was Reza's sanctuary.

Governess Samantha Hayley had cordoned off the jungle and declared it a prohibited zone, shielding Reza and his assault force from discovery. Severe fines for trespassing discouraged citizens from even thinking about venturing into the area.

When rebels went to nearby towns for R&R, they had to keep a low profile, and recruiting was absolutely forbidden. The last thing Samantha wanted was to attract the CDF's attention. Any whisper of rebel activity in Colony Five would draw them there. Her people had no desire to get dragged into the war, and Samantha was going to ensure they weren't, all while assisting the Coalition however she could.

Arson and Sariah led the way. Randy and Kesley trailed behind the group, keeping each other company.

"I'm assuming that building is Reza's lair," Randy said to Kesley, his eyes examining the plain, windowless square structure. Once again, Kesley served as his guide through the unfamiliar.

"Yep, Governess Hayley had it constructed for him," she replied. The group went by a waterfall that flowed into a stream. "It's pretty basic. The main room functions as a communications hub, and the other room is Reza's study."

Randy swatted at a swarm of buzzing insects. He saw a massive open-air hangar beside the building. Inside it, Hammer Fall's assault ship—a base-class vessel equipped with sleeping stations—sat grounded. "Where'd you guys get the ship?"

"The Falgoah got it for us."

That surprised Randy. "The Falgoah are helping you guys?"

"Yeah, we formed an alliance with them. They've supplied us with weapons and other resources. They've even volunteered for the assault force. All they ask in return is for Reza to reinstate them to their land."

Randy had studied the conflict between the Falgoah and Chalderat clans thoroughly. Reinstatement of the Falgoah to their land would reignite the blood feud. He knew that letting the two clans continue to duke it out wouldn't be smart. He was sure Reza knew that as well. There needed to be a plan for reconciliation. Randy hoped Reza had one that was solid.

The group passed mobile showers and rows of large waterproof canvases stretched between poles. Beneath the canvases, up to twenty-five rebels slept in sleeping bags or on cots.

"So why aren't you guys using the ship for housing?" Randy asked Kesley.

"It just arrived two days ago," she replied. "The technicians are still installing the stealth-cloak emitters. Reza doesn't want anyone aboard until they're finished."

"How long has the assault force been here?"

Kesley took a few seconds to think before answering. "About two months now. They've been training with the Reldaldri mechsuits and other weapons."

The group stopped. Ahead of them, rebels inside improvised shelters rested. Arson gave instructions to his men, and they tapered off, some going left and some going right.

"Wait here," Kesley said to Randy. She went up to Arson and Sariah to talk to them about something.

While waiting for her, Randy scanned the jungle. He saw a small earth-colored quadruped masticating a fallen bough with its elongated teeth.

Kesley returned to Randy as Arson and Sariah walked off together, holding hands.

"So what's up?" Randy asked.

"C'mon, follow me." Kesley motioned for him to come with her. "You'll be staying with me in my field hut. Built it myself."

Reluctant, Randy squinted. "I'm staying with you?"

"Either that or you can crash with several others under one of the outdoor shelters. But I figured you'd want a little more privacy." In an overly chirpy tone, Kesley said, "Besides, my company's priceless, and *youuuu knowwwww* you enjoy it. Don't play." She winked.

Randy preferred the privacy of Kesley's hut, but he wasn't keen on dealing with her cheeky and occasionally pushy demeanor. He sighed in resignation. "Alright, fine. Let's go."

They stepped inside a log-wood hut with a thatched roof. The interior was sparse, just a bed, table, washbasin, and shower spigot.

"Get some shut-eye," Kesley told Randy. "In about three hours, Reza's going to update everyone on the new timeline for Hammer Fall. I'll be back by then. Got a few things to take care of." She paused at the door, remembering something. "Oh, Arson wanted me to let you know that Sariah will be giving you and Jarius a crash course on operating the Reldaldri mechsuit tomorrow, since you two are joining the assault force."

"Got it. Thanks."

Kesley left Randy to his own devices, going out the door.

Randy lay on the bed, his mind replaying the events that had turned his life upside down. The fact that he was now a Coalition rebel seemed crazy. His thoughts drifted to Stacie. He wondered how she was handling the revelations he'd dropped on her.

Exhaustion overtook him, and he shut his heavy eyelids.

Three hours passed. Night had fallen.

Kesley returned. She'd gotten cleaned up and was dressed in a tank top and shorts. She gently shook Randy awake from his sleep.

His eyes fluttered open. "So, the big moment has arrived, huh?" he asked groggily.

Kesley nodded.

Randy climbed out of bed, and together they went outside into the starlit night. The entire assault force had assembled in front of Reza's sanctuary, large spotlights illuminating the area. Anticipation hung in the air. Everyone was eager to hear from the Coalition leader.

Nocturnal creatures croaked in the background, blending with the indistinct murmur of the crowd.

Kesley spotted Arson and Sariah. She took Randy's hand, and her long strides dragged him forward.

Randy kept a comfortable distance from his father, avoiding eye contact and saying nothing. He crossed his arms over his chest, his eyes fixed on the doors of Reza's sanctuary.

Near Jarius, two Falgoah women were conversing. Like their male counterparts, they had taupe skin, ebony hair, slanted eyes, and a single set of scales extending from their forehead to their nose. Both wore something resembling black jumpsuits. Noting their uncanny resemblance, Jarius assumed they were sisters.

Randy became impatient. *So how long are you going to make us wait, Reza?*

Speak of the devil. The double doors of the sanctuary parted, and Reza emerged, his masked face cloaked in shadow underneath his cowl. He wore a black leathery ensemble with cybernetic strength-augmenting braces coiled around his arms and legs like armor. He set forth at a controlled pace, and three armed men followed behind him in perfect formation.

As he advanced, the crowd fell into hushed reverence. Voices died. Movements stilled. All eyes focused on him. He passed between two tall, flickering torches, their light dancing over the metal of his augmentations.

The holo transmitter at his feet, a disk mounted to a four-foot pole, cast pale light onto his figure. It captured and projected his image across the Coalition intranet, transmitting him in real-time to every faction's base.

He pressed a button on his mask. His voice, amplified and altered by the vocoder, thundered over the assembly. "My fellow freedom fighters, human and Falgoah alike, we stand here bound by a single truth: The Commonwealth Government must fall. And I am honored to stand here tonight among the ones who will bring it to its knees."

Enough grandstanding. Get on with it, Randy thought.

"Your valor will bring equality to Satellite One and return the exiled to their rightful planet. The Falgoah were wrongfully banished from Zelaforia. During the ceasefire, a militia secretly armed by the Chalderat attacked them. It was an underhanded tactic to continue exterminating the Falgoah. In light of that, the Falgoah had every right to break the ceasefire.

"They will be returned to their homeworld, and we will have equality. But Operation Hammer Fall must happen sooner than planned, because a madman now holds the Commonwealth's highest office, Cornelius Gould." The wind bent the flames of the torches. "We have proof that, backed by one of the Eight Elite, he orchestrated the assassination of Jared Kerner. And that's not all. Our insiders confirm Gould has built a secret arms-development facility. This darksite is manufacturing deadly new weapons the CDF will use to snuff us out.

"Jared Kerner was a reserved man; Gould is unpredictable, a wildcard. As Chief, he'll worsen our oppression. He'll impose harsher restrictions on the occupied colonies. He'll even initiate unwarranted surveillance on the unoccupied colonies, something he admitted in his debate with Chairwoman Amaechi.

"This is why our timeline must change. Instead of striking in seven days, we strike in three."

As Randy glared at Reza, a wave of worried susurrations swept through the crowd, too quiet to make out, but clearly laced with concern. The shortened window of preparation understandably unsettled some rebels.

"I know this is burdensome," Reza admitted. "Those training to master the Reldaldri suits will now have to push harder, and newcomers will need to learn faster. But I believe in all of you."

One rebel clapped, breaking the tension. Others joined in. A few cheered. The applause loudened, washing away hesitation as renewed confidence invigorated everyone.

"Governess Hayley has arranged a grand feast for us tonight," Reza added. "So enjoy it."

To Randy, it was clear: Delivering a good meal was Reza's way to pacify nervousness and boost morale.

After a final glance at the crowd, Reza disappeared into his sanctuary, his cowl snapping in the wind.

Randy's face pinched. The inciter of the Independent Movement didn't impress him. He wondered if Reza was the savior people claimed he was or just a false messiah chasing power. Driven by a need to uncover the truth, Randy broke into a sprint. He was done speculating. He would confront Reza face-to-face.

Arson shouted, "Randy, wait!"

Reza's three armed guards trained their rifles on Randy.

Arson raced toward the standoff, with Kesley flanking him.

Jarius crossed his arms and shook his head. *There you go again, Randy, rushing headlong into trouble. That's how you got into this mess . . . and somehow dragged my ass along for the ride.*

"Stand down!" Arson ordered the guards. As Reza's top commander, his authority held weight. The guards complied, lowering their weapons to the low-ready position.

Kesley parked herself beside Randy. "What the devil were you thinking?"

Arson scowled at his son, and a note of reprimand edged his voice. "Reza doesn't have an open-door policy, Randy. You can't just waltz into his domain and expect to get social time with him whenever you feel like it, just like you can't barge into your commander's office anytime you want."

"Is he afraid to talk to us 'underlings'?" Randy asked forwardly. "Does he think he's superior to us, his obedient pawns?"

Overhearing the commotion, Reza stepped back outside. "Randal Scott, I assure you I'm no elitist."

"Sorry, sir," Arson said. "My son's . . . been skeptical of the Coalition . . . and you." He shot Randy a sharp sidelong glare. "But I *think* he's coming around."

"It's alright," Reza said coolly. "Perhaps I can ease his skepticism. If your son wants an audience with me, he shall have one. I'll answer whatever questions he has, within reason."

"Thanks," Randy said.

He, Arson, and Kesley moved forward.

They entered Reza's sanctuary and walked into the central room, where comms equipment chirped and trilled.

Reza said, "Kess, Arson, remain here. I will speak to Randal alone in my study."

"Sure," Arson replied.

Randy and Reza went through the door ahead.

Reza settled into one of the chairs at the wooden table. Randy took the chair opposite him, more than ready to kick off the Q&A session.

Reza twined his fingers together on the table. "Alright, Randal, speak your mind."

"I want to know who you were before you became this . . . great influencer? What turned you into a revolutionary?"

Reza gathered his thoughts. "I was a Guardian, a private. My company was deployed to Zelaforia. Our mission was to assist the High Council in ending the civil conflict between the Falgoah and Chalderat clans. One day, my squad was ordered to open fire on a group of Falgoah warriors who had already surrendered. I refused to take part in the distasteful act." His voice quaked with rage. "They were defeated. There was no need to kill them. But Secretary of Defense Cornelius Gould had enacted a kill order. We were to take no prisoners.

"After my insubordination, I was reassigned from active duty to the Reserves. My new company was later activated to suppress the miners' strike in Colony Four. During that mission, I witnessed another cruel, senseless act. My squad was ordered to open fire on unarmed miners. Just like on Zelaforia, I refused. Consumed by rage, I attacked my squad leader. That was the final straw for CDF

Command. They gave me a dishonorable discharge, for refusing to become a heartless killer."

Again, Randy recalled his drill sergeant saying every enemy was to be dealt with ruthlessly. Even the slightest hint of compassion could mean execution on the spot for a Guardian. "Seems like the CDF adopted a culture of brutality," he said.

"Yes, CDF Command believed that culture was necessary for the survival of the New Humanity. They thought the CDF had to be as merciless as possible to protect humanity in its vulnerable state. A species will go to great lengths to protect itself."

Randy voiced the thoughts churning in his mind. "The RUC was seen as an enemy to the New Humanity, because they were threatening to take away resources from the Commonwealth as a whole. So that ruthless brutality was unleashed on them, even though we're all human beings."

"Yes, but compassion is a strength, not a weakness. I believe it's time for the CDF to evolve its culture and for the central government to be purged of corruption. It's time for a fair and just Commonwealth."

"So what happened after you were discharged?"

"I embarked on a journey of introspection, wandering the colonies as a drifter. I survived off the credits I had and took on odd jobs here and there. As a lottery beneficiary, I considered the colonies home. Not wanting to live a life of insignificance, I contemplated my place in society. During this journey, I saw people suffering from the poor living conditions the government seemed to be doing little to improve. Instead, they were busy profiting from planetary-impact missions on protectorates.

"Driven by the realization that the central government was a source of both good and significant wrongdoing, I understood the necessity for change. I donned this disguise, used the net to speak out against gross injustice, and urged others to resist. My goal was to ignite awareness, and the Independent Movement was born, a result far beyond my wildest hopes."

"So how'd you become the Coalition's leader?"

"To my dismay, the CDF crushed the RUC. The remaining resistance formed the Coalition of Rebel Factions. But they lacked direction. Needing a leader, I stepped in to take command, and they immediately accepted me, since I was the driving force behind the Independent Movement. Now, we're poised to end the central government's malign ways for good, which, I must stress, is affecting civilizations throughout the entire galaxy, not just the Commonwealth."

Reza keyed his electronic bracer, and a holo bloomed to life. He tapped a planet, enlarging the projection. "This is Uandorais," he said. "The Cogrull government has accepted Commonwealth protectorate status. The CDF is helping that government destroy the rebel forces threatening to overtake it. But the CDF has no right to interfere in those rebels' righteous stand."

"How do you know it's righteous?"

"Like colonists, they're merely demanding better of the established order. They despise the Commonwealth for derailing their revolution. People in other protectorates share the same feelings. It could be only a matter of time before Commonwealth antagonists, opposed to our planetary-impact missions, strike Eden soil or the colonies.

"Thom Kerner and Cornelius Gould set our republic on a path that must be reversed. Parliament members have become complacent with the Commonwealth's wrongful planetary-impact missions, because the government profits from them.

"With too few politicians willing to redirect the Commonwealth's course, our mission is crucial. I wish it could have waited until after the results of the election. Perhaps Oviereya will win. If she does, I know she would work tirelessly to turn things around. However, the extent of the change she could achieve is uncertain. She would face resistance from obstinate Parliament members determined to undermine her efforts. Many of them are corrupt and have made deals with the Eight Elite.

"Even if Oviereya could bring about considerable change, the colonies can't wait a year, especially with Gould as Chief. Something needs to be done now."

Randy, a stickler for detail, asked, "So what if everything backfires? What if the uncorrupt Parliament members don't want to cooperate with you in creating a new government? Though they may not have ties to criminals, most of them still believe in adhering to AEGIS's stratification of humanity. Have you thought about all that? Do you have a contingency plan?"

No one could easily pressure Reza into answering questions he didn't want to answer. Sidestepping the questions, he said, "You'll receive more information when the time comes." He stood. "You should go enjoy tonight's meal."

Randy followed Reza to the door and exited the study.

"Get your questions answered, Randy?" Arson asked.

"More or less." Randy remained skeptical of Reza.

Arson, Kesley, and Randy left the building.

Reza went through the rear door of his study to the wooden outdoor deck and rested his arms on the balustrade. His talk with Randy about his past sent his mind down memory lane . . .

Atop the roof of his temporary duty station, Ahmed Hawsawi —the man who would become Arman Reza—nursed a cigarette between his lips.

The sky was aglow with shades of orange and red as the last rays of sunlight pierced the clouds.

The roof-access door shrieked open. Ahmed glanced over his shoulder. His best friend, Lance Grisham, emerged.

"Thought I'd find you here," Lance said. The curly-haired blond plucked a cigarette from his front pocket. "Mind if I join you?"

"Not at all." Ahmed returned his gaze to the city's geometric architecture, structures of edges and angles.

Lance walked up to the parapet, taking up a spot beside his friend. "What's on your mind?"

Ahmed sighed his frustration, uncertainty muddling his thoughts. "Just wondering what the *hell* we're doing here."

Lance chuckled. "You know why we're here. The Noshkanu province is a protectorate. The deal is that the Commonwealth provides the High Council with military assistance to squash the Falgoah uprising in exchange for bitrium and other minerals."

Ahmed replied in a voice of disapproval. "So the CDF is a bunch of contract mercenaries, is that it? Just fucking guns for hire?"

Lance laughed. As long as he wasn't doing anything pro bono, he'd execute all orders without question. "Basically. The government likes to call us peacekeepers, equalizers, or interventionists. We restore harmony to civilizations, reduce crime when governments can't, and defend worlds when they're unable to protect themselves. You know, all that righteous drivel. But it's all for a price, though.

"We've earned a reputation for this heroes-for-hire stuff throughout the galaxy, and the central government is using that rep to benefit the Commonwealth." He tossed his cigarette onto the rooftop and scuffed it out with his boot. "Anyway, we swore to obey the orders of the Chief Executive. We don't get to choose what missions we like or dislike. We don't get to decide what's right or wrong. The only thing we get to do is execute orders, my friend. And we get paid to do it, so I really don't give a fuck."

Ahmed exhaled a stream of cigarette smoke, grimacing. "Well, *I* am a thinking man." He aimed a thumb at himself. "And I'm not sure the CDF should be meddling in disputes over territorial rights. Our being here feels wrong." His conscience troubled him. This mission felt morally dubious for a man of honor like him.

Lance drew his lips into a smirk. "Careful, if Sergeant Bartel heard you talk like that, she'd probably blow a hole into your 'thinking man's' cranium." He shaped his fingers into the form of a gun and pretended to fire a shot. "*Pa-chow.*" Ahmed frowned. "After all, the—"

"I know, damn it," Ahmed interrupted. "It's just like Senior Instructor Wells said: 'The Commonwealth is always righteous.' Maybe that's just cliché bullshit. No government is always righteous." He puffed his cigarette. Then he expelled his next thought, saying, "Fuck, how come the Union cheerleads our efforts to play savior across all these worlds?"

Lance replied, "It's all about presentation. If the central government shows how a planetary-impact mission aligns with the Union's goal of promoting its benevolence and attracting universal allies, they consent to it *(unaware there might be details omitted or ulterior motives)*. Lucky for the Commonwealth, right? 'Cause we got debts to pay, and these missions are helping us pay 'em off.

"But I *do* have to admit, the Union seems to be getting a little concerned about our campaigns of 'good deeds' on other worlds. Eyebrows are being raised." He checked the time on his wristcom. "Hey, we need to head inside to get shelled for tonight's op."

Ahmed dropped his cigarette onto the rooftop and crushed the butt under his heel . . .

As Reza stood on the deck outside his study, his mind recapped the aftermath of that op . . .

Amid their razed campground, eighteen Falgoah clansmen—some just teenagers—held their hands aloft in surrender. The eviscerated bodies of their comrades, who had fought to the death, littered the ground, lying in their own viscera and entrails.

A squad of Guardians in M-X01s trained their rifles on the survivors, red tagging lasers marking them for execution.

A shudder racked Ahmed's limbs. He was horrified. In a firefight, even if it didn't always sit right with him, he'd had no choice but to shoot back. In those do-or-die moments, it was easy to forget the humanity of those trying to kill him. He was a soldier, and so were they, all warriors on a battlefield. His instinct had always been to make it home alive, to help his comrades do the same. But this was different. These people had put down their weapons. They had surrendered. They were no longer a threat.

"C'mon, they've given up! They're unarmed!" Ahmed shouted.

The squad leader, Sergeant DaSalvo, nonchalantly said, "The CDF's orders from Gould are to take no prisoners."

Ahmed's face flushed red from anger. "But this isn't right! Some are just kids! What fucking sense does this make?"

"We don't decide what's right or wrong, Private. We just follow orders."

Hoping to get some support, Ahmed glanced over at Lance.

Lance ignored Ahmed's help-me-out look. He was in full compliance. *Ahmed, this is no time to be a Falgoah sympathizer.*

The hands of some Guardians quivered with unease.

"Fire!" DaSalvo ordered.

Triggers clicked. Crackling gunfire swallowed the frenetic

screams of the dying clansmen. Mowed down, they lay massacred en masse.

Ahmed, the only one who hadn't fired, couldn't desensitize himself to the slaughter. Disgust hardened his features.

DaSalvo marched up to him. He retracted his faceplate, showing his enraged countenance to Ahmed. "Private Hawsawi, you were ordered to fire!" A throbbing vein bulged from his forehead.

Ahmed's faceplate unsealed. He scowled. "Fuck your orders, and fuck Gould."

"Your insubordination will be reported up the chain of command, you understand, Guardian?"

"Whatever."

DaSalvo's faceplate clamped back down. Life scans detected nothing. Mission accomplished. "We destroyed the camp, and all the clansmen here are dead. The cleanup crew will begin body disposal." That meant the cleanup crew would cremate the bodies via flamethrower or dump them into the ocean. "Let's go."

Ahmed stared at the shot-up bodies, silent. These people wouldn't even get a proper burial.

"Ahmed, let's go," Lance said as mechboots thumped away. Ahmed didn't move. "Ahmed, come on!"

Chin down, Ahmed waved Lance off. "Go, Lance, I'll catch up."

"Don't ruminate on this shit too long. It's done. End of story." Lance left with the others.

Ahmed walked past huts fire had gutted, searching for a sign of life. His heart sank to the pit of his belly. He felt appalled. How could anyone numb their soul to what happened here?

The crackle and pop of crisping flesh and bone made his stomach heave.

He coughed hard, smoke strangling his lungs. His mind reeled, reflecting on what had truly transpired here. Under the Commonwealth Government's auspices, he had participated in the Chalderat's systematic cleansing of the Falgoah.

There were Guardians in his platoon who, like him, hadn't wanted to be part of this slaughter. They had remorseful souls, as he did. But they were bound by duty and couldn't risk a reprimand for refusing to obey orders or voicing their disapproval. But was obeying orders worth weltering your soul in the blood of people who had done you no harm? Not all planetary-impact missions were like this, though. The CDF had helped defend worlds against some of the universe's most vile wrongdoers.

Flying predators circled above, hunting for carrion.

While passing the blackened bodies of small children, Ahmed heard shallow breathing coming from a woman.

His searching eyes found her. She was injured but alive. Trying to flee from him, she crawled past the charred bones of friends, nails clawing grooves into the dirt.

Ahmed went to her. She stared at him, eyes wide and terror-stricken, her lungs fighting for oxygen.

He crouched beside her. "I'm not going to hurt you," he said gently. His helmet's external sound port relayed his words in the Falgoah's language.

The woman's heart skipped when she saw a syringe pop out from Ahmed's wrist.

He injected a healing accelerant and pain suppressant into her wounded leg. Then he straightened to full height.

He racked his helmet and commanded his Shell to release him. Couplings unlatched. He unsnapped his harness and exited the Shell to appear as nonthreatening as possible.

The stench of burning flesh hung in the air.

Ahmed mentally instructed the CPU of his standing war machine to continue translating his words in the Falgoah's language through the external sound port.

With the pain of her wound dulled, the woman managed to stand and hobble around. She pinned a hawkish glare on Ahmed and quickly snatched up a plank of wood.

She swung at him.

He dodged. "I don't want to fight!" His Shell translated and echoed his words.

She swung again, the plank slamming into his gut.

He fell onto his back. "I'm sorry!" His Shell translated.

The woman raised the plank, ready to bash in his skull.

With no choice, Ahmed drew his sidearm and fired a fatal shot into her chest.

She crashed to the ground, a geyser of dark orange blood spurting from the bullet hole.

Ahmed got to his feet and holstered his pistol. *No.* He lowered his chin, staring at the woman's lifeless body. *The way she reacted to me . . . I've become a monster to these people.*

A weary Ahmed sat at a metal table in a barren, windowless room, the audible buzz of a lone light bulb overhead adding to the weight in his chest. In front of him sat his platoon sergeant, Sergeant First Class Alicia Bartel.

"You're a lucky man, Private Hawsawi," Alicia said. "For your insubordination, you're being kicked off active duty and reassigned to the Reserves. No more full-time benefits. No steady pay. But it's a far cry from being cashiered."

Ahmed exhaled a shaky breath. "Fine," he said quietly. "Okay."

Alicia slid a datapad across the scarred surface between them.

"Just need your print to make it official."

Ahmed placed his thumb on the signature box of the v-doc. He stood, chair scraping softly behind him, and exited.

Outside the door, Lance was waiting. His eyes studied Ahmed's dejected expression. "So was the consequence of not pulling that trigger worth it? Was it worth it being a Falgoah sympathizer?"

Ahmed paused. That word—sympathizer—carried so much venom. It was how the CDF silenced compassion, how it defamed Guardians who expressed sympathy for the enemy. "Recusing myself from mass murder was every bit worth it."

"And what did you gain? You just threw away a full-time military career, something we worked our asses off for."

Ahmed turned his head just enough to glance over his shoulder. "What I gained was my soul." He walked away.

Twenty-eight miners on strike in Colony Four, protesting the Commonwealth Government, stood outside their work facility. Their voices roared, fists pumping handmade signs.

A squad of Reservists in M-X01s confronted them.

The sergeant in charge stepped forward. His Shell's external sound port megaphoned his voice. "YOU ARE RESOURCE HARVESTERS IN THE EMPLOY OF THE CENTRAL GOVERNMENT. RETURN TO WORK IMMEDIATELY! THIS IS YOUR FINAL WARNING!"

"Screw you!" a man shouted from the front. He hurled a stone that bonged off the sergeant's faceplate.

The miners burst into cheers. More stones followed, pelting the Guardians' Shells.

The sergeant C-commed his squad. *<<Alpha Squad, crowd has turned hostile. Kill parameters are relaxed. Turn selector switch to lethal*

and open fire on my command. >>

Safeties disengaged, rifles locked and loaded.

Ahmed's face contorted with reproach. He opened a private C-comm channel to the cutthroat sergeant. <<*Wait, why are we using lethal rounds?*>>

<<*Gould's given us authorization to go lethal when we see fit, and I see fit right now, Hawsawi.* >>

Ahmed was on the verge of snapping at the mention of that name—Gould, the Secretary of Defense. He spoke to a woman among the miners through their Link. <*Priscilla, get out of here.*>

<*Why?*> she asked.

The sergeant said, "Alright, prepare to—"

Ahmed tackled him to the ground, armor banging against armor. "This is madness! I didn't sign up to be a murderer!"

"Off me!" The sergeant whammed his armored knuckles against Ahmed's faceplate, knocking him aside and spiderwebbing cracks across his visor.

Priscilla gasped.

The sergeant stood up. "Open fire, goddammit!"

Staccato gunfire erupted. Miners scattered in a panicked frenzy, desperately fleeing the onslaught.

"No!" Ahmed screamed, watching a spray of crimson squirt from Priscilla. Her body jerked grotesquely, reacting to every bullet shot through it.

Being Linked with Priscilla made the execution a shared nightmare for Ahmed. Dizziness and nausea bum-rushed him. Bile rose in his throat. His body absorbed the keen pain of every bullet. Fighting to stay upright, he was on the precipice of blacking out.

After the gunfire ceased, six bodies lay sprawled in the dirt, Priscilla among them. Their blood soaked the ground in dark glistening pools. Message sent.

The sergeant in charge said, "Let that be a lesson to all you peons: Don't bite the hand that feeds you."

Ahmed's legs gave out. He plummeted to his knees beside Priscilla's body. His heart thrummed in his ears, and his lower lip trembled.

Blood gushed from the holes in Priscilla's chest and from her mouth, a macabre reminder of the brutal cost of defiance.

She brought a quivering hand to the side of Ahmed's face, tears of farewell flowing from her entrancing azure eyes. < *Goodbye, love, I* —> She smiled wanly, and her weak hand hit the ground. As her thick-lashed lids closed, she wheezed. Then her lungs failed.

Ahmed cradled her body in his arms. The world around him blurred, colors bleeding into each other. Then, as the mental aftershocks of experiencing something akin to death overwhelmed him, he slipped into unconsciousness.

Ahmed barged into the visiting Secretary of Defense's office. "You killed her!" he shouted belligerently.

Cornelius jumped from the chair behind his desk. "Security, escort this man out of my office!"

Two men rushed in and seized Ahmed by the arms.

He writhed and thrashed against his subduers' grip, hands clawing for Cornelius' throat.

"How the hell did he get in here?" asked the bearded security officer.

"He forged a level-three pass somehow," his colleague replied. "Tricky bastard."

"Don't worry, Sir, we'll get him outta your sight." The bearded officer yanked on Ahmed's arm. "C'mon, asshole."

Cornelius gestured for them to halt. "Wait a moment." He

moved around his desk with deliberate slowness, hands clasped behind his back. He clutched Ahmed's jaw, fingers digging into bone. "What have I done to . . . unhinge you, Guardian, hmm?"

Ahmed's eyes were bloodshot from tears of rage. "One of the people killed today during the miners' strike was my lover. Her name was Priscilla Kitzron. And it was *you* who killed her! You and your damned permission to use lethal force whenever! Everything falls back on you, you heartless son of a bitch!"

There wasn't a trace of remorse in Cornelius' icy eyes. "No, she got herself killed by revolting with her fellow miners," he said, his tone offensively cavalier.

"She wasn't a miner! She was a missionary from Eden taking a stand with people who'd become her friends!"

Cornelius let go of his Ahmed's jaw. "Whatever." He shrugged dismissively. His indifference was a slap in the face. "Either way, her death was her fault."

Ahmed screamed a primal, heart-wrenching sound.

Cornelius said to his security officers, "Go ahead, remove this vermin from my sight."

The officers hauled Ahmed out of the office.

He received a dishonorable discharge after that act of defiance, and he had no regrets . . .

Wanting to take down the Commonwealth Government, Reza saw the Coalition as a godsend. It was exactly what he had prayed for: his own army.

He had declared that his army would be different from the CDF. It wouldn't employ the cutthroat tactics Gould had sanctioned. It would only kill when absolutely necessary. The torture of prisoners or the rape of women would be severely punished. The Coalition would be a fighting force guided by high moral standards.

Reza initially told his troops the plan for Hammer Fall was to expose the government's corruption by seizing the Parliament Building's broadcast center. Then he'd work with the people and righteous politicians to create a new, equitable government. But months ago, his vision shifted. He concluded: *He* knew what was best, *he* knew the direction the Commonwealth should take, *he* had the solutions for helping the colonies.

He didn't want to risk a new government enacting an agenda that diverged from his. He didn't want to deal with disagreements or red tape. To ensure his vision prevailed, he decided his leadership was all the Commonwealth needed for the foreseeable future. He didn't care if people labeled him a dictator.

After releasing the information indicting the corrupt politicians, Reza knew the people of Eden wouldn't feel a shred of sympathy for them, or for the Eight Elite. But he also knew they wouldn't want him to become the overall ruler of the Commonwealth. They'd demand new leadership chosen through a democratic process. Well, too bad for them, he thought. There was no room for error. This wasn't a time to take chances.

A collaborative effort to build a new government meant the introduction of too many ideas, the clash of differing viewpoints. Reza already had the blueprint. And his blueprint was the only one that mattered, the only one that needed to be enacted.

He also decided the corrupt needed to face true justice. Leaving their fate to the judiciary system, especially Cornelius', was out of the question. He'd be the sword of justice, the overall juror of the wicked. And his sentence for them would be death. The executions would definitely include Cornelius and the Eight families.

He wrestled with this decision. He still wanted his soldiers to believe in the ethos he had established, the ideals that made them better than the CDF. But as a man's positions and conclusions evolved, so did he.

Doubt crept into his conscience as he continued gazing out over the deck. Was this new direction, this compromise in his belief system, truly the right way to go?

The familiar warmth of a gentle hand graced his shoulder. A warmth that could only belong to . . . her. But he knew that warmth was an illusion manifested by his cerebral implant. The Quilgarian tech was using his mental transcript of Priscilla's distinct touch to recreate past sensory experiences.

Priscilla's disembodied serene voice said, *Know that you are doing the right thing, my beloved.* Her likeness materialized, glowing softly. She wore the white dress from their first date.

But—

She pressed a finger against Reza's lips. The touch felt astonishingly real. *Shhhh, you know Gould must be killed,* she said. *And you can't risk letting anyone else build a new government except for you. Don't let what I fought for be in vain.*

A lump formed in Reza's throat. *No, never.*

Then do what must be done. Priscilla faded back into his mental diary, along with her comforting presence.

Reza blinked back tears. It felt good being consoled by her, even if she was only a hallucination. And no, there was no going back to the original plan. He realized what he had to do to usher in the next chapter of the New Humanity.

• • •

Randy had gone back to the hut. He'd already showered and changed clothes before Kesley entered. Sitting on the bed, he reflected on his conversation with Reza, the upcoming operation, the government corruption, and the CDF's misuse of military power and lack of accountability.

When he completed BCT and MOS training, his outlook on the war was simple: The Coalition was the enemy, the CDF was the galaxy's righteous warriors, and his father was a murderer and traitor that needed to be taken out. But now he'd been enlightened.

Basic Training conditioned Guardians to believe that the Coalition and anyone who opposed the Commonwealth Government were the enemy. But Randy learned the Coalition's intentions were noble, and he found out Arson wasn't the villain he had once thought him to be. And though he disagreed with Arson's decision to leave his family and fight for the Coalition, he realized it wasn't right to assassinate the man's character.

The Coalition wasn't the enemy. The CDF wasn't the enemy. Arson wasn't the enemy. The true enemies were Gould, corrupt politicians, and the Eight Elite, along with widespread ignorance and a system that discriminated against colonists. The Coalition was the force dedicated to defeating them. But there was something about Reza Randy wasn't on board with.

Kesley was leaning against a wall, arms folded. "You haven't said much since we left Reza's sanctuary," she commented.

"Not much to say," Randy replied tersely.

"Well, what do you think of Reza? You satisfied since you got a chance to talk to him mano a mano?"

Randy squared his jaw, distrust registering across his face. "Right now, I find it hard to trust many people. We'll see what happens after Operation Hammer Fall."

Kesley laughed. "Such a tight-ass."

Randy got up from the bed, brows knitted. "*Excuse me* for being skeptical. We're bringing this war for colony equality to Eden soil. We could very well kick-start humanity's next holocaust if things go wrong. I think I have a good reason to be a little antsy, don't you think?" Stacie suddenly entered his thoughts, and he began pacing in a circle.

"Would you sit down and take it easy," Kesley said.

"I'm just thinking about a . . . friend of mine, a Guardian."

"The woman you mentioned? Stacie? The one who was out cold when I picked you up at Bravo Force's camp?"

"Yeah, I hope she's okay. And . . . to be honest, I'm still not sure if I'm doing the right thing here."

Kesley sighed and sashayed up to Randy, hips swaying and lips smiling. She slapped her hands onto his shoulders, making him wince. "Stop pacing and sulking, Mr. Worrywart." She chuckled. Randy frowned in response. "Relax, we're about to change the *entire* Commonwealth for the better."

Randy raised an eyebrow—a silent "screw-you" gesture. "Relax? You want me to relax at a time like this? I don't think—"

Kesley fused her lips to his, silencing him.

Blindsided again by an uninvited—but not unwelcome—kiss, Randy gently pried her off him. Color rose in his cheeks. "Um, I'm sorry. I can't—" His mind flashed back to Kesley slipping off her shirt at her home, and to the kiss she planted on him that day. Suddenly, temptation ensnared him.

Kesley egged him on, necking him and sucking face, coming on stronger by the microsecond.

Randy's curious hands made an exploratory excursion over her voluptuous body, traveling the arc of her hips and groping her everywhere within reach. Losing self-control, he captured her well-fleshed backside in a vicious squeeze that made her loins rumble. His restraint was fading fast. Sex drive overtaking him, he ached to divest Kesley of her clothing.

Thinking of Stacie, Randy rejected Kesley's advances, pulling himself away. "This can't happen, Kess. We should—"

Kesley put a finger to his lips, shushing him. "Lighten up, soldier boy. You need to forget about the CDF and all that other past crap. That's over. You're one of *us* now, a Coalition freedom fighter, and it's time to celebrate." Unwilling to cede, she pasted her lips to his again, melting away his protest.

Randy's mind and body urged him to give in and go for it. *No, that's enough,* he told himself, but kept touching Kesley through her clothes, imagining how it'd feel to touch her in the buff. He tried to force himself to desist to no avail, his desperation for sex growing worse.

Kesley backed him against a wall and crashed her lips into his like she owned him. Her kiss was a goddamn assault—wet, sloppy, and unrelenting. She drew back just enough to smirk, their shared spit glistening her lips.

"Knock it off, Kess. I mean it," Randy said mildly but sternly, trying to let her down easy.

Kesley molded her breasts to his chest and brought her mouth to his ear. "And if I say no?" Challenge laced her voice.

Before he could answer, she jammed her tongue into his mouth. She bit his bottom lip and then sucked it gently. Again, she kissed him, while brushing her fingers against the bulge in his pants.

Randy tried to muster some semblance of resistance. He wanted to stop this—he should stop this—but hell, it was hard to.

Thoughts of Stacie reentered his mind, and he tore his lips away from Kesley's. He clenched her biceps and spun her, trading places and pinning her against the wall to restrain her.

Kesley said playfully, "Right where you want me, huh?"

Randy let go of her arms and stepped back. "Enough. We're done." His expression told Kesley he was serious.

"Come on, let me properly reward you for saving me from that creep." Kesley dragged her shirt overhead, and her plump breasts spilled out from underneath.

Randy's eyes were drawn to her beautiful nipples and areolas.

Kesley took his wrist and flattened his hand against her right breast. "Go on, have your way with me." Torn between loyalty to Stacie and his undeniable attraction to this chesty redhead, Randy cupped a generous handful of the soft, supple mound, squeezing it possessively. Its shape felt good in his palm.

Kesley reached down, grabbed Randy's ass, and yanked him closer, plastering him against her salient proportions. She whispered, "I know you're angry, agitated, and stressed. Let me provide some relief. Make love to me. You know you want to."

Thoughts of Stacie prevented Randy from giving in. He craned his head away from Kesley. "I'm sorry, I can't. I—"

"What's wrong?" Kesley furrowed her brows. "Am I not fuckable enough for you?" Silence followed.

Randy glanced at her bare chest before diverting his eyes. He was stressed to the max, and Kesley was offering herself up to him as an outlet. His conscience and libido began playing tug-of-war.

Kesley's eyes narrowed into slits, and her lips pursed. "Fine, forget it." Feeling undesired and embarrassed, she turned to leave. "Maybe you just ain't man enough to handle an older woman," she muttered out of spite. "Maybe you're just a fucking kid who still has daddy issues. You can just—"

Randy's hand shot out, snatching Kesley's wrist. He pushed her down in front of him, the sound of her kneecaps hitting the floor audible. His fingers fumbled with his belt buckle, then nearly tore off his zipper.

As he shoved his pants and boxers halfway down, his aroused, rigid cock sprang free from confinement. Kesley was impressed with the length his pants had concealed.

In less than a beat, Randy had his cock stuffed in Kesley's mouth. His hand fisted a hunk of her hair, controlling her head as he jerked his hips back and forth. A part of him had longed to shut her sassy mouth in this manner.

She licked the underside of his member and swirled her tongue around its head, taunting the sensitive skin. She then opened her mouth wide and took in all his girth, slurping noisily.

With her lips tightly sealed around him, she pulled back in an extra-slow suck, only to devour him whole again.

Randy's conscience screamed at him, reminding him he had a girlfriend. He hated how much he wanted this, how horny he was right now. As he spontaneously sped his pace, Kesley's hands found purchase on his thighs. He drove his cock past her uvula, lodging it in her throat, and ejaculated.

After a strangled, gurgling sound left Kesley, she gulped. Then she released him. Cum and saliva drizzled down her chin.

Still horny, Randy fed his cock to her again. A thrill arose when her nose smacked his pelvis. Gripping her skull, he forced her head to move in sync with his rhythm. Her mouth wasn't the orifice he truly wanted, but it would have to suffice—a compromise between his sexual desires and his commitment to Stacie.

Kesley took him like a pro, her lips, tongue, and teeth working together to ravish him.

Randy had to admit that the sight of her slavishly sucking his cock while sitting on her heels topless was a huge turn-on.

But as he continued deep-throating her, a small voice in the back of his mind told him wrong was still wrong. The clarity hit, and he mustered the discipline to withdraw from her mouth.

Guilt and shame washed over him. Enough was enough. It was time to leave and get his head together.

Before he could zip up, Kesley stood and wrapped her hand

around his still-hard dick, stroking it. "Are we gonna fuck or not?"

Randy said, "I can't—" Just then, Kesley fondled him demandingly. His resolve was now hanging by a thread.

He clutched Kesley's wrist to halt her advances, but he failed to actually remove her hand, her caress so damn soothing.

Kesley said, "Look me in the eye and tell me you don't wanna get it on tonight, don't *need* to." She stroked faster, pushing Randy closer to capitulation. She literally had him by the dick.

Succumbing to seduction, Randy latched onto her hair, pulled her head back, and clamped his mouth over hers. Kissing a path down her body, he suckled the hardened peaks of her breasts. As he indulged, his erection burgeoned even more.

Kesley's body was thick, fleshy, and curvy. It was a succulent, gorgeous shape, and he couldn't resist this opportunity to feel and taste it. Right now, he was dying to get her panties off.

Kesley helped him out of his shirt, fingers skimming his taut muscles. In turn, he worked her shorts down her legs. Then he stripped himself naked in a frenzy.

Randy hoisted Kesley up by her shapely thighs and dumped her onto the bed. Tresses tumbled over her forehead in a sexy disarray.

Like a vulture on carrion, Randy clawed her panties' waistband and tugged. The fabric slid down her broad hips with a whisper of resistance, electrifying him. He yanked more aggressively this time, and the stubborn material surrendered, emitting a sharp, exhilarating *rip* that made his pulse race. He wanted her goddamn panties gone. One final, determined pull tore them clean off, turning them into refuse. Almost instinctively, he crushed them in his fists before hurling them across the room.

Randy sank his knees into the mattress on each side of Kesley, an animalistic thirst in his eyes. Her naked body lay sprawled out before him; it would take a superhuman effort not to fuck her.

Kesley said, "Hey, I can't conceive children, so don't be afraid to go all out, if you know what I mean."

Adrenaline and testosterone building, Randy was more than ready for the coup de grâce. He reached below and wedged his stiff member into Kesley inch by inch, savoring every second. As he plugged himself all the way into her cleft, a wheeze of elation escaped her lungs, and her back arched, breasts jutting upward. After pulling out almost entirely, he plunged back inside her.

Thoughts of his jeopardized career as a Guardian, his strained relationship with his father, and the ceaseless stresses of war consumed Randy's mind. These frustrations fueled every punch of his cock into Kesley's willing body.

"Harder," she gasped. "Don't hold back. Let it all out." She was begging him to harness the anger inside him to amplify her own pleasure, anger he'd been harboring since his mother's death. It was a mutual exchange, a balance of needs—his release for her satisfaction. She was into being dominated and manhandled in the bedroom, something all her partners found stimulating.

Randy was happy to grant her request. He clamped his hands around her ankles and forced her legs to fold back until her joints cricked. He now had her knees smashed against her shoulders, so he could drill deeper into her. His grip intensified as he fucked her into the mattress, cock dunking into her at a downward angle.

Randy accelerated, his tempo feral—savage. He hammered into Kesley with the untamed, primal energy of a man pushed to his limits by life. His future in limbo, he was desperate to unload all the tension roiling inside him. Every sobering thrust into Kesley seemed like catharsis.

It wasn't long before she was a trembling wreck. She relished being fucked as roughly as possible—nothing compared to it.

She struggled to breathe as an orgasm slammed into her. She

came so hard she saw stars, and couldn't even think.

Still holding her ankles down, Randy stretched her legs wider, more harshly than intended. Her submissive body squirmed in ecstasy, every inch of him impaling her nonstop.

"K-keep going," she panted. *Show me what your dick can do.*

Randy's cock became a battering ram, its head pounding her cervix with each vigorous stroke. *This is what you wanted, Kess,* he thought. She'd given him permission to go no-holds-barred, to fuck her senseless. So he kept spearing her relentlessly.

After pulling out, Randy turned Kesley belly-down and yanked her hips into the air. The sight of her bent over—face down, ass up—rocketed tingles up his spine. He ran his eyes over the fullness of both cheeks, then slapped his hands onto them. A resounding *whack* reverberated through the room. He kneaded *all* her ass meat with total abandon, feeling it mash against his fingers.

Not wasting another second, he buried himself to the hilt inside her. The recoil of her ass flogged him as his hips worked.

Soon, a cacophony of clapping noises filled the room, flesh striking flesh without pause.

Believing he'd gotten his fill, Randy reached down to extract himself. Kesley's rear cheeks quivered as he snapped his hips back, a wet *plop* punctuating his exit. Thick, gooey strands of neohuman cum sagged between the head of his shaft and her entrance.

As she tried to push herself up, Randy clutched the back of her neck, keeping her facedown. "No, not yet," he commanded gently. He hadn't gotten his fix after all. He rammed into her again, his thrusts rocking her forward and rubbing her face against the mattress.

Every bed-shaking thud of his hips rippled Kesley's ass. While clinging to the sheets, she bit down on them, muffling a choked whimper that was half protest, half desperate plea for more.

Randy entwined her arms behind her back in a tight crisscross and threshed her cheeks with the full brunt of his loins.

Kesley was in absolute submission, letting him do as he pleased. It had him pumped up. There were no parameters given to him. Anything and everything was welcomed by her—as long as it wasn't harmful and was consensual.

He pulled out and flipped her onto her back. His cock was still thick and throbbing. He grabbed her thighs and spread-eagled them. Then he lined himself up and embedded his cock in her. The impact nearly made her eyes protrude from their sockets.

While Kesley cried out in ecstasy, Randy's mind became a battlefield, the image of his mother's death flashing behind his eyes. He saw the explosion, the flames, the fucking nothingness that was left. Kesley had volunteered to be his outlet, and he had promised himself he'd "hold nothing back," as she requested.

The bed frame shuddered and groaned, screws threatening to pop loose, but he didn't give a damn. Let the bed break.

Kesley took Randy's wrists and maneuvered his hands to her throat. "C'mon, get a little rougher, a little freaky," she demanded, her voice low and seductive. *Don't disappoint me, soldier boy.*

Randy pressed his thumbs against her windpipe, not hard enough to completely restrict her breathing, just enough to stifle a groan. And the masochist in her loved it. He smothered her mouth with his to mute the next groan—a kiss that was more bite than lips.

He then moved his hands from her neck to her shoulders, his full weight pinning her down. His thrusts were a steady force that wouldn't let up—an overwhelming force.

"Harder," Kesley begged. "Give me the roughest you've got."

Her demand was a balm on the angry fire engulfing every cell in Randy's body, music to his ears. His cock pistoned in and out of her dripping slit like a machine that couldn't switch off.

Kesley's nipples stiffened into pebbled cylinders, noticeably jutting out for attention. Leaning down, Randy imprisoned one inside his mouth, teeth grazing the morsel just enough to make Kesley mewl. As he suctioned her other nipple, she writhed beneath him, hyperventilating.

One push into her after another, he fell deeper into a trance that made him forget everything but her intoxicating presence.

"Oh, shit," Kesley hissed. A seismic orgasm hit her. Randy continued to fuck her through the convulsions quaking her body, his cock disappearing balls-deep into her over and over.

As if it were a remedy to his bottled-up frustrations, he pummeled the area between her wide-open thighs at an unrestrained pace, satisfying both their needs.

Kesley wound her legs around him, commanding him to bring it—to do his worst. *This is what I want. Fuck me.* Her heels dug into his ass, cramming his cock as far down as it could go.

With a final, ferocious stab—one pleasing to Kesley—he came. His cum filled her to the brim, oozing out of her and pooling on the sheets. He yanked his cock out, done painting her insides white.

Coming down off the adrenaline rush, his entire body seemed to breathe a sigh of relief. Taking a break, he collapsed beside Kesley. His erection remained rock-hard, pointed toward the ceiling and coated in his jizz—and still spurting.

Kesley had heard stories about the unreal prowess of Highborn men in bed. It seemed the rumors were accurate. However, she hadn't anticipated an experience so orgasmic, so incredible.

She closed her eyes. "So, finally worn out, huh?" she huffed with a laugh. Her eyes popped open when she felt Randy's tongue lick a trail of saliva up her thigh. Rest time was over. She didn't even have time to gather herself before Randy was on her again.

Sparing not one bit of Kesley's flesh, he dropped slobbery kisses all over her body and plucked on her erect nipples.

Insatiable, he dragged her closer, sliding her across the sheets. After shoving her legs apart again, he teased her soaked entrance using the head of his cock. Apparently, he wasn't done yet.

In a sudden move, Kesley rolled their bodies. Now on top, she mounted him—impaling herself on his cock.

Delight drove him crazy as she glided up and down his length, clapping her ass against him. She was a woman on a mission to claim him, to fuck him.

The beads of sweat tracing the curves of her body dripped onto his chest as she worked.

With a quick motion of her hand, she flipped back the hair that had cascaded over her shoulder. Then she paused her hips. "So, you done doubting the Coalition?" she asked, breathing raggedly.

Randy said in an irate tone, "Shut it. I'm still not convinced Operation Hammer Fall is the right move, *okay?*"

Kesley scowled. She had shown him the colonies' deplorable conditions, and he'd seen her nearly get raped, yet he was still waffling? Fuck that. An inferno ignited within her. She viciously jerked her hips, riding him with a ferocity that was almost cruel.

"Damn it, Kess," Randy grunted, "ease up."

Kesley was beyond taking it easy. She was sick of his indecision. "No," she said aggressively, nails scratching his pecs. If he insisted on being so obstinate about joining the Coalition, she figured maybe she'd use him for sex and then be done with him.

Randy was fed up with her too—fed up with her pushiness, her taunts. He counter-fucked her, upthrusting into her and dribbling her jiggly ass cheeks between his fingers.

Kesley retaliated and matched his aggression, grinding herself against him. She clenched her walls around his cock, like she was trying to strangle it.

Randy and Kesley were now simply hate-fucking each other. And Randy was determined to win the skirmish.

Irritation from her calling him "soldier boy" and prodding him boiled over. He jackhammered into her punishingly until euphoria had her whimpering, her head snapping back and arms going limp at her sides in defeat. He'd won the skirmish. *So much for her temper tantrum.* He grabbed her waist, burying his cock so deep he swore he could feel her heartbeat against its tip.

He sat up and leaned all the way forward, toppling Kesley backward. As her back met the mattress again, his cock slipped out of her. Barely a tenth of a second went by before he reentered.

He continuously crashed his hips into hers, a fresh dose of adrenaline in his system. There was no lull, no respite—just consecutive, unyielding thrusts. And his tongue raided her mouth with the same dominance. The urge to fuck her was inescapable.

Kesley rocked uncontrollably beneath Randy, her overstimulated body unsure if it wanted more or wanted to escape for a reprieve. Her moans devolved into desperate, incoherent utterances as he drove into her obsessively. She couldn't string together a single word, only gasp for oxygen.

Randy had gotten Kesley buck naked for one reason: to gratify himself. And for all he knew, this could be his last night in bed with a woman. So he was going to maximize it—fuck Kesley until she couldn't take any more.

Losing himself in his desires, he fastened his mouth on her breasts, while squishing his pelvis against hers, and clamped his teeth down on a tight, throbbing nipple.

Kesley broke out in shivers, and she slapped her hands over her face as if she'd reached her breaking point.

But Randy wasn't about to let her tap out—not yet. This was the home stretch. He wrestled her hands away from her face and crushed her wrists to the mattress. His eyes warned her to brace herself for the finale—and she expected him to deliver.

Since Kesley derived so much pleasure from pain, Randy wrapped his hands around her throat and choked her just enough to blur the line between agony and arousal.

"That all you got?" Kesley panted, continuing to push him.

Randy tightened his fingers, watching her teeter on the brink of unconsciousness. This almost felt criminal—but so good.

Kesley coughed, spewing saliva as her eyes rolled back. Randy didn't let up. She'd agreed to be his plaything tonight, given him certain liberties, and he intended to finish on a high note. He slammed into her without mercy, filling her again and again. His thrusts pulverized her cervix like he was trying to grind it into dust.

He looked for her to give him a sign that he was going too far; she gave none. She craved the edge, the abandon, the moment when control slipped away. It lit something inside her. She wasn't just allowing this; she was urging him on. She was daring him.

He accepted her challenge, keeping up his hyperaggressive pace. She'd probably wake up sore tomorrow.

When he let go of her throat, she gasped desperately for air. Using one hand, he smashed her face sideways into the mattress, and then he pounded so forcefully that cum splashed out around his shaft. After emptying himself inside her, he wiped his cock in his palm and smeared cum over her stomach and breasts—as if branding her as his. But the night wasn't over yet.

CHAPTER SEVEN

Under a gazebo, a spindly pale priest with wizened skin stood on a round platform. He finished Jared Kerner's eulogy, ending with "Amen."

Solemn-faced family members in dark clothing, including Jared's wife and child, rose from the white plastic chairs surrounding the platform. They wept and sniffled.

Cornelius walked up to Mei Ling. "You have my condolences," he said. "Jared was a fine man." He actually managed to sound authentic.

"Thank you," Mei Ling said, strangling a sob. In one arm, she cradled the tricornered Commonwealth flag—a gift customary to the ceremony—that had been given to her. Taking her daughter's small hand, she said, "Come, dear." She wiped at her eyes as she and her daughter made their way to the parking lot. "Thank you again, Chief Gould."

The gazebo emptied, leaving only Cornelius and Thom Kerner behind.

Thom gazed out at the headstones of deceased servicemen,

servicewomen, and dignitaries. Beyond the grand stone markers, a coruscating blue ocean stretched to the horizon.

"Again, I'm sorry about your son, my friend," Cornelius said.

A warm wind brushed their faces.

"I won't pretend my son was some prime example of manhood or set the bar for excellence, but"—Thom sighed—"he didn't deserve to be murdered by these Coalition treasonists."

His son's murderer continued his charade. "Yes, and these treasonists will pay for their cowardly crime."

Thom closed his eyes, reserving a moment of silence for his son. When he reopened them, he said, "Tell me, Cornelius, what of Area 14?"

"Still fully funded and operational. I would never allow our work to be disbanded. I'm actually heading there after I depart from here. Of course, I kept the program a secret from Jared. I had to. He would've terminated it otherwise."

"Yes, he would have," Thom agreed, knowing his son all too well.

"I will move the Commonwealth toward self-sufficiency and cut the Union's leash, just as we planned."

Thom nodded. "Yes, all in due time."

The two old war veterans shook hands and parted ways.

Cornelius' limo and a three-car motorcade sped down a winding solar-paneled street bordered by a mossy green bog.

In the wake of the Union's harsh ultimatum—to end the civil war within five days—and Jared Kerner's assassination, which Cornelius had pinned on the Coalition, fear and apprehension gripped the Parliament. Under pressure, many of Cornelius' critics granted him the authority to proceed as he saw fit to achieve the

Union's desired outcome, which was exactly what he had hoped would happen.

They finally permitted him to initiate surveillance on Governess Hayley, whom the CDF suspected of aiding the Coalition. He also immediately signed an executive order halting the issuance of travel passes, fully quarantining Satellite One's population from the rest of humanity.

Conlan had dispatched an intelligence team to Colony Five. He informed Cornelius they intercepted communications between Hayley and Arman Reza, giving Cornelius all the justification he needed to deploy troops and impose martial law.

"When the occupation force arrives in Colony Five, they'll take Hayley into custody, and we'll get answers," Cornelius said to Gillian, who sat beside him. "Perhaps she'll even lead us to Reza's whereabouts. I will also be expanding our martial-law operations in colonies One, Four, and Six. We'll deploy unmanned aerial drones to monitor sector zones and track movement into and out of private residences, and troop numbers will be raised. The Coalition *will* be flushed out."

Jared Kerner had objected to the idea of omnipresent surveillance. He believed drone use would infringe on citizens' privacy. He thought people should at least have the freedom to move about unmonitored. Patrols were ample enough for him. But Cornelius harbored no such qualms.

"I damn well hope the Commonwealth loses its incorporated status," Cornelius said. "We'd be better off. But it's my colleagues' belief in the Union's usefulness, and their fear of losing them as allies, that pushed them into giving me more authority to deal with the Coalition."

"It's like you taught me: Fear is one of the greatest weapons at your disposal," Gillian commented. She looked out the window at the foggy wetland. The scenery held a beautiful yet eerie ambiance that felt tranquil to her.

Small green arboreal creatures hopped and croaked among the trees, bushes, and bramble.

"How long before we reach Area 14?" Gillian asked.

"Not long."

Cornelius and Gillian were on their way to Area 14, a secret military arms-development site where the next evolution in Defense Force weaponry was being created. Cornelius kept the site's existence hidden from the Parliament and the public because of the unsanctioned weapons in development there.

Only he and Thom Kerner knew it existed. He had even kept it off Jared's radar. The former Chief, whose freewheeling nature was a noted fault, had simply let Cornelius handle all military matters, including arms development, without his personal oversight. Jared never kept himself abreast of where the military's funding went. He trusted Cornelius completely. It was just another responsibility Jared didn't want to be bothered with. If he could shirk a duty and delegate it, he did, and left it at that.

Gillian waited anxiously. Cornelius had promised she would bear witness to groundbreaking feats of military technology no one could yet fathom. He hadn't told her, however, that unsanctioned experiments were in progress.

She couldn't imagine anything surpassing the feats of the plasma-energy weaponry and mechanized combatwear that alien tech had helped develop. The arms in production at Area 14 were the reason Cornelius was confident the Commonwealth could defend itself without Union support.

The bog transitioned into a more eye-pleasing flatland. A short distance later, the limo arrived at a windowless oval facility with a gray exterior. There was a menacing phyocrete wall encircling its perimeter, and there were no signs indicating its purpose.

Cornelius lowered his window. As soon as the guard in the security booth saw the Chief, he punched in a code on his console. Then the security wall's gate slid open.

The limo and motorcade followed an access road leading to the rear of the facility. Gillian's brows quirked when she heard an earth-shaking clang. She wondered what could make such a colossal sound. The limo passed a sign that said WARNING! TESTING GROUND AHEAD! The noise grew louder.

The limo rolled to a slow stop. Gillian's heart lurched at the intimidating sight before her.

A thirty-foot-tall mechanized contraption of neutral grays, with rotary gun-cannons for arms, stomped over the phyocrete grounds. Winged, orb-shaped aerial drones banked downward at the giant metal monstrosity. They fired twin pairs of missiles. Air around the machine vibrated and crackled. An energy shield blossomed, intercepting the projectiles, then shimmered out.

The mech's gun-cannons spun up and ejected a stream of rounds, tearing the drones from the sky.

Through a nearby tower's megaphone, a man said, "Test one complete!"

The mech's cannons whined to a stop, steaming and hissing.

Cornelius exited the limo.

Gillian followed. "Incredible," she said.

Cornelius grinned proudly as he admired Area 14's invention. "Yes, we call it a Juggernaut. Weapons of war like this will enhance our forces' combat capability in the occupied colonies and across all Mission Worlds."

Gillian pointed at a young Guardian standing near the mech. "Wait . . . is he controlling that machine via cerebral interface?"

"Yes," Cornelius confirmed.

Gillian's face hinted at her indignation. This was morally wrong. The only authorized implant modification was for Shell CPU interface. Cerebral implants weren't supposed to control military devices such as flyers, vehicles, or war bots like this. "But it's unlawful to reformat a cerebral implant for that!" she protested.

Cornelius answered mildly. "I plan on getting that changed soon."

Gillian chided him, saying, "Yes, but until then, it's prohibited, and if we're discovered, we'd be—"

"Quiet," Cornelius cut her off. "The Parliament is blind to everything happening here, as is the rest of the Commonwealth. We're not going to be discovered."

Gillian's face betrayed her discomfort.

"Initiating test two!" blared the voice from the tower.

Seven drones converged on the Guardian. With a thought, he malfunctioned two of them, and gravity sent them crashing to the ground. He took control of two others and fired their weapons at the remaining drones, destroying them. He then made the two he had mindjacked crash into each other. Their wrecked metal forms plummeted to the ground.

Gillian watched wordlessly. Implants weren't supposed to be modified to hack electronic systems. *This isn't right.*

"Test two complete," the tower operator announced. "Good job, Private Salcedo."

The private smiled, proud of his performance. But an explosive headache altered his expression into one of horror. He clutched his head and screamed his throat raw, crumbling to the ground.

Two medics in white rushed over. One took a knee and checked Salcedo's vitals using a handheld forensic scanner. The device beeped, flashing a grim notice. Salcedo's life had come to an abrupt end.

Gillian stared in shock. "Wha-?"

"Yes," Cornelius said with regret, "we're still in the beta phase of cerebral-implant modification. We have yet to fully mitigate the strain on the mind when operating a Juggernaut or hacking electronic systems. He lasted longer than the others, though."

Gillian gasped. "Others?"

"Yes, ten fatalities so far. But all for a good cause."

Gillian frowned. *So the end justifies the means?*

Another medic arrived, pushing a rolling capsule gurney.

Gillian said, "Were they aware they could die, being guinea pigs for these . . . experiments?"

The medics placed Salcedo in a white body bag and zipped it up.

"They knew there was risk involved," Cornelius responded emotionlessly.

Gillian, once a Guardian herself, could no longer contain her outrage. Her voice hardened. "What of their families?"

The medics deposited Salcedo into the gurney.

Cornelius said, "Their families were told they were deployed to a colony or were on a tour of service for a protectorate. As far as they will know, their children died nobly in combat."

A lie, Gillian thought. Heat flooded her veins. She had been on board with Jared Kerner's assassination, believing he was a threat to the Commonwealth, but exploiting innocent soldiers, in the name of strengthening the CDF, was extreme.

Cornelius, not one to listen to diatribes for too long, stepped off and motioned for Gillian to follow. "Come, let us go inside. There are more marvels for you to witness."

Part of Gillian didn't want to know what other illegal machinations were being concocted in this clandestine program.

They crossed the width of the testing ground and entered a

metal back door set into the phyocrete wall of the building.

Trailing behind Cornelius down a quiet nondescript hall, Gillian wrestled with her thoughts. *This isn't okay,* she kept telling herself silently, but she was trying to convince herself otherwise. She had placed too much faith in her mentor's leadership to abandon it now.

They turned into another hall.

Ahead, two double doors parted as they neared, revealing a laboratory. Inside, men and women in white lab coats spoke scientific jargon.

On a bed, a Guardian in battledress sat upright.

A gray-bearded scientist studied the data displayed on the beside monitor. "How are you feeling?" he asked the Guardian.

"Just a little woozy," he replied.

"So what's going on here?" Gillian asked Cornelius, unenthused.

"More implant modification. This lab compiles data from all the Nerve Centers on Eden, Satellite One, and every Mission World. After thorough case evaluations, I determined that, despite the CDF's mental conditioning, one major issue is that some Guardians begin to feel empathy for our enemies, such as the Falgoah or the Coalition."

Cornelius tapped a sequence of buttons on a computer panel. Case files of "enemy sympathizing" involving Guardians flashed by on a screen, including Ahmed Hawsawi's.

"The implant updates being made here include empathy dampening, only while Guardians are in their Shells," Cornelius said. "It's for the best. Empathy is an Achilles' heel. Guardians must perform at their peak when engaged in combat. These . . . feelings simply get in the way. The modifications will lead to a more focused, sharper soldier, one unburdened by emotions that might compromise their fighting ability."

Gillian grunted. What Cornelius was proposing was altering the human psyche, creating Guardians stripped of sensitivity and mercy while in combat. To her, sensitivity and mercy, tempered by proper judgment, were virtues.

Cornelius believed he was acting in Guardians' best interests, but to Gillian, these implant modifications didn't seem congruent with his intentions.

Seeing Gillian's discomfort, Cornelius gripped her shoulders delicately and softened his tone—a rare show of compassion from such a blackhearted man. "Gillian, listen. I can see you're uneasy about what I've shown you. But I need you to have faith in me, as you always have. I know what's best for the Commonwealth and the CDF."

Speaking ever so persuasively, Cornelius continued his bid for Gillian's trust. "For goodness' sake, I was a soldier too. It's not my intention to extinguish a Guardian's life if it can be avoided. What's being done here is for the betterment of all Guardians. They need this technology. It will lead to a stronger, more efficient fighting force and a reduction in Guardian casualties. This is what's best for the CDF."

Coaxed into acceptance, Gillian said wistfully, "Fine."

"Come, let's leave and get a meal. You've seen enough."

They left Area 14.

•••

Knuckles rapped against the door of Randy and Kesley's hut.

"Hey, Randy, you up yet, man?" came Jarius' voice from behind the door. "Training starts in a couple of minutes."

Randy stirred awake. "I'll be right out," he muttered sleepily, rubbing his eyes.

He and Kesley lay tangled together naked atop the rumpled,

cum-stained bedsheets, their body sweat commingling.

Sleeping quietly without a stitch of clothing on, Kesley was an eyeful for Randy to wake up to.

Randy's implant piped sensations from last night into his body, causing a thrill to run down his spine. In a reflexive response, he splayed a hand across Kesley's rear end, caressing its pronounced shape.

He'd experienced the most carnal sex of his life, climaxing more times than he could remember. Kesley had consented to things other women never had—like letting him tie her arms to the headboard while he acted out his fantasies, even rousing her from sleep by thrusting into her whenever he craved more sex. He couldn't get enough; it was as if he'd been possessed. He'd never been with a woman so uninhibited, so kinky.

Already, he was getting hard again. But then he thought about Stacie. Flashbacks rushed through his mind: them enduring BCT together, him sitting by her bedside when she battled infection, dancing at the graduation banquet, and other moments of significance. Guilt seeped in. He had broken their covenant to stay exclusive and be in a committed relationship.

Last night, he fucked the heck out of a woman nine years older than him, had given her the best she ever had. For a young man fresh out of college and the Academy, it should have been a notch on his belt. In the heat of the moment, it was thrilling, but now he felt stupid for jeopardizing his relationship with Stacie all for the short-term satisfaction of a one-night stand.

Randy peeled himself away from Kesley and scooted out of bed.

After washing off under the shower spigot, he walked to the clothing rack and got dressed in a khaki T-shirt and dark green trousers.

While he laced his boots, dread gnawed at him. What would happen when Stacie found out he had sex with another woman? He could try to keep last night firewalled from her, but she'd know something was up. And he didn't want to lie to her.

He'd just made his life more complicated. *Way to go, Randal.* He glanced back at Kesley, who was still asleep. *Last night was a mistake, a dumb mistake. What came over me?*

He valued the positive influence both Stacie and Kesley had on his life, and he found them both attractive. He even had a crush on Kesley. But his heart was with Stacie. She was the woman he truly loved and wanted to build a future with. He knew he had majorly screwed up. He should've left the hut to distance himself from the temptation of getting into bed with Kesley.

Randy finished tying his boots, gripped the door handle, and pulled slowly. Hinges squeaked.

He quietly stepped outside, where Jarius and Sariah were waiting for him.

Jarius wore a black T-shirt and a pair of beige camo-pattern trousers. Sariah was already in her Reldaldri mechsuit, now being referred to as a Hardsuit.

"Let's get going," Randy said in a serious tone.

Sariah strode forward. "Alright, boys, follow me."

The trio trekked down a steep grassy hill, Sariah leading the way.

"So," Jarius said to Sariah, "are we gonna get the chance to try on those fancy Hardsuits and do some hands-on training?"

"Of course," she replied. "You're not just getting a demo. Two men will meet us at the training site with your suits."

"Awesome." Jarius then pinged Randy's implant.

"Yeah, right," Randy whispered, "we're cool, but not that cool."

"C'mon, man, just for a few minutes. Don't want her to hear

what I have to say."

"Alright, fine, just for a few minutes." Randy accepted Jarius' Link request.

Jarius' lips spread into an intrusive smile. *<So, how was it banging an older woman? The babe's got almost a decade on you, right?>*

Randy had a beleaguered look plastered across his face. He had kept his intimate night with Kesley mentally shielded from any snooping. *<What are you talking about?>* he asked, faking cluelessness, but he was doing a poor job of it, judging by his blushing face.

Jarius chuckled. *<I ain't no idiot, dude. You don't sleep with a smoking-hot man-trap like that and not smash her. Besides, I happened to walk by and couldn't help but eavesdrop a little. I heard more than socializing going on, if you know what I mean.>*

<Is my personal business all you wanted to bug me about?>

Jarius shook his head. *<I've been wondering if this is worth it. I'm convinced these rebels are good people, but do you really think we can go up against the CDF and pull this invasion crap off without a hitch?>*

<Don't know about 'without a hitch,' but I think our odds are . . . fifty-fifty.>

With arched brows, Jarius said, *<And that's enough for you?>*

Randy shrugged. *<It's gonna have to be, because there's no going back to the company. Not for me, anyway. You can still opt out of this and go back, though. Is that what you want?>*

Jarius pondered. *<Nah, guess I'm in this for the long haul with you, bro.>*

Waterfalls, green trees, and unusual plant life made the walk quite scenic.

Randy knew he or Arson might well die in the battle ahead. Was it time to stop being standoffish and try to mend fences with his father?

Go ahead, do it, Kathleen's melodious voice echoed inside Randy's mind. *What would it hurt?*

No, Mom. N-O, no. His reply sounded resolute.

This battle might be the last time you see each other. Either of you could be killed, Randy. For the last twenty-four hours, you've been thinking about Linking with your father. That would allow him to feel and understand your pain. It would allow you to feel the love he has for me, and the love he has for you. Are you afraid that exposure will soften your heart? Are you afraid that love will dissolve your anger and remind you why you once revered your father?

The trio arrived at a grassy clearing surrounded by trees. There was an immense lake in the middle of it. "This is it," Sariah said. "This is where we'll train."

His thoughts interrupted, Kathleen's voice left Randy's mind.

Sariah stood facing her trainees, ready to prime them for combat. "Hardsuits operate both similarly to and differently from a Shell. They're similar in that they're thought-operated," she began. She pointed to the tech around her head. "We don't have implants. This neural-sensor headset allows cerebral interfacing by scanning brain activity and transmitting our thought-commands to the CPU." The headset, created with alien technology far too complex for her to understand, was something she avoided going into detail about.

"A Shell's CPU is inside the helmet." She turned around. "The Hardsuit's CPU is located inside the diamond-shaped protrusion midway down the back." She pivoted to face forward again. "A regenerative alloy makes up parts of this suit's armor," she explained. "From what little I understand, it's basically a composite of artificial, robotic cell-like organisms. When the suit takes damage, these nanites self-replicate to repair it."

"Do these suits have an AI Combat Assistant like Shells?" Randy asked.

"Negative," Sariah replied.

Randy wondered who had the superior hardware. Shells might've had a helpful, invaluable AI assistant, but they couldn't self-repair, meaning they couldn't absorb as much damage as the rebels' Hardsuits. And from what little Randy had seen, Hardsuits might even have a slight edge when it came to energy-based firepower.

During the attack on Arson's base, he'd seen a single energy sphere splatter a shelled Guardian all over the bay, like what happened to Emilia. And according to his father, Hardsuits could sustain the use of plasma energy longer than Shells. They could also fly.

Sariah continued her instruction, covering the weapons cache and how to generate energy spheres using their hands.

Thirty minutes in, two Falgoah men on a hover skid brought Hardsuits for Randy and Jarius. It was time for some hands-on training.

• • •

Not particularly wanting to, but left with no choice, Stacie exercised her privileges as a daughter of the Eight. High-ranking military officials on Eden, well aware of who she was, granted her temporary leave from duty, much to Lars' displeasure.

She stood outside the gate of a CDF launch port, dressed in a semiformal chic red blazer, a black flexwear jumpsuit, and red zippered heels.

Clifton arrived in a luxury-class flyer to chauffeur her.

Stacie tapped her foot and clucked her tongue, patience waning. The second the flyer touched the ground, she picked up the black gear bag containing her clothes and scurried up to it.

The canopy hissed upward, and the rear cargo compartment clicked open.

Stacie slung her bag into the rear compartment, slammed the hood down, and plopped into the front passenger seat.

The canopy lowered and snapped shut.

Clifton took the flyer aloft, into moderate air traffic.

"Where are Mother and Father?" Stacie asked with an edge, disgusted by her parents' devious secrets. "I've been trying to call them since I got to the station," she added, tapping her wristcom.

"They're on Babylon Island with the other family heads for a recreational convocation and business assembly."

Stacie had been to the man-made island once, when she was seven. Faint preconscious memories, awakened by her cerebral implant, fast-forwarded through that day: women with fancy hairstyles in flashy regalia, men in pricey suits, hovering valet golems toting Highborns' luggage and shopping carryalls. The memory ended with her looking out the window of her father's limo at a beach packed with partying young adults drinking and laughing.

"Take me there. Now," she demanded.

Clifton winced at her pushy, assertive attitude. "You can't just disrupt a conclave whenever you—"

"The hell I can," Stacie snapped. She wasn't in the mood for any opposition whatsoever. "So take us there. That's an order."

The CDF launch port disappeared into the distance as the flyer sped past gleaming obelisk-shaped office towers.

An irritated expression crossed Clifton's face, deepening the grooves of his forehead. He thought Stacie needed to be verbally disciplined, but alas, he was merely a servant. After sighing away his protest, he said, "Just as bullheaded as your mother, I see."

"Then you can thank her for my stubbornness."

And your vicious tongue as well. Clifton veered into the left air lane, adjusting the flyer's trajectory to go to Babylon Island. "From your tone, I assume something is troubling you."

"Damn right." Stacie brought up a holo-menu from her wristcom and opened four files detailing her family's corrupt dealings, each in its own window. "Did you know about this?"

Clifton activated the flyer's autopilot. "Madam Spencer, your parents have amassed great wealth, and no, not all of it was earned by virtuous means. But that's how the game is played. The Eight families are profiteers. When they see an opportunity to profit—even at the expense of others—they take it.

"Their methods for generating wealth may not align with your moral tenets, but those methods allowed the Eight to become the alpha of humanity and live a lifestyle most people can't even comprehend.

"It was the Eight families' unfathomable wealth that protected them during the destruction of Earth Era, when pillagers, murderers, rapists, and scavengers ran amok in lawless streets devastated by Armageddon . . . when billions died from the aftereffects of alien biochem weapons unleashed by warmongering fools . . . when global environmental destruction caused by those same weapons ravaged the planet."

Clifton would never forget the downfall of Earth Era, every memory a grim reminder of humanity's darkest days. "Chronic drought. Food-supply shortages. Caustic rain eating the flesh of children. All before your time, girl. Perhaps had you witnessed such horrors, you would be more grateful for what the Eight have built for themselves." He smiled and added, "And as a plus, I get paid handsomely thanks to your family's wealth."

Stacie's expression hardened. "The Eight's criminal ways are unacceptable. *Period.*"

Clifton sighed and retook the controls.

Thirty minutes later, Babylon Island came into view. A single causeway connected it to the mainland.

Stacie gazed down at a six-story spiraling white structure at the center of the island. It was the building where the family heads had assembled.

The Eight Elite funded and created the artificial island strictly for themselves. It was off-limits to the public, the authorities, the military, and even the politicians who ran the Commonwealth, unless invited. No one but the Eight and their guests knew what happened on Babylon. And what happened there stayed there. If it didn't, all tattletales ended up on a missing-persons report.

A golden aerial yacht cruised overhead, carrying super-rich young men and women in swimwear who were dancing to a pulsating beat.

Suddenly, the flyer's comm system crackled to life. "This is Babylon Transit Authority. State your identity and purpose," a man's voice demanded.

"I am Elias Clifton II, dutiful servant of the Spencer family. I have Madam Stacie Lynette Spencer aboard. She requests permission to land."

"Stand by." After a brief pause, the control operator came back on the comms line. "I'm afraid Madam Stacie Spencer isn't on the guest registry. I'll have to—"

Stacie leaned forward, planting her palms on the dash. She lowered her mouth close to the mic and said, "Dispense with the nonsense, mongrel, and permit us entry." Definitely like her mother, Clifton thought. "Or my parents will have manacles strapped to your ankles and throw you into the ocean." She definitely wasn't in the mood for opposition today.

"Permission granted," the control operator said hastily.

Clifton dropped the flyer's altitude and touched down on the island's landing port, where other fancy flyers were parked. From there, he led Stacie to a deck full of land vehicles available for guests.

A spotless dark blue car that had a sunroof caught Stacie's eye. Clifton opened the right rear door for her. She settled into the back seat while he placed her bag in the trunk. Then he slid behind the wheel and powered on the car.

As Stacie got comfortable, the intelligent seating system adjusted to her frame.

The car left the landing port, rolling down a solar-paneled throughway. Stacie watched sandy beaches and tropical plants go by.

On one beach, a bare-chested fat man wearing sunglasses and a wide-brimmed hat lounged on a chair. His personally selected servant of the day—a young woman with slate-gray skin, striking yellow eyes, and butterfly-like ears—wore almost nothing below the waist and was naked from the waist up.

She delivered a foamy drink to him, placing it on a nearby table.

Exerting control over his "party favor," he yanked the chain attached to the choker around her neck, pulling her onto his lap.

All along the beach, other young outer-species women wore little to nothing, with bonds of servitude around their necks. Some bore visible welts from whippings. They were nothing more than merchandise to their handlers.

Stacie cast her angry eyes on Clifton. "Those women are obviously not here of their own accord."

"Babylon Island provides exotic luxuries to the Elite's guests and patrons, who are connoisseurs of . . . eclectic extravagances forbidden elsewhere in the Commonwealth." Nothing but sinister men and women with dark, twisted desires.

Drunken Highborn lay on the beach atop blankets and danced to loud music. Two topless women wearing bikini bottoms, both strikingly attractive, flirted with two ripped men. Stacie had long since grown sick of the senseless, decadent party lifestyle.

The car continued into the island's micropolis, leaving the beaches and boardwalks behind for a mishmash of stores, bars, nightclubs, and shady establishments.

An electronic banner outside a Pleasure Station scrolled text from left to right: WELCOME TO GOODTIMES UNIVERSAL: A TREASURE TROVE OF OUTERWORLD PLEASURES BEYOND YOUR WILDEST IMAGINATION.

Hyperrealistic holos of nude alien women flickered outside the entryway, rendered in provocative poses.

Revulsion prickled Stacie's skin. Everything about the island felt sleazy.

The car pulled up to the tall, imposing spiral structure where the family heads had gathered, slowing to a stop at the roundabout.

"The family heads should be in the fifth-floor dining suite," Clifton informed Stacie. "I will wait for you here." He hoped everything would remain civil. A heated Stacie and her mother in the same room were a surefire recipe for catastrophe.

Stacie got out, stiff-faced, and proceeded down a cobblestone walkway. At the large front door, a concierge awaited. He opened it as she approached, and she entered a vestibule replete with tall white pillars, spraying fountains, chandeliers, lounge couches grouped around coffee tables, and mosaic art. There was also a bar and a restaurant.

To her right sat a small, compact attendant at the reception desk. She had pink pigtail buns and wore a teal one-piece skirt that rode high on her thighs.

The attendant put down the e-zine she was reading on her tablet and focused her attention on Stacie. "Greetings, ma'am. Can I assist you with anything?" she asked while adjusting her round wire-rim glasses. Her kind green eyes and peppy voice made her the perfect greeter.

Stacie looked at the unending spiral staircase that rose to the topmost floor. Definitely a no. "Where are the elevators?" she asked curtly.

The attendant aimed a manicured red nail toward a hallway. "Down that way, ma'am."

Stacie's eyes followed the direction of the attendant's finger. Without another word, she passed two well-dressed staff members.

Midway down the hall, a cleaning golem whizzed around, vacuuming.

Stacie approached a set of five elevators. She entered the one in the middle and pressed 5.

The elevator doors clicked shut, and the car hissed up the translucent shaft. It ascended to the fifth floor and stopped. *Ding.* The doors parted.

Stacie walked down a lengthy carpeted catwalk to a pair of mahogany-colored doors with gilded framing. Behind them: the clinking of utensils and dishes, hearty conversation, and mouthwatering aromas.

Nervous and discouraged, Stacie gnawed her lower lip while gripping one of the door handles, and sweat rolled down her face. Was barging in on the Eight's gathering a smart move? Was anger overriding sound judgment? Chin held high, she plowed on and opened the door, making her grand ingress into the rotunda-shaped dining suite.

Fashionably dressed in the finest clothing G-credits could buy, the eight family heads sat around a circular table, a gourmet feast of unique delicacies spread before them. All were avaricious men and women whose thirst for wealth and power had driven them to obtain it using the darkest of means if necessary.

Stacie fixed her smoldering blue eyes on her parents. Darlene wore colorful makeup and a sequined turquoise dress. Patrick was clad in a posh three-piece black suit. "*Mother, Father,*" Stacie called out loudly, sucking the energy out of the room.

The conversation stopped. All eyes stared at her.

Darlene flicked her hand in a dismissive gesture. "Stacie, wait outside. We'll be with you shortly."

"No, Mother, right *now,*" Stacie demanded.

Darlene's jaw tightened, her daughter's disrespectful tone infuriating her.

The family heads at the table snickered and uttered severe remarks in hushed tones.

From beneath bushy brown eyebrows, a heavyset man—whose prominent features included a large mustache and bulbous nose— eyed Patrick and Darlene with amusement. "It's been a while since I've seen Stacie." He chuckled at their daughter's impudence. "She's blossomed into a beautiful young woman but clearly lacks the grace and manners expected of a lady of refinement."

Gales of laughter from the family heads irritated Patrick and Darlene.

Darlene clapped a palm to her forehead, embarrassed. *Damn child.*

Patrick shook his head. His daughter's indiscretion incensed him.

Darlene sprang up from her chair and skirted around the table to Stacie. She gripped her daughter's arm by the bicep. "Come," she hissed.

The door snapped shut as Darlene dragged Stacie out of the

room.

Stacie tore her arm loose. "What are the Eight Elite, Mother, a bunch of crime lords? What are you and Father a part of? I know about the corrupt dealings. I know about your illegal transactions with Chief Gould."

"Power isn't acquired by playing by the rule book, Stacie."

"It's wrong, all of it. The slave trade, money laundering, bribery —"

Darlene jabbed a finger at Stacie. "What's wrong is you barging in here and disgracing the Spencer name."

I was foolish to come here. What did I think was going to happen? "No, what's wrong is you constantly berating me, treating me like some child, like a piece of clay to be molded into your warped idea of perfection. I've had enough! You and Father can both go to hell for all I care!" Stacie spun and stormed off.

Darlene's fury coalesced, her face flushing red. She dashed up behind Stacie, grabbed a fistful of her hair, and yanked hard, wrenching her head back. Glaring into her daughter's eyes, she said, "I'm sick of your tantrums. I will no longer tolerate your defiance, you ungrateful little brat." She yanked harder. "You will respect me. Do you understand?"

"Let go! You're hurting me, Mother!" Stacie screamed, stifling the urge to strike Darlene—something she had been forced to do many times before.

Darlene clutched Stacie's hair tighter. "With you being such a . . . *nymphomaniac*, you're lucky you haven't—"

Stacie twirled and slapped her mother across the face.

Darlene staggered backward and tumbled to the floor. She arched her brows in disbelief, lip bloodied.

Chest heaving, adrenaline pumping, Stacie stood tall. She felt lighter, as if a boulder had been lifted from her shoulders. Striking her mother to expel years of pent-up rage was like therapy.

Darlene got up and seized Stacie's shoulders. "You dare hit me, you classless little degenerate?"

Mother and daughter scuffled, shoving each other into the catwalk's guardrails. Beads broke off Darlene's sequined dress.

Hearing the commotion, Patrick burst out of the dining suite. He saw the catfight escalating out of control. "Stop! What the hell is going on out here?" His eyebrows came together. "The family heads are inside thinking you've both gone insane! We are all intelligent adults, for goodness' sake!"

Darlene and Stacie separated.

The baroness cleared her throat and straightened her dress, trying to recover her dignity.

Patrick hurried to her side and gently dabbed the blood from her lip with a handkerchief. "What the hell has gotten into you, Stacie?"

Stacie scoffed and pointed at Darlene. "Ask your wife." Patrick trembled, visibly pissed off. "You want access to your daughter's mind again, Mother? Well, here!" She pinged Darlene's implant. Darlene accepted the request, restoring her maternal Link. "Here it is, Mother! All of my pain! All the anger from your abuse! All of my *fucking* hate!" Stacie pushed years of unspoken anguish into Darlene's mind.

Three family heads stood in the doorway, wondering what was going on.

A deluge of intolerable pangs wracked Darlene's brain. She gasped, queasy, squeezing her eyes shut.

Every physical and emotional wound she had ever inflicted on Stacie overloaded her nervous system, bringing her to her knees. She shuddered, heart vibrating, mind unraveling.

"What's wrong? Can't take it, Mother?" Stacie said coldly,

determined to make her suffer to the highest extent possible.

Darlene wheezed raggedly, struggling to hold herself together. Explosive migraines detonated in her skull, driving her into the depths of psychic agony. Tears streamed down her face. Unable to focus long enough to deLink, she screamed, "Stop it!"

Patrick intervened, saying, "Enough of this!"

Stacie severed the Link, for her mother's sake. Her head throbbed from the psychic backlash. She exhaled a long, quivering breath. She didn't know how she had just weaponized her emotions. It had been instinctive. The Quilgarian nanotech had a plethora of enigmas to be unlocked and understood, some good, some bad.

Patrick helped Darlene to her feet. With her mind marred and body swaying with vertigo, her knees buckled, but he caught her and held her upright.

Darlene said nothing. Her body spasmed, shivering uncontrollably.

Blood dripped from her nose, staining the carpet. She had never known pain like this.

For the first time in Stacie's life, she saw something unfamiliar in Darlene's expression: guilt. Real human guilt. She had been humbled. Mission accomplished.

A growl rumbled in Patrick's throat. He activated his wristcom. "You want to be a self-made woman, Stacie? Fine. But don't think you can spit in our faces while living off the fortune we built." He stabbed several holokeys with his finger. Then came a confirmatory chime. "I have reduced your account from two hundred million credits to fifty thousand."

He tapped his wristcom's centerpiece, dissolving the holographic interface. "The villa we bought you is now in your name. You're on your own. Talk to us when you come to your senses." He glared disappointedly at Stacie. "You have until sundown to stay on Babylon. Then you're no longer welcome."

Stacie's heart jumped. She had gone from princess to pauper. But keeping a firm voice, she said, "Fine, wouldn't want it any other way." She strode down the catwalk, heading to the elevators.

• • •

Samantha Hayley, Colony Five's governess, was a lottery beneficiary who had returned to Satellite One to improve the lives of her people. But she believed that declaring sovereignty from the Commonwealth and provoking the wrath of the central government was foolhardy. So did most of her constituents, according to the "illegal" exodus polls. Her daughter, however, had disagreed.

Living in Colony Four, Samantha's daughter had fought for colony independence during the Three-Week War, and paid the ultimate price.

Determined to ensure her daughter's sacrifice hadn't been pointless, Samantha began secretly supporting the Coalition of Rebel Factions, unknown to her people but suspected by the Defense Department. She had assisted with arms acquisition and had provided a safe haven for Reza and Hammer Fall's assault force. That was the extent of her willingness to help. But Conlan's intelligence team had blown her cover.

She sat at a shabby wooden desk in her bare-walled office, wearing a white blouse and charcoal-gray pencil skirt. A single framed picture sat on the desktop, a photo of her daughter at nineteen, the age she was killed in action.

Transmitting from his study, Reza appeared on Samantha's computer screen.

"Something is amiss," she said, sipping from a mug of warm liquid. "Several CDF starships landed at our port, without prior notice from the Defense Department.”

“Of course not,” Reza replied. “That’s not Gould’s MO. He prefers the element of surprise, especially when he’s up to something nefarious.”

“Well, when air-traffic control requested their purpose, the response was vague—just that they had orders from the Defense Department and couldn’t disclose more. BUSs, combat flyers, and armored assault vehicles deployed from those ships, which worries me.” Samantha’s professional posture cracked a little.

“This is clearly a military occupation of Colony Five.”

Samantha steepled her fingers. “But on what grounds? There’s no evidence linking me to the Coalition.” She wasn’t careless. She had made sure no trail led back to her. Or so she thought.

“Gould isn’t Jared Kerner,” Reza said. “He’s a shrewd madman, one who bucks the system or manipulates government leaders into supporting his schemes. Be careful, Sam. If—”

Samantha’s assistant’s voice came from behind her office doors. “You assholes can’t just barge in here!”

Sounds of a scuffle ensued.

Samantha’s brows lifted, and her heart skipped a beat. She glanced at the doors, then back to her screen. “Arman, something’s going on. We’ll have to continue this later,” she said quickly. She mashed a button on her keyboard, and the screen went dark.

The office doors swung open. Three Guardians in black combat gear forced their way past Samantha’s assistant, who was trying to block their entry. Two of the intruders were privates; the third wore a captain’s chevrons.

The gangly pale-faced officer stepped forward as his two burly subordinates wrestled with the assistant. “Governess, I’m Captain Felix Moss,” he said. “I’m here to initiate martial law in Colony Five.”

Samantha responded in her businesswoman voice. "What for, Captain? There are no opposition forces here."

Felix sneered. "There's nothing I hate more than a liar. Privates Ashcroft and Taggart, restrain her."

Samantha's jaw set. "Don't any of you dare touch me."

Felix's men shoved the assistant aside and advanced.

Not backing down, the young man marched up to Felix and grabbed his shoulder. "Call off your goons, or—"

A gunshot cracked.

Samantha let out an "eek" and said, "Ritz!"

Ritz crumbled to the floor with a guttural cry, clutching his thigh where Felix had shot him. He groaned, cursing under his breath.

Felix smirked. "That's what you get for putting a hand on a captain of the Defense Force." He lifted his boot and stomped down on the wound, causing Ritz to scream. "Dumb little pipsqueak." He shot two rounds into Ritz's skull.

Samantha recoiled in horror. Then Ashcroft and Taggart seized her arms. "Release me!" she demanded, twisting and writhing.

Taggart clamped a hand around the back of her neck and slammed her upper body onto the desk, knocking over the picture of her daughter.

"Stop struggling, Governess," Felix said. He set a cube-shaped instrument near her face. The device hummed to life, its circuitry glowing with kaleidoscopic light—an Area-14 invention.

Samantha doused her fear with courage and stayed resilient. "What is that thing?" The privates' hands pressed harder, keeping her folded over the desk. Now the first throbs of an excruciating headache hammered at her skull.

It was easy to see that Felix relished her discomfort. "It's called a Mind Sweeper. It's bypassing all the safeguards in your cerebral implant. Once done, it'll Link your implant to mine, letting me probe your mind for your communications with the Coalition."

Fighting to maintain her firewalls against the waves of nausea and delirium attacking her, Samantha rasped, "Bastards . . . you have no right to . . . trespass into my mind." Her breathing grew erratic. "This violates . . . consent law."

Felix scoffed. "Desperate times call for desperate measures, Governess. Chief Gould has authorized us to do everything within our power to prevent the Commonwealth from losing its incorporated status." His implant pinged, connecting to hers. Success. Time for the test. *<Hello, Governess, nice to——>*

Face slick with perspiration, Samantha screamed fiercely and pushed the interloper out.

She writhed, but the privates' hands didn't budge. Tremors overtook her body as she remained pinned flat.

Felix reared back, impressed by her willpower. "You're headstrong, Governess. I'll give you that." He gripped a fistful of her short honey-brown hair and lifted her head. "But you *will* break," he guaranteed in a cold timbre, then let go of her hair.

Felix breached her mental defenses and ravaged her thoughts, foraging through layers of memory.

Samantha's vision clouded and cleared in rapid succession. Her insides squirmed, the liquid contents of her cup threatening to resurface.

A stream of her most cherished memories flowed into Felix's mind: her wedding day, her husband's funeral, her daughter at sixteen in a white T-shirt and yellow beach shorts, laughing as she spun a hula hoop around her hips on the beach.

<Pretty kid you had. Too bad the little whelp's dead,> Felix said.

Samantha tried to muscle herself up, painful twinges in her arms, but the privates had her overpowered.

At last, Felix found Samantha's communications with Reza.

He disconnected the Link. "Well, now we've proven you're the treacherous conspirator bitch we thought you were."

The privates released Samantha. She pushed herself up, but her equilibrium was so impaired by the throbbing aftershocks of the mind rape that the room tilted and swayed, and she collapsed to the floor.

A fuzzy haze clouded her vision as she gasped between breaths. She said to Felix, "I hope you suffer the most horrific death, you lowlife piece of filth." A storm of emotions raged beneath the surface—violent ones.

Felix laughed. "So, the prohibited zone is just cover, to keep people from stumbling across your rebel friends." He tapped his wristcom. "This is Captain Moss to Yankee and Zulu battalion commanders. I'm sending you coordinates. Reza and his rebels are there. All other forces continue martial-law operations." He eyed Samantha. "Take her to a BUS and detain her," he ordered Ashcroft and Taggart.

Samantha's vision slowly swam into focus. She glared at her tormentor, the message in her eyes clear: She wanted him dead.

Ashcroft and Taggart picked her up from the floor and locked cuffs around her wrists. Knowing resistance was futile, she offered no struggle and silently allowed them to take her into CDF custody.

• • •

Randy and Jarius had completed their training for the day. Along with Kesley, they were traveling to a nearby town in a rickety zipsled—a roofless utility hover vehicle—to celebrate at a tavern.

The sled was outdated and simple: a flat platform with two seats in the front, a long bench in the back, and two wings with can-shaped plasma boosters mounted underneath. Coalition mechanics had also installed a pair of cheap, low-powered laser cutters to provide basic offensive capability.

They passed rows of large rectangular shipping containers that had been converted into single-person living units.

"I've been inside one of those," Kesley said from the back seat. "They're nicer than you would expect."

The sled left Container Row and entered a part of town with modest buildings and residential homes, nothing near Eden quality, but far more upscale than anything in Colony Four.

Two blocks from the tavern, Randy parked the sled on a lay-by. The trio got out to walk the rest of the way. Passersby regarded them with suspicion.

"So why are these people giving us dirty looks?" Jarius asked, eyes darting left and right.

Kesley replied, "It's a small town. Locals know we're not from here. They probably think we're from an occupied colony, which means we could be rebels. These people don't want the central government breathing down their necks. They think challenging the central government is downright crazy and unnecessary."

"So, not all colony folk welcome each other with open arms."

"Nope."

Once inside the tavern, Randy, Jarius, and Kesley ordered drinks and took a window-side booth. Their voices competed with the din of loud conversation, merry guffaws, and clinking glasses. Both young and old patrons were having a good time.

Thirty minutes in, Kesley excused herself to the ladies' room, leaving Randy and Jarius sitting side by side at the table.

Jarius thought about how the establishment, though not bad, didn't measure up to Eden standards: no server golems, no pictographic holo-menus, and a plain, drab interior. *We live like gods compared to these people,* he thought. He took a sip of his drink and asked Randy, "So, you having any second thoughts about this operation?"

"Right now, it feels like the right move. Do I trust Reza completely? No. But I guess we'll find out if he's a wolf in sheep's clothing."

"What if he does turn out to be just a power-hungry dictator?"

"Then . . . he'll be stopped." How? Randy didn't know. "What about you? Any doubts?"

"I think I'm sticking with this rebel thing for now."

"Your choice. It's not too late to bail." Randy raised his glass mug to his lips and chugged his beer. At the bar, he saw a father and his eighteen-year-old son sitting on high stools. A dusky-skinned barmaid with long, curly raven hair, wearing a red dress and an oblong shawl, poured ale into their mugs from a glass decanter. They toasted, then quaffed their drinks together.

Watching them revived pleasant memories for Randy, memories of him and his father. He remembered when Arson took him for his first drink when he was eighteen.

"Thinking about your old man?" Jarius asked.

"Yeah, just a good memory." Randy gritted his teeth, and his brow furrowed. "Before he betrayed Mom and me."

"What went down was hella fucked up, but it was an accident. Your dad's not a bad guy. If you're gonna proceed with joining this mission, I think you should make some kind of peace with him. There's no guarantee one of you ain't gonna be six feet under when this is over.

"I'm glad I made peace with my biological dad after my mom remarried. The man died a year later in a freak vehicle crash, and if I hadn't forgiven him, I would've carried that regret forever."

Randy took a swig of beer. "If I'm dead, making peace with him won't matter."

"It will to him," Jarius countered.

"Well, tough for him. And if *he* dies . . . well, don't worry, I think I can live with myself. He's been dead to me for quite some time anyway." Randy kicked back more of his drink.

"Enough of the tough-guy act, dude. Be real with yourself. You ain't fooling me."

"Just drop it, man."

"Okay, fine." Jarius took a gander at the ladies' room to see if Kesley was coming out, then grinned. "So, who's better in bed, Kess or Stacie?"

Randy slammed his mug down after taking a gulp. "*Drop it.*"

Jarius said, "You got the hots for her, don't you?" Randy returned to his drink, annoyance showing in his body language. Jarius continued teasing him. "You like those jugs of hers. That wit."

Randy's mind played back a memory from last night . . .

Following their rest break, Randy bent Kesley's torso over the side of the bed. She demanded a hard slap on the rear, so he obliged with a smack that stung her perfect, round cheek. She told him to do it again. The next smack left a red mark.

Getting down to business, he nudged his foot against hers to widen her stance. With his cock stretched to the limit, he gripped her wrists and drew her arms back while propelling his loins forward. The drumbeat of flesh slapping flesh once again filled the room.

It wasn't long before he was thrusting into his own cum, droplets of it leaking out from between Kesley's thighs. At a brutal tempo, he pounded her sinfully attractive ass.

Randy blinked out of the memory. "Listen, what happened between us was just . . . a fleeting moment. It was a one-nighter, no strings attached. Kess was simply . . . a temporary fuck buddy, and she's cool with that. She wanted to have some fun, that's all. But what happened last night was a stupid mistake. It *wasn't* right. I . . . got caught up. And let's be clear: Stacie is the *only* woman I want."

"Well, Stacie's gonna be furious when she finds out what went on between you and Kess."

"No fucking kidding. I'll deal with it when the time comes."

"Good luck with that."

Just then, they heard Kesley chatting with a patron. She made her way back to the table—her braless breasts bobbing—and sat down in the seat facing them. She lifted her glass, holding it high. "A toast to equality, fellas," she said merrily.

Jarius raised his own glass. "Sounds good to me."

Randy's expression stayed neutral. *I don't think we should shout out things like "equality" here.*

The rims of all three glasses clinked.

The comm-set on Randy's belt chirped. He put his mug down, placed the device against his ear, and pressed the talk button. "Scott here. What's up?"

Arson answered from the other end. "Reza wants everyone back pronto. He believes our location has been compromised. We're leaving for Eden ASAP. As soon as you get back, head to the ship."

The comm-set beeped and went silent.

Randy clipped it back to his belt. "That was my father," he said in a hushed tone. "We need to head back now. Our location may no longer be safe. We're leaving for Eden today."

"Sounds like our operation might happen sooner than planned," Jarius whispered.

Suddenly, Felix appeared on the tavern's wall screens. "People of

Colony Five, I am Captain Felix Moss. I am responsible for establishing martial law and am your duly appointed viceroy for the foreseeable future. We have removed Governess Hayley from her position and placed her in our custody."

Heads faced the screens. Randy, Jarius, and Kesley looked at each other in alarm.

Felix said, "She was aiding Coalition forces in their attempt to ruin our great republic. To neutralize this cancer, the CDF will conduct patrols and search homes. I do not wish to complicate your lives and will make every day as trouble-free as possible."

Grumbles erupted among the tavern patrons.

A red-bearded, chubby man whammed his table with a fist. "They think they can just barge into our homes? That's fucking home invasion!"

Another man at a table stomped the floor. "This is the rebels' fault. Why can't they just give up?"

Felix said, "Please do not worry; your privacy and dignity are at the forefront of our concern."

Yeah, right, Randy thought.

"When we root out the cancer, life in Colony Five will go back to normal," Felix assured everyone watching. "I am ordering all citizens to return to their homes for the rest of the day. You may resume daily activities starting at oh-eight-hundred tomorrow, but you must adhere to your new seventeen-hundred curfew and all established moratoriums."

"That's bullshit!" a man shouted, making a displeased gesture.

"Hush," warned a thickset busty blond woman. "If Guardians hear you say things like that, you might end up in front of a firing squad."

BUSs pulled up outside the tavern, chuffing and rumbling. Shelled troops clogged the streets.

Kesley's body tensed.

Jarius got up from the table. "Come on, guys, let's hightail it outta here."

"You don't have to tell me twice," Kesley said, rising to her feet.

The trio strolled out the door casually, remaining low-key.

"You think Hayley ratted us out?" Jarius asked quietly, scanning streets overcrowded with Guardians directing civilian foot traffic.

"Not by choice. The CDF has ways to loosen lips," Kelsey replied, well aware of the CDF's harsh interrogation methods, like injecting pain analeptics into prisoners.

More patrons filed out of the tavern, gabbling.

Guardians' external sound ports megaphoned their instructions to citizens as they coordinated the evacuation. People swore and uttered complaints. BUSs growled to a halt, and more shelled Guardians poured into the area, armor clacking.

"Everyone, go home!" shouted a Guardian who was possibly three blocks away.

Citizens spewed invectives and epithets.

Already, a few overly disruptive men and women were being rounded up.

Funny how these people stayed submissive until they got shitcanned, Kesley thought.

A man in his sixties yelled above the clamor. "The Coalition was right: You guys are just a bunch of no-good brutish thugs!"

A Guardian triggered his rifle. A loud *blam* made people shudder. The slug the Guardian had fired punched into the man's sternum, then exploded out his back.

A brilliant spray of blood splattered across the ground.

Bystanders gasped. A mother shielded her toddler's eyes. A husband pulled his wife close. Several women swooned and collapsed.

"Let that old geezer serve as an example," the Guardian announced. "We declare any dumbfuck who insults the central government or the Defense Force an enemy of the Commonwealth, and we will execute them on the spot."

Kesley grunted. "Son of a bitch didn't have to do that. That old guy was no threat. Was he afraid he was gonna damage his state-of-the-art combatwear with sticks and stones or something?"

Randy gripped her shoulder. "Hey, Kess, keep your voice down. We need to maintain cool heads and get the hell out of town."

The trio quickened their pace, separating themselves from the rest of the crowd.

Shells' Oracles conducted facial recognition scans to identify rebels.

Kesley entered a Guardian's field of vision.

"Identity confirmed: rebel Kesley Whittaker," the Guardian's Oracle said. A red pop-up displayed the data that profilers had logged:

Name: Kesley Michelle Whittaker
Age: 31 / **Ethnicity:** Caucasian / **Gender:** Female
Occupation: courier for Dynamic Relief Provisions
Rebel affiliation: the Coalition of Rebel Factions/Colony Four
Comments: last seen fleeing a rebel camp in Colony Four

The Guardian centered Randy in his reticle. Kesley's data vanished, replaced by a new pop-up. "Identity confirmed: rebel Randal Scott," his Oracle warned.

Name: Randal Eugene Scott (turncoat)
Age: 22 / **Ethnicity:** Caucasian / **Gender:** Male
Military Occupational Specialty/Rank: Land Combatant/SPC

Rebel affiliation: the Coalition of Rebel Factions

Comments: last seen fleeing a rebel camp in Colony Four with rebel Kesley Whittaker

The Guardian aimed his visored gaze at Jarius and consulted his Oracle for an ID:

Name: Jarius Don Ford

Age: 22 / **Ethnicity:** Black / **Gender:** Male

Military Occupational Specialty/Rank: Land Combatant/SPC

Jarius had no rebel ties logged. *Damn, another convert,* the Guardian deduced. He shouldered evacuees aside as he advanced toward the trio. "You three—Randal Scott, Kesley Whittaker, Jarius Ford—halt!" he barked as he stalked forward.

Jarius said, "Run like hell."

The trio broke into a mad dash for their zipsled.

"Stop those three!" The Guardian's eyes tracked them.

Gunfire thundered.

Men and women screamed, and children squealed.

The orderly evacuation had unraveled into chaos.

"Are they fucking crazy, firing while civilians are still evacuating?" Kesley said. Her leg muscles burned as she kicked up her pace.

The trio reached the sled and leapt in, Randy at the controls, Jarius in the passenger seat, and Kesley in the back.

Randy flipped a switch to ON, and the sled's start-up sequence activated.

Bullets whizzed past.

Jarius' nerves were on a razor's edge. "Come on! Come on!"

"Calm down and stop screaming in my ear!" Randy snapped.

"This thing's an antique! It takes time to power up! You know that!"

Behind them, three shelled Guardians sprinted toward the sled.

Kesley reached into a gray cloth satchel and pulled out a plasma grenade. "I'll take care of them." Randy and Jarius looked back at her. "Never leave home without one."

Randy raised a hand. "Wait, Kess. The engine's almost ready. That thing is deadly. They may have families. If we can avoid—"

"I ain't waiting to get killed, Randy." Kesley thumbed the detonator stub and lobbed the grenade. It clunked to the phyocrete and exploded.

Plasma force warped, twisted, and charred the Shells, and it injured the Guardians inside.

Damn it, Randy thought, hating that the Guardians had been badly hurt, maybe even suffered life-threatening injuries.

The yellow ENGINE READY light blinked on, and the laser-cutter indicators flashed green. Antigrav lifters pushed the sled off the ground, and Randy fired up the plasma boosters.

Dust swirled.

The sled started off slow, then accelerated. More Guardians shot at the vehicle, but it was already out of range.

<<*Let 'em go,*>> the sergeant in charge said to all Guardians. <<*We know where they're headed, straight for the jungle compound. Battalions are already en route there, so they'll get what's comin' to 'em. Let's not waste ammo and time goin' after 'em. Let's focus on clearing this area as ordered.*>>

• • •

The zipsled finished a stretch of barren road, entering the jungle to the crackling of gunfire and the sight of dancing flames.

Randy, Jarius, and Kesley had seen the smoke from a distance, confirming their fears: The CDF had made their incursion into the rebels' hideout.

Upon reaching the no-entry point, the trio spotted a breach in the security fence.

Gunned-down rebel bodies lay sprawled across blood-soaked grass. The CDF had destroyed the first line of defense.

Wordless, Randy surveyed the carnage as the sled crept forward at low speed.

Fire crawled, burning the camp's shelters. More gunfire crackled.

I hope the CDF hasn't gotten to our ship yet, Randy thought. He pressed the accelerator. The sled picked up speed as it passed a trail of devastation.

The hiss of energy weapons and the thunder of automatics grew louder. The trio was getting closer to the heart of the battle.

The zipsled sluggishly climbed a steep incline, its engine groaning. At the top, the trio reached level ground and found themselves front and center of a gun battle, Guardians and rebels exchanging shots.

A mini launcher rose from a Guardian's shoulder panel. A scattershot of rocket pods ejected. The marble-sized plasma bombs erupted in a rebel's face, tearing away skin and muscle. He screamed and fell to the ground, cradling what was left of his face.

A bronze-skinned rebel woman with dark ropes of hair hoisted a blaster cannon over her shoulder. She fired an energy blast that blew a Guardian's arm clean off.

A rebel man had a wounded woman in a fireman's carry, hauling her to safety.

Jarius said, "Damn it, where are our armored troops?"

Randy swerved around a tree. "Aboard the ship, preparing to get the hell out of here."

"So these guys are just—"

"Volunteer sacrificial lambs," Randy finished. They were brave souls who'd volunteered to forfeit their lives so their comrades could escape and end the war. He remembered a truism that a drill sergeant had said: *In war, you don't get to save everybody.*

Rebels manned bipod-mounted blasters, launching booming shots of spherical energy.

A heavy thudding sound echoed from deep within the trees, quaking the ground. Frightened rebels turned toward the source.

Branches crunched. Something massive was coming.

A Juggernaut stomped out of the trees, its motorized joints whining. Weapons lockers opened. Slugs, energy blasts, and missiles spat out in a barrage as its torso rotated ninety degrees.

A panicked rebel woman fired wildly at the giant walking arsenal. Unfazed by her small-arms fire, the Juggernaut brought its enormous foot down on her, squashing her into a bloody smear.

"What the hell's that thing?" Jarius yelled.

"It's gotta be a Juggernaut," Kesley replied.

"How do you know what it is?" Randy asked.

"You heard Reza back at the sanctuary. Our intel said Gould's developing advanced weaponry at some secret military test farm. One of them is a Juggernaut, a high-tech robot that's completely thought-controlled."

"No way," Randy said. "That type of implant modification isn't legal."

Kesley scoffed. "Tell that to Gould."

What the Commonwealth would become under Gould's leadership frightened Randy. The madman was going too far.

Three more Juggernauts emerged from the trees' concealment, each cerebrally piloted from control-free cockpits. An energy beam from one Juggernaut sawed a rebel in half, bisecting her.

Randy mashed the acceleration pedal to the floor.

Air slapped the trio's faces as the sled whooshed past bloodshed and burning jungle, scraping against outstretched tree limbs as it neared the hangar.

At the hangar, Randy braked and cut the engine.

Rebels were double-timing it through the rear bay door of the ship.

Randy snatched the comm-set from his belt and contacted Arson. "Dad, we're here."

Arson replied, "Hurry the hell up and get inside the ship. Our troops can't hold the CDF back much longer."

"Let's skedaddle," Kesley said. She hopped out of the sled.

Sariah ushered rebels inside. "Come on, move it!"

Randy, Jarius, and Kesley rushed into the ship. Sariah slipped in with the last trickle of rebels.

The ship rolled out of the hangar and climbed into the sky.

Weapons fell silent.

A Guardian watched the ship vanish into the atmosphere. *Damn, bet Reza's aboard.*

The CDF had come close to taking out the Coalition leader. Close, but no cigar.

• • •

Felix Moss barged into the BUS where Samantha Hayley was being detained. He stomped past buzzing electronics, weapons racks, and storage lockers.

He slid back the cell door's grille cover and peered in at Samantha sitting on a metal bench. His scowl made his foul mood obvious. "Reza has escaped. Where is he going?"

"Like I'd tell you," Samantha snapped, eyes full of loathing.

Felix gave a wicked smile that stretched from ear to ear. "Perhaps I missed some vital information the first time I probed your mind." He rubbed his hands together. "Let's do it again, shall we, Governess?"

Terror reflected in Samantha's eyes. She didn't want to face that agony a second time.

Felix opened the flap of the black bag hanging on his shoulder, pulled out the Mind Sweeper, and powered it on. The latticework of circuitry gleamed ominously.

Pain stabbed Samantha's head as the device tore into her memories. A headache flared instantly. She couldn't take it. "No! Alright, I'll tell you!"

Felix shut off the Mind Sweeper. "I'm all ears."

• • •

On Babylon Island, Stacie strolled the marble-block promenade of Kirkstone Park, marshaling her thoughts and processing her societal demotion. It felt strange no longer being "modern-day royalty," no longer being the princess of the Spencer family. And though her parents had caused her pain, it felt odd to be completely out of touch with them.

On a pavilion, musicians played instruments. Around them, onlookers sipped drinks, laughing and enjoying themselves. A leggy female jogger, wearing purple gel leggings, dashed past Stacie, her white tank top darkened by patches of sweat.

Stacie crossed a footbridge and sat under a tree beside a pond. She needed to reflect and clear her mind.

A woman in a sundress sauntered by, hand in hand with her boyfriend.

Stacie pondered. If she hadn't interrupted the family heads' get-together and caused a scene, if she had just kept her cool, maybe she could've stayed in the Eight and dismantled it from within. Maybe she could've even convinced her parents to turn over a new leaf. *Damn, if I had just played it smarter.*

And yes, she would miss the chauffeuring, the extraneous

spending, the ability to have anything she wanted. She just didn't want to be totally defined by her ascribed status. That was why she had joined the CDF. And she didn't want dirty money involved in sustaining her lifestyle. Anyway, now her identity was solely wrapped around being a Guardian. Apparently, that was all she had left—that and Randy.

Her wristcom beeped a warning notice. She pressed the center disc, and a holo-message hovered above her wrist. It said that all Guardians on Eden, whether they were on active duty or on leave, were being called to action under a declared State of Emergency. They were to report to Defense Force HQ immediately.

Once there, she'd be temporarily assigned to a unit on Eden.

She knew something major was about to go down. Her duty was all she had now. There was no more time to continue dwelling on how she could've confronted her parents differently.

• • •

The Coalition assault ship had exited Hyperspace Leap and was en route to Eden at a speed that afforded the rebels aboard five hours of rest.

Rebels had claimed the foldout wall-berths in no particular order, bedding down for their brief respite.

Randy slept fitfully, tossing and turning. In his dream, he again wrestled with his conscience. He and Kathleen stood in a void of darkness, a pillar of light shining down on them.

This battle may be the end of either of you. Don't miss this opportunity, Kathleen pled. *Link with your father and begin restoring your bond.*

Again, no! Randy said.

Kathleen rested a hand on his shoulder. *Do it, Randy, for yourself . . . and me.*

Randy jolted awake, his mother's words still in his head. He rubbed his palms over his face. *Okay, Mom, fine. Have it your way. You always knew what was best.* He swung his feet onto the floor and pulled on his boots. With soft footsteps, he left the sleeping station, careful not to disturb the napping rebels.

The ship was quiet, save for the low rumble of its engines.

Randy rounded a corner, stepping into a ribbed gyre-shaped corridor, and saw Reza gazing into space through a long window.

Reza prayed everything would go according to his will.

Wishing Priscilla were there to comfort him, Reza felt a warm, loving ambiance swarm around him. Then the apparition bearing her uncanny resemblance appeared once more.

Don't worry, everything will go well, my love, Priscilla said.

"Thank you. I will always be grateful for the serenity you brought to my life."

Who is he talking to? Randy wondered.

With just that brief exchange of words, Priscilla disappeared.

Randy approached Reza. "Who were you talking to?"

Reza spun toward Randy, his boots squeaking against the smooth floor. "Randal, you heard?"

Randy nodded.

Reza said, "Well, a woman was killed during the miners' strike. She was my lover. We were Linked at the time of her brutal death. My mind was tormented as she was executed. It was as if I experienced death with her. Since then, my implant seems to draw on my memories of her—her voice, personality, the clothes she wore—to conjure a lifelike hallucination whenever my heart cries out for her." He turned back toward the window. "Then again, maybe it's the trauma. Maybe I'm losing my mind."

Randy edged closer. "It's the same with me," he shared. "I see my mom sometimes. It's so real."

Reza craned his head sideways, looking at Randy. "So, I'm not the only one."

"No, you're not." Randy stepped beside him, gazing out the window at a drifting asteroid belt. "What do you think it would take to get rid of these . . . phantasms? An implant cleanse? A full implant replacement?"

"Perhaps reconciliation with—or elimination of—whatever caused the pain." For Reza, that meant killing Gould.

Getting back on track, Randy said, "Do you know where my dad might be?"

"The stockroom, I believe. Take a left at the second junction and keep going. You'll see it."

"Thanks."

Reza extended an open palm. "A pleasure talking to you, Randal Scott. And I appreciate you lending your talents and abilities to this fight."

Randy hesitated a moment, as if he might be shaking the hand of someone up to no good. Out of common courtesy, he grasped Reza's hand and shook it. Then he headed to the stockroom as Reza walked in the opposite direction.

In the stockroom, Arson was inventorying armaments and Hardsuits.

The circular hatch's lock mechanism cycled open.

Randy appeared in the hatchway. "Dad," he said, voice low, mind unsettled. He was unsure if this bonding attempt was a good idea. Linking with his father, the man he had once wished dead, still felt bizarre.

Arson clipped his datapad to his utility belt. "Yeah, Randy, what's up?" He sounded unenthused, tired of his son's repeated criticisms, yet he understood the pain behind them. Even so, the back-and-forths had become exhausting.

Randy came down the metal ramp below the hatchway. He

started the conversation casually. "I saw some crazy stuff out there, things that shouldn't even exist."

Arson said, "You mean the Juggernauts?" Randy nodded. "Well, that's just one more reason we need to stop that madman. Word from our insiders is he's developing some kind of implant modification that dulls Guardians' empathy during combat."

Randy's brows rose. "Totally insane."

"Yeah, I know. But I have a feeling you didn't come here just to chat about that. What's on your mind, Son?"

Randy shed his reluctance. "Since we're headed into the fight of our lives, I wanted to kinda bury the hatchet."

"Kinda?"

"I'm not going to pretend I suddenly agree with your decision to leave Mom and me. I'm not going to be fake and phony."

Arson boosted himself up into a sitting position on a container and crossed his arms. "Alright, Son, I'm all ears."

"I've seen the conditions the people of my birth-colony have had to endure. I've seen decent people get mistreated by the CDF. I understand that your heart told you to do something, to take a stand. I still wouldn't have left my family. But knowing Mom, I don't think she'd want me to hate you. I don't think she'd want us to be at odds. I can't say everything's going to be the same, though."

Silence settled between them.

"Anything else, Randy?" Arson asked.

"Yeah, I . . . want us to Link. I think it'll help me understand you, and you understand me. And maybe that'll start some kind of healing process . . . for me."

For a moment, Arson was at a loss for words. He hadn't believed his son would ever want to Link with him again. "Okay, Randy, let's do this." He slid off the container.

Randy bobbed his chin. "Be prepared. Mom and I were Linked

when she died. You're going to feel all of that pain, understand?"

"Son, I've endured incredible physical and mental ordeals."

"None like this," Randy guaranteed. "Ready?"

"Yes," Arson replied confidently.

Randy forwarded the Link request. Arson's implant pinged.

Nervousness rose in Arson, but he held his composure. He accepted the request, and the interchange of emotions, thoughts, and times passed proceeded.

Arson revisited the moment Kathleen was killed, diving into Randy's anguish. Head swimming, tension permeating every limb, he dropped to his knees. He clutched his skull and was unable to form a coherent word. Suddenly, a whirlwind of agony swallowed him.

Randy journeyed into Arson's thoughts that night. He heard his father's voice cry out, *"Wait, someone's still in there! Intel said the building would be vacant tonight!"* Then the explosion replayed. Arson's undeniable love for Kathleen, his guilt . . . *all* of his emotions crashed into Randy like a tidal wave, overloading his mind.

A fog of self-condemnation hanging over him, Arson sat sobbing in the corner of his flyer that night, a broken man. He grieved for days.

Randy then encountered another memory . . .

Arson was in his quarters. Wracked with guilt, he had wallowed in self-loathing and battled suicidal thoughts for days, reduced to a shell of the man he once was.

He held a pistol to his head, staring at a photograph on the table—a picture of him and Kathleen on their wedding day. He whispered a prayer to God, asking forgiveness for his sin, seeking peace with his maker. Only death, he thought, could free him from his pain.

Just as he was about to pull the trigger, Sariah walked in, startling him. "Sariah, what are you—?"

She gasped, rushed to him, and slapped the gun from his hand. It clattered to the floor.

"Killing yourself is not the answer! Get off your guilt trip, Commander!" Sariah threw her arms around Arson. "Kathleen wouldn't want you to end your life. You have too much to live for. Too much to do. The Coalition needs you. Your son needs you. *I* need you."

Arson hugged her, weeping . . .

The memory faded. A lump formed in Randy's throat, and a tear rolled down his cheek. This moment marked a turning point in his estranged relationship with his father.

Arson sat on the floor with his back against the container. He settled his chin against his chest. Now he fully understood the mental trauma Randy had suffered, being Linked with Kathleen during the explosion that killed her—and nearly ripped his soul out. He understood why Randy had rejected his pleas for forgiveness for so long, and maybe, he thought, Randy shouldn't forgive him. Guilt, shame, and humiliation—all his personal demons—resurfaced, dragging him back into the abyss of self-disgust.

Randy extended a hand. Arson stared at the gesture, uncertain why his son would ever forgive him.

"Come on, Dad, get up," Randy said kindly.

Arson took his hand.

Randy helped lift him to his feet.

Kathleen's death had shattered them both. Each had lost the woman he cherished more than life itself.

They stood there, facing each other. Neither of them was sure what to say.

Tears streamed down Randy's face, not for Kathleen, but for Arson. With their minds Linked, he had experienced a man's grief for his wife and the crushing guilt of having caused her death.

Randy felt empathy for Arson, the kind that only Linking—a radical concept made reality—could unearth, as it had been foreseen.

Arson broke the silence, voice cracking. "You should go rest up for the operation."

Randy swallowed and cleared his throat. "Yeah, I think I should." He hugged his father with love and forgiveness. Then he left through the hatchway.

Arson closed his eyes. His son had forgiven him. His son loved him.

He returned to work, fighting off tears of relief.

CHAPTER EIGHT

The Defense Department raised Eden's threat level to red—the highest level. Cornelius had broadcasted an emergency address to the citizens of Eden, informing them that the CDF had detained and interrogated Governess Hayley for collaborating with the enemy. He said she had confessed that the Coalition planned to invade Eden, though she didn't know the exact day or time.

The fight was now coming to humanity's motherworld.

Pandemonium ensued. To secure the streets, the government mobilized the entire CDF and ordered all citizens to remain indoors under a full lockdown until further notice.

Stacie, in battledress, was en route to Defense Force HQ in an air-cab. Below, in Cornerstone City's Terence Plaza, authorities and Guardians were overseeing a large-scale evacuation. Tiny figures and vehicles bustled across the plaza's colorful tiles.

The cab soared past Cornerstone's aerial shopping center, a floating globular structure with wrap-around windows. For the first time, it was a ghost town.

All throughout Eden, it felt like doomsday was approaching,

and Stacie had that eerie calm-before-the-storm feeling, the kind that comes right before all hell breaks loose.

Thoughts of her lover surfaced. She was worried. Randy's message said he was scoping out the other side, the Coalition. He wouldn't actually join them, would he? No, she knew him better than that. Whatever phase of confusion or doubt he was dealing with, he'd come back to the CDF.

The Coalition couldn't possibly poison his mind against her. He held the CDF's values dear and had sworn to protect the Commonwealth from all enemies, foreign and domestic. His personal standards and morals were too strong to be corrupted by Coalition tricks, propaganda, or doctrine.

Boy, she wished he were with her right now. He was like no other man she had met. He knew just what to say to console her. He knew how to work her body in ways that left her breathless and yearning for more. For him, it was virtually a cinch.

She closed her eyes and accessed the feeling of his powerful, tender touch from her cerebral implant's sensory archive. The sensations suffused her body and mind with a dopamine rush. *Randy, I miss you. I need you.*

Elation coursed through her like wildfire. Her breathing changed, the rise and fall of her chest quickening. Deriving pleasure from her lover by using stored recollection data was the next best thing in lieu of actual intercourse with him.

Focusing her thoughts on the mission, she logged out of her sensory archive. *Keep your head in the game, Stacie. Keep your head in the game.*

Stacie's cab landed outside the gate of Defense Force HQ's base. After she got out, the craft ascended into roaming mode and vanished into the sky.

A male guard emerged from a small outbuilding, the security

control center. Stacie identified herself as a Guardian. The guard scanned her retina, confirmed her enlistment, and granted her access to the base.

A comm pedestal was located a few feet beyond the gate. Stacie flipped up the plastic cover and pressed the large red button to request transportation. Five minutes later, a white self-driving commuter van slowed to a stop beside her, its engine barely audible.

She stepped aboard. Inside were five other Guardians in battledress.

"Next stop: Ferrington Gate," said the van's computer.

The side doors sealed, and the van accelerated smoothly.

A screen mounted to the ceiling displayed a newscast. Every headline focused on the looming rebel invasion.

After the van delivered the other Guardians to their destinations, it delivered Stacie to hers.

She stepped down from the van. The doors closed. Electronics chirped, and the van drove off.

Outside, CDF HQ buzzed with frenzied activity. Outbound convoys rolled from motor pools, officers barked orders, NCOs shouted, and Guardians hastened here and there. A sense of urgency electrified the air.

Stacie entered the towering white building. To get directions, she tried to flag down the Guardian jogging in her direction. "Excuse me, Private, could you tell me where—?"

He made a beeline right past her for the exit. "Sorry, no time, toots."

She frowned. *Toots? Damn misogynist.*

More Guardians ran past her, boots clacking against the floor.

Stacie located a directory module, used it to find her temporary company commander's office, and proceeded.

As she neared the office's door, sensors detected her presence, and it slid into the wall. A man in battledress with a captain's rank sat behind a wooden desk. A computer faced him; a polished award placard faced outward.

Stacie rapped on the doorframe three times and recited the procedural spiel. "Specialist Spencer requesting permission to enter, Sir."

"Enter," the captain said.

Stacie went into the office. The door closed automatically behind her.

Standing at regulation distance, she locked her heels together, rested her arms firmly at her sides, and then saluted. "Specialist Spencer reporting for duty, Sir."

"I'm Captain Samuel McBride. At ease." He opened a drawer and placed a datapad on the desk. "I just need your biometric signature to finalize your temporary unit transfer."

"Yes, Sir." Stacie stepped forward, rested her palms on the desk, and studied the detail of her service sketch. She raised her chin, her eyes fixed on McBride in confusion. "Excuse me, Sir, this v-doc has my rank listed as sergeant. I'm—"

"Not anymore," McBride said. "A Staff Sergeant Jason Mansford submitted your name for promotion." Stacie flinched, caught off guard. "He included a service critique citing above-average performance and noted that you've shown strong leadership aptitude as a sub-lead."

Stacie thought that "high leadership aptitude" was laying it on a little thick.

McBride said, "All documentation was approved. Unless, of course, you'd rather stay a specialist."

"Uh, no, Sir," Stacie replied.

Though she had helped take down the Scott Faction, she knew

she hadn't served long enough, hadn't done enough, to truly deserve a promotion. But Jason had a soft spot for her. He saw something in her, which was why he handpicked her as Alpha Team's sub-lead. And hell, she wasn't about to turn down a promotion, earned or not.

She pressed her thumb to the v-doc's signature box. Her temporary unit transfer was now official.

"Excellent," McBride said. "Area B-4 is Delta Company's AO. Your platoon sergeant will get you squared away. Now go, get out of my sight."

"Yes, Sir." Stacie did an about-face and exited. Her promotion stroked her ego. *Now "Sergeant Spencer." Yaassss!*

She went to Area B-4, linked up with her platoon sergeant, got assigned to a squad, and hit the company armory to get shelled. Not long after, her platoon boarded BUSs and headed for the Parliament Building's yard. There, they joined the largest assembly of Guardians they had ever seen.

On the yard, prefabs had been set up as chow facilities and perhaps even barracks.

Bound by the Oath and a sense of duty, the Guardians were ready to give their lives to protect Eden soil. The sheer audacity of the Coalition in bringing the war to their turf ignited a fervor.

No one knew when the invaders would arrive. Until then, the Guardians would remain alert and stay ready.

Though Stacie felt prepared to face whatever the Coalition threw at her, she didn't like being this exposed. Out here, she felt like a sitting duck waiting to be picked off. But there was nothing she could do about it.

• • •

At the rear parking deck of the Parliament Building, a motorcade of limousines and CDF armored vehicles rolled in. The chairmen and chairwomen of the Parliament sat inside the limousines. Armed Guardians in light body armor opened their doors for them and began escorting them inside.

While walking toward the entrance, Chairman Jeff Hutchinson glanced at Oviereya, who was right beside him. "Is this really the safest place for us?"

"Is there any place safer?" Oviereya replied, her sleek dark braids swaying as she strode forward.

With no better ideas, Jeff changed the subject. "These rebels are biting off more than they can chew. Do they really think they can beat the Commonwealth Defense Force? We've spent years and billions transforming the CDF into the most fearsome fighting force of the Interplanetary Union."

Oviereya knew not to underestimate the Coalition. "Threat assessments suggest the Coalition has acquired advanced wearable armaments that may rival or surpass our Shells. They've also enlisted the Falgoah. We don't know their numbers, and we can't predict the full extent of their firepower. But this day didn't have to happen.

"We let systemic oppression fester far too long. This attack on Eden is the result of our neglect."

"The colony citizens are lucky to have what they have," Jeff snapped. "They should be grateful."

More limos arrived. Doors clicked open.

Oviereya's strong features hardened in visible offense at her colleague's lack of compassion. "Nonsense. Edenites became comfortable being the New Humanity's ruling class. They expected colonists to remain their proles. Their unspoken motto was, 'Someone has to do the dirty work, but not me.' For years, colonists were treated like lower lifeforms, and colony advancement got thrown by the wayside."

"Eden had to come first, and must evolve further, if our republic is to become the intergalactic superpower needed to protect humanity," Jeff replied. "Both Edenites and colonists have roles to play. Those roles have different responsibilities, yes, but are equally important. The colony proletariat's role will only grow in value as we expand to trading-partner and Mission Worlds for resource harvesting.

"Face it, Amaechi, AEGIS put the right gears in the right places. We risk stalling humanity's progress if we deviate from the socioeconomic structure it laid out."

Oviereya said pointedly, "The way we live is starkly different from the way they live. Ensuring basic human dignity is no deviation. It's a moral obligation."

"We'll improve life in the colonies eventually. Just not now."

"That mindset is why we've arrived at this unfortunate climax."

Jeff grunted in irritation, signaling the end of the exchange, as the security detail escorted them through twin tinted glass doors into the building's atrium.

• • •

The assault ship's cloaking field had worked like a charm. The ship had made unauthorized planetfall without detection.

Hardsuit on and headgear racked to his side, Randy strode down the corridor that led to the troop hold. He'd be joining Gold Force in the occupation of the Parliament Building, along with Jarius and Kesley.

He saw Kesley staring out of a window. Not part of the Hardsuit element, she wore a royal-blue getup cut close to the body, overlaid with armor attachments—unpowered combatwear provided by the Falgoah. It was being referred to as "protective combat uniform (PCU)," and served as the underlayer for the Hardsuit, like a sleeve.

Randy took up a spot beside her.

"This is paradise," Kesley exclaimed. The splendor of the land and the sprawling metropolises were unlike anything she had ever seen.

"Yeah," Randy said, "sorry you had to see Eden for the first time under these circumstances." He placed a hand on her back. "After things settle, I promise I'll take you for a joyride in my sports cruiser."

Kesley spun to him with a thankful smile. "'Kay, sounds good. Thanks." On the spur of the moment, she grabbed the back of his head, threading her fingers through his wavy hair, and claimed his mouth in a fiery good-luck kiss.

Randy quickly pulled away, thoughts turning to Stacie.

"Something wrong?" Kesley asked.

"I just . . . have to get going. It's almost time for the big shebang," he said, moving on. "Stay safe out there, Kess."

"You too, Randy."

As he neared the entry hatch to the troop hold, Randy saw Sariah up ahead. "Hey, Sariah, wait up."

She paused and faced Randy. "What's up?"

He edged closer. "I Linked with my father."

"Yes, he told me."

"Well, I wanted to say thank you. Thank you for stopping him from taking his life."

"I was just doing what a friend would do. Now let's get on with this mission."

Inside the troop hold, armored rebels stood, gripping the wall railings' handholds.

On the eve of change, precombat stress shook the rebels' limbs.

The pressure was on.

"We are now in position over the target areas," the helmsman said over the intercom.

"Alright, all forces, we'll be airdropping into hot water," Arson said. "As you know, the element of surprise has gone to shit. We've got a huge welcoming committee waiting for us down there. After we neutralize them, we'll deploy the shield generators. Avoid taking any lives if possible. These soldiers are just doing their jobs." *So many Guardian lives are about to be put at risk. What a screwed-up situation.*

"Let's do this!" a man shouted energetically, boosting morale.

"Yeah!" came a woman's voice.

Arson commed the helm. "This is Arson. Open the drop doors."

The whirring sound of the floor splitting open signaled the start of what would be the Coalition's most important battle.

The ship hovered above the Quad, cloaked from the naked eye.

Randy swallowed. This would be his first time fighting in the Hardsuit. His cram session with Sariah had gone well, but he still wasn't used to the suit. It felt strange going into battle without heightened awareness or an AI Combat Assistant—like being back in Basic Training, using the outdated M-X01 Shell. The Hardsuit was superior to the M-X02 in some ways, inferior in others. Maybe they were about even.

His heart beat faster as he waited for his father's command. Bringing war to Eden was nerve-wracking, but necessary. He and the others aboard this ship carried the promise of a new Commonwealth in their hands. Ridding his mind of worry, he composed himself for the fight to come.

"Gold Force, you're up first," Arson said.

Tasked with taking the Parliament Building, Gold Force let go of the handholds and leapt out. They ignited their vernier jets to control their free fall.

Wind howled against their armor.

On the Parliament Building's yard, shelled Guardians looked skyward. "Holy shit, it's them!" one shouted.

"Take the fuckers out!" an NCO bellowed.

Guardians' Gatling guns, their primary weapon, vibrated to life and hosed the sky with slugs.

"Come get some!" a Guardian roared.

A CDF armored land vehicle launched a missile.

One rebel, unable to dodge in time, stared wide-eyed as the missile closed in. "Holy Shi-!" An explosion flashed.

Rebels opened fire mid-fall, their energy blasts strafing the ground. Fountains of dirt, grass, and phyocrete splashed upward.

A blast from above blew a fist-sized hole in a Guardian's solar plexus. His feet backpedaled, and he fell sideways.

The Rebels' air-to-ground fire didn't let up. Guardians cursed, shooting upward.

A blaster lowered from the assault ship's underside and accumulated plasma energy. It released an enfilade, forcing Guardians to spread out.

Four robo-cannons rose from their underground compartments. Autoloaders chinked and clanked, chambering explosive rounds. Dual launch chutes fired, sending the projectiles streaking toward the assault ship.

Rebels in the sky intercepted the incoming projectiles with energy blasts, detonating them midair.

Hardsuits made landfall, dropping onto the battlefield.

A horde of Falgoah dispersed from the ship in needle-shaped, triangular-winged fighter bombers. The craft swooped down, unleashing a blitzkrieg on the Guardians below. As explosions flung Guardians like rag dolls, the Falgoah pilots shouted their war cry and pumped their fists.

More armored rebels landed.

Randy jetted into the air. He conjured an energy sphere with his hands and hurled it at one of the robo-cannons. The resulting explosion tore it apart, spraying metal fragments across the yard as flames consumed what remained.

Randy landed just as a blur of bullets zipped past him.

Boom! Shrapnel rained from above. The pace of the battle was accelerating.

This is maddening, Jarius thought. There was no cover, no concealment. There was no way to be strategic. This was an open, all-out gunfight to the last man and woman.

A Guardian's shoulder blasters struck down two Hardsuits. Jarius had the Guardian in his visor's crosshairs. He hesitated to pull his rifle's trigger. This wasn't easy on the soul. He couldn't balk now, though. He had chosen his side.

He pulled the trigger, and a blast of energy shot from his rifle. The Guardian slumped to the ground, a steaming hole in his torso plating. *Damn, this just feels wrong.* He fired two more blasts, striking down another Guardian. *Man, I really don't like firing on my own compadres.*

His shots drew the attention of two Guardians. They turned their weapons on him, firing.

Pulses of energy streaked past him. "Shit!"

He didn't know if the Guardians he'd taken down were dead, but he had no time for guilt. It was fight or die.

He ignited his vernier jets and soared above the melee. The two Guardians still targeting him adjusted their aim, but he took care of them with well-placed blasts before they could fire again.

He landed. *The faster this ends, the better.*

Kesley manned the top-mounted laser turret of a combat hover vehicle.

The rebel at the controls swerved the vehicle alongside one of the robo-cannons.

Now, Kesley thought. Her gloved hands tightened around the twin grips of the gun as she thumbed the firing studs. Twin flashes of energy burst forth, and the cannon became a heap of burning wreckage.

"Hold on!" the driver yelled. "Incoming!" He veered to the left, barely dodging a missile. It slammed into the ground behind them, the explosion juddering the vehicle's frame.

Close one, Kesley thought.

A Guardian lunged at Randy with a plasma saber. Randy sidestepped, grabbed the Guardian's arm, and threw him over his shoulder. While the Guardian lay dazed on his back, Randy drove a plasma-charged punch into his faceplate. The concussive blow knocked him out cold.

Randy was doing his best to disable Shells without killing, but deep down, he knew he wouldn't make it through this battle without taking one single life.

Around him, the brutality of war escalated. Rebels and Guardians gunned each other down.

Suddenly, Randy's implant pinged and buzzed. *Stacie. She's near.*

Weapons roared from all directions.

Stacie, engaged in close-quarters combat, buried her plasma saber into a Hardsuit, melting armor and filament. She summoned more power to the blade, and it grew—flickering wildly. *Ciao, baby.* Her implant gave her notice of Randy's presence. *Randy?* She jerked her arm back, ripping the blade free. Then the rebel crumpled.

Purple sparks scattered as Stacie shut off the saber. Her

implant, like a compass, guided her to Randy. His signal grew stronger the closer she got to him. As her eyes skimmed the grisly battlefield, her implant directed her to the Hardsuit straight ahead.

<Randy, what are you doing?> she asked.

Randy pivoted. *<Stace!>* He retracted his face guard.

Stacie edged closer. *<So, you did join them!>* Her voice carried a mix of shock and betrayal.

"You saw the files," Randy said. "Something needs to be done."

Stacie raised her faceplate. Her eyes mirrored her disappointment at Randy's decision. "Yeah, there's a lot of corruption in the government," she said, voice low. "And . . . my mother and father are part of it." Her brows knitted. "But that *doesn't* mean you join a bunch of terrorists. Corruption can be fought another way. We took an oath to defend the Commonwealth."

A shot-up Falgoah bomber plummeted from the sky, air whistling, and crashed into the ground in a puff of fire.

"You say there's another way," Randy replied, "but what is it?"

"I don't have an answer," Stacie admitted. "And it's not our job to have one, anyway. But I know turning your back on your duty is . . . is just plain wrong. The CDF Code of Military Justice makes that clear."

A rogue missile struck the ground nearby. *Boom!* Randy and Stacie's hearts pounded. Chunks of earth flung up and rained back down. That was a close call.

Relieved, Randy resumed the conversation. "This mission isn't just about the corruption. You've seen how colonists are treated, how they're forced to live. Before we went to Colony Four, everything we believed was just an assumption. We could only imagine what life was like for colonists, but imagination couldn't truly grasp the inhumanity of their reality.

"Now we've seen how horrible they have to live. I've even witnessed Guardians brutalize innocent people without cause. Edenites hear those stories and just brush them off as rubbish, just 'Coalition propaganda.' They tell themselves, 'Things can't be *that* bad.' But they are.

"Stace, the government needs to change. The CDF needs to change. And the institutional injustice inflicted on the colonies must end."

"So Reza's going to usher in a new era of equality and not seek any payback on Edenites? And after this magical new era begins, we'll all sing Kumbaya around bonfires together, right?" Stacie scoffed and shook her head. "Give me a fucking break."

Displeasure settled on Randy's face. "You're making a mockery of the genuine hope I, and so many colonists, have."

"No, I'm making a mockery of your stupid fairy-tale thinking, to drill some sense into your head, because I need the Randal Scott I know to wake up." Chopping the air, Stacie's hands punctuated her tirade.

Randy stood firm in the face of her criticisms. "I've been awoken alright, awoken by the reality of what needs to happen."

Stacie wished he'd come back to his senses. "Randy, are you for real right now? You help put in place an oligarchy, then what?"

"No, Reza's not putting himself in power. He plans to work with politicians who aren't in the Eight Elite's pocket, and with the citizens of the Commonwealth, to build a new government that serves everyone." Trying to win his war of words with Stacie, he left out, *I hope.*

Stacie threw up her arms. "My God, do you hear yourself? Take the blinders off, Randy!" This was so uncharacteristic of the Randal Scott she knew.

In the distance, the maelstrom of thudding explosions, zaps, and gunfire went on endlessly.

Randy sighed. "Stace, I know you never thought you'd hear me say stuff like this, but I need you to trust what I'm saying."

<*What's gotten into you?*> Stacie began probing his mind to unearth what had driven him to stray from the Oath. She found his travels with Kesley, his talks with Arson, and . . .

Randy tried to prevent her from digging further, saying, <*Stace, there's no need to—*>

Stacie's lips parted. A lost expression blanketed her face. She trembled, Shell rattling.

Her mindscan had uncovered Randy's night of enthralling sex with Kesley. She absorbed his sensations. She absorbed the thrill of every touch, every kiss.

She summed up her feelings in just a few words. <*You motherfucking son of a bitch!*> Her infuriated expression disappeared behind her faceplate. Hot plasma crackled from her armguard, and her saber materialized.

She swung the energy blade at Randy, screaming a curse.

He re-formed his face guard and dodged to the side, but not fast enough to avoid receiving a gash in his shoulder plating, which regenerated in seconds. "That night was a mistake. A big mistake."

"Enough!" Stacie kicked Randy, jamming her foot into his gut.

He "oomphed."

Stacie's face was red-hot. "Not only have you joined the enemy, but you sleep with them too!" Her voice was the harshest Randy had ever heard it. "You betrayed your duty, but you also betrayed *me*! *Me*, Randy, the woman who dragged you out of your emotional withdrawal from society! The woman who broke you out of . . . being a loner! The woman who made you smile time after time since your mother's death by the very people you now ally yourself with!" All true, Stacie had been his lifeline—a lifeline out of sorrow

—and had helped him rebound from all the hurt, breathing life back into his soul.

"We had a covenant, Randal Eugene Scott! We agreed to only you and me! We agreed for us to be exclusive! But you betrayed me for some . . . some rebel bimbo."

It was strange for Randy to hear the words "You betrayed me." That was exactly how he had felt about his father. "Stace, I don't want to fight you!"

She wasn't listening. A launcher sprang up from her shoulder. It fired two missiles in quick succession.

Randy thrust his plasma-charged hands forward, generating an energy screen. The missiles hit, erupting into fiery bursts.

The shield dissipated on his command. He shot back using his palm blaster. Stacie instinctively crossed her forearms. The energy blasts struck her, breaking off shards of armor.

"Stacie, no more! Let's end this!" Randy begged.

The memory of Randy's night with Kesley still burned fresh in Stacie's mind, stoking her rage. She had felt Kesley's lips and body overpowering Randy's resolve to respect their relationship.

She vaulted high into the air, letting out a roar of outrage, and slashed downward in a vertical arc toward Randy.

He rolled over his shoulder just in time. The blade sizzled past him and burrowed into the ground. Damn, her reflexes were lightning-fast, he thought, and she was showing no leniency. Hell hath no fury like a woman scorned, he figured.

Locked in their own skirmish, the ex-couple ignored the larger battle raging around them.

Not wanting to hurt his former lover, Randy dove at her, wrapping his arms around her waist. They clunked to the ground, with him on top.

Randy held down Stacie's wrists, the servos of his arms

groaning.

Her Shell's joints hissed as she struggled to break free.

Unyielding, Randy asserted more pressure. "Stop fighting, Stace," he pled. Any other time, he would've enjoyed being on top of her, but not today.

She was now vulnerable. He could've disabled her Shell right then. But tied to her by emotion, he held back.

Capitalizing on Randy's moment of weakness, Stacie drove a knee up and knocked him off.

Turning the tables, she shut off her saber, power-leapt into the air, and crashed a knee into his torso as she came down.

Randy winced. That blow packed a hell of a wallop.

Trapping him between her thighs, Stacie began clobbering his helmet with wild, furious blows. *Fucking traitor.* The teasers and naysayers had hurt her. Her parents had hurt her. And now her lover had hurt her. Her heart cut open, the fury, sadness, and pain bubbled to the surface, making her cry. *Fuck you!*

Disoriented by the barrage, Randy thought, *Gotta get her off.* He fired a close-range shot from his palm blaster, sending her flying. A blast at that distance was dangerous, but he'd held back enough power to damage only the Shell, not the woman inside.

Lying on her back, suit smoking and crackling, Stacie mentally kicked herself. *Sloppy of me. Damn sloppy. I should've been watching his hands.* Her anger had blinded her.

As she rose, Randy quickly launched a taser coil from his bracer. It clamped onto her Shell, and a plasma charge surged through the cable.

Pain smashed into Stacie. On her HUD, CONDITION 8 flashed, code for "not good." Then: SYSTEM OVERLOADING. The charge shorted out circuits and severed her implant-to-CPU connection. Feeling vanished from her arms and legs. All coherent thought and her consciousness receded.

She collapsed onto her back and would be comatose for a while.

Randy deactivated his face guard. Exhausted, he inhaled deeply and exhaled. *Sorry, Stace.* Hurting her tore at him.

He leaned in, removed Stacie's helmet, and tossed it aside. Then he rolled her facedown and palmed the Shell's manual release.

The armor expanded from her body, sliding panels unsealing with a series of chinks.

Randy reached in, gripped her under the arms, and wrestled her free from the suit. He hefted her onto his shoulder, carried her a few paces, and gently propped her against the side of the Parliament Building.

He gazed out at the bodies of Guardians and rebels lying on the yard and cringed. Being both a Guardian and a rebel, watching lives being lost on both sides weighed heavily on his soul. *I sure hope you're wrong, Stace, dead wrong. I hope this turns out alright.*

Spasmodic gunfire echoed. Falgoah bombers landed, and their pilots jumped out, firearms in hand.

Rebels began filing into the Parliament Building. They had suffered fewer casualties than projected. Their Hardsuits' plasma-based firepower had compensated for their lack of numbers.

• • •

Standing on the assault ship's bridge, Reza observed the battle sites below on a battery of screens. His forces were mopping up the last of the Guardians protecting the targets, doing their best not to kill.

Over the ship's comm, Reza heard Arson report, "Reza, I've gotten word that we've taken the Parliament Building." The Coalition had also taken the Academy, which had been evacuated. "I'm now infiltrating the Chief Executive's Manor, and shield generators are being put in place for each building."

"Excellent. A job well done," Reza replied proudly. "When you have Gould, bring him to *me*, in the broadcast center of the Parliament Building."

"Roger, sir."

Reza's mind recapped Priscilla's death. The moment he'd dreamt of for so long had finally come to fruition. It was time for Gould to die, by his hands.

Another set of screens off to the right showed blipping icons representing CDF vehicles. Waves of Guardian forces were being redistributed from the streets of Cornerstone to the Quad.

"Lower the ship into the shield generators' range," Reza ordered his helmsman, who sat at the primary control station.

"Yes, sir." Navigational instruments chirped.

The craft descended, then held a fixed altitude above the Parliament Building.

• • •

Inside the Chief's Manor, Arson and Sariah, encased in their Hardsuits, surveyed the bodies of unarmored Guardians they'd had no choice but to hurt. The four rebels in PCUs who were with them stood watch, their faces grim as they worried about the wounded.

A Guardian in battledress groaned, his side gashed.

Arson estimated the young man to be between eighteen and twenty-two. He deactivated his face guard and knelt beside him. "Here, let me help," he said gently. A syringe extended from his wrist. He plunged it into the Guardian's side, medicating the wound. "That should numb the pain and help you recover."

The Guardian murmured, "Why—" He coughed. "Why . . . are you helping me, *Arson Scott?*"

"Because I don't want you to die. I don't want *anyone* to die. You're just a man doing his duty."

The Guardian managed more words, the pain and bleeding slurring his speech. "If you don't want . . . anyone to . . . die, then wh-why the . . . invasion?" He coughed again.

"This operation had to happen, son. The central government is corrupt, and—"

Sariah cut Arson off, knowing now wasn't the time for talk. "Love, we have no time for this. We have to keep moving."

"You're right." Arson straightened and reactivated his face guard. "Stay alert and stay alive, everyone. Let's move." To the young Guardian, he said, "You'll be fine."

A rebel named Saul said, "I'll take point, Commander Scott." Holding an energy gun with a two-handed grip, he rounded a corner and ran straight into four unarmored Guardians. "Oh, shit!" He immediately retreated around the corner as bursts of machine-gun fire roared.

While in a crouch, he snatched his last stun grenade from his bandoleer and rolled it toward the Guardians.

It exploded in a bright blue flash, unleashing a paralyzing shock wave that knocked the Guardians unconscious.

"Clear!" Saul rose from his crouch.

Sariah said, "According to the building schematics, the next hallway leads to the Chief's office. Let's move."

Unshaken and unworried, Cornelius sat calmly at his desk with his fingers twined. His deadpan face showed no stress or concern. In contrast, Gillian, standing beside him, wore a look of helplessness.

Her worried eyes darted between the door and her mentor. In a low, uncertain voice, she simply said, "Sir?"

"We surrender and remain calm," Cornelius replied inexpressively. "Don't show them any fear."

Gillian nodded. "Yes, Sir." *How does he remain so dauntless in a situation like this?*

"Reinforcements will arrive soon, Juggernauts and more weaponry from Area 14. The CDF will eventually overpower the Coalition's invasion force."

The office doors blew inward. A veil of smoke drifted into the room. Arson, Sariah, and the four rebel fighters stormed inside, bringing their weapons to bear.

Cornelius got up from his chair, composed and unintimidated. He and Gillian lifted their hands in surrender.

Arson commed the assault ship as his men kept the two at gunpoint. "This is Scott to Reza. We have Gould."

Arson's headgear comm squawked. Reza replied, "Excellent. You know where to bring him."

"Yes, sir." Arson opened his face guard and pointed to two of his men. "Kaiden and Mateo, detain the woman with the surrenderees. Tend to their needs as best you can. If they need water or anything, take care of it."

"Right," Kaiden replied. He and Mateo each took one of Gillian's arms and led her out of the room.

Arson grimaced at Cornelius, disgust twisting his features. "See? We're not like you."

Cornelius chuckled. "Obviously. I don't start wars against my own people."

Arson spun on his heel. "Saul, Otto, bring him."

Saul strode up and jabbed the muzzle of his rifle against Cornelius' spine. "C'mon, dirtbag. Move."

"Sariah," Arson said, "I'm headed to the Parliament Building. I need you to stay here and take command."

"Roger that," she replied.

They exited the office.

• • •

Inside the now-occupied Parliament Building, rebel fighters were unwinding. The energy dome produced by the shield generators outside had secured the perimeter, for now.

Stacie, in her sleeve, sat against a wall. Her hands were cuffed behind her back, and her eyes were closed. Randy sat beside her in his PCU. He also had his eyes closed.

Across from them, Jarius sat against the opposite wall, now out of his Hardsuit. He watched a newscast on his wristcom. The footage showed Juggernauts and more shelled Guardians surrounding the energy dome outside. The crawl at the bottom of the newscast said COALITION FORCES WIN FIRST ROUND: PARLIAMENT, ACADEMY, AND CHIEF EXECUTIVE'S MANOR OCCUPIED.

The camera drones of another newscast showed clandestine armed groups loyal to the Coalition's mission obstructing Guardians attempting to leave Eden's streets and reach the Parliament Building. These groups had long awaited this day, the day the Commonwealth Government would fall. Reza had counted on them to show, counted on them to be inspired and rise up.

Kesley came over to Jarius. Randy and Stacie's stillness gave her pause. "They asleep or something?"

Jarius shook his head. "Naw, suspended animation. They're just having a little heart-to-heart in a dreamscape, a reality generated by a cerebral implant."

"You Highborns and your fancy brain chips." Kesley plopped down beside Jarius. "Randy mentioned a Stacie. That her?"

"Yeah." Jarius cut off the newscast.

"So, what's their deal?"

"They're lovers deeply bonded by a Link."

Kesley raised an eyebrow. "He never said they were sweethearts, but I kinda suspected. Were things working out between them?"

"Yeah, they were, at least as far as I know. But now they're on opposite sides of the war. And to make matters worse, there's you. If you and Randy hadn't shacked up, I could've easily seen them continuing where they left off, if this war ends in some sorta consensus. But now, with you in the picture, their relationship is *really* on the fritz."

"Hey, I didn't make him do anything he didn't wanna do, and like I said, he never told me he was serious with anyone."

"Would you have still come on to him if you had known?"

A hesitant silence followed. "Like I said, I didn't make him do anything he didn't wanna do."

"Fair enough." Jarius glanced over at Randy and Stacie. *I wonder how things are going. Maybe they can patch things up. Then again, maybe they were two incompatible souls from the start.*

In the dreamscape, Randy and Stacie stood in an expanse of sand, under a magnificent sky of dreamy colors. Blue ocean waves crashed against the shoreline. The beach was a place they were both fond of. Randy had chosen the ideal backdrop for an attempted kiss-and-makeup session.

Stacie wore a greenish-blue one-piece swimsuit and a sheer sarong. Randy wore a white T-shirt and red beach shorts.

As the drama between him and Stacie unfolded, Randy said, "I'd do anything for you, Stacie. You *know* that. *Anything.* Even take a bullet. As for what happened with Kesley, I was frustrated, tired, angry, confused. You name it. I needed an escape. I needed to take my mind off everything. She's attractive, a temptation. My judgment was impaired, and . . . well . . . it just happened. I'm sorry I hurt you. It's not like I'm head over heels for her or anything." He hoped he could repair his damaged relationship with Stacie.

Stacie's emotions were feverish, to say the least.

Her eyes glowed. The air hummed, loud and shrill. Fragments of the dreamscape tore away, shattering into splinters. The rupture revealed a window into Randy's memory of his night with Kesley.

Kesley's high-pitched whimpers reverberated through the air, Randy thrusting into her.

"That looks like willful abandon to me," Stacie said.

Randy refiled the memory, and the dreamscape mended itself. Shamefaced, he bowed his head. "I'll do anything to make it up to you. You're the one I—"

"No. No more bullshit!" Stacie's volatile emotions quaked the dreamscape. "You want her? Fine. You want to be a rebel? Fine. I don't give a fuck." The world around them wobbled and shimmied. The beautiful beach scenery eroded into nothingness as the ethereal construct Randy had created deteriorated.

"Stacie, listen. I know I fucked up, but—"

"Enough!"

Darkness smothered them both.

Randy and Stacie opened their eyes, returning to the hall. Jarius and Kesley rose from the floor.

"You okay, Randy?" Jarius asked.

Randy said nothing. His expression gave the answer: no. Could he ever redeem himself in Stacie's eyes? He got to his feet and walked off. "I'll be back. Just need some breathing room." It was clear he'd get no forgiveness from his former lover.

Stacie shot a furious glare at Kesley. *Rebel bitch,* she thought, biting her lip.

"I'm gonna check on some of the others," Kesley said to Jarius, then walked away.

Now it was just Jarius and Stacie.

"Stace, you alright?" Jarius asked, concerned for his former sub-lead.

"What do you think?" Stacie's body ached from combat, her lover had been with another woman, and she was being held captive.

"Yeah, dumb question. Sorry."

"How, Jarius? How could you join them?"

Jarius took a breath. "I know it seems wrong, and I had doubts. But I think joining the Coalition for this operation is the right move. Believe me, I'm not happy about fighting Guardians."

"If you're so uncomfortable with fighting your own comrades, then why'd you join the Coalition and betray the Oath?"

Jarius leaned his back against the wall and crossed his arms. "Because . . . the shit we were taught wasn't right," he said thoughtfully. "The colonies need help. But that's not all. I was viewing some articles the central government didn't approve of, and the Nerve Center warned me to stop, like I don't have the right to view whatever the hell I want.

"Also, I'm pretty sure Lars was gonna blow me away just because I wondered if there was some legitimacy behind the CFP protesters' actions. You get that, Stace? I was gonna get blown away by my superior. Apparently, being a freethinker is a career killer in the CDF, *literally*.

"Now the Coalition's discovered that Gould has empathy-dampening modifications in the works for our implants, meant to keep us from feeling any regret for the people we kill. That's some scary shit, if you ask me. And that's not the future I want for the CDF. Hell no. Something had to be done, Stace, and the Coalition seemed like the answer. That's all I've got to say."

Stacie closed her eyes and withdrew into her thoughts, still unconvinced the Coalition's invasion was a good thing. She wondered how this standoff was going to end.

• • •

In the broadcast center, located on the top floor, Reza waited for Cornelius to be brought to him. From here, he could have the net filters overridden to release the corruption files and take over all vidcast transmissions, delivering his message to the entire Commonwealth.

A set of metal steps led to the upper-level deck of the room, where one of Reza's technicians sat at the operations console. He was ready to upload the corruption files upon Reza's command.

Patience wearing thin, Reza thought about Priscilla's death, bullets tearing into her body. He remembered reaching for Cornelius' throat, only to be held back by his cronies.

The reinforced metal door slid open. Two rebels in tactical gear escorted Cornelius in at gunpoint.

At last, the moment Reza had been waiting for had arrived. "So, we meet again, Cornelius."

The Chief's posture remained calm and composed. He had survived countless wars and battles; no masked man or barrel aimed at his back could shake his fortitude. "So, I assume we've met, before you decided to hide your face," he said dryly.

"Yes, we have," Reza replied.

"Who are you?" Even in captivity, Cornelius spoke demandingly.

"You'll know soon enough. But first, the Commonwealth must hear the truth about you and your corrupt colleagues."

Cornelius drew his eyebrows together. "What the devil are you talking about?"

Reza said nothing more. He stepped onto the cylindrical pedestal protruding from the floor and signaled the technician to begin the vidcast.

The eighteen-year-old keyed a command on the console.

Above, a dome-shaped installation bathed Reza in a pillar of light. The Commonwealth's net orbiters in space broadcasted his image and voice to every watchable device on Eden and Satellite One.

The technician gave a thumbs-up. "Uplink is green. You're live, sir."

"Citizens of the Commonwealth, I am Arman Reza, leader of the Coalition of Rebel Factions." Reza gave another hand signal. The technician pressed the yellow "send" button. "On the net, you'll now find evidence revealing the true nature of many of your elected leaders. Some members of the Parliament are good men and women; others are among the most vile people to ever hold office. They have forged insidious deals with Eden's wealthiest class, the Eight Elite.

"The Eight are more than just businesspeople expanding their enterprises throughout the cosmos. They're a criminal syndicate. That's why we, the Coalition, have taken control of key government buildings: to oust the scum who degrade our republic and keep colony citizens under the thumb of oppression. Go online. Access the files. See the truth for yourself.

"I encourage all Guardians who abhor these corrupt politicians to lay down their arms and allow a new government to rise."

All across the Commonwealth, people were accessing the leaked files.

Reza continued. "I will take the reins of government to enact the change we so desperately need. As for the unfit, their time is over. Judgment begins now, with Cornelius Gould." He gestured to the two rebels flanking the Chief.

"Move," one of them ordered, shoving Cornelius forward.

Cornelius' frown deepened. The two rebels forced him up onto the pedestal and into the transmission beam, both of them training their weapons on him.

Reza slowly reached for the pistol holstered at his side and brought it to the back of Cornelius' head. "Do you feel fear, like Priscilla Kitzron did?" he asked, voice colder than death.

Cornelius said, "I have no idea what the hell you're talking about."

"Years ago, in Colony Four, there was a miners' strike. Guardians shot and killed a woman. Her name was Priscilla Kitzron. She was my lover. And I was the Guardian who barged into your office that day."

Reza had jogged Cornelius' memory. "You? You're Arman Reza?"

"Yes, *me*." His anger compounding, Reza pressed the gun harder against Cornelius' skull. "And you weren't contrite in the least. Even now, you show no remorse. You're truly a soulless human being.

"People like you should be erased from existence. You're responsible for Priscilla's death. And you allowed defenseless Falgoah to be slain in cold blood for no reason. No reason at all!"

Reza's mind resurrected images of the destroyed Falgoah village. Then a montage of treasured times with Priscilla blinked through his thoughts. With her death about to be avenged, he wondered if she was smiling down on him from Heaven right now.

He heard her voice whisper, *Finish it, my love.*

The gun barked once. Cornelius' body thunked to the floor, his blood sprinkling everywhere. Reza fired three more rounds into the corpse, his own scream transforming into a ragged sob.

Shell casings tinkled across the floor.

Reza dropped to his hands and knees, the gun slipping from his grasp. He dragged air into his lungs and exhaled. *It's done, Priscilla.*

Priscilla's ghostly, translucent incarnation materialized in front of him. *You did it, my love. Let your mind be at peace now.* She faded away, blowing a kiss.

The technician's heart flew into his throat. *Public executions? This isn't right.*

"Sir, are you okay?" one of Reza's men asked him.

Reza's voice regained its strength. "I'm fine." He stepped back onto the pedestal, standing beneath the transmission beam. "Citizens of the Commonwealth, I am your new leader for the foreseeable future. I will be the one to shape this republic into what it was always meant to be." He kicked Cornelius' dead body. "Not this piece of trash. And the other corrupt officials, now in custody here in the Parliament Building, will be next to face justice."

A disturbed expression crossed the technician's face. This wasn't the plan. The Coalition was supposed to hand power over to a transitional government and let the judiciary system try the corrupt officials fairly. Reza had promised to collaborate with the new government and the Commonwealth's people to achieve a win-win for both worlds. Instead, he had just declared a dictatorship.

• • •

Arson had met up with Randy, Kesley, and Jarius in the hallway. The four of them were watching the livecast on the tablet Arson held.

Arson scowled and flung the tablet against the wall. Reza was supposed to help usher in a new government, not take control. There weren't supposed to be any public executions. Judgment was supposed to come from the courts, not the barrel of a gun. And now, Reza had made himself judge, jury, and executioner. Tyranny wasn't what the Coalition stood for. It wasn't what Arson Scott stood for.

So much for the Coalition's idolization of Reza, Randy thought. "I knew it," he said bitterly. "I knew there was something shady about him. He's just another hypocrite, another authoritarian hiding behind a cause."

Stacie, still sitting restrained, pinned a scalding glare on Randy. "Well, Randal, how does it feel putting this autocrat into power?"

"Enough, Stace. I don't have time for a verbal sparring match. We need to figure out how to fix this mess."

"Oh, *whoop-de-do*, now you have to clean up the shitstorm *you* rebels created."

Randy frowned. "You're acting like a child again."

"*Again*? What the hell are you talking about?"

"Yeah, *again*, like when you—"

"Hey, you two," Jarius cut in, "save the melodrama for later. We've got bigger problems."

Kesley chimed in. "Well, I can't say I'm not glad that lunatic is dead." She shrugged, palms up. "And if those corrupt Parliament scum, who kept us colonists in the gutter, end up in front of a firing squad, so be it. Suits me just fucking fine."

Randy chided her, saying, "No, Kess. That kind of senseless brutality is exactly what the Coalition was fighting against. And I didn't join the Coalition just to put another nutcase in power."

Jarius, hearing Reza's voice continue, grabbed the tablet from the floor. Its screen was cracked but still working.

Reza said, "Even as I speak, my knights are infiltrating the estates of the Eight's family heads, bringing the sword of justice to them as well."

Stacie gasped. "My parents!" She looked up at Randy hard-eyed. "And you—who I let touch me, make love to me—helped put this murdering piece of garbage in power, who just sent his bozos to my family's doorstep to murder them. Damn you, Randal Scott."

Kesley showed no sympathy for Stacie. "Yeah, well, maybe your mommy and daddy shouldn't have been a couple of crooks."

"Cut it out, Kess!" Randy shouted. "I know you've suffered under the government, but what Cornelius is doing is wrong."

"Randy's right," Arson said, his voice stern. He had known nothing about the kill squads. Reza had made plans in secret, behind his back and the backs of all the Coalition's commanders. So much for transparency and trust. "Reza's changed. At some point, his heart darkened. This isn't the man I believed in."

Chin lowered and lips sealed, Kesley felt regretful and embarrassed.

Stacie sat in silence, tears beading down her cheeks. Her relationship with her parents had never been perfect, but she had never wanted them dead, not even after all of her mother's parental cruelty, or their illegal dealings.

Good memories surfaced: her mother cradling her as a child, fun outings during her teenage years, warm family dinners where life lessons were passed down with sincerity and care.

Randy's heart ached for Stacie. This wasn't how things were supposed to turn out. He reached out to her cerebrally, only to find she'd terminated their Link. Undeterred, he sent a new Link request, hoping to reestablish their rapport. She rejected it, slamming the door on their relationship. It was far too early for any reconciliation, if there could be any at all. The hurt was still raw, too deep-seated inside her.

No, Randal, you don't get to have access to me, Stacie thought. *You can keep your rebel playmate.*

Arson opened a door to a conference room and gestured. "Randy, Jarius, Kesley, in here, now."

Randy spoke to Stacie softly. "Hey, don't go anywhere."

Stacie refused to make eye contact with him. "Not like I could leave without getting caught." It was true.

Randy followed Arson, Jarius, and Kesley into the room.

As they entered, motion sensors activated the overhead lights. A square crystalline table, surrounded by ten chairs, dominated the modest space.

"So what are you thinking?" Jarius asked Arson. He rested his nervous hands on the back of a chair.

"I didn't join the Coalition to put some tyrant in power." Arson felt duped. "I respected Reza and his vision. But somewhere along the line, he let power get to his head. He's not trying to work with the people or the uncorrupt officials to build a new Commonwealth. He wants to impose his own order. He's become just like Gould and Ritter, and men like that are dangerous."

"So, what, we become the Four Mutineers and take him out?" Kesley asked.

"*Yes*," Arson replied definitively. "If we don't, the fighting's only going to continue, and more young men and women are going to die. Reza was supposed to release the files and call for peace, to end this homicidal insanity. I don't want to see *anyone* else lose their life: Guardian, rebel, Highborn, colony-born . . . *no one*."

Jarius scoffed. "After we take him out, then what? The battle ain't gonna stop just because he's dead, and it's only a matter of time before the CDF figures out a way to knock out the shields. Both the CDF and the Coalition are gonna fight for their respective sides until the bitter end. The bloodshed is only gonna continue, right here on Eden soil, unless—"

"Unless we get what we want, *reformation*," Arson finished for him. "An armistice needs to be agreed upon."

Randy joined the conversation. "So once Gould's dead, who's next in line for the Chief Executive seat?"

Arson replied, "That would be the chairperson with the next highest ranking position to the Secretary of Defense, the

Chancellor of the Supreme Judiciary, Oviereya Amaechi. And we've got her here, being held with the other Parliament members in their meeting chamber."

"Okay," Jarius said, "Oviereya, as Chief, would represent the Commonwealth, but who'd represent the Coalition in this truce negotiation?"

For Arson, that was an easy answer. "Me." He was Reza's top commander, unquestionably the number-two man of the entire Coalition.

Randy thought, *In other words, the right people on both sides finally get into power.* And both were originally colony citizens.

Arson said, "Alright, we've got a plan. Let's put it into motion. Randy, come with me. We're going to get Oviereya and bring her back here to this room."

Randy was more than ready to end the war. "Let's do it."

Arson and Randy left the room, stepping back into the hallway.

When Randy heard Stacie whimpering, he paused. Tears streamed down her face.

Concerned, Randy said, "Hey, wha-?" He saw the tablet Jarius had left beside her. Onscreen, Reza was broadcasting images of the slain family heads, proof of execution sent by his kill squads. Among the dead were Patrick and Darlene Spencer. "I . . . I'm sorry, Stacie. If there's—"

"Just leave me alone," she choked out, sniffling and sobbing, mucus dripping from her nose.

"I—"

"Son, come on," Arson said sharply. "She needs space. Let her grieve."

Damn it, Randy thought. *How'd I let things get this messed up between us?* He turned away as Stacie cried loud and hard.

Side by side, rifles slung, Arson and Randy moved down the

hall and came to a single guard posted at the chamber doors.

"I need Oviereya," Arson said insistently.

"Yes, sir." The guard opened the door. All too easy.

Arson and Randy went into the spacious meeting room. The guard held the door open behind them.

The chairpersons sat around a glass-topped round table.

Despair was thick in the air.

Staying in character, Arson leveled his rifle at Oviereya. "Chairwoman Amaechi, get up and come with us."

A burly chairman at the far end of the table frowned. "Arson Scott. The infamous deserter comes home to—"

"Quiet!" Arson snapped. His eyes didn't leave Oviereya. "Chairwoman Amaechi, I need you to comply."

Without a word, Oviereya rose from her swivel chair and rounded the circumference of the table toward the father-son duo.

Arson grabbed her arm roughly, pulling her forward. She trailed behind him, stumbling to keep pace. "Move it." As they exited the room, he said to the guard, "Thanks. Keep up the good work."

Arson's compliment made the guard proud. "Yes, sir."

Walking back toward the conference room, Arson stayed behind Oviereya, rifle trained on her back. Randy walked beside her, rifle at the low ready.

In the hall, rebels exchanged quiet thoughts about Reza's new course of action, some agreeing with it, others not.

"Executing people isn't right," a man said.

A woman with rainbow-colored hair replied, "Who the hell cares? Those officials are scum. Reza's just cleaning house."

Divisions were already forming within the Coalition.

Oviereya whispered to Randy, "You're Randal Scott, Stacie Spencer's boyfriend and son of Arson Scott, yes?" She gave him a sidelong glance. "I understand why you joined the Coalition. A lot of young men and women defect after seeing how colonists live." Randy marched forward in silence. "I'm sorry the war has reached this point," Oviereya continued. "My fear is that it's spiraling toward a senseless, all-out massacre. Perhaps there's still a way to prevent that from happening, to finally—"

"Agreed," Randy said. "Believe it or not, my father and I are on the same wavelength as you."

What does he mean? "Where are you taking me?"

"To a conference room where you and my father can work something out in private to end this war. You're both now the de facto leaders of the opposing forces."

Oviereya looked flummoxed. "But Reza is still alive, isn't he?"

"Not for long," Randy replied bluntly.

They reached the conference room door.

Stacie still sat on the floor, her eyes full of grief. Jarius stood near her. The second she saw Oviereya, her heart brightened—during what was otherwise a dark time. "Oviereya!"

Oviereya met her gaze compassionately. "Stacie, I saw the vidcast. I'm sorry. I know you and your parents were often at odds, but I also know you valued the wisdom they passed on, and the ways they tried—however flawed—to shape your life. I'm grateful Darlene allowed me to be her midwife. And I'm honored your parents trusted me as your caretaker. I—"

Arson interrupted. "There'll be time to catch up later." He opened the conference room door. "Chairwoman, Randy, inside."

Before going into the room, Oviereya reached out to Stacie through their long-established Link. *<Stay strong.>*

<I will,> she replied.

Arson, Randy, and Oviereya entered the room.

"Please sit," Arson said amicably to Oviereya.

Oviereya pulled out a chair and sat down at the table. Arson and Randy took their places opposite her.

Arson kicked things off. "You already know who I am. Reza's changed, and not for the better. We never wanted a dictatorship. My son and I are going to stop him. But once that's done, the fighting won't just magically end. I'm proposing a ceasefire so we can work out an action plan. All the Coalition wants, Chairwoman Amaechi, is equality."

Oviereya gave a solemn nod. "Arson Scott, you have my word. Once Reza is dead, we'll make a plan for colony progression."

Randy said, "And what about the other chairpersons, the ones not tied to corruption? Are they going to back this plan? Most of them still cling to AEGIS's blueprint for humanity. Honestly, they're a bunch of spineless conformists."

Arson replied, "Anyone in Parliament who's hesitant to restructure the oppressive systems born from that damn computer will have to make a choice: peace or more war. And I *guaran-damn-tee* that if any of them resist, the Coalition will keep fighting. I'll lead that fight myself if I have to. But we're trying to give peace a real shot. After Hammer Fall, the Parliament should be smart enough not to blow this opportunity.

"Chairwoman, once we've dealt with Reza, we'll take you to the broadcast center. Together, you and I will call for a ceasefire."

Oviereya longed for the war to end. "Agreed."

Arson left the chair. "Alright then. Randal, let's go. Chairwoman, please stay here."

Randy and Arson exited the room into the hall.

"Things on track?" Jarius asked.

"Yeah," Randy confirmed.

"Where are you two headed now?"

"To take care of Reza," Arson answered.

Stacie said nothing.

Arson and Randy took an elevator to the top floor.

"Any idea of how we're going to pull this off?" Randy asked.

Arson held up his rifle. "Yeah, we blast him."

Randy, always the planner, said, "What if we're outnumbered by a security detail?"

"There's no time to account for every variable. We'll just have to adapt to whatever situation we encounter."

The elevator hissed to a stop, and the doors slid apart.

They approached the broadcast center. The building was secure, but Reza had expected potential dissent from rebels unhappy with his new direction, so he ordered that three guards be posted at the door.

"We're here to see Reza," Arson said.

"Hand over your rifles," the lead guard ordered. "No weapons are allowed inside."

Shit, Arson thought. *There goes option one.*

He and Randy surrendered their rifles. The other two guards patted them down thoroughly. One pulled a small blade from a hidden sheath in Arson's boot and stared at him incredulously, waiting for an explanation. There went option number two.

Arson said, "Sorry, oversight. I forgot I had that."

"Alright, you're clear, Commander Scott," the lead guard said.

The guards stepped aside, and Arson and Randy entered.

Reza sat at a metal desk, which had been brought from another room. "Arson, Randal, what brings you here?"

Randy said to Arson, <*Other than Reza, there's one guy on the control deck. Not sure if he's armed. What now?*>

Arson's eyes locked on the pistol holstered at Reza's side. <*I'm going for his gun. Just back me up.*>

<*Gotcha.*> Randy glanced at the big red square on the wall

panel, the emergency lock for the room. Once activated, no one could open the door from the outside without the passcode. <*I'll trigger the lock when it's time. That'll keep the guards out.*>

Arson stepped up to Reza. Randy stayed by the door.

"What's going on, Arman?" Arson asked. "The Coalition's ethos is based on the principles of life, respect, and proper conduct. Not death and domination. What you're doing—taking control, choosing who lives and dies, building a government without public input—is wrong."

Reza rose from his desk and placed a hand on Arson's shoulder. "You're a noble man, my friend. I understand your discomfort. But trusting Satellite One's future with others is too risky. I have to be the one to forge the new republic."

"This will only divide the Coalition. It already is."

"If—"

Now, Arson thought. He reached for the pistol, but Reza was faster. He captured Arson's wrist in an ironclad grip.

"So you chose to betray me," Reza said, mask hiding a disappointed expression. His grip tightened in anger.

Reza, strength enhanced by the cybernetic implements he wore over his arms, lifted Arson with both hands and hurled him into a metal rack. The equipment on its shelves scattered.

"Damn it!" Randy palmed the big red square button on the wall panel, locking the door.

"What's going on in there?" one of the guards shouted from the other side.

The technician wondered whom he should back. His conscience began to tilt toward Arson and Randy.

Randy lunged at Reza, tackling him. They hit the floor, wrestling furiously. Randy ended up on top of Reza, hands clamped around his throat.

"Get off me, fool!" Reza slammed an elbow into Randy's face and knocked him off.

As soon as Reza got to his feet, Arson lunged at him from behind. They tumbled across the floor.

From the control deck, the technician made a split-second decision. He tossed his energy gun down to Randy. "Heads up!"

Randy glanced up and snatched the weapon from the air with a one-handed grab, a feat of hand-eye coordination only an enhanced human could pull off.

Arson and Reza scrambled back to their feet, still trading blows.

Randy took aim. "Dad, move!"

Arson dove out of the line of fire, and Randy pulled the trigger. An energy blast roared from the gun's muzzle, blowing a simmering gap into Reza's chest.

His blood showered the floor as his body fell.

Randy breathed raggedly. *It's over.*

Arson said to the technician, "Thank you. What's your name, son?"

"Arwen. Arwen Dukes," he replied.

"Arwen, you made the right call today."

"Yeah, I didn't become a freedom fighter to help a dictator take over the Commonwealth."

• • •

Inside the broadcast center, Oviereya and Arson stood shoulder to shoulder on the pedestal, under the beam of the relay transmitter above.

Oviereya began the address. "Guardians of the Defense Force, Chief Gould is dead. Though I would've preferred he face trial, I do not mourn him. With his death, I now serve as your new Chief Executive. I am ordering you to stand down."

Arson then spoke. "Coalition rebels, Reza betrayed us. He no longer represented our ideals. My son and I did what had to be done. The war is over. Oviereya and I, as respective leaders of our combat forces, have agreed to a ceasefire."

The rebels and Guardians outside stood down. The energy shields around the Parliament Building, Academy, and Chief Executive's Manor flickered off.

This day marked the advent of a new dawn for the Commonwealth.

CHAPTER NINE

DAYS AFTER HAMMER FALL

In the Chief Executive's Manor, Chief Executive Amaechi sat at the table of the master stateroom with the other Union leaders. Each wore a translator earpiece.

ZorKeld said, "We have reviewed your summary of recent events and reached a decision. The Commonwealth may keep its incorporated status. We have high hopes for you, Chief Amaechi."

Days of worry lifted from Oviereya's shoulders. "Thank you," she replied. "The Commonwealth will live up to the mandates of the Union Charter, ensuring equality for all its people and no more bloodshed."

From Durgraso came a skeptical snort. "It had better."

Ziltilda, clad in a garment of crisscrossing brown leather straps and a spiked choker, spoke. "I believe there is nothing more to discuss." All the Union leaders rose. "Good luck, Chief Amaechi, we will be watching the Commonwealth's progression closely." With an ice-cold edge to her tone, she added, "Very, *very* closely."

As the others departed, Queen Pappalonie, looking glamorous in her jewel-studded bodysuit, approached Oviereya. Her bracelets and anklets jangled. She wrapped her arms around the new Chief. "Let me know how Taramassia may help, if needed."

Oviereya nodded silently.

After everyone had left, she sat at the table, pondering. There was a long road ahead. Healing the divides would take time.

Many Edenites questioned why the central government was being subservient to "terrorists." They resented the idea of letting the rebel fighters walk away scot-free. In their eyes, the rebels deserved punishment for starting an "unnecessary war" and bringing violence to Eden soil. They also didn't like that a colony-born Chief had taken power, fearing she might act against their interests.

On the flip side of Oviereya's dilemma, there were colonists who had unrealistic expectations of the central government.

She'd have to calm the irrational fears of Edenites and earn their trust. At the same time, she would need to show resolve to her own people, some of whom believed that, with a colony-born Chief in power, all their demands would be granted swiftly. Even with all troops recalled from the formerly occupied colonies, tension remained high. If progress took too long, another wave of unrest could follow.

Yes, Oviereya loved her people, but she wouldn't bow to every demand, especially those that were currently beyond the realm of possibility right now.

Besides the pressure of having to remain neutral and satisfy both colonists and Edenites, Oviereya also faced anxiety from not knowing how the upcoming elections would turn out.

Judges would try the corrupt politicians, and special elections would determine their replacements. However, Oviereya predicted that most of the open seats would likely be won by candidates with the same mindset as their predecessors, due to Edenites fearing a colony-born Chief and colonists being outnumbered at the polls.

As for next year's election for her own seat, she knew her opponents would use the deaths of Guardians and Edenites' fears about a colony-born Chief as talking points and political attacks. She had no illusions that her victory was guaranteed.

No one had ever said that leading a post-civil-war Commonwealth would be easy, but she was determined to rise to the challenge.

She sighed and left the room. It was time to travel to Zelaforia for a meeting with the Noshkanu High Council regarding the return of the Falgoah to their land.

• • •

Stacie swam through the huge outdoor pool behind her villa, which was nestled in lake country and enclosed by a white picket fence.

In the tranquility beneath the water, her mind quieted, finding relief from the pain of her parents' death. But unease and confusion continued to gnaw at her. She had killed rebels, rebels who may not have been the villains she believed them to be. Yet weren't they responsible for the war, and all the bloodshed that came with it? She had only followed orders. But whose orders? A corrupt government, no more virtuous than the insurgents it condemned? The constant need to justify the war and the lives she had taken was tormenting.

She longed to leave the past behind and move forward with her life. Thankfully, the CDF provided excellent mental health therapists for Guardians struggling with the psychological aftermath of the war. If she needed their services, she'd go.

At the alert dong of her front-door sensors, she bobbed to the surface of the pool. Then she swam to the edge and pulled herself onto the deck.

The sunlight made the water on her naked body glisten, accentuating every muscle and curve.

Her wet feet slapped against the dry walkway as she headed to the back door. Suddenly, her waterproof wristcom vibrated. It was her estranged lover, trying once again to rekindle what they had. She brushed aside the damp blond strands clinging to her forehead, looked down at her wristcom without emotion, and pressed the "dismiss" button. *Give it up, Randal. You're in my rearview mirror now.*

Inside her home, she slipped into a velvet robe, left open down to her navel and closed at the waist with a cloth belt tied in a knot. The skin-pleasing diaphanous material showcased the attractive silhouette beneath.

Wearing slippers, Stacie crossed the hardwood floor of her living room and opened the front door. Her unannounced visitor was a man dressed in a navy-blue suit and black top hat, his grizzled beard framing his wrinkled face.

"My name is Gerald Remington," the man said in a British-sounding accent. "I was your parents' financial custodian."

Stacie leaned against the doorframe, arms folded. "And?" she said impatiently. She was ready to get to the point of Mr. Remington's visit so she could return to her leisure.

"Your parents' will bequeaths their entire fortune and all of their assets and possessions to you, Madam Spencer."

It took a moment for Stacie to register Gerald's words. "Me?"

"Yes, their millions of G-credits, their homes, vehicles— *everything*." He held out a datapad. "I just need your signature." Without hesitation, Stacie pressed her thumb to the device. "That's it. The transfer is complete."

"Um . . . thank you."

"If you need my services, Clifton knows how to reach me. Have a good day." Gerald descended the short set of phyocrete steps.

Stacie went back to her living room. She sat on a sofa and crossed her legs. "Coffee," she said to her housekeeping golem. The ovoid-shaped hover bot brought her a foam cup of her favorite brew, made from Satellite One's best beans. She took the cup from its pincers. "Go complete the rest of your chore log." The golem burbled in response and floated away.

Stacie raised the cup to her lips. Had her parents meant to leave everything to her, or had they simply been killed before removing her from the will? Nonetheless, she had claimed her birthright. She'd gone from princess to pauper to queen, queen of the Spencer fortune. Irony.

As she sipped her coffee, she made a decision: She'd buy herself out of her contractual obligation to the CDF and use her wealth to help others, as wealth should be used. She was sure the other seven families' heirs would take control of their parents' criminal empires and continue their corrupt legacies. She had no intention of letting that happen.

An idea had come to her days ago, to assemble her own private combat team to thwart the other seven families. Now, with her parents' fortune, she finally had the means to turn her idea into reality.

She already had potential recruits in mind, Guardians she'd served with, including Jason Mansford. If they were willing, she'd buy out their contracts from the CDF so they could join her mission.

She took another sip of coffee and smiled. She'd be the start of a new era for the Spencer family name.

•••

Randy and Arson were at Kathleen's grave.

Arson stooped and set down a bouquet of colorful flowers, then rose to his feet. Moisture welled in his eyes. "I love you, my dear. I'm sorry for what I did. I love you with all my heart."

Randy placed a comforting hand on his father's back. "She knows."

Arson wiped away a tear. "So, how are you holding up?"

Randy's inner turmoil was reflected in his face and voice. "I . . . I've been having disturbing dreams about the battle. They wake me at night. Killing Guardians who were just upholding the Oath hurts, no matter how few. It doesn't matter if it was five hundred or five. And just when you think the pain is gone, it boomerangs right back. It . . . lingers in your mind."

Some of the casualties might've been bigoted thugs, like the Guardian who tried to rape Kesley, and Randy felt no sympathy for them. But there had been no way to tell them apart from well-intentioned Guardians who were simply miseducated—raised in a system that told them they were superior to colonists—and had their biases reinforced by CDF doctrine.

Just like Randy, grief hung over Arson like a storm cloud. "Well, all I can say is we did our best to preserve as many lives as we could.

"I know it won't make the pain go away, but the central government was responsible for the war, just like the Union leaders said. The blood is on *their* hands. They're the ones who oppressed the colonies, attacked the RUC, and declared martial law. If you try to beat someone to a pulp, they're going to fight back. The *government* was the reason armed dissidence happened."

"Yeah, true," Randy said in a melancholic tone.

"How is Jarius holding up?"

"We're all grappling with psychological scars from the war, but Jarius is strong. He'll overcome this, just like the rest of us who endured the fight."

Arson nodded. "Too often, the collateral damage of war is the soldier's mind." Getting emotional, he paused to compose himself, then changed the subject. "So, what's next for you, Son?"

Randy sighed, clearly worn out. "I'm taking a break from military life." He needed a respite from bloodshed. "I promised Kesley I'd show her around, take her for a ride in my sports cruiser. Maybe we'll go on a road trip."

"And Stacie?"

"I've tried calling. She won't answer. I guess our relationship is really over. If I could fix it, I would. But who knows, maybe a miracle will happen and she'll give me another chance. We'll see."

"They say time heals all wounds."

"What about you? Where are you off to now?"

"I'm going back to Colony Four to help my people in any way I can."

"Sounds good."

Arson held out his hand. "It's been great working with you, Son."

Randy grasped his hand, shook, and then pulled him into a heartfelt embrace. "I love you, Dad. Take care of yourself."

They released each other.

Arson said, "I'm proud of the man you've become, Randy. Your mother would be too." He began walking down a gray stone-block path, unaware of the unseen threat that had him in the crosshairs of a rifle.

As Randy watched his father leave, he said, *<Aunt Wells, I know you're there. Come out and put the rifle down.>*

Merriam stepped out from behind a tree, a sniper rifle slung over her shoulder. *<He needs to die, Randy. He needs to pay for my sister's death.>*

Randy saw everything he had been in Merriam's grimace. He saw pure hatred for his father. <*No. My mother—your sister—wouldn't want him to die. Her death was an accident.*>

Merriam's blood ran hot.

Randy said, <*Let go of your hate. Conquer the rage, like I had to. Stop being selfish and think about what Kathleen would want. Besides, Chief Amaechi exonerated all Coalition fighters of any war crimes. If you pull that trigger, you're murdering an innocent man. Is that something you want on your conscience?*>

Merriam's teeth chattered. <*Damn it.*> She stomped off, thoughts swirling. *These traitors cannot just go free. Someone needs to set things right.* She wondered whether she should challenge Oviereya in the coming election.

Randy went to his sports cruiser, climbed in, and started the engine. The vehicle hovered into the air and glided away from the cemetery.

At last, he felt relief now that the war was over.

End

About the Author

Michael J. Brooks holds a BA in Art and an MFA. He is a member of the Independent Book Publishing Professionals Group (IBPPG), and his first novel, *Exodus Conflict*, was a finalist of the 2013 Next Generation Indie Book Awards, in the sci-fi/fantasy category; earned honorable mention from the 2013 London Book Festival, in the science fiction category; and received five stars from *Readers' Favorite.*

As he currently tries to balance his busy life in Washington, DC, he seeks to write fiction novels which are not meant to be only entertainment but to address some of the most crucial issues of our time and explore the trials of being human. He hopes to create characters that people can relate to and stories that will have an impact on them long after they are finished reading one of his novels.

Contact Michael J. Brooks at: authormbrooks@gmail.com

Follow Michael J. Brooks on Twitter at: @AuthorMBrooks

www.authormbrooks.com

www.ingramcontent.com/pod-product-compliance
Lightning Source LLC
Chambersburg PA
CBHW061101210726

48294CB00001B/252